Garden of Shadows

Garden of Shadows

Amy Marie Turner

Copyright @2024 by Amy Marie Turner

ISBN-979-8-218-52035-9
ISBN-13: 979-8-218-52036-6

Names: Turner, Amy Marie, author
Title: Garden of Shadows/Amy Marie Turner
Description: First edition| Fauve Press: Colorado

Cover: Flowers of the Pomegranate, painted in Teneriffe ©Marianne North/Kew Royal Botanic Gardens
Cover design by Amy Turner
Map: Image taken from page 308 of 'O'Shea's Guide to Spain and Portugal. Edited by J.
Lomas. Eleventh edition. Alamy, Inc.

Epigraph and Dedication

My little boat,
take care.
There is no
land in sight.

~Charles Simic, The Wind Has Died

To feral women who fight conformity.
And to the brave ones that love us.

Also by Amy Marie Turner
Linnea Wren Mysteries

Voyage of the Pleiades (South America)
Garden of Shadows (Spain)

CONTENTS

| vii |

| VIII | –

Map of the Alhambra

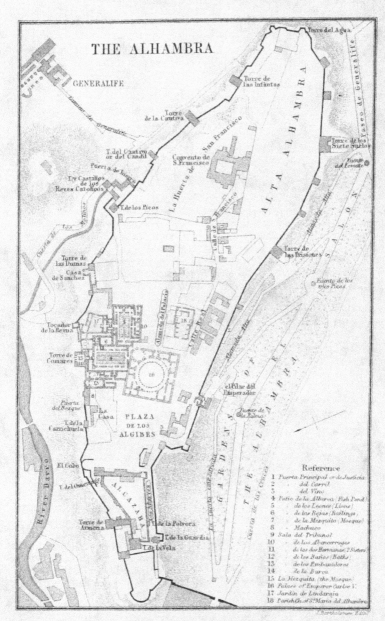

THE ALHAMBRA

GENERALIFE

Torre del Agua

Torre de las Infantas

Torre de la Cautava

ALTA ALHAMBRA

T. del Cautivo or del Candil

Convento de S. Francisco

Torre de los Siete Suelos

Puerta de Hierro

Fuente del Tomate

Los Castillos de los Reyes Católicos

E. de los Picos

SALON

Torre de las Prisiones

Torre de las Damas

Casa de Sanchez

Fuente de los tres Picos

Tocador de la Reyna

Torre de Comares

el Pilar del Emperador

Fuente de las Palmas

Puerta del Bosque

La Casa

T. de la Carnichuela

PLAZA DE LOS ALGIBES

GARDENS OF THE ALHAMBRA

El Cubo

T. del Omar

ALCAZABA

Torre de Armería

T. de la Polvora

T. de la Guardia

T. de la Vela

RIVER DARRO

Paseo de Generalife

camino de Generalife

San Francisco

La Huerta de San Francisco

Calle de San Francisco

Cuesta de los Arboles

Cuesta del Palacio

Calle Real

Avenida Alta

GARDENS OF THE ALHAMBRA

Cuesta empedrada

Cuesta de los Coches

Reference

1 Puerta Principal or de Justicia
2   del Carril
3   del Vino
4 Patio de la Alberca (Fish Pond)
5   de los Leones (Lions)
6   de los Rejas (Railings)
7   de la Mezquita (Mosque)
8   Machuca
9 Sala del Tribunal
10   de los Abencerrages
11   de las dos Hermanas (2 Sisters)
12   de los Baños (Baths)
13   de los Embaxadores
14   de la Barca
15 La Mezquita (the Mosque)
16 Palace of Emperor Carlos V.
17 Jardin de Lindaraxa
18 Parish Ch. of Sta Maria del Alhambra

J. Bartholomew, Edinr

Published by A. & C. Black, London.

Cádiz

Chapter One

I tapped the driver on the shoulder. "*Señor, deténgase aquí, por favor.*" He nodded in acknowledgment, steering the horses from the flow of traffic. To Matias, I added, "This is Hugh's address."

After months at sea, Cádiz was a feast for the eyes, an appealing contrast of stark buildings against turquoise seas, rust-colored lanes, and azure skies. Throngs of people and horses clogged the streets. My previous visits to Cádiz had been brief resupply stops; we'd rarely ventured further than the docks. After months on a ship, my brain was dizzy from the colors and sounds.

We wobbled to a halt at a buff-colored multistory house with a watchtower perched on top.

It took me a moment to gain equilibrium after descending from the cart. An ornate knocker in the shape of an owl sat at the center of Hugh's door, its whimsical expression daring me to knock. I tapped the ring, and it reverberated on the wooden surface. Nine o'clock in the morning was an unfashionable hour for visiting by London standards, but Hugh wouldn't want us to wait.

The butler who opened the door was pocket-sized, but his disdain was enough for two men. I attempted to disarm him with a winsome smile. "*Buenos días. Me llamo Lady Wren. Soy pariente de* Lord Holloway. *¿Está disponible?*"

He scowled and replied in accented English, "Lord Holloway does not wish to be disturbed. Return later."

"He'll forgive me," I reassured the man.

"I'm sorry, señora, but—"

My impatience to see Hugh wouldn't tolerate a delay for formalities. As he continued to ramble, I leaned around him, pushing through the door into the vast entryway. "Hugh! Arise, you lazy man! I know you're here."

The butler remained on the threshold, speechless at my audacity.

Matias came around him, apologizing under his breath.

A barrage of footsteps followed the slam of a door down the hall. Hugh emerged, wrapped in his dressing gown, with a piece of toast between his fingers. "Linnea! You arrived early!" He tossed the toast aside, spreading his arms in welcome. "Let's get a look at you."

Decorum abandoned at the door; I pelted across the entryway.

His familiar bergamot scent filled my lungs, easing every muscle in my body. He was slimmer, his chestnut hair threaded with more silver. There was a lightness to his being—his facial muscles were relaxed, his movements loose. He, likewise, perused me from head to toe.

The *Cormorant* did not have any mirrors, but I assumed Matias would have intervened if I'd appeared untidy. I was about to say as much when another man entered the hall.

He was a few inches shorter than Hugh and at least ten years younger. He had broad shoulders and a narrow waist, and dark gray breeches hugged his muscular thighs. He also wore a dressing gown. And he was barefoot.

Was he . . . ? Had Hugh . . . ?

Hugh flushed as my astonished expression shifted from the man back to him. His mouth was agape, absent of sound.

As Hugh composed himself, the man spoke, hand outstretched. "You must be Linnea—er, Lady Wren. I am Antonio Navarro. I have been looking forward to meeting you." His handshake was firm, his chocolate-brown eyes lambent with intelligence.

Hugh cleared his throat as el señor Navarro released my hand. "Antonio is an inquiry agent recommended by, er, acquaintances. To help find Felicity Ward." The men exchanged a meaningful glance. "And he is my . . . friend."

My concerted effort to mask my amusement at his awkwardness made the corners of my mouth dance. El señor Navarro hid a grin behind his palm. Hugh glowered at us, which unleashed my suppressed laughter. It echoed off the walls of the hallway.

Embarrassed by my outburst, I tried to shift the topic of conversation. "It's lovely to meet you. Hugh, may we stay with you? Our hired driver is waiting to unload the cart."

"We?" Hugh peered over my shoulder, acknowledge Matias. "Ah, Mr. Ward, I didn't recognize you. Welcome."

Matias approached our trio with a quizzical look in my direction as he accepted Hugh's handshake. I'd written Hugh from Valparaíso but neglected to mention that my relationship with Matias had become more than professional. Confessing such a monumental development in a letter hadn't seemed right, so I'd delayed. And here we were.

A sheepish grimace communicated what I couldn't say aloud.

Hugh's glacial-blue gaze promised a later discussion of this turn of events. With a nod, he addressed the butler: "Alberto, please have their trunks delivered to the green room at the rear of the house."

The butler, satisfied by Hugh's acceptance of us, called for the footman. In a whirl of fabric, Hugh turned with a beckoning wave, el señor Navarro on his heels.

Matias bent to my ear and whispered, "You didn't tell him about us?"

"There wasn't time. He knew that I—we—no, I didn't tell him."

Matias pivoted toward the front door. "Perhaps I should find somewhere else to stay. I don't want this to be awkward. Or do you think he expects me to have proposed?"

Clasping his hand to stop him from fleeing, I interrupted, "All is well. And I don't want or expect a proposal. Hugh won't judge us, obviously."

He tilted his head toward the two men. "Yes, another thing you kept secret."

I kissed his stubbled cheek, towing him toward the breakfast room. There had better be coffee . . . a lot of coffee.

A giant plush bed dominated our bedchamber, beckoning as a siren song. When I was two steps from the bed, overwhelming fatigue conquered me.

More than three months had passed since we'd departed Chile—half a year since our violent confrontation with Matias's half brother, Lucien—yet I still had nightmares frequently. They'd been impossible to hide while sharing a berth with Matias on the *Cormorant*. Hidden away from the rest of the crew, we would whisper into the night, sharing stories of our lives until exhaustion claimed us. Our waking hours had been suspended in a comfortable bubble, but in my dreams, I'd revisited the blood, violence, and my fears of losing Matias.

Now, I didn't sit so much as collapse onto the coverlet.

"Are you well? You were on deck early this morning."

"Well enough. I was anxious to see Hugh. At least they found Mrs. Ward."

Lucien, Matias's half brother, had confessed that his mother, Felicity Ward, had been the mastermind behind the murders we had attempted to solve on the *Cormorant* and Chiloé Island. Her ultimate plan had been for Lucien to murder Matias and enable her to receive his inheritance. Hugh had followed Felicity from England to Spain, hoping to delay her long enough for our arrival.

Over breakfast, Hugh and el señor Navarro had informed us that she had attempted to flee Spain when she'd learned Hugh was in Cádiz. She'd had one foot on the gangplank when el señor Navarro confronted her. She was in custody, but Matias would have to give evidence to the British consulate before she would be deported to England.

Matias reclined on his elbows next to me on the bed. "There's no guarantee she'll be charged. If we hadn't arrived, there would have been even less of a chance."

"Captain Hastings is sailing on the evening tide. Should I send him a message and ask him to delay? Would you prefer that we return to England when she does?"

Matias's exhale was exasperated. "Who knows how long it will take to deal with her? No need to involve Hastings and the crew. But I can stay alone to attend to Felicity if you want to go."

I hadn't even considered leaving without him.

"No, we'll endure this together." *Unless you want me to go.*

I refused to say what else was on my mind.

Matias flopped onto his back, the mattress dipping beneath us. His lack of response hung between us. Instead, he brushed his fingers along the inside of my wrist. The contrast of his callouses against my softer skin sent a shiver up my spine.

The casual affection between us was mesmerizing in its unfamiliarity. Matias was a physical being, always administering kisses and gentle caresses. I was surprised to find it reassuring rather than smothering.

"So, Lord Martin prefers the company of men? Or is it not exclusively men? Were you aware of his inclinations?"

I supposed we were finished with the other topic.

I tugged at my bootlaces and kicked my boots to the floor. Wiggling my unrestrained toes was bliss. "Of course I was aware. He and my Uncle Liam were together. But Hugh's love life is personal. I would never gossip about him. And in England, it can be a death sentence."

Matias ran a fingertip along my spine. "You know I would keep his secret."

"It wasn't my mine to tell. It had nothing to do with you being trustworthy. Until now, I wasn't sure whether Hugh had had another relationship since Liam. If he has, he's been very, very discreet."

"Are you concerned about el señor Navarro?" Fortunately, Matias sounded curious, not disgruntled.

I took in the room's decoration while I pondered my reply. The furniture was minimal but well maintained. And modern. Not a family home, then. "Not at first glance. Hugh is happier. That's enough for me."

"He does seem content."

"Content." I snorted. "That's tepid. Are *you* content?"

He captured my stockinged foot, tickling the arch until I thrashed on the bed.

When we both recovered our breath, he sat up. "We should get up. It's not even one in the afternoon."

I groaned, draping my arm over my face. "Do you want to get your interview with Felicity Ward over with today?"

He meandered across the room to open the balcony doors and let in the street noise. "No, I need to be in the right state of mind. I want to approach her with a logical strategy."

I forced myself to leave the bed, snaking my arms around his waist and resting my head against his back. "What are we going to do after Felicity departs? Do we find a ship to England right away, or do we stay awhile? What would you prefer?"

"We could stay for a bit. A naturalist I assisted lives in Cádiz. I wouldn't mind meeting with el señor Fernández. He studies wolves in the Sierra Morena. And it would give you and Lord Martin time together as well."

I nodded, rubbing my forehead across his silk waistcoat. "I'll let Hugh know while you unpack." I squeezed his waist before leaving the room.

Chapter Two

We strolled shoulder to shoulder along the Avenida Campo del Sur, toward the Plaza de la Catedral. The road was too narrow for privacy. Strangers pressed against each other practically cheek to jowl, vying for their fraction of space.

We turned into an expansive plaza. Palms ringed the vast square, and the rich, buttery color of the cathedral reflected the intense midday sun. Hugh inclined his head toward the benches scattered along the outskirts.

"Being together is a gift," Hugh said when we were seated. Matias had stayed behind to unpack, send a letter to el señor Fernández, and decide what to do about Felicity Ward. "Let's begin with you."

My fingers clenched with nerves. In my letters from Chiloé, I had glossed over our situation. Hugh had gone to a great deal of effort to secure funding for our expedition to Chile, but the fact that a murder investigation and romantic entanglement had thwarted my research aims was not something we could share with our supporters. Their dissatisfaction would affect future endeavors, not to mention both of our reputations.

Two children ran from one side of the square to the other, a welcome distraction that gave me the courage to speak.

"You know about Lucien Ward's capture, and what we uncovered about Felicity Ward's plans. Matias handed Lucien over to the British consulate in Ancud. They were unsure if he would be transported to England or the Antipodes. Your letter arrived a few days before our departure, so we altered the schedule to dock in Cádiz." Fussing with the folds of my skirt, I hesitated over my next words. "Chiloé was . . . fascinating. There was so much to explore, but my plant surveys didn't uncover any rare specimens. I want to write about the contrasts of the different areas—the coast versus the forest. On the Chepu River, I camped in an isolated cypress grove for several weeks. It should be an interesting monograph subject, a comparison of the current plant distribution and discussion of how the impact of grazing on the island may result in one type becoming dominant."

He spread his palms on his thighs, his brow furrowed. My heart plummeted. Was this confirmation of his disappointment?

"Hugh . . . if you are displeased with my efforts . . ."

He released his arms and rested a hand on my shoulder. "I'm not. Your observations sound compelling. There are few studies that have elucidated such comparisons. However, it doesn't explain why you didn't tell me about Matias."

My eyes traced the steep sides of the cathedral upward to the crenellated, Moorish decorations on the roof. A pool of shame deep within me boiled to the surface. "I didn't succeed with a fraction of my goals. The murder investigation—and Matias—distracted me."

Hugh reached for my hands, prying them apart. "Why are you distressed? You couldn't ignore the murders. And you and Matias . . . I suspected you would suit. He *might* be worthy of you."

"But I went to Chile to prove my worth as a naturalist, to identify and learn about new plants." I squinted at the hazy sky, trying to maintain control. "Not to fall in love."

"But love trumps all, my dear. You've always been your harshest critic."

I scoffed. "I don't know. Vile rumors about me have circulated for years. My behavior following the shipwreck fueled people's certainty that I was a drunk at best, and a whore at worst." A downy feather from a dove drifted from the rooftops, shuttling to and fro on the breeze. "This will give substance to their gossip. My failures never fade. No one will fund future endeavors when rumors start circulating about my behavior in Chile. Love is insubstantial by comparison."

Hugh twisted to face me on the bench. "Do you really believe that? Are you that jaded?"

Perhaps I did, and perhaps I was. A woman's value was proved through marriage and childbirth, whereas a woman like me—a woman who refused those shackles—lived under a constant cloud of judgment. I was satisfied with that path, but I didn't want to see Hugh or Matias affected by it. As soon as word of my failures reached England, opportunities would vanish. There was a possibility that I wouldn't even be able to return to my position at the Chelsea Physic Garden.

Hugh shook his head at my lack of response. "I understand your concerns, but other people have experienced less-than-ideal collection trips. Some lose their specimens, or contract tropical diseases. Everyone knows this is part of the risk with our work."

"You know the standard is different for a woman."

"And what about love? Isn't Matias's love worth the risk?"

A wash of heat engulfed my cheeks. We hadn't determined how we would move forward with our relationship; traveling aboard the *Cormorant* had kept reality at bay. Could our relationship stand up to the challenges that were sure to come? I had my doubts, and I suspected Matias did as well.

"I know how difficult it is to balance your career with those you love." Hugh had not lost his uncanny ability to discern my thoughts. His tone turned sharp. "But my situation with Liam was even more complicated. We could never reveal our relationship, never share it with anyone but trusted friends. When we were alone, we could ignore the judgment of society and the threats to our safety, but our relationship was conducted in the shadows. Do you understand? We lived with the persistent fear of being exposed. On the other hand, we did not have to deal with the complications of everyday life. We rarely had reason to be annoyed with each other. When we were together, it was as if the rest of our lives was suspended." He gripped the edge of the bench. "You and Matias are free to show your affection. Don't squander it!"

I respected his experience, but our situations were not comparable. "As long as we remain unmarried, our relationship will be a source of speculation. It will be used against us. Given the English's obsession with reputation, there will be consequences. Neither of us has ever balanced work and a relationship."

"He left his family in Chiloé to come with you."

"Exactly. What if he has regrets and grows resentful?" Even speaking those fears aloud turned my stomach. They lived in the deepest, most insecure part of my soul.

"Why are those the inevitable outcomes?"

My Uncle Liam had loved Hugh—of that, I had no doubt. His loyalty had been fixed; his devotion maintained until he died. And Hugh had felt the same for Liam. How did you tell someone with that experience that at some point in your life, you had decided that you were flawed beyond repair? Damaged in a way that meant a great love story would never be yours? As a logical person, I had accumulated evidence over the years to prove my theory to the point that it now felt indisputable. Matias would eventually see it for himself.

And he would leave.

A tabby crouched low to the cobbles, stalking an oblivious pigeon pecking at the remains of a pastry. The cat wiggled its rump, striped tail undulating. Who would win? Heedless pigeon or the murderous cat?

Hugh's boot bumped the side of my shoe. A swift change of subject was in order. "Can we talk about you?"

"Me?" He pointed at himself. "There is nothing to share beyond what you already know. After my tedious lung ailment, I itched for adventure. It took little prompting to follow Felicity Ward to Spain."

"And you met el señor Navarro when you arrived?"

Hugh's cheekbones darkened to a charming, rosy hue. "Yes, a friend with a home in Cádiz recommended Antonio."

"Is the nature of your relationship with him more than"—I waggled my eyebrows—"professional?"

His face resembled a pomegranate. "I—I don't—it's not appropriate."

I took his hand, wishing to convey support. "You deserve to be happy, Hugh."

Hugh glanced around us. "We have . . . something. After Liam died . . . Christ, this is embarrassing. Desire and attraction, they perished as well. I didn't expect to meet someone that made me feel . . . that made me feel, I suppose."

"If he has sparked something in you, then it is a good thing. A wonderful thing."

His shy smile glowed with contentment. "We are enjoying the moment and trying not to worry about the future."

Could I do the same? Stay present with Matias instead of focusing on what would happen?

"How do you acquire a knack for not worrying about the future? Can you teach me?"

Hugh rubbed his chin, where a fine dusting of stubble was growing. "Maybe it comes easier with age? You have to grow into your vintage." We erupted with laughter, dispelling any remaining tension. "You don't have to have all the answers. Now that you and Matias are staying in Spain for a while, perhaps you can chart a new course."

We found el señor Navarro and Matias in a snug library, deep in discussion in Spanish. Their conversation trailed off when we entered. El señor Navarro grinned at Hugh, a dimple flashing low on his left cheek. "Did you have a nice walk?"

Hugh settled into a worn leather chair. "We did. We walked to the cathedral."

I joined Matias on the brocade settee. The maid delivered a tray of tea and pastries, then scurried from the room. I allowed the men to serve themselves before leaning in for my cup. "Were you and el señor Navarro discussing Felicity?"

Matias nodded. "I was asking him for advice on how to handle the consulate tomorrow."

El señor Navarro brought Hugh a cup, then took the seat next to him. Once he was settled, I asked, "Señor, do you believe it will be enough to secure her an escort to England? It's our word against hers, with only a few letters, Edmund Ward's journal, and Lucien's confession as evidence."

"Please, call me Antonio. And we've scratched the surface of the situation—Hugh passed along just enough information for us to have her detained. Can you tell us the rest?"

Matias and I exchanged a look. I wanted him to be the one to tell this story.

"My half brother confessed that Felicity Ward sent him on the *Cormorant* to threaten and kill me and anyone who got in his way. She wished to claim my inheritance, which I was unaware of at the time. In his efforts to target me, he killed two men, Tomas and Cristobal. Lucien also attacked Linnea."

Hugh's teacup tipped, spilling some liquid into the saucer. "What? Linnea, you were attacked? You never said!"

I cringed. Yet another thing I had failed to share with Hugh. "Matias, please continue."

"After we discovered where he was hiding and who he was, we lured him to my cousin's farm for a confrontation. Linnea stabbed him and he was severely injured, so we were able to confine him to the village gaol."

Hugh again interrupted, "You neglected many details, my girl."

Matias cleared his throat. "While Lucien was in gaol, he confessed to Felicity's plan. We decided to hand him over to the British consulate. They took custody of him in Ancud before we received Lord Martin's letter about Felicity Ward fleeing to Spain."

While Matias was speaking, Antonio had retrieved a notebook. He finished writing, then flipped the pages back. "I followed her movements once she arrived. She came to Cádiz about a fortnight before Hugh. She took up residence at the Ilustrísimo Señor Conde de Cádiz's palace after becoming acquainted with the conde while in London. One assumes they are close friends or lovers. Mrs. Ward has taken advantage of the conde's acquaintances to garner invitations to gatherings of high-ranking businessmen and lesser royalty that reside in Cádiz. Hugh did not attend any events, but she was alerted to his presence, nonetheless. As you know, I caught her at the docks as the ship was casting off."

"Someone warned her? Who else knew?" Matias asked.

Antonio closed his notebook with a snap. "A rumor of Hugh's presence alone might have been enough to prompt her escape."

I watched Matias process this information. From the moment we departed Valparaíso, he had been anticipating his confrontation with his stepmother. Our frequent discussions about her had kept our experiences fresh in our minds.

Matias's hand curled into a tight fist on the settee. "The sooner she is on a ship bound for England, the sooner she is out of my life."

Chapter Three

Hugh was subdued at dinner, muttering about stabbings under his breath while toying with his butter knife. Antonio rushed him from the table, an arm slung over his shoulder.

After I returned to our bedchamber, I considered finding Hugh to apologize. His health had been precarious while we were in Chile; my evasiveness had been intended to spare him additional distress. Before I found the energy to act, though, I fell into a deep sleep.

And woke to an empty bed in the morning.

Rubbing at my gritty eyes, I entered the breakfast room. Matias sat at the table alone, staring into a half-empty coffee cup. His stiff shoulders relaxed when my fingers sifted through the dark waves of his hair.

"Where were you last night? Did you get any sleep?"

He tipped his head against my palm. His eyes were the color of conifer needles, accentuated by dark purple circles beneath them. "I went for a walk around the city until my mind quieted. The settee in the library was adequate for a short nap."

I slipped into the chair next to him. "You were worrying?"

"You should eat." Matias was trying to distract me.

"You are more important. I will eat after."

He poured a cup of coffee. "Have some coffee. We know you need it."

I held the cup in one hand, covering his hand with the other. Matias sighed, resting his head on my shoulder.

"I allowed myself to hope that once we arrived in Spain, we could close this chapter. Banish Felicity Ward from our lives. With her gone, we could begin to think about the future." He returned upright and tossed his napkin onto his empty plate. "Even if I am successful and she returns to England, it will not be enough—not to lessen the guilt I feel over Cristobal and Tomas's deaths. If I had never set foot on the *Cormorant*, on Chiloé, they would be alive. Justice will not bring them back."

Matias's cousin Maria and her husband, Jaime, and I, had all insisted that Matias was not responsible for Cristobal and Tomas's deaths, but those were just words. If I could take on that burden for him, I would. Instead, all I could do was listen and continue to reassure him. He would have to forgive himself.

He turned our hands to kiss my knuckles. "Will you come with me to the consulate?"

"Of course I will."

"Good morning," Hugh spoke low so we wouldn't be startled.

Matias dropped my hand like a hot coal. My knuckles struck the wooden surface.

"Ouch." I rubbed at the sore spot, then joined Hugh at the sideboard, surprised at Matias's reaction. Hugh seemed in better spirits, though. At some point, I would need to apologize for my evasiveness.

I filled my plate with toast and delicate slices of *jamón*. Hugh also made his selections, then followed me to the table.

I added a slice of *jamón* to some bread and slid it onto Matias's plate. Hugh watched our interaction with a knowing gleam in his eyes. "You're off to the consulate this morning?" he asked.

Matias cut a slice from his toast with care. "Yes, I have an appointment at ten o'clock. I have asked Linnea to attend the interview."

"Would my presence be of help?"

Matias took another bite, mulling over his offer. We had discussed Hugh's involvement on the journey here. While it might help our case to have an earl present, Matias did not wish for him to become entangled in Felicity's schemes. "Assuming all goes as planned, we should be fine, but the offer is appreciated."

I watched Matias as discreetly as possible while he finished eating. There was a slight tremor in the hand that held his knife. He laid his cutlery on the side of his plate and rose from the table without making eye contact with either of us. "I'm going to refresh myself. Linnea, I'll find you when I'm ready to leave."

We watched him shuffle from the room.

"Is he well?" Hugh whispered.

"As well as he can be, considering his family tried to kill him and he has to confront the instigator of that scheme today. Not to mention the discovery that he has inherited his father's properties in England, a place he hasn't lived since he was twelve. And leaving behind his newfound family on Chiloé. He is coping."

"At least he has you."

I took a sip of coffee. Would I be enough? These doubts had tormented me prior to committing to this relationship and had only grown stronger as we crossed the ocean from Chile. How long before he regretted what he had given up? We had come to Spain so he could confront Felicity Ward, but where would we go from here? The fact that we had both avoided discussing the issue had to mean that he was as conflicted as I was.

"Yes, he has me." My appetite had vanished. "I'm going to take a walk in the garden. Enjoy your breakfast."

Hugh's perceptive stare burned between my shoulders as I exited the room.

Matias met with a group of consulate officials while I squirmed on an uncomfortable chair in the anteroom. The moment I began to fidget, though, they emerged.

We were shown into an ornate parlor to wait for Felicity Ward. The officials assured us they would observe our interaction through a slot cut into a painting and reiterated that we must extract a confession from her within this room. My guess was that they were watching through the painting of an amorous, cross-eyed bull frolicking beneath an oak grove.

I turned from the brooding bovine to observe Matias yanking on his cuffs and smoothing the front of his waistcoat as he paced the room. "Are you ready for this?"

He strode to the covered window and twitched open the heavy velvet curtain. "I'm angry. Staying calm may not be possible."

"We need her confession, and then you'll be free of her."

"Will we? If we're fortunate, there will be a trial, which may prolong her presence in our lives."

As I was about to respond, a familiar shriek came from the corridor. "Do you know who I am? Mora will not stand for this. Release me immediately. This is harassment!"

We stood side by side as the door flung open and slammed into the flocked walls. Felicity Ward stepped inside, halting on the threshold.

"You!" she spat. "What are *you* doing here?"

As she glared at Matias, I examined the woman who had been the mastermind of violence against us. After becoming acquainted with her son, Lucien, the resemblance was uncanny. Her face was pale, lips pursed in disgust.

"Felicity, do you remember Lady Wren?"

Her poisonous gaze slid sideways. A jolt of anger sizzled through my body when our eyes locked. She hadn't witnessed the brutality perpetuated by her greed. She wasn't the one who'd found Tomas and Cristobal, their bodies defiled with slashes, dead in pools of blood.

Meanwhile, we lived with those horrors.

Matias gestured to several chairs gathered around a small marble table. "Won't you join us?"

Felicity Ward folded her arms, refusing to move. "I have nothing to say to you."

"No one is coming—nor will they—unless you speak to us."

"I prefer to wait."

But Matias's icy tone was a warning she should have heeded. Matias removed Edmund Ward's journal from where he had tucked it alongside a chair cushion. The *thunk* when it hit the table cracked her facade.

Felicity blanched. "Where did you get that?"

"From your son, of course."

"My son! Is he here?" Her nervous eyes darted about the room.

"He is not."

"Lucien would never give you that journal. What have you done to him?"

Matias riffled the pages of the book. "Felicity, do you love your children?"

"What a stupid question! Of course I love my children." She seemed irked, not distressed for Lucien.

"If you knew one of them was going to die, would you do anything to save them?" Matias asked placidly.

"Are you threatening my children, you foolish boy? I don't care who you are, I will scream down this building."

"Go ahead. The consulate authorized my presence. I have proof that you conspired to kill me in a scheme that led to the murder of two innocent people and the attempted murder of another." Matias's eyes flashed with fire. His early nervousness was absent. His manner reenforced my confidence as well.

Felicity glared at him, searching for a crack in his composure. Her forced laugh was tinny. "This is a farce. You are deluded."

"You aren't surprised to find us alive?"

She scoffed. "I have no idea what you are talking about. No one will believe such outrageous lies."

I interjected, "They will, because your son confessed. To me."

Felicity swayed suddenly, gripping the chair back for stability. "What do you know of my son?"

"Where do I begin?" I tapped my top lip. "He knocked me unconscious and abandoned me in a cave. Upon our second meeting, well . . . I stabbed him."

She moved faster than I expected, skirting the chair to throw herself at me, her hands gripping my neck. "You *shrew*! What did you do to my son?"

I tugged at her forearms, gasping for breath, but she was surprisingly strong.

Her voice came from a distance. "I'll ruin you, you bitch! It will take nothing! Everyone already says you are a scheming, talentless whore—"

The compression on my neck vanished, but I couldn't seem to get air in my lungs. Felicity continued to screech a deluge of various threats against me.

Matias's voice rose from the cacophony. "Linnea, are you well?"

My vision cleared enough to see he had pinned her in a chair, her wrists shackled in his hands, his body angled between us.

Breath rasped through my burning lungs. I croaked, "Fine, I'm fine."

Felicity took advantage of his distraction, shoving past him to race for the door. She traveled a few steps before Matias tackled her to the ground like a jaguar on a peccary. The sound she emitted when she hit the rug was porcine-like. Two consulate officials charged into the room while I struggled to my feet.

Matias rolled, pinning her arms behind her back.

"Get your hands off me! The conde will see you punished!" she howled.

Matias frog-marched her to a plush chair. Felicity fought Matias's grip, kicking and spitting.

"Calm yourself," he ordered.

Her hazel eyes glinted in fury; lips twisted in an unattractive sneer. "Have your say," she hissed.

Matias relinquished custody of her to an official.

"First, you blackmailed Lucien into traveling to Chile to murder me. Lucien killed one man on the ship during our voyage to South America, and another man in Chiloé. He struck Lady Wren and left her in a sea cave, assuming she would be unable to escape. And he attacked me—and might have succeeded with murder—if Lady Wren had not stabbed him. Lucien was held in gaol until his wounds healed. During his imprisonment, he confessed. He was transferred to the custody of the British government and shipped to England. Once he arrives, they will determine whether his fate is to hang, be transported, or receive a prison-hull sentence."

As Matias spoke, Felicity's face grew paler. Her bottom lip trembled.

"The British government is aware of your role in this scheme, Felicity. As a mere mister, I don't merit their attention, but Lucien attacked a member of the aristocracy"—he gestured to me—"and now so have you. They will not allow that to go unpunished."

At least my title was useful for something.

She glared at us, but there were signs her composure was fragile: a slight quiver to her chin, fear in her eyes. "You have no proof. This is a fantasy created by a vengeful stepson."

"We have your letters and Lucien's testimony."

"My son would never." She fisted her hands in her skirt.

"But he has. Make no mistake, Felicity, he will die at the end of a rope or on a prison hull unless you admit your guilt," Matias said dispassionately.

Felicity sneered, taking the measure of the others in the room. She was tallying the count in her mind: four against one.

A mustached official spoke. "Mrs. Ward, the British consulate will transport you to England for trial. It would be best if you went quietly."

She struggled to her feet, back ramrod straight. "Nothing will come of your accusations. Mark my words, I will not board that ship. I have friends with more influence than you can imagine. You and your whore are insignificant bumps in my plans. I am unconcerned."

Felicity tried to fake nonchalance as she whirled away, but the officials took up her arms, halting her flounce from the room.

Matias watched the closed door until her voice faded down the hallway.

"Do you think it was enough?" I asked him, rubbing at my bruised throat.

He came to my side to examine the skin of my throat, no doubt noting how my body continued to quiver from the surge of adrenaline. "I hope so. Are you sure you are well?"

"A bit tender," I admitted.

He kissed my damp temple. "We should return home. I'm going to have a quick word with the officials."

I turned toward the windows, replaying Felicity's words. Knowing she was in custody should have been comforting, but seeing her was only a reminder of the months of threats we had endured. Of my attack on Lucien, the violence of which lingered in my subconscious. Felicity Ward was slippery; she wouldn't go anywhere willingly. And her comment about us being a small part of her plan made me uneasy. Would the threats continue?

What damage had she already incurred in England?

The acceleration of my heart seemed thunderous in the quiet room. Could she have killed Matias's father, Edmund? Was that where this had started, not Matias? And if she had started rumors in England, had my fears about the destruction of my career already come to pass?

Chapter Four

Matias tried to insist on staying with me, but I could tell he needed a distraction. Our meeting with Felicity had raised a swarm of conflicting emotions in him. So, after I promised that I would rest, Matias headed off to an appointment to meet with his colleague, el señor Fernández.

The echoing desertion of the house was too much to bear. After a hopeless attempt to nap, I fled toward the lemony late-afternoon sunshine in the garden. Cooler temperatures were chasing away the heat of the day, coaxing the plants to release their aromatic oils. Lavender and rosemary bushes were familiar, fragrant evening companions; they also resided in my garden at Holloway House. These Spanish varieties were different, though—the aroma sharper, more medicinal.

Only some of the vegetation in Spain was familiar, though. My previous visits had been to the northern part of the country, with brief stops at the port of Cádiz. Andalusia was a new, unknown landscape. I wouldn't be opposed to staying to explore. Returning to England wasn't appealing, especially if Felicity Ward had already spread gossip about Matias and me.

"Here you are." Matias followed the wandering path to my side.

I plucked a blooming floret of lavender, twirling the stem between my fingers. "Hello. How was your meeting with Fernández?"

Matias confiscated the sprig from my hand. He raised the floret to his nose, breathing deep. Not since Chiloé had Matias's face been this peaceful. "Once he begins talking, he's impossible to interrupt. When we traveled together, he put an entire table of men to sleep by monologuing about the behavior of alpha-female wolves. He didn't even notice the snoring." Matias batted my nose with the lavender. "Fernández has a trip planned soon to track a declining population of wolves in the Sierra Morena. He wants to determine how many individuals remain."

A slight breeze ruffled the overlong strands of hair around his face. His eyes gleamed with excitement. Meeting with el señor Fernández had been the tonic he needed after that scene with Felicity. A burble of pre-monition danced along my spine.

Matias lounged on the bench, nudging my thigh with his knee. "Fer-nández invited me to visit Granada to view his collections . . . and asked if I would like to accompany him on the excursion to the mountains."

A wave of alarm pulsed through my veins. I snapped off a branch of rosemary, parting the needles from the stems with nervous plucks. What would I do? I didn't begrudge him taking this opportunity—far from it—but what would it mean for us?

For me?

"Did you give him an answer?"

"No, I wanted to discuss it with you. There's much to consider. My responsibilities in England are waiting, as well as ensuring that Felicity stands trial. What do you wish to do?"

I flicked the bare rosemary stem to the paving stones. "My leave from the Chelsea Physic Garden was indefinite. Their opinion of me may have changed after our trip. It is possible I won't have a position there anymore. Did you hear what Felicity implied when she attacked me? If she was circulating disparaging gossip about us before she fled to Spain, the damage is already done."

Matias shot from the bench, flushing an alarmed sparrow from the hedge. He paced toward the brick path, chest heaving in distress. "That damned woman. She's already taken so much from us. I owe it to Tomas and Cristobal to see it through, to ensure that she is charged. Lucien killed them because of me. Justice is a worthy goal, but I'm weary of her vitriol." He halted in front of me, head bent, resigned. "I'm sorry. You don't deserve this. If I hadn't—"

I halted his apology by grabbing his wrist. "No, she deserves your anger, but nothing more. What's done is done. Rushing to England now isn't going to change that. If you want to go with Fernández, you should. I'll support your decision, mi amor."

His finger pressed against the underside of my chin. A luminous glow from the low sun surrounded his head, obscuring his face. His voice rough with emotion, he murmured, "You've never called me that."

It took a moment to register what he was referring to. The endearment hadn't been a conscious decision.

"I—I—um—"

He brushed his calloused thumb over my lower lip. I shivered at the sensation. He traced a path from my shoulder to my fingers, intertwining them with his as he resumed his seat on the bench.

Despite the swirling unknown of the future, his presence was soothing, a point of stability.

A whisper of a kiss brushed my hair. I turned his hand, rubbing his knuckles against my cheek. "Do we have to decide today?"

He nuzzled my neck. Small birds returned in a flock to surround us, hopping around the nearby shrubs and communicating in chirps. Matias chuckled. "An immediate decision isn't possible, anyway. Every single thought of mine just vanished."

My laughter startled the birds into flight when he swept my knees up, drawing me onto his lap.

Cradled in his arms, I listened to the thump of his heart and watched the branches swaying above us in the breeze. My heart felt so full, it ached. Yet there was a dark cloud cast by Felicity Ward's actions that I knew we would have to deal with eventually.

Matias recounted our morning at the consulate to Antonio and Hugh as I stared out the door, clinging to those last peaceful moments in the garden.

Would I go with Matias to Granada? I wasn't ready to face the consequences of my Chile trip, or Felicity Ward's whispers. Her gossip would be bolstered by my lack of research results. If I could write a monograph or two while I was here in Spain, it might quiet at least some rumblings.

I took a sip of a whiskey. The burn of the alcohol was but a brief distraction.

If I didn't go with Matias, would that be the end of our relationship?

"We could all go to Granada."

I swiveled at Hugh's suggestion. Matias must have told them about el señor Fernández's invitation.

Antonio nodded in agreement. "I have a house in Granada, and there is a client that has been demanding my return. I've delayed as long as I could while we waited for Felicity Ward. If you do not object to living together, there is plenty of space."

Matias came to my side, his eyebrows lifted in anticipation. "Linnea? What's your opinion?"

My opinion was that this conversation would be better to have in private. But that ship had sailed, quite literally, with the *Cormorant*. Going to Granada would help Matias, and besides, it wasn't as if I had an alternative in mind.

"I've never been to Granada. I'd love to visit the Alhambra." I silenced my internal concerns about the future of my career. That was for me to figure out when there wasn't an audience.

Matias's broad smile at my words was worth any discomfort.

The butler entered to inform us that dinner was served. Antonio and Hugh followed him, debating the details that would need to be addressed before leaving. With a last glance through the window, I turned to follow.

I should have felt content having the two men I loved with me, but instead, I felt more alone than ever. Today had been a reminder that my fears about the consequences of forming a relationship with Matias were real, and eventually, I wouldn't be able to outrun them.

Chapter Five

After the meal concluded, I stumbled up the stairs. Someone had closed the windows in our chamber, but Matias and I both preferred fresh air. I flipped the latch, allowing the breeze to rush in. I sat on the casement, wrapping my arms around my knees, trying to get a grip on my spiraling panic.

A dog barked on the street below. I strained forward, almost toppling when Matias spoke from behind me. "Are you not happy with our decision to go to Granada?"

Regaining my balance, I replied, "It will be an adventure for both of us, I'm sure."

He paused to retrieve a book from the bedside table. "If that is the case, why is your mood so low? You hardly said a word at dinner."

The dog launched into a fury of barking. Taking advantage of the interruption to temper my words, I finally ventured, "We've had a busy couple of days. I'm trying to absorb the changes."

Matias along the wall below me, stretching one leg out, bending the other to rest an elbow on his knee. I appreciated how he listened; he gave weight and consideration to my words. "But it is more than that, isn't it?"

My chest was tight. My words tumbled forth in a burst of constricted air. "What if we can't do this? Find a way forward together?"

A moth flew between us, trapped against the glass pane, bashing toward the light. We watched in silence. Seconds passed, every doubt closing in on me. Pressure increased in my chest. I rubbed at my breastbone. But when Matias spoke, the bands of anxiety loosened.

"Maria and Jaime were the first couple I've witnessed in a relationship with love, partnership, and respect," Matias said thoughtfully. "Jaime and Maria's love isn't built on guilt and recrimination, or a constant battle for dominance. Until we lived with them, I wouldn't have been able to describe an ideal marriage."

I wrapped my arms tighter around my legs. Wasn't what they had rare, though? Was it even achievable for two very independent people such as us?

I lowered from the casement to join him on the floor. When I crawled toward him, he opened his arms. The buttons on his jacket freed beneath my fingers. I worked my arms beneath the fabric, allowing him to take my weight as I nestled against his chest.

"I want to believe what Maria and Jaime have is achievable, but all I've seen are struggles between competing desires—or submissive capitulation, always by the woman," I whispered.

"I think it takes dedication, like anything worth doing," Matias spoke into the crown of my head.

"But what if you grow to resent me, or I you?" My throat was strained, almost choking out my question.

"Then we decide how to navigate it. Love exists when everything is going well *and* when it isn't."

I buried my face in the front of his shirt. "No one has ever loved me."

"How can you say that? Hugh loves you. Your Uncle Liam loved you. I'm sure your parents did as well."

My shock at having shared such a vulnerable thought made me retreat, putting some distance between us. "They are family. They're obligated to love me."

Matias cupped my shoulders. "Maybe the more you accustom yourself to being loved, the more it becomes a habit. I can help with that."

He swooped me up in his arms, throwing me over his shoulder. The suddenness of the movement and his mischievous grin knocked the breath from my chest. It rushed back in via laughter when he deposited me on the mattress.

Crawling up the bed, he pinned my hips in place between his knees. His eyebrows furrowed in concentration as he unbuttoned my blouse, then trailed a line of kisses along my collarbone before pausing to free the rest of the buttons.

"Do you feel my love now?" he queried, pushing aside the jumps to nuzzle my breast.

I tangled my fingers in his silky hair. "Maybe. A little."

He nipped the skin next to my navel. I squawked, batting at him. "Cheeky. I guess I'll need to work harder."

I rubbed my knee against his obvious bulge. "Hmm. Seems plenty hard to me."

"Behave," he scolded. Without warning, he flipped me onto my stomach.

As he alternated between pinning me down and stripping away my clothes, I went limp. In the months we'd been together, I'd realized that with him, I could relinquish control. The more dominant Matias was, the more I could release the demons that seemed to plague me. With other lovers, I hadn't trusted that they would see to my pleasure.

While I was starting to float away in thought, he had removed his clothes as well. He pressed the length of his bare body against me.

"Get out of your head," he demanded with a swat to my arse.

The snap of pain was unexpected. Exquisite. My gasp transformed into a groan as he caressed the smarting skin. His fingers traveled down through the crease, where he found me already aroused.

I canted my hips, wordlessly begging for more. He teased me with his cock, inching in and pulling out without thrusting. As I whimpered into the mattress, Matias paused, leaving me bent over, wanting, throbbing while he pulled the pins from my hair. Winding my braid around his fist, he murmured in my ear, "I'm going to make you feel it—my desire, my love—when I bury my cock in you."

He punctuated that statement by slamming into me.

My back bowed in pleasure. I felt his guttural moan vibrate through my ribs. His movement was relentless, hurling both of us toward a pinnacle. Yet it remained out of reach. My begging came out in frantic pants. "I need . . . I need . . ."

"I know," he replied, rolling us as one so we were facing each other on our sides.

I wound my leg higher on his hip, propping my arms on his shoulders so I could cup his head in both of my palms. He entered me on a slow slide, and we both sighed in relief.

This was what I wanted: to stare into the depths of his eyes. His pupils were blown wide, almost obscuring the green of his irises. Damp strands of hair stuck to his temples. His lips and cheeks were rosy with exertion. He was glorious.

Our hips moved in a wave, drawing us closer together until every part of our bodies touched.

Matias rested his forehead on mine. "Can you feel it, mi amor? Us. Love. Please don't deny it anymore."

His words, and the friction of our skin, were enough to catapult me into the heavens. I shattered, clutching at him, and he followed me over the edge.

Chests heaving, the dampness of our skin mingled, adhering us together.

We remained on our sides. His fingers toyed with the strands of hair that curled around my face. I traced his bold brows, brushing the soft mink of his eyelashes. We didn't discuss his plea, or my reluctance.

Matias fell into a heavy sleep while I remained awake, watching his chest rise and fall. Alone, I continued to wage a battle with my fears. Part of me was convinced that despite my fathomless love for him, this wouldn't last.

A click of the door, followed by the rich aroma of coffee, jolted me awake. Matias came around the side of the bed, perching his hip on the disaster of linens to offer me a steaming cup.

"I was worried you were going to sleep all day. If anything would rouse you from the dead, it is coffee."

I tucked the linen under my arms and sat against the pillows, balancing the cup. A sigh of pleasure escaped with my first sip. Matias laughed.

I scrutinized him while I took a second swallow. He was dressed in daytime finery: a black, fitted morning coat over a cobalt waistcoat. He was clean-shaven and fragrant; a spicy blend of his juniper soap mingled with the scent of coffee.

"You're fancy for this early in the day." I trailed my fingers over his smooth jaw, tugging on his collar to bring him closer and dust our lips together. "Very handsome. Good morning. Where were you?"

"Finish your coffee. We have things to discuss."

The liquid burned my esophagus. What now? I didn't taste the next swallow that I forced down.

"I went to el señor Fernández's first thing this morning to accept his offer to travel with him to the Sierra Morena. His house was in a frenzy because he's leaving for Granada in a few days. I made arrangements for us to follow him on the new rail line." He plucked the cup from my hand and finished the dregs with a single swallow. He hummed a tune while he opened his trunk and was folding his clothes before he noted that I was frozen in place. It had been ages since I had seen Matias energetic. "I thought we agreed. Have you changed your mind?"

Eyeing the empty cup, I wished for more, although abstaining might be prudent, given the hammering of my heart. I'd agreed to this, so why was I panicking now?

I flung the coverlet aside and headed for the privacy screen, ignoring Matias's scrutiny. "It's fine. I didn't realize things would move so fast." I snatched my dressing gown from the screen, securing the tie forcefully.

His voice filtered through the barrier. "I'm sorry. Perhaps I rushed a bit. I thought we agreed."

"I understand." But my reassurance was flat.

On some level, his response registered—something about Fernández, wolves, the train—but I couldn't hear it over my rapid breathing. The toothbrush clattered as it fell from my hand into the basin. I wrapped my fingers around the edges of the porcelain, my head buzzing as if infested with a swarm of bees. What would I do in Granada? What if he took over all our decisions?

Why couldn't I speak and assert myself?

Breathe, Linnea, breathe.

"Linnea?" He peered around the corner of the screen.

Agitated, I pushed past him, rambling on my way across the room to distract from my overwrought state. "A new train line? We should arrive in half the time. I assume we should take our belongings since we might not return?"

When I threw open the lid to my trunk, the contents were a blur.

Whether my distraction was effective or not, Matias left to return to his tasks to give me space, leaving off a discussion for now.

Granada

Chapter Six

We had arrived a few days earlier. Rapid transit on the new rail line had left me little chance to get a handle on my conflicted moods. Upon arriving, everyone had scattered to their responsibilities. Matias was meeting with el señor Fernández every day, and Hugh and Antonio were busy with Antonio's various inquiries.

As my restlessness grew, my nightmares became more severe, a twisted recollection of storms and stabbings. Loath to disturb Matias, I would slip from the bed to retreat to the garden. Today, when I'd returned to dress for the day, he was gone.

Hugh's distressed voice in the breakfast room stopped me in the hall.

"I wish to stay, Antonio, but I have responsibilities in England. I received a letter from Sir Thiselton-Dyer, the director of Kew. Rumor has reached him that Linnea's research in Chile was a failure, compromised by a romantic entanglement with a colleague. The *Cormorant* and the rest of the crew haven't arrived to contradict it yet. I've written to him to reassure him, but if my letter isn't enough, I may have to return to England to soothe his ruffled feathers."

A starburst of emotion blasted my chest wide. I slid down the wall, ending in a heap on the floor. I was certain Felicity Ward was behind this. What would I do? Should I tell Hugh I overheard him?

From my heap on the floor, I heard their conversation carry on. "I don't intend to tell Linnea. Not yet. It will only cause her distress. With luck, I can resolve it from here. Please be patient with me."

"Understood. We'll return to this discussion, Hugh. I want a future with you," Antonio replied. "I know you mean well, but I'm not sure it is the right choice to keep this from Linnea. Consider how hurt you were with her for the same reason."

As Antonio spoke, I managed to get my feet under me. I had to leave. I had to make sense of what I'd heard and decide what to do next.

Inside my pocket was a map Antonio had drawn of the neighborhood. He'd mentioned a market at Plaza Larga northwest of our house.

I set off in that direction on wobbly legs.

Antonio's sketched map was a surprisingly accurate representation of the city, given how complex navigating proved to be. Granada was a lopsided grid of streets.

I traced my finger along my route, choosing to turn right. Roads disappeared into alleys or ended in stone walls. More than once, I ended up turned around, dizzied by the lack of landmarks. If not for the helpful locals, my decision to venture from the house would have resulted in a frustrating morning.

My body hummed, a potent combination of my earlier distress and my relief at slipping into anonymity.

Upon rounding a tight alley, the street widened into a hectic plaza. As suggested by its name, it was narrow and long, the bricks broken by embedded stones that formed a swirling pattern. Midmorning light spilled across the ancient walls, turning them the color of baked scones. Occupied benches dotted the plaza, but I found an open seat next to a pair of elderly women passing each other wedges of an orange as they observed the market crowd.

I exhaled, winding my fingers together. The walk had helped lessen my immediate turmoil to a low simmer.

"¿Señora, quiere una rodaja?" the woman asked, offering me a slice.

"*Por favor, gracias,*" I responded. The tangy citrus exploded in my mouth, tickling my throat. My tongue tingled from the intensity of the juice. We rarely had citrus when traveling.

With a nod to the ladies, I left the bench to meander through the stalls. The tempting arrangements of fresh bread and ripe vegetables made my stomach grumble. I purchased a string bag and filled it with oranges from a precarious pyramid. After slinging the contents over my shoulder, I selected a *tostada* from the neighboring stall—vibrant, red tomato smashed into the bread, piled with slices of *jamón*.

At the corner café, I nibbled my *tostada* and sipped coffee while taking in the unobstructed view of the market. Granada's essence was different from that of Cádiz. Cádiz was a bustling port town preoccupied with business and defense; it was precise and formal. Granada, on the other hand, was unpretentious. Music drifted in the air and people moved to its rhythm, loose-limbed, with ample time to reach their destination. The susurration of activity soothed me.

My career had seemed destroyed after the shipwreck. If it was possible to rebuild then, it would be once again.

My contemplations were interrupted by the sound of a gathering in the far corner of the plaza, grouped around a woman standing on a small movable stage.

Curious, I finished my breakfast and joined them.

"People are suffering. Families were devastated by the epidemic, their children orphaned. Now their homes are being snatched up by the rich. They want our neighborhoods! We must act!"

The crowd shuffled, rumbling in agreement like a flock of restless chickens. A young man standing near the woman glowered from beneath the brim of his hat.

"The king is an infant! His regent mother is a pawn controlled by politicians who will do everything they can to prevent change." A beam of sunlight highlighted her face, illuminating her keen, amber-colored eyes. "Foreigners arrive every day, trying to change our country. These extranjeros support those in power and their obsession with raza. They will live in these houses! Sagasta is corrupted by money and power!"

Our eyes met over the crowd. The hatred in her stare seared through me with such force that I rocked on my heels. Beads of perspiration formed along my hairline and neck.

The restless animosity of the crowd was palpable. I scanned the faces, hoping to connect with someone, but those around me avoided making eye contact. I fled across the square before the mood of the gathering became aggressive.

The woman began speaking again, yet the sensation of being watched continued to sizzle between my shoulder blades.

As I bolted down a side lane into a quiet residential street, an angled cobble broke my stride. My ankle twisted, pain shooting through my leg.

I leaned against a nearby wall and unfolded the map to confirm my location, willing the throb to subside.

As I stowed the map in my pocket, a flicker of movement less than a block away drew my attention. After Lucien stalked and attacked me on Chiloé, my vigilance had heightened whenever I was alone. Doing my best to ignore the twinge in my ankle, I hobbled away, my footsteps disconcertingly loud, echoing off the buildings.

As I slowed to pretend to remove a pebble from my shoe, my fears were confirmed: Someone was indeed following me. They stuck to the shadows, but the brim of their hat occasionally caught a beam of sunlight.

I clutched my hand into a fist, the bite of my fingernails in my palm helping to ward off the panic.

Up ahead, a shop door stood open. I soothed my escalating fear by parsing the situation: There were other people on the street, and my dagger was in the sheath of my boot. I increased my speed, sidling through the doorway into the shop. No one was at the counter.

I hid beneath the windowsill, waiting for my follower to pass.

A few moments later, a man paused in front of the shop. He was stout, his rolled shirt sleeves displaying muscular forearms. His short-brimmed hat sat low, shading the upper half of his face.

Had he been part of the crowd at the plaza? If so, I didn't remember him.

He lingered at the intersection at the end of the street. Footsteps came from the rear of the shop, their owner whistling a lilting tune. I took a risk and exited, not wanting the attendant to find me.

Staying close to the wall, I waited for the watcher to turn in the opposite direction. When he did, I darted away, taking a circular route that looped toward our house. I kept glancing over my shoulder, expecting to see him until the portico came into view.

I ran up the steps, soundlessly closing the door.

I collapsed against the heavy wood. My knees trembled, and the linen of my blouse was sticky with sweat.

Antonio appeared at the entrance to the study. "Linnea? Are you ill?"

I stepped away from the door, bent over with my hands on my knees to draw in deep, cleansing breaths. He pressed his warm palm to the center of my spine.

"I'm well, I'm well. Just a moment."

He clasped my elbow and guided me to the study. "Would you like water? Something stronger?"

Exhausted, I lurched into a chair. It was still a bit early in the day, but I accepted the dram of whiskey he offered. Antonio waited, propped against the edge of his desk.

After a bracing swallow, my breathing steadied. "I was followed from Plaza Larga."

His eyebrows shot high. "A thief?"

I hesitated, recalling their behavior. "If he were a thief, he would've approached me. He wanted to see where I was going."

"Did they see you enter the house?" He flicked a concerned look toward the door.

"I don't think so. I lost them in the shops."

Antonio uncrossed his arms to grip the wooden surface. My fear was receding and quickly being replaced by embarrassment. He and I hardly knew each other, and I had entered his house like a madwoman, sweating and stammering. And this was after his conversation with Hugh earlier, where he'd shared my failures in Chile. Mortification fanned the flames of a blush across my face.

I straightened, collecting the tattered remains of my poise.

"There was an interesting rally at the plaza. A woman was speaking about people losing their homes, how the cholera epidemic gave the wealthy an excuse to take over neighborhoods. When the crowd noticed I was listening, they weren't pleased." I rolled the glass between my palms. "Do you know anything about it?"

He shifted his stance, his expression curious. "They were bold to risk discussing such subjects in public. Can you describe the speaker? And tell me more about what was said."

"She was tall for a woman but shorter than you. Dark brown hair and extraordinary eyes—amber, shrewd. Hostile, even. She said Sagasta is corrupt and that the rich would continue to force them from their homes. And she used the word *raza*. Race?"

Antonio was reaching for his notebook but paused, tapping the pen against his chin. "*Raza* means more than race. It implies a failure, a blemish that needs to be removed. It assumes that uniformity is superior. One of those attending followed you?"

"I couldn't say for certain. Don't they want recognition for those of different backgrounds? To argue against the idea of someone being superior to others? Isn't that the opposite of *raza*?"

Antonio rolled his shoulders. "Indeed, that was probably what she intended. Some people in Spain remain discontent with the state of our country and government. Rampant corruption and prejudice have destroyed our dreams of a republic. When the new constitution was passed, it was supposed to divide the power between a republic of the people and the monarchy, but it is more complicated than that." He tossed his pen on the desk with a sense of agitation in his sharp movements as he settled into his chair. "We have a republic, but the leaders are the same people advising the monarchy. It rotates between the conservatives and the liberals, but their differences are not so great. In the past twenty years, the divisions between classes have continued to grow. King Alfonso was loved, especially because of his response during the cholera epidemic. Those charitable actions took his life. It will be many years until his heir, the young king, will rule. His mother, the regent, is influenced by Sagasta, our current prime minister. He's aging and will soon retire. There is no clear path forward for our country."

What he described was familiar; Spain and England struggled with similar issues. It wasn't those with money and power who shouldered the burden when times were difficult.

"People are growing restless and discontent with the uncertainty?" I asked.

"Yes."

"You don't agree with their cause?"

Antonio clenched the hand that rested on his thigh. "As an inquiry agent, I try to remain impartial. Not a simple thing when it's your own country. I'm not a devoted monarchist or a socialist. They hired me to monitor these groups, so that's what I'll do. It isn't judgment, it's information." He rolled down his sleeves, buttoned his cuffs, and picked up his jacket from the desk chair.

I considered what he said. Was it possible to remain so removed? What did it say about Antonio that he felt he could be?

"What if the monarchy uses the information you gather to harm people?" I wished to reveal more about Antonio's character, and if I could trust him with Hugh.

He threaded his arms through the sleeves and tidied his lapels, considering my question. "It's a chance I must take. I can't refuse a request from the regent. I'm going to the plaza to see this woman. They've probably moved on, but I'd like to be sure. Are you well enough to be alone?"

"Of course."

He paused at the threshold. "We received a last-minute invitation to a reception at the Alhambra this evening. You and Matias were included. Matias was here when it arrived and was certain you would be interested. Is that the case?"

I sat taller in my seat. The Alhambra? Of course I was interested. "Yes, I'm anxious to see the garden."

Antonio buttoned the top fastening of his jacket. "Excellent. It starts quite late. We'll need to depart around eight thirty."

As his footsteps receded, I swirled the remaining liquid in my glass. Antonio had given me much to think about. Perhaps while I was here, I could learn more about the political situation in Spain. Or volunteer to assist Antonio with his investigation?

But what if my actions this morning had led someone dangerous to the house? Clammy gooseflesh coated my arms.

With the last swallow of the whiskey, I abandoned the glass on the sideboard. We didn't need to depart for the reception for hours. A hot cup of coffee, my dressing gown, and a pile of books were the comfort I needed.

Chapter Seven

The deep wine color of the dress gave our bedchamber a ruby glow. Under my hand, the nap of the fabric was sumptuous, a less expensive silk rather than the heavy velvet one would expect of this color. When I spied the modern silhouette in a shop window in Cádiz, I knew it was fated to be mine.

At the moment, the hundreds of tiny buttons that secured the back of the dress had me second-guessing my purchase. Antonio employed a few people: a footman, Severiano, who answered the door at night; a cook, Sarita; and a maid of all work, Felipa, who worked a couple of hours each day. Everyone had departed after the midday meal, and Matias hadn't returned. Buttoning the dress on my own was not possible, short of dislocating my shoulder.

I untied my dressing gown and tossed it on the coverlet. Across the room, my distorted image displayed an abundance of skin draped in fancy underthings. I usually avoided corsets, but the fit of this dress demanded one: black satin sprinkled with vibrant embroidered vines and flowers, paired with a set of matching drawers. It was the most decadent lingerie I'd ever owned.

Despite the worries that had plagued me since I'd overheard Hugh and Antonio's conversation, I tried to dig deep for strength. The woman in the reflection pushed her shoulders back, emanating confidence—with a touch of provocation.

Huffing in amusement, I lifted the dress and wiggled it over my head.

As crimson silk obscured my vision, a distinctive *click* came from behind me. The shroud of fabric vanished from my hands.

Matias draped the dress over a nearby chair. The heat of his gaze scorched a path from my toes to my head.

"Where did you get these?" he murmured, running his palms over my ribs to rest under my plumped breasts.

"In Cádiz. They aren't my usual style, but . . ."

His dumbfounded expression said everything. He tore his eyes from my satin-encased curves to notice my heightened color. A sly grin tipped the corners of his mouth. "Are you embarrassed?" He wrapped his arms around my waist, brushing his nose against a curl that clung to my neck.

"It's . . . different from what I normally wear."

He kissed the corner of my mouth, spearing his fingers in my loose hair. "You are beautiful in anything, but I'm not opposed to you exploring fancy underthings."

I tilted my head, giving him access to my neck and losing myself in the sensuality of his lips—until I remembered I hadn't seen him today, or told him what happened to me. "How was today? Are you making progress with Fernández's collections?"

He didn't reply. Instead, he used his weight to lower me onto the bed.

I resisted the descent, pressing my hands to his chest. "Matias, wait. The reception, and—"

"We have time."

My resistance crumpled under his commanding tone. It took only seconds for him to spark a fire within me. And right now, I wanted to escape more than anything, to remember how it felt when it was only us, and the world went away.

He dropped to his knees between my thighs, obliterating my thoughts.

As I'd suspected, there was no opportunity for discussion. After pleasuring me witless, he fastened my gown and rushed off to bathe. Dressing my hair took an eternity and a mountain of hairpins.

Hugh and Antonio were chatting at the bottom of the stairs, Hugh dusting Antonio's lapels with affection. I waited at the top, watching the tender moment between them, acquiring the fortitude to descend. It would be my first encounter with Hugh since overhearing their conversation about the letter from Kew.

Mask firmly in place, I took the first step.

Hugh beamed when I came into view. "My dear, you look marvelous. That color is fantastic."

"Thank you, Hugh. You look handsome."

He twirled his toucan-topped cane, spreading his arms. Matias swept up my elbow without me noticing he'd arrived.

I was speechless at his appearance. His dark waves were swept off his face, except one that kept flopping over to frame his arresting eyes. He also glowed with sartorial elegance in the same suit he had worn to meet Fernández in Cádiz, tonight with a silver waistcoat.

My regard must've been plain. He dipped low to brush his lips against my jawline. "You look delectable."

Remembering where his lips had traveled earlier, I tightened my grip on his arm.

Hugh's voice shattered the lascivious images that had already begun to flood my imagination. "Are we ready to depart?"

He and Antonio looped arms as they proceeded out the door.

Matias waited for me to climb the stairs into the carriage, then whispered in my ear, "We have unfinished business."

I whipped my head around. He had seen to my pleasure earlier but hadn't allowed me to return the favor. "Is that so?" I teased. "Whose fault is that?"

He followed, chuckling under his breath.

My wander through the city this morning had allowed me to glimpse some of this area of Granada called the Albaicín, but our slow progress in the carriage made for a more leisurely view. As we approached the edge of the Darro River, the Alhambra loomed on the other side of the canyon, framed by the distant peaks of the Sierra Nevada mountains. According to Washington Irving's account, it the Alhambra was a medieval Islamic palace, a formidable feature on the skyline that had fallen into disrepair. The formerly magnificent fortress had been abused over the years, first remade into a royal dwelling and then abandoned. It had even been used to house gunpowder during the Napoleonic Wars.

Major restoration was now happening at the Alhambra, transforming it inside and out. I'd heard that the redesigned gardens were being brought to life. It was the type of project a botanist dreamed of being involved in—or they did, when they weren't being ostracized from their profession.

The reality of my situation kept drifting away, only to fall upon me again with the force of an anvil. I tried to shake it off, pressing my face to the carriage window as we clattered over the bridge.

Illuminated rose walls filled our view as we ascended the hill.

Antonio gestured to the entrance. "We'll enter through the Puerta de la Justicia." The Gate of Justice. How fitting.

From within the confines of our conveyance, the expanse of stone was intimidating. Crossing the plains on foot in medieval times would have meant days under the vigilance of that ominous beacon.

A line of men waited to greet us at the entrance, dwarfed beneath intimidating arches. Torches glowed from within the square watchtower, lighting the twin expanses. One of the guards handed me down from the carriage. I proceeded straight to the walls of the Alhambra.

Face-to-face with the humbling edifice pockmarked by age, I gave in to the urge and removed my glove to touch the surface. My hand served as a necessary anchor when I arched my neck to get a view of the carved keystone.

"It's the hand of Fatima, the *hamsa*. The five fingers represent the pillars of Islam. It is also a symbol of protection," Antonio said.

"It's stunning."

Hugh urged us toward the archways. "Wait until you see the inside."

We passed through the tower along a walkway that ascended in a curve and led us into a vast courtyard. Across the canyon, the lights of the city were sparkling pinpricks. Antonio and Hugh charged across the plaza, but Matias and I lagged, staring in wonder at the palace built by Charles V.

"Hugh." I planted my feet, ready to protest. We were passing sculptures, obelisks, and the enormous palace itself, all without a second glance.

He gestured ahead. "We should've directed the carriages to drop us at the other gate. We're very late. You'll have to wait to sightsee. The reception is in the Nasrid Palaces. Hurry along."

With a grumble that made Matias snort in laughter, I followed.

Part of the wall was disassembled between the Palace of Charles V and the Nasrid Palaces. Men waited on both sides with torches to direct us through the opening. The crowd was audible as we passed through a small courtyard and through the outer walls.

I was again immobilized with wonder when we entered the building. Above us, a canopy of tiles spiraled in dizzying geometric designs that danced in the flickering torchlight. Despite having been built as a fort, it was airy, an amalgam of outside space and interior mathematical perfection. It tempted the visitor to linger and absorb every inch of creation. My mind struggled to absorb the grandeur.

Antonio interrupted my reverie by nudging us into the infamous Court of the Myrtles. Elevated torches along the pool reflected the dark water in the middle. A receiving line of people snaked along one side in a procession of opulent fabrics and jewels. When we passed into the luminescent area, a man whose girth tested the strength of his jacket rushed toward us.

"Ah, Señor Navarro! How are you this evening?"

Antonio gave a slight bow and gestured to Hugh first, as was appropriate. "I'm well, Señor Suárez. May I please present Lord Martin, the Earl of Holloway, Lady Wren, and el señor Ward? El señor Hernando Suárez is overseeing the restoration of the Alhambra on behalf of the government."

As a group, we dipped into gestures of respect. El señor Suárez captured my hand as I rose from my curtsy. "Lady Wren, we are honored that you are in attendance. I understand you have vast expertise when it comes to gardens."

My mind blanked at his compliment. Suárez took advantage of my distraction to lead me away from the others. "Please allow me to escort you into the reception."

I frantically looked over my shoulder at Matias, but he looked equally helpless in the face of this overeager man.

"Er, thank you, Señor Suárez. You may call me Linnea."

"Ah, indeed. *Una rebelde*, eh?"

"No, it's just—" I braced myself for this recurring theme in my conversations this evening. My title came from a family I hardly remembered and represented privileges I rejected.

I craned my neck around, glancing forlornly at the myrtles and espalier trees as Suárez towed me toward a large group of people. "Come, come, I'll introduce you to the rest of our honored guests."

We moved through a gauntlet of greetings: Some shook my hand, some bowed or curtsied, but with most, I exchanged a *besito*, one on each cheek.

A handsome roué interrupted our slow progress, pushing ahead of the others in line.

"Lady Wren, may I please present the Ilustrísimo Señor Conde de Granada Graciano Gonzalez-Gomez."

The conde took advantage when he leaned in for a *besito* and looped our arms together. I was getting fed up with being manhandled. Too much resistance would create a scene, so I allowed him to guide us . . . for now.

Suárez sputtered in indignation in our wake.

"Ilustrísimo Señor, you foiled el señor Suárez's plans."

My icy tone didn't faze him. He waved his hand. "El señor Suárez cannot always have his way. A woman as beautiful as you shouldn't be stuck in a line. I want you to meet some people—your people."

I redoubled my efforts to free my arm when I caught sight of our destination: a pack of haughty aristocrats with curled lips and ostentatious jewelry in abundance. Agitated at the prospect of being trapped with them, I searched beyond, hoping to spot Matias. They closed ranks, caging me within their circle.

"Good evening, friends. I would like to introduce Lady Wren. Lady Wren, this is la señora Lourdes Sánchez-Martín. She is assisting with the restoration."

Though our time in Spain had been limited, I was familiar with la señora Sánchez-Martín. She was a sought-after garden designer. What I knew of her work was impressive. I admired how she continued to modernize her designs, breaking away from the traditional approach to gardens.

"Ah, Lady Wren, I've heard of you. El señor Navarro and I have friends in common. He mentioned that you have expertise in medicinal plantings. I would love to ask your opinion." She moved us toward a small bench tucked against a carved arch.

A young man occupied the seat built into the niche. He rose as we approached.

"Ah, Señor Pelayo, we didn't mean to disturb you. We'll find somewhere else to chat."

"It's quite all right, señora. I must locate my family before they come looking for me."

"Señor Alonso Rodriguez Pelayo, may I introduce Lady Wren?"

As the young man leaned in for a *besito,* his unique fragrance enveloped me. He smelled of cloves, bay leaves, and whiskey. It was unusual, a welcome change from the cloud of floral perfumes. He was a handsome young man in his mid-twenties, with wavy, dark hair and cocoa-rich eyes.

"Do you work at the Alhambra, señor?" I asked as we drew apart.

"I do not, but my family is involved." But el señor Pelayo was distracted. He edged around us, close enough for me to note the gleam of perspiration along his hairline. "Will you excuse me? I see someone I must speak to."

He darted away without waiting for a reply.

"Young people." La señora Sánchez-Martín shrugged. She seated herself on the bench, spreading her skirts with an elegant flick of her wrist. "Lady Wren, I would like your opinion on something. I've had requests from clients to include imported flowering plants from southern Africa. Do you think that we risk the seeds escaping from the gardens?"

Grateful for her rescue, I was willing to discuss any topic as long as it kept me away from those people.

We spoke of the advantages of planting native specimens in gardens. La señora Sánchez-Martín grew animated when she spoke of the difficulties of pleasing clients.

At a pause in our conversation, she settled nearer, the strong scent of hyacinth wafting toward me. "There is another reason I wished to speak to you privately, Lady Wren. I hope that now that we are a bit more acquainted, I can persuade you."

I was confused at her turn of conversation. "Persuade me?"

"Yes. You see, I have several projects underway in Cádiz, but I was summoned to Granada because they have an immediate need for a gardener. When I heard you had arrived, I thought maybe we could assist each other."

My fingertips tingled. Assist each other?

Glancing at the crowd that was moving toward the dais, she continued, "One of the gardeners directing the restoration had to leave immediately for a family crisis. I hoped that you might step into that role."

My astonishment must have been evident. She was quick to provide reassurance.

"It would not be taxing. The plan is already set. You would be responsible for following it."

I was stunned by her invitation. To be involved in a restoration on this scale was an opportunity most botanists would never experience. I would be a fool to pass it up.

La señora Sánchez-Martín rose from our hideaway. "The speeches are about to begin. I can see that I've startled you. Unfortunately, I will need your answer by tomorrow." She offered her hand.

I shook her hand and mumbled a goodbye, still adrift in my astonishment.

A few moments later, Matias drew alongside me, raising my hand to the crook of his elbow. "Where did you sneak away to?"

"I was hiding in a corner, talking about plants."

"Somehow, I'm not surprised."

I smiled up at him. "Matias, I've had the most extraordinary offer."

Bearing two glasses of wine, Hugh interrupted, "You look as if you need this."

"Oh, goodness, yes." My throat was dry from speaking with la señora. I wanted to escape this reception and flee into the gardens. I took a step toward the exit.

Hugh laughed, snagging my sleeve. "I know what you are thinking. You can't bolt. We must stay for the speeches."

I sighed, resigned to my fate. "Have you met these people?"

"A few of them. Antonio and I don't socialize with this class of people."

"You mean your fellow aristocrats?"

He waved his hand. "Yes, well."

"Any chance I'll be able to tour the grounds?"

"Maybe after," Hugh replied.

Antonio joined us with a drink for himself and one for Hugh. The crowd turned toward the head of the pool as a woman with gravity-defying hair took her place upon the dais and launched into a loud aria. Matias, knowing my hatred of opera, covered his mouth to smother his mirth at my expression of horror.

Chapter Eight

After the aria and three rambling speeches, my desire for quiet was a desperate, clawing necessity. Matias discerned that my poise was disintegrating and offered to keep the others occupied.

I was tempted to kiss him at that moment, but we didn't need to draw any more attention.

Winding through the Palace of Charles V, I emerged on the edge of the Generalife. The external torches on the palace walls, combined with the third-quarter moon, bathed the vast garden in light.

The Chelsea Physic Garden occupied four acres, the Generalife closer to thirty-four. Beds, trees, and pocket courtyards stretched across the hillside, spilling onto the shadowed edges. Distant lights from the Alhambra and the Albaicín glittered across the river, a barrier between worlds. Unifying the space into a design scheme was a heady prospect. My fingers itched to tackle it.

At the height of its occupation, the Generalife had been home to the sultan's summer palace, the beds cultivated to feed the inhabitants of the palace and fortress. Many years of neglect were being repaired. Heaps of rich soil marked the fresh beds, gleaming new rocks transformed the trails into streams of moonlight, and feral cypress groves crept from the banks of the Darro to colonize the borders.

A map formed in my mind, delineating the new from the original areas. Established roses, pomegranate trees, and myrtles dominated the shrubs. Plantings of spirea colonized the fresh beds. Thus far, the fundamental structure was being discarded for the creation of small, knot-like gardens, interspersed with existing courtyards and waterways. The possibilities were intriguing. I wouldn't be allowed to change the design, but there were ways to be innovative with the plantings.

With one final, guilty glance toward the noise of the reception, I lifted the hem of my dress and fled along the white, pebbled pathway.

My body tingled with an effervescent rush of excitement. To have the opportunity to make my mark on a project of this scale would be a significant boon to my career. It was what I needed, given the talk circulating about me.

I rubbed the glossy leaf of a myrtle between my fingertips. Tendrils of a breeze swept up from the canyon, blowing wisps of hair off my face. The caress of air was a whisper, a sign that this place was my destiny.

I was so engrossed in my glow of purpose as I approached the Alhambra that I didn't notice the body until I was less than a foot away.

Facedown, they were a few steps from the outer walls of the fort.

"*Disculpe, ¿se encuentra bien?*"

No response or movement.

I nudged them with the toe of my slipper. Still nothing.

I wrapped my skirts around my knees and knelt. Judging by the person's clothing, it was a man.

"¿Señor?"

He didn't move.

I discarded my gloves from my trembling hands. Under my bare fingers, his shoulder was muscular. After a shake didn't receive a response, I wiggled two fingers under his cravat.

His skin was cool, but not cold. There wasn't a pulse from his carotid artery.

I ignored the nausea that surged at the confirmation he was deceased and instead registered the surrounding details, knowing they would be important. Palms down against the ground. Clean, short fingernails. From the cut and material of his suit, he was a reception attendee.

I searched the entrance to the reception. A server stood inside the archway on the fringes of the crowd.

Stumbling over, I addressed him in a shaking voice. "Señor, I'm unwell. Can you find my companion?"

"Of course, señora."

"His name is Matias Ward. He's tall like you, with wavy, dark brown hair and green eyes. He's wearing a silver waistcoat. Oh, and he has an English accent." Matias's accent wasn't truly English, but to most Spanish people, it would sound so. "He might be with a man of similar height who has gray hair and is carrying a cane with a bird on top."

Heart hammering, I returned to the prone man.

From this angle, three sets of footprints were visible. Mine led to the Generalife. Two other sets also pointed away from the body, taking the same path toward the Generalife, but veered off toward the entry gates. The man's shoes were shiny, handmade, and smaller than either of the prints.

Low voices approached. Matias and Antonio were coming toward us.

I scowled. Why had Matias brought Antonio?

Matias spoke as they drew near. "Are you well? Oh." He halted when he saw the body.

"What happened?" Antonio squatted. "Is he alive?"

"There isn't a heartbeat," I croaked.

Matias knelt on the other side of the victim. Antonio placed a hand on the man's shoulder. "Let's roll him over."

Matias levered from his side while Antonio gently guided the man toward us. As the body shifted, so did the stench of vomit. It was foul. The plackets of his jacket were damp.

"He was poorly before he died," I said, choking down an involuntary retch. Another scent wafted in the air: cloves. The implications of the familiarity of that scent almost made me retch again. "I—I know him. I met him at the reception."

Antonio propped an arm on his knee. "Alonso Rodriguez Pelayo. One of the king's cousins."

We stared at one another; the air heavy with significance.

"The king's cousin? That's not good." Matias's understatement mirrored what we were all thinking.

Heavy sadness pressed down on me. A couple hours ago, this handsome young man had kissed my cheek. Now his skin was pale, red veins blazing in the whites of his eyes.

"Antonio, look at his eyes. Strangulation?"

Antonio gulped, massaging his temples. "He also could've suffocated on his vomit. I must find Suárez and alert him to the situation." He rose to his feet. "You'll both stay while I go for assistance? This must be discreet."

Matias replied, "Yes, we'll stay."

I didn't want to stay. I wanted to be as far away from this situation as I could get. Why were we fated to be left with a corpse—again?

A few steps of distance would help. I shifted my weight to rise when I noticed his shoes.

"He didn't walk in the Generalife. There's no dust on his shoes. And the other two sets of footprints are larger." The hem of my dress was caked in dust. He couldn't have walked in the gardens without dirtying his shoes. "He wasn't here when I left the reception."

Matias shifted closer. "You didn't pass anyone?"

"No, nor did I hear anyone. But the Generalife is huge, and I walked only a small portion."

My eyes traveled from the body to Matias and the night beyond. Our location was unfamiliar, but the situation wasn't. Horrible memories of Cristobal and Tomas's murders sat with us. At least this man hadn't been brutally stabbed.

"What are the chances that this is happening to us again?" He was also thinking of those other bodies.

"One in a million?"

"It's uncanny."

"Last time, the murders were connected to—" As soon as I spoke, I felt awful. I reached across the body to snag the sleeve of his jacket. "Apologies. You didn't need to be reminded."

He gripped and squeezed my hand. "It brings it back, doesn't it?"

"Antonio is the inquiry agent. It won't be our concern. The government has their own people, unlike rural Chiloé," I tried to reassure us both.

Antonio approached with Suárez, heads together. Antonio gesticulated, pointing toward us. I came to my feet, shaking the soil from my gown.

"Señor Suárez, Lady Wren found el señor Pelayo."

El señor Suárez pressed his fingers to his temples. "This is distressing. Señor Navarro, what do you believe happened?"

"As I said, Lady Wren discovered him when she returned from a walk in the Generalife. Based on the evidence, we believe he was ill. Are you aware of any health conditions he may have had?"

"No, no, el señor Pelayo was healthy. He is . . . ahem, *was* a young man."

"I assume you will contact an official to examine him? We didn't see any obvious marks that would indicate an attack."

"Ay dios. No one can know. I'll send for the doctor who serves the royal family. Señor Navarro, you must be present for the examination. If this is murder, your services will be required."

Antonio began speaking, but Suárez ignored him to shout orders to the staff person lingering near the entrance.

I walked around the body to Matias's side, reaching for his hand. "Er . . . Matias and I can leave, I presume?" I wanted distance between us and that body. The last thing we needed was to be involved in another investigation.

Antonio gave us a distracted nod. "Yes, yes. I'll have questions for you later."

We didn't hesitate as we hastened toward the ebullient crowd inside.

In our absence, the reception had turned boisterous. Free-flowing wine, combined with desperate social climbers, was a riotous stew. Dionysian in its inebriation, but with expensive jewelry.

A painful contrast to the scene we'd left.

Hugh hovered at the edge of the crowd, waiting for Antonio. Our wide-eyed, addled state must have been clue enough that he wasn't with us.

Hugh steered us to a quiet alcove. "Something has happened?"

This wasn't the place to explain. "Yes. I think Antonio will be occupied for a while. Matias and I would like to go home."

Hugh didn't argue. "I'll call the carriage for you. I'll wait for Antonio, though. We can take a hired hack when he's finished."

Matias followed Hugh, leaving me alone in the alcove. "Why don't you go to Antonio? I'll ask for the carriage."

La señora Sánchez-Martín sidled in as soon as Matias was out of sight. "Are you bored with the party? I am."

Earlier, I'd found her company charming. But the events of the night had plunged me into a whirlpool of memories. My enthusiasm at her offer had dimmed.

"You disappeared. Did you tour the gardens?"

Was it my imagination, or were her shrewd eyes predatory? I had yet to reply to any of her questions, yet my cool manner didn't dissuade her unsettling eagerness. Perhaps it was my heightened emotional state, but our interaction was . . . strange. "I did. I couldn't see much in the dark, but it was intriguing."

Matias caught my eye from across the room. He waved toward the door. Our coach must've arrived.

Relieved, I turned to her to take my leave. "Señora Sánchez-Martín, please forgive me. It appears my carriage is ready."

"I must return to Cádiz tomorrow. Did you make a decision?"

My plummet from elation to grief—and the peculiarity of our interaction—made me uneasy. It tempered my eagerness, but not enough to decline. "Yes, I'm willing. You'll send the details?"

"I will." She clutched my arms and kissed my cheek. "Our meeting tonight was fated."

Her insincere laugh haunted me as I traversed the drunken revelry to Matias.

Chapter Nine

We were silent as the carriage navigated through the neighborhoods, lost in our private thoughts. A young man was dead. Why had he been killed?

As we descended into the Albaicín, the looming Alhambra felt portentous, rather than promising.

Once we arrived, each step into the house took effort. My shoulders sagged with weariness. My feet guided me along the hall and into the library, but sleep wouldn't be possible yet. My recurring nightmares were flickering in my mind, merging with visions of Pelayo's body.

I poured a glass of water from the sideboard, rather than something alcoholic. Matias folded into a chair with a resigned sigh. "Would you like some water?"

He nodded. I handed him the filled glass and poured another.

"I keep seeing Tomas and Cristobal." His voice was an anguished whisper.

My sip of water helped lessen the choking emotion that rose within me. "I know."

Matias raked his fingers through his hair. "What did you speak to la señora Sánchez-Martín about?"

In the chaos of finding Pelayo, I had forgotten to tell Matias about our conversation.

"We spoke about plantings, but that turned into an offer. She asked if I would fill in for a gardener who has been called away . . . to assist with the restoration of the Generalife gardens."

He jerked up in his chair. "That's incredible! Why didn't you mention it earlier?"

"With the discovery of Pelayo, I didn't think . . ."

Matias quirked his brows just as Hugh stumbled into the library, interrupting him from parsing my evasion.

Hugh freed the knot in his cravat with a grimace.

"You decided not to wait? Can I get you something to drink?" I asked, moving toward the sideboard.

Hugh nodded, taking the chair next to Matias. "Antonio sent me away. He wasn't sure how much later he would be. They are waiting for the doctor."

Antonio must've told Hugh what happened.

"Are you well? Antonio said you found the body," he said to me.

Was I well? Adequate words to describe my state remained out of reach. Horror at finding another body. Grief for the life lost. But what happened to him wasn't about me.

"Pelayo, the man who died, deserves our focus."

Hugh hesitated before imbibing. "You knew him?"

"We met this evening. Briefly."

We lapsed into silence. I suspected Matias and I were wrestling with similar memories. I drifted to the shelves, searching for volumes on Spanish botany.

When Matias made a whiffling noise, we both turned toward him. His head was propped on his chest, muffling a second, louder snore.

I whispered, "Seeing that body was a shock for Matias. An upsetting reminder of Lucien Ward's crimes."

Hugh gave me a concerned look. "It took more of a toll on you both than you've admitted."

He was right. In the weeks since we'd arrived in Spain, the cracks were spreading.

I wandered to the settee in the corner with my pile of books, running my fingers over the velvet brocade. In the past, alcohol and sex were how I had coped. I couldn't lose myself in that destructive spiral again. Matias and I were physically intimate, but something was shifting.

When Antonio arrived, I was paging through a guide to the flora of Spain, wide awake and being serenaded by Matias and Hugh snoring in their respective chairs. Antonio stopped to pour himself some water, then glanced at them and at me, and tilted his head toward the garden.

I followed him into the courtyard.

Trust wasn't easy for me, and even harder to earn when Hugh was involved. He was my only family, and he was in love with Antonio. I wasn't sure if Antonio reciprocated Hugh's devotion. But for Hugh's sake, I was willing to build a relationship with him, despite my embarrassment that Hugh had shared my failures with him.

He rubbed his eyes in exhaustion. "I wanted to see if you are well after stumbling across that nasty scene."

Wasn't it typical of the British that we always claimed to be well? Maybe it was because I didn't feel British after so many years elsewhere, or perhaps because I knew Antonio's query was genuine. Whatever the reason, I was truthful. "You're aware that this isn't the first time I've discovered a corpse. Does one become accustomed to it?"

"Only monsters." His tone was as bleak as his expression.

"Did the doctor say what killed him?"

"The doctor believes he was poisoned."

Antonio's response made the hair on my arms rise with foreboding.

An animal shuffled in the vines above us. I peered upward, searching, but the moon had set hours ago. We were in the deepest hours of the night, absent of any hint of dawn.

His rough exhale stirred the delicate bougainvillea petals that hung around us. "I shared that information because I need your help."

"Me?" I squeaked. "What can I do?"

"The doctor believes the poison came from a plant. His rapid death, vomiting, and skin discoloration are consistent with vegetative poisoning, although the doctor couldn't confirm which caused his demise—the plant, or the suffocation."

Shivers gave way to full-body trembling. I wrapped my arms tight around my waist to calm my physical reaction. I knew what he was asking. "I'm not an expert on poisonous plants."

"You may not be an expert, but you'll know which plants in the Alhambra are deadly. We can arrange for you to have a detailed tour of the garden. Given your reputation, the staff would not question your presence. But if you would rather not be involved, I can ask someone else."

My first impulse was to refuse his request. I had been offered a position at the Alhambra that would help me rebuild my reputation. Matias and I had investigated murders before, and I wasn't anxious to do it again. Would my position and relationship be in jeopardy if I got involved? I did have the knowledge to assist, though, and if it helped seek justice for an innocent victim . . .

"Er, a tour won't be necessary. La señora Sánchez-Martín asked me to assist with the Generalife restoration."

Antonio froze in his fiddling with a dried leaf. "She did? That's . . . fortuitous. Does that mean you agree to help?"

This entire night had been a runaway carriage careening toward a cliff. We had learned during the investigation on Chiloé that the more time passed after the crime, the more likely evidence would be comprised or removed. We would need to examine the scene as soon as it was light.

The fact that I was planning the next step implied that I was already committed. But I wouldn't get too involved. My role was simple: Identify the plant, and let Antonio deal with the rest.

"Ye-e-es?" I betrayed my hesitancy.

"Maybe you'll feel certain after a few hours of sleep. It's almost morning. Let's rest while we can."

Hugh and Matias were still asleep. We exchanged wry looks and roused our men.

Matias followed me from the library, yawning. In our room, he dropped to the edge of the bed and motioned me over to unbutton my dress.

Once the dress and stays were loose, I retreated behind the privacy screen. The silk fabric of my dressing gown and the scented water in the basin were soothing.

"You're suspiciously quiet. Don't fall asleep in your clothes," I scolded.

The thud of boots hitting the floor came from the other side of the room. Matias's face was contorted in a yawn when he joined me behind the screen, fumbling blindly for the tooth powder. After giving my face a last swipe with the cloth, I ceded the space.

The topics I needed to discuss with Matias were mounting. The Alhambra position. Another murder investigation. What I'd overheard from Hugh.

We faced each other from opposite sides of the bed. Lines of tension were etched in his face. Now wasn't the moment.

I sat on the bed and slid my legs beneath the coverlet. The cool sheets against my skin were exquisite. I rolled to my side, away from him. I would tell him about the investigation, but the speculation about me created by Felicity Ward? That would devastate him. Was it wrong to keep that a secret?

My mental debate didn't last. Like a snuffed candle, my mind went dark.

My doubts about helping did not diminish overnight. Neither did my vocal conscience.

But I wasn't ready to discuss my concerns with anyone, and Antonio preferred silence in the mornings. We sipped our scalding coffee between nibbles of *tostada*. When his familiar notebook appeared on the tabletop, that was my cue to top off my coffee cup.

Finally, Antonio cleared his throat. "May I share details from the doctor's examination? To provide some insight?"

I nodded.

"Pelayo had convulsions before he vomited."

My stomach swooped.

Antonio watched my expression. "Is this too much?"

"No, no," I reassured him. "Go on."

"The doctor isn't sure that poison would've killed him outright. If he hadn't fallen, he might've survived the dose. So, the plant might not be the ultimate cause of death."

Hot liquid burned the back of my throat, my coffee threatening to reappear. "Pelayo might have lived if I had found him earlier?"

Matias's voice penetrated my accelerated breathing. "Are you well?" He cupped my knees through the fabric of my skirt. "You're pale." He turned to Antonio. "What did you say to her? What's going on?"

His strident questions returned me to awareness. I patted his hand with fondness, my voice gentle. "It's fine, Matias. Give me a moment. Please, have some breakfast."

With a lingering, concerned expression, he retreated to the buffet.

I faced Antonio. "We'll return to the Alhambra this morning?"

"Yes. Knowing what we know now, we need to examine the area around where you found Pelayo and notify Suárez of your involvement. I assume you planned to meet with him anyway, to arrange your duties at the Generalife?"

"I missed something," Matias grumbled as he pulled out a chair.

Antonio rose from the table as Matias sat. "Shall we meet in the foyer in half an hour? Is that too soon?"

"That's acceptable."

Matias's knuckles were white around his utensils. As he waited for me to speak, I twirled the cup in its saucer, searching for the right way to phrase it.

His patience broke as I was searching for the words. "Are you helping with his investigation?"

Whatever I replied, he was going to be unhappy about my involvement. Since when did I need to share all my decisions with him? He wouldn't be here in Granada. I didn't answer to him or anyone. I dampened my rising ire. "They suspect Pelayo was poisoned with a plant. Antonio has asked for my assistance in identifying it. Since I'm going to be in the Generalife anyway—"

"Are you sure this is a good idea?"

I drank the dregs of my coffee without tasting it. Didn't he believe I was competent enough to know what I could handle? Hadn't I proved myself to him, at least?

"I found him. I have plant knowledge and access to the Alhambra. Wouldn't you?"

Matias's puzzled expression at the vehemence of my reply tempered my flare of anger a bit. "Yes, I would. I did. But things are different for you. Even if I'm not here, Hugh could help."

My voice was steely. "Are you saying it is different because I am a woman, or because we are in a relationship?"

His eyebrows shot up in alarm. "What? No, that wasn't what I meant."

I slid my chair from the table with such force, it wobbled. As I steadied it, a wave of dislocation blurred the room in front of me. Was this truly what he believed?

"I need to gather some things from our bedchamber. Are you meeting with Fernández?"

"We're going to begin planning for our trip."

"Until tonight, then," I replied, exiting the room.

Chapter Ten

Antonio didn't remark on my mood while we traveled to the Alhambra, but I thought it unlikely that my agitation was concealed after my exchange with Matias. I drew upon every one of my reserves of professionalism to push aside my emotions.

On our way to meet Suárez, we passed through several courtyards. They were busy with workers repairing the damage from the reception-turned-bacchanal.

Our conversation ended up being as dizzying as that party. Suárez was delighted that I had agreed to fill in for the absent gardener. He'd handed over a letter from la señora Sánchez-Martín and was about to dismiss us when Antonio disclosed my role with his investigation. And that was when Suárez turned peculiar.

"There's no need for an inquiry. This is the work of anti-monarchists. Identify their leader, and you have your criminal."

Antonio folded his arms, shifting his weight to his heels. "With respect, señor, we don't know for certain that it was the socialist group. The doctor believes Pelayo was poisoned. Lady Wren will assist me with identifying the culprit."

Suárez ignored him, riffling through his desk drawers. When he raised his head, his expression was one of disinterest. "Fine. Do what you feel you must. She can help when she isn't working in the Generalife. You must excuse me—I'm expecting a group of sponsors."

With a glance between us, Antonio and I left. We waited until we had passed into the courtyard before speaking.

"He believes it was the socialists. Is there any point in an investigation?" I asked once we were out of range for eavesdropping.

"It is the opposite of what he said last night," Antonio replied.

"I wonder what changed?"

Antonio shrugged. "Who can say? Let's proceed as we planned. Do you need me to accompany you?"

"No. I'll begin where I found Pelayo." I folded la señora Sánchez-Martín's letter and slipped it into my pocket. "And then draft a list of plants."

"I'll leave you to it."

As I approached the site of Pelayo's death, my instincts bade me to wait. To calm myself, I closed my eyes, releasing my senses like scouts deployed to collect information.

The essence of the gardens infused my body: the perfume of plants, the water flowing, the hundreds of years of people working this land. Around me, gardeners debated where to start, their voices amplified by the walls of the Alhambra. Leaves swished in the orchard.

There were more birds than people in the Generalife. They were active in the cooler air of the morning. Swooping wings. Conversational calls, not alarm notes.

Motionless, I waited. A slight breeze stirring my skirts was the signal. It was a sense—the movement of air, a settling within.

The footprints from the previous night had been swept clean. The only indications of Pelayo's last resting place were soil dried in clumps and a slight depression in the earth.

Kneeling in the dirt, I unsheathed my knife, teasing at the lumps of dirt. Warm air had dried the soil, leaving only the clumps as indications that there had once been liquid here. Pelayo must not have eaten for several hours prior to vomiting. The poison had likely been delivered through a drink of some kind.

Sitting on my heels, I surveyed the empty Generalife. It was an expansive, lonely place, as if it were holding the grief of what had occurred.

Blowing a strand of hair from my eyes, I squinted at the position of the sun. I had been here for at least an hour, maybe more. Five more minutes, and then I would focus on compiling the promised list of plants.

I used the flat side of my dagger to sift through the soil, digging the blade deeper at a scooping angle.

A dark brown, jagged fragment appeared at the surface, then vanished. I swirled the blade again. With minute movements, I coaxed it onto the metal.

At first glance, it appeared to be vegetative, with an odd, thick texture. My hand lens hung on a leather strap around my neck. I bent closer without disturbing the specimen, using the lens to examine the striations.

"Buenos días, señora."

The lens fell from my hand, jarring the carefully balanced blade. I swallowed a curse, twisting in my undignified position to glower at the interloper.

A young woman dressed in a faded, rose-colored frock stood nearby, her expression eager. I addressed her in Spanish: "That path will lead you into the Generalife."

She pointed to my lens. "Are you looking for insectos?" She spoke in accented but clear English.

"Er, no. Plants."

"Plants? That small?"

"Pieces of plants." I blew the dust from my lens, assuming she would take a hint, given my terse responses. I searched for the spilled fragment. Fortunately, it hadn't been covered by the soil yet.

Instead, she knelt across from me. "¿Es usted la jardinera inglesa? My name is Pilar Molina." She offered her hand.

I wiped my palm on my thigh and extended my stained fingers. "I'm Linnea Wren. You're a gardener?"

"Sí, pero no soy una experta como usted." She settled the folds of her skirt beneath her knees. The hem was decorated with embroidered flowers. A plain pinafore was tied over the top, her pruning shears half spilling from the pocket. "We were told there was an accidente last night. Is this where it occurred?"

Given Suárez's wish for discretion, I was surprised the staff had been informed. The less said, the better. "Er, yes."

"Would you mind if I practiced my English?"

She vibrated with the radiance of youth. Her dark, braided hair rested on her shoulder, her eyes the color of shiny chestnuts. Did I have anything to offer this bright young woman? Having been raised by my uncle and on ships, I was usually inclined to form friendships with men instead of women. Maria, Matias's cousin, was the only female friend I'd had in many years.

"Not at all."

"Can I help?"

Fumbling with the lens strap, I returned to my examination. "I'm searching the ground for any information that could help us understand."

"You're using that to look at the soil?" She pointed at my hand lens.

"Yes, it's a device that magnifies."

"Did what happened last night involve plants?" Her eyes sparked with unmistakable intelligence. Was her innocence an act?

I folded a handkerchief around the blade, saving the fragment to examine. Pilar watched as I stowed the cloth in my pocket. "Pilar, you know what occurred last night, don't you?"

A rosy flush bloomed on her cheeks. "Sí, señora. Someone was murdered."

She either wasn't a practiced liar, or she was an accomplished actress. The latter possibility tempered my response. "What do you want from me?"

She avoided making eye contact, shifting on her knees. "I wish to learn from you. I've worked here for a short while and want to gain more skills. But the other jardineros don't associate with the workers. But as you are una mujer, I thought . . ."

My sigh was involuntary. Did she want to learn from a fellow woman, or did she think that because I wasn't a man, I would be more gullible to disclosing information?

Then again, did it matter? If she wanted to observe, I wouldn't turn her away. Uncovering her motivations could wait for another day, when I wasn't sleep deprived.

"I would welcome you assisting some other day. I'm finished for now. It was a pleasure to meet you."

I veered toward the lower garden. Once within the shade of a courtyard wall, I watched her. She hadn't moved, her face pinched in an expression of frustration. Was I being overly suspicious? Maybe she *was* just seeking a mentor. She didn't deserve my insolence.

I would make more of an effort the next time we met.

At our morning meeting, Suárez had motioned toward an area that contained the offices—temporary, narrow rooms wedged between the Palace of Charles V and the Court of the Lions. Calling these flimsy spaces "offices" was generous. A lopsided door opened into the one set aside for the absent gardener; it was a glorified closet containing a dodgy desk, a questionable chair, and a few planks of wood propped on bricks that I assumed was supposed to be a bookcase. The gardener's priority had been an organized basket of tools.

At least we agreed on that.

I was tentatively lowering myself into the chair when voices resounded through the walls. Suárez's brittle tenor was recognizable.

"I couldn't refuse. What would you have me do? It was her choice, not mine," he snapped.

Another voice rumbled further down the corridor, a warm baritone that was hard to discern.

The thin walls did not allow for privacy—a fortunate discovery. I wondered who "she" was in the context of this argument.

Deciding not to risk the rickety chair after all, I remained standing and unfolded the letter from la señora Sánchez-Martín that Suárez had passed to me during our meeting.

Lady Wren,

Thank you for taking this assignment. We are fortunate to have your expertise. I've enclosed a map of the beds. Please begin with the ones indicated. Once those are complete, consult with the other gardeners to determine how to proceed. I will be traveling, but you can reach me in Cádiz if you need information. My address is below.

Señora Lourdes Sánchez-Martín

The bottom half of the letter was a drawing of the Generalife, the beds numbered and located near the courtyard I had sheltered in earlier.

After another cursory examination of the office, it became obvious that it wasn't secure enough to store the handkerchief with the plant. The door was flimsy, and the desk drawer did not lock. As anxious as I was to begin working, I would have to remove the evidence first.

The curtains in the library billowed inward when I entered. Someone had left the doors open. Antonio wouldn't have been that careless; the wind must've blown them open.

I scanned the house garden. Heavy flower heads bobbed in the breeze. The garden's sole occupants appeared to be orange-winged butterflies and pollen-drunk bumblebees.

I reluctantly closed the door on the peaceful scene to return to my task. After finding a secure place for the pod, I would return to the Generalife to search for poisonous plants.

A small wooden side table across from a window seat would make an adequate place to view my discovery. Bright beams of light fell upon the scrap of vegetation, illuminating details I hadn't been able to see in the garden. These weren't the characteristic patterns of a leaf.

A bit of stem? Not the right shape. A pod? That would explain the strange texture. Which plants in the Generalife would have pods now?

Leaning against the library wall was a stack of books I had pulled from the shelves the night before. A guide to the plants of southern Spain might be useful, but there were many plants in the Generalife that had arrived from elsewhere. I selected a pamphlet on plants for the garden that had been recommended by la señora Sánchez-Martín.

The front door slammed. Antonio's shout followed: "¿Hay alguien en casa?"

"*Estoy en la biblioteca,*" I responded.

Antonio swept into the library and over to my temporary workspace. "What is that?"

"A bit of a pod from where we found Pelayo. I've no idea what it's from yet."

He squinted at the tiny piece, raising a skeptical eyebrow. "Do you think this is the plant that poisoned him?"

I fiddled with the edge of the cloth. "Maybe, maybe not. It could be detritus. Regardless, it was the only thing I found."

Antonio retrieved a pen from the stand on the table. He sat in a chair facing me and crossed his ankle over his thigh.

The scratch of the pen against the paper of his notebook jangled my nerves. Did he doubt me?

"It isn't much, I know. With luck, something else will come to light once I can search the garden," I babbled, trying to reassure him. Embarrassed by my atypical behavior, I changed the topic. "I've been considering our conversation with Suárez this morning. Do you think he will try to obstruct the investigation?"

Antonio's foot dropped to the floor; the sound muffled by the thick carpet. "Suárez is a powerful man. If we defy him, he will cause problems. But in this case, I don't answer to him. He's unlikely to affect my future inquiries, try though he may."

"Could he be involved in Pelayo's murder?"

Antonio paused, smoothing a hand across his chin. "I wouldn't think so. He's a staunch royalist. He wouldn't associate with the socialists—if they are responsible."

An ornate clock on the mantel gave a discordant chime. I waited for the sound to fade, working up the courage to ask a personal question. "Does he know you and Hugh are—"

"No." His reply was sharp.

I pushed on. "Does anyone know?"

Antonio shifted in his seat. "Our laws are not as strict as those in England, but my relationship with Hugh isn't something I flaunt. We've been living together. It wouldn't be difficult for someone to draw conclusions." He steepled his hands, watching me over the tips of his fingers. "Hugh is not the first. I had one other long-standing relationship several years ago. It didn't affect my work then, and it is unlikely to now."

His candor was appreciated, even if it didn't alleviate my concerns. I didn't want Hugh to be harmed by Antonio or anyone else. "What can we do to appease Suárez?"

"He's stubborn, high-handed. He puts on airs. We shouldn't dismiss him as a suspect. Our best course is to keep our findings confidential for as long as possible."

"Can you keep this secure?" I offered the linen.

He carried it to the clock on the mantel, where a tiny drawer sprang from the base. Inside was a gold key. "Now you know where the key is hidden."

He locked the bundle in his desk.

My ability to contain my restless energy was fading. "Bringing that here was more important than cataloging plants. I'm going to take advantage of the remaining daylight and return to that task. You'll let Hugh and Matias know?"

Antonio tipped his head in agreement. As I reached the door, he added, "Do you know what makes a good inquiry agent? Curiosity. And you have that in spades. It's only dangerous when our curiosity blinds us to the facts."

Chapter Eleven

B lue hour: the territory of owls and errant botanists. *And bats*, I thought, as one swept from the branches of the gnarled cypress above my head.

The Generalife had emptied while I filled my notebook. Ambient light was minimal, and this was the darkest corner of the garden.

I rested my aching spine against the rough bark of the trunk with a sigh of relief. Searching for a seedpod among this abundance was ridiculous. It could've blown in from anywhere.

I thought of Antonio's cryptic observation. Was I trying to make the evidence fit the story, or was it fact?

Thus far, restoration efforts had been focused on the area around the buildings. The bottom of the garden, past the orchards, was still wild. In a gust of wind, cypress branches brushed together; their rustles and clacks made an unpleasant grating sound. Gooseflesh pebbled my arms despite the sultry July air.

Pushing away from the tree, I went to retrace my steps. It was easier to navigate in the garden proper, away from the trees.

A tingling at the base of my neck made me stumble over a rock in the trail. Was someone watching me?

A partially collapsed wall provided temporary shelter from which to listen. I heard a slight shuffling sound, but it could've been the trees.

I imagined the specters of those who'd lived in the Generalife, who'd died in these gardens, ravaged by wars and disease. My hands tightened into fists against the fabric of my skirt.

Why is it that in the moments you don't want your brain to conjure disturbing things, it goes straight for the murky corners?

I waited a few moments, every sense quivering, but no one emerged from the gloom. The glowing walls ahead were beacons of safety.

As I escaped via a side gate to the street parallel to the walls, I was thankful for the lamplight. Circles of illumination led from the corner to the carriage stop, but I didn't truly feel safe until I was sitting inside a hack.

Severiano opened the door as I ascended the stairs on shaky knees. The ride had given me a chance to reflect. Was my state heightened because of my nightmares, or because of the watcher from Plaza Larga?

But I was determined to allow logic to prevail. Why would someone follow me, anyway?

"*Buenas noches*, Severiano. Are the gentlemen dining?"

"No, señora. Everyone is away for the evening."

"Ah." Just as well. I wasn't ready to face Matias after this morning. "Did Sarita leave us dinner?"

"She did, señora. Would you prefer to eat in the dining room?"

I had no desire to sit alone at an enormous table. "Can you leave a tray in the library?"

"Sí, señora. If you give me a few moments, I'll bring it to you."

"No need to rush, Severiano. I'll bathe first."

I retreated to my bath, ready to be cleansed of the dirt from today. When I emerged, my tray was waiting in the library.

As I ate, I propped my notebook open to scan my list. There were numerous plants with pods that grew in the region.

As I added another one to the list, Matias appeared in the doorway. "I knew you must be here. I followed the fragrance of your soap." His fingertips danced along the base of my hairline, leaving warm trails of sensation over my skin.

"Like a truffle hog?" My tone was acerbic. I was still angry, and my attraction to him was irritating when I wanted to hang on to my frustration.

"Gruñe, gruñe," he muttered, burying his nose in my neck.

I shivered. Damn him. "What does that mean?"

"*Oink, oink* in Spanish. Did you find anything?"

I spun my pen in my fingers. "Maybe something, maybe nothing. How was your day?"

"I was with el señor Fernández, studying maps and sorting gear. We're planning to depart in a sennight or less."

My heart gave an uncomfortable lurch at the prospect of being parted. "That soon?"

He nodded, taking a seat and putting his feet up to recline on the garnet brocade chaise that faced the garden.

Logically, I knew our separation would be temporary. But logic didn't apply to my heart's reactions. In Chile, after we reunited, we'd had a few days of perfection. On the *Cormorant*, the nighttime hours had been our refuge, and we'd made the most of them. Of course, there was physical intimacy, but within those walls we'd built another kind of vocabulary: whispered stories of our past, the good and bad, the accomplishments and failures. We never ventured into the future, though—no further than our arrival in Spain. We hadn't discussed the consequences of our relationship and Matias's decision to leave Chiloé either. Despite our discretion, we knew there would be rumors about us. And now I knew that gossip had turned destructive—at least, for me. After our argument this morning, I was wary of our stability.

From my place at the table, my eyes traced his silhouette. My love for him was fierce and terrifying, comforting and painfully vulnerable. Was it strong enough to hold us together, or would we drift apart? I considered again if I should share with him my concerns about what Felicity had done in England.

"Linnea?" As if he could sense my inner turbulence, Matias motioned me to his side.

In a daze, I went.

It was as unconscious as breathing to settle my head on his shoulder. But the steady thump of his heart beneath my ear wasn't enough to drown out my thoughts. If I allowed him to take on some of the burden of my worries, would it deepen his resentment? Would he pull away like he did when he thought being with him would harm me? Did he wish he had stayed with his family in Chile?

"Are you sorry you left Chiloé?"

Surprise moved through his body, muscles flexing my cheek. "Where did that come from?"

His shirt button was half out of its hole. I resisted the compulsion to flick it open. Seduction would be a welcome delay to this conversation.

"You seem to be in a rush to leave. I wondered . . ."

His sigh was deep, the movement rocking my head and heart. I sat up to spring from the chaise. His hesitation was his answer.

He halted my retreat, grabbing for my hand.

"Wait a moment. Let me explain. The past several months have been a whirlwind. Capturing Lucien, you, my decision to leave Chiloé, a burning need for justice . . . and then we arrived. As happy as I am that Felicity is in custody, my quest to secure her was a distraction from everything else."

My arms wrapped around my body, creating a buffer to the pain. "You regret coming." My voice cracked on the last syllable.

"I miss Chiloé, Jaime, and Maria. But I wouldn't trade any of it for you. I knew what I was choosing when I boarded that ship, and it has been worth it. We are worth it."

His expression pleaded with me to understand. But it was too late. My defensive walls were going up. "You may not always feel that way."

Matias moved his hands up my arms to frame my shoulders. "I'm not running from you, mi amor. Studying wolves with Fernández will help me build my professional experience. When you were offered the chance to work in the Alhambra, I thought it was the perfect solution. It is also an opportunity for you to show your talents."

I probed at the tender wound his words had opened. Did I believe him? What would the distance do to us? Would he decide it wasn't worth the sacrifice? That his career was more important?

Matias sensed my wavering. "Trust in what we feel for each other. It will be enough. And please promise that you'll be careful with this investigation."

"I don't think I'll be involved for long. All I need to do is identify the plant used to kill Pelayo. Antonio is the professional."

Matias clasped me to him. "I'll worry for you anyway. Not because I don't believe you are capable, but because I don't wish to see you harmed."

I listened to the unfaltering rhythm of his heartbeat until voices in the hallway interrupted us.

Chapter Twelve

Our chamber looked as if it had been ransacked. Two open trunks stood in the center of the room, one organized, the other over-flowing with clothing, books, and letters. The offender sat cross-legged on the floor, holding a thick taxonomic book in each hand.

"Everything has to fit in the trunk, or on my back. Books are cumbersome. How do I choose?"

My vision blurred with sudden tears. I blinked to clear them. Over the past week, I hadn't allowed myself to think about Matias's departure, choosing instead to focus on my search of the gardens and the restoration—although that hadn't worked, either, since I hadn't located the plant used to kill Pelayo.

Winding my way through the piles, I considered his selections. "Take the one that has the most applicable information. Or cut out some pages, so you can take both."

"What? I can't cut up a book!" He lowered the larger of the two to a precarious pile and added the other to the organized trunk. "It will have to be that one. Cold-weather clothing is bulky. I haven't had to worry about warm layers. We had chilly days on Chiloé, but a thick wool jumper was always adequate."

"Especially the jumpers Maria knits. One feels as if they are wearing the whole sheep."

He shook out one of Maria's creations, folded it, and added it to the trunk. "I have my journal, paper, plenty of ink, and writing implements—"

"Specimen preparation materials?"

"Scalpels and sand. I don't want to deal with liquids. Will you pass me that book?"

I picked up a small leather volume. The cover was cobalt blue, freckled with salt stains. "This looks familiar."

The deckled edge of a scrap of paper slipped from the pages. I recognized my handwriting. Before I could tug it free, he snatched it. "It's my journal," he mumbled.

Ah, that was why I recognized it. I'd left a note in that book when we were at Maria and Jaime's. "Is that from me?"

"It is. I save all your letters."

Matias was affectionate, but I wouldn't have guessed he was also romantic.

"Can I read it?"

His sly grin reminded me of my letter's salacious contents. "Don't you remember what it says?"

I flushed, examining the piles of clothes. "It's been too long."

I was being coy. Of course I remembered. My body had been on fire for him, deranged by unfulfilled lust, and it had led me to writing some slightly wanton phrases.

He crawled toward my feet. "I recall every word."

"Do you?"

He tossed the book in the trunk. "You made explicit promises involving your hands."

"That doesn't sound like me . . ."

"You remember. I know you do."

His fingertips crept up the inside of my calves. Feathery sensations caressed my skin as his hands ascended from my ankle to the top of my stockings. He traced the outline of the fabric where it rested against my thigh. My garter loosened; the stocking slumped around my ankle.

"Does this mean you've finished packing?"

"Hmm," was his response. My second stocking met the same fate.

Desire set my blood afire, a swelling of desperate need. Matias's hands toyed with the tapes of my drawers as he came to his feet.

Then I surprised him by dropping to my knees. "Don't you want—"

"I intend to deliver on my promise first."

His hand tangled in my hair as I tugged loose the fabric of his shirt. I watched him as I slipped the buttons open. His cheekbones bloomed with the flush of arousal, lips parted and panting as I moved higher.

My mouth watered with anticipation. I licked a trail down each of the muscled ridges on his abdomen. Matias dug his fingers in my hair, knocking hairpins loose. My plait swung free. One hand snaked up his body. I pressed my palm to the compass-rose tattoo on his chest, over his heart. "Will this compass help guide you to me?"

Instead of answering, he bent forward to press our lips together. With one hand, he cradled my jaw, his other palm smoothing over my braid. "I don't need the compass."

"No?" My lips and fingers returned to their downward trajectory. I flicked open the closures on his trousers to a delightful surprise. "You forgot something."

He chuckled. The muscles of his abdomen gave a delicious ripple. "I wanted to wash my underthings."

I pushed away the sides of his trousers to reveal his other tattoo, the stars of the Southern Cross, sprinkled across his hip. When my tongue traced the pattern, his composure fractured. His moan vibrated the skin under my lips. "Do you remember the first time I did this?" I murmured.

He flexed his hips in an unmistakable invitation. "I was ready to beg you to continue south."

I took his hint, running my tongue along the head of his cock. Some women didn't like performing this act, but in my opinion, it was a pledge of trust, an agreement to vulnerability. Relinquishing control of your pleasure to another.

I drew out the act, slowly exploring every inch of him and communicating my esteem, my love, by worshipping him. I was lost in the flavor of him when he pulled on my braid, drawing my head away.

"If you don't stop, I'm going to—"

"That's the idea."

"Not today. Not now." He lifted me by the shoulders, so I was forced to stand. Our kisses slowed, a pause in the climb to desire's ascent. "Let's move to the bed. I don't want a quick fuck on the rug."

"But there's much to be said for a wild fu—" He stopped the word with his tongue. I laughed. "To the bed, then."

"Matias!" Hugh's voice rang through the closed door. "A delivery has arrived for you."

Matias swore. He looked down at the trousers around his ankles. I could see he was considering whether Hugh would leave us alone.

"Matias?" he called again, accompanied by the loud thumping of boots on the stairs.

Matias wriggled into his trousers, shoving his swollen cock and his shirt into the waistband and buttoning them as he stomped toward the door.

Stars winked off one by one as the morning crept across the horizon. I counted them as a distraction from the chill of the air. A blanket knitted by Maria swaddled my shoulders, it's comforting fragrance of sheep and Chile an embrace. The dense wool also absorbed the occasional tear. Despite the tight lock I was trying to maintain on my emotions, they continued to escape via my tear ducts.

Matias slid his arm around my waist. "You needn't wait."

Within the shelter of his body, I turned my face into the fabric of his shirt, breathing deep and memorizing his scent, his shape. "I'll wait until you go."

"I want to carry that bloody trunk upstairs and return to bed."

I tried to be pragmatic. "You'll be exhilarated for the adventure once you're on the road."

Wheels crunching on stones shattered the tranquil morning. Matias stepped to his trunk, and the severing of our bodily contact fractured my poise.

What if attraction, love, and companionship were a matter of proximity? Hugh had been the first stable presence in my life since Liam died, and even with him, I maintained a sliver of emotional distance. I was always anticipating the inevitable return to loneliness. I recalled what Matias had said about love being trust. How did one learn how to trust after a lifetime of building walls to protect oneself?

A large traveling cart approached with several donkeys tethered to the rear. Two men rode in the back with the trunks while a white-haired man drove, and another walked alongside.

I remained in the shadows, paralyzed by dread. Matias supervised the loading of his luggage and gestured to me. It took effort to move. I folded the blanket, placing it near the door before joining him. The driver of the cart shifted impatiently as we approached.

"Lin—Lady Wren, this is Señor Bartolome Fernández."

"Ah, the famous Lady Wren. It's a delight to meet you. How kind of you to see Mr. Ward off. Such a devoted friend."

Matias and I exchanged an amused look: friends, colleagues, lovers. Explaining our unconventional relationship was a challenge.

"Furthering our acquaintance will have to wait for another day, my lady. Our journey awaits! Mr. Ward—"

Matias led us around to the rear of the cart. The men perched on the trunks stared, unembarrassed. Their presence made the moment awkward. "Our camp is remote. I don't know how often we'll be near villages, but I'll send letters if I'm able."

"I understand." I squeezed his fingers. "Safe travels."

He rested his forehead on mine for a second. It was as much as we dared with his colleagues watching. "Please be cautious, Linnea. Let others assist you."

The cart rolled, and Matias followed. I faced the door, wiping the last of my tears.

A firm grasp spun me around.

Matias's warm lips moved against my cold mouth. A sob shuddered from my chest. He whispered, "I love you," before loping to join the others.

Even knowing he wouldn't hear, I replied, "I love you too."

Squaring my shoulders, I imagined the barriers firming around my heart. The portcullis was closing, the locks jangling.

Chapter Thirteen

Centuries of cultivation had compacted the soil, and forcing a spade past the surface was difficult. It had been years since anyone had cared enough to nurture it. I added a handful of rich topsoil to the hole, mixing it with the tired substrate. A bead of sweat trickled between my shoulder blades. My palms burned with new calluses from the shovel handle.

Lowering myself to my knees, I selected another clump of grass to place in the row. These sun-loving grasses would establish easily, transforming a corner of the garden into a golden, rippling sea.

My lower back protested against the unfamiliar physical labor. I stretched my fingers toward the sun, elongating my spine and overworked muscles. The wide brim of my hat blocked the direct sun from my face. A layer of gritty perspiration coated my body. Rising with the sun to say to goodbye to Matias seemed days ago rather than hours.

"Señora . . . ah, hello."

How did Pilar move without sound? And when did the garden become crowded? I blinked at the hectic activity. "Good afternoon, Pilar. Are you here to assist me?"

"Sí, señora. I finished weeding in the upper garden and saw you."

I gestured to the pile of grass tufts. "As you can see, there is plenty to plant. And please call me Linnea."

We transplanted in quiet companionship for several minutes before she spoke. "I'm surprised to find you laboring in the garden."

I pressed the soil around the grass with a solid *thwack*. "Are the other gardeners not working?"

Her cheeks flushed, either from the sun or from embarrassment. "Oh . . . there is, ah, cotilleo? How do you say in English?"

I thought for a moment. "Gossip?"

"Sí, g-gossip, that you are aristocrática."

My grip around the stems was excessive. This was the price of traveling with Hugh. Rumors of my title were hard to avoid. "I didn't grow up with the aristocracy, nor do I claim a position among them."

Pilar retrieved another clump of grass. "Why not?"

She was young and curious. She didn't mean to be insulting, I reminded myself while I breathed deeply, summoning patience. But my silence must have belied my frustration.

"Perdón, señora. My questions are bold," she mumbled.

"My uncle cared for me as a child. He was my only family. After he died, I went to a girls' school. I began working as a young woman. My godfather didn't come into my life until I was an adult. He also became my employer."

Her eyes rounded in astonishment. "Your godfather forced you to work?"

"I wanted to work. Needed to."

"If I had the choice, I wouldn't work another day."

"I enjoy what I do, but it is necessary."

Pilar twirled the trowel, her eyebrows narrowing in bewilderment. "Are you not wealthy, señora? Married?"

A low throbbing in my left temple warned me of an imminent headache. My exhaustion and emotions related to Matias's departure were catching up to me. "I'm neither wealthy nor married. My father had a title but not the money. I've always wanted to work, to make my own way in the world. A woman does not have to rely on a man to accomplish things."

I didn't mean to snap at her. My reactions were intemperate and out of proportion, I reminded myself. It was bloody embarrassing.

A worm had been dislodged with the weeds. I prodded it gently on its way.

Pilar feathered the stems through her fingers. "It's uncommon to meet a woman, an older woman—older than me, that is—who doesn't have children or a husband."

That observation sat between us as we continued our task to the sounds of the other people in the garden.

I brooded over my behavior. The layer of protection I kept in place had been scraped raw when Matias left. My head, my heart . . . all of it was a bleeding gash. And I was lashing out like a wounded animal.

"Señora"—Pilar's voice dipped—"are you happy?"

Bloody hell. Was the woman clairvoyant?

I squinted from beneath the brim of my hat. Her head was bent, fixed upon the hole she was digging in the bed. The sun glinted off her braided sable hair. She wasn't asking about the state of my heart. She was trying to understand the path my life had taken.

I considered her question, determined to rein in my moodiness.

"I've been fortunate. People believed in me and helped me. Trying to forge a career as a woman in a man's world means working harder, longer, and better than anyone else, usually without acknowledgment and without complaint. After the struggle, now *I* have the freedom to determine my path. But it wasn't easy." I adjusted the pad beneath my knees.

Fuck. I didn't have it anymore, did I? Thanks to my impulsive actions and Felicity Ward.

"Do you think I could do it too? Travel the world?" Her tender wonder was a stark contrast to the brutal reality reeling through my mind.

I had a choice: I could allow my cynicism to push Pilar away, or I could put my selfish preoccupation aside. Even from the depths of my murky brain, I knew my decision. "If you set your mind to it, you could achieve your goal. It would not happen quickly, but I would help."

Pilar chewed her lower lip, flipping clods of soil with the tip of her trowel. "You would help? Why?"

I shrugged. "When I needed it, someone was there."

She frowned, assessing me. I stifled a laugh at the irony. When Hugh had approached me at Kew, offering a job and a home, I'd kept one hand on my dagger, convinced his intentions were dishonorable. When you've been on your own, the last thing you're willing to do is rely on someone else.

Earning trust took time. I could wait.

Pilar came to her feet when I did. Grasping the handles of the wheelbarrow, I gestured at the next bare area. "How did you come to work at the Alhambra?"

"Me?"

I placed wooden stakes on the plot in a pattern while waiting for her response.

"May we speak in Spanish? My English, it—"

"Of course."

In Spanish, she continued, "My father died before I was born. My mother, when I was two. I was raised by my aunt and cousin. My aunt died, like many others, from cholera. Now there is only my cousin and me. We are poor, but also rich. My aunt owned the small house where we live. Many of our neighbors are being forced to leave. Rich people want the land. I've taken on extra work in case we are forced to move."

It was the same situation the rally at Plaza Larga had seemed to be about. "Can they do that?"

"They can because the government supports them. My cousin says people are desperate, and the wealthy are purposely making life hard for us. Our neighborhood lost many people to cholera. We were fortunate to survive, but we may lose our home."

"Does your cousin work at the Alhambra?"

"She works at a print shop. I also work at a café, but I prefer the garden."

"Your cousin is not married?"

"No, señora."

"Then I'm not the only unmarried adult woman you know," I teased.

"I suppose, but my cousin, she is . . ." Pilar's head swiveled as if worried about being overheard. Who would she be concerned about? "Ah . . . focused on other things." At that, Pilar retreated to the far end of the bed.

Interesting that the subject of her cousin had caused Pilar to halt our conversation. I wondered what she meant by "other things."

Pilar remained at a distance, effectively preventing me from asking. We continued with the grasses until she placed her tools in the pocket of her pinafore. "Señora, I must go."

"Apologies. I hadn't realized it was late. Good evening, Pilar."

She hurried toward the palace. As I piled my tools into the wheelbarrow, I watched her move along the trail. She paused at the base of the stairs where Suárez was descending, headed toward the Generalife.

Instead of proceeding up the stairs, she darted along the path toward the other gate. He didn't appear to have noticed her.

Why was she avoiding Suárez? Had he been inappropriate to her?

"Señora! Señora! Lady Wren!" he panted, halting in the middle of the trail.

The rungs of the wheelbarrow slipped from my hands, the legs slamming into the stone path. "Señor Suárez, how may I assist you?"

"Have you made progress?"

"Yes, several of the empty beds are planted. They look much improved. Tomorrow, we'll address the neglected courtyards."

He sliced his hand through the air. "No, no. Progress on the investigation. Have you determined what killed Pelayo?"

"I . . . I have not." My grip on the rough handles forced a splinter into my palm. "Restoration tasks—"

"Shouldn't you have some idea?" he interjected. "El señor Navarro claims that you are an excellent botanist, yet we haven't seen any evidence to that effect."

Pinpricks of heat sparked under my skin as my anger flared. The wound in my palm throbbed. "Señor, I've prioritized my duties in the garden, as that is the primary reason I was hired. If you would prefer that el señor Navarro appoint someone with more experience, that can be arranged."

He flicked a leaf from the bucket of the wheelbarrow. The corners of his mouth twisted in an arrogant sneer. "You have a sennight to identify the plant. If you cannot meet that deadline, I will assume that you cannot meet the requirements of a position at the Alhambra. Do we understand each other, señora?"

He didn't wait for my answer, striding off in a cloud of smugness.

The fiery sensation in my body turned to ice. Was he threatening to dismiss me? What the bloody hell was that?

I continued to seethe as I made my way to the office. My hand required immediate attention. After storing the wheelbarrow and wiping down my tools, I lit a candle to examine where the splinter was jammed deep into my flesh. The dodgy chair shrieked, echoing off the parchment-thin walls. Tilting the wound toward the light, I used the tip of my dagger to tease the wood loose. The sharp pinch of pain was a welcome change from the noise in my head.

It took careful excavation to locate all the bits in the wound. I squeezed the sides, flushing it until I could do a more thorough cleaning.

Matias's absence waited for me at the house. I wasn't ready to face an empty bedchamber, but I couldn't stay here. After blowing out the candle, I fled the stuffy confines.

The Court of the Myrtles was never empty during the day. Workers used it as an access point between the main buildings and the Generalife. As a result, I hadn't lingered here since the reception.

Darkness turned the ebony waters of the pools fathomless. A scythe of moonlight reflected on its surface. My face was turned upward, toward the stars, when a scraping sound made me snap my head around.

A figure emerged from near the entrance. Alarmed, I braced myself, fingers poised to draw my dagger.

"Señora Wren?" It was an unfamiliar woman's voice.

"Yes." I cleared my throat. "Can I assist you?"

She stepped into the faint moonlight. A shawl was draped over her head, covering her hair and most of her upper body. She was tiny, several inches shorter than my diminutive height. Her dark eyes were wide. There was something familiar about her facial features.

"Do we know each other?" I asked.

"No, we've never met," she replied, drawing closer so that we stood almost toe-to-toe. "Are we alone?"

Who was this woman? I didn't get the impression that she was dangerous. "I believe so."

Reaching out, she grabbed my forearm in a forceful grip. "Señora, I need your help. Alonso Rodriguez Pelayo—he was my brother."

My body recoiled. Her brother?

I laid my hand over hers in consolation. "I'm so sorry for your loss."

Her eyes filled with tears. One of them escaped, a glinting streak against her cheek.

"We don't have much time. My name is Izabelle. Alonso and I only had each other. We've lived in Granada since we were small children. Our parents remained in Jamaica and shipped us to Spain to be raised in the homes of various aunts and uncles. Alonso received his inheritance years ago, but our parents insisted on an arranged marriage for me. My husband is convinced Alonso's death is too much for me. We are leaving for Jamaica immediately."

It was a great deal of information to absorb. Why had she sought me out?

"Señora, I'm sorry to say that your brother was deceased when I found him. If you were hoping he communicated something to me . . ."

She squeezed my arm tighter. "No, Señora Wren, you don't understand. I heard your name when my husband was discussing Alonso's death with our cousin. I know you are assisting el señor Navarro with the investigation. But I don't trust him. He works for my cousin."

Wait, did she mean— "Your cousin?"

"Yes, the regent."

My eyes widened in shock. Regent. The queen.

The jangling of bridles reached us over the walls of the Alhambra. A carriage must be waiting outside the near gate. Izabelle's distraught glance in that direction confirmed my suspicion.

"I must go. Señora Wren, I came to you because you are the only person I trust to find out the truth about Alonso's death. My parents do not care, and our family insists it was the socialists. I know it wasn't. He had friends within that group."

A soft whistle wafted through the night air.

She began to walk backward, away from me. "Please, señora. I know we don't know each other, but I have no one else. My husband won't listen. No one will listen. You are my only hope. You mustn't tell anyone. You know our family is powerful. If they knew I asked you . . ."

My brain was reeling. How could she ask this of a stranger?

"But . . . why me?" I managed, chasing after her.

"It has to be you. We have no one else."

Izabelle flicked the shawl over her head and ran for the entrance. I followed, but the carriage was already leaving when I reached the gate.

Chapter Fourteen

Five days.

Five days had passed since everything went pear shaped. Matias left. Suárez threatened me. And then there was Izabelle, Pelayo's sister.

Years ago, I'd experienced a similar but more fraught upheaval when the ship I was on had gotten wrecked on an island, and my body was irreparably shaped by a lost pregnancy. In the matter of a few hours, my life had imploded.

When I returned to England, incapable of dealing with the physical and mental devastation, I went through a phase of alcohol-fueled evenings in gambling hell. Mornings found me lolling, semiconscious, on the floor of my cottage. From that angle, as I lay sprawled on the threadbare Aubusson carpet, my shelves had mocked me, packed as they were with journals and books. A few of the publications had been mine, others written by those I admired. Their judgment was menacing, a chorus of condemnation that drove me into melancholy.

Only a woman.

Never enough.

Too weak.

On the rare days I felt cheeky, they received a two-fingered salute. More often, I was immobilized, pinned to the rug by their castigation. By my shame.

Years of wisdom stood between those unwise behaviors and now. I knew healthier ways of coping—or I thought I did. Yet here I was, treating the Alhambra as my hermetic fortress. Missing Matias. Obsessing over my conversation with Izabelle. Wallowing in worry about the demise of my career. My concentration was fleeting; I bounced from garden duties to searching for the poisonous plant. I wasn't getting anywhere with identifying what killed Pelayo. At least the areas I was responsible for in the Generalife were seeing progress.

On top of my inner turmoil, or maybe because of it, I avoided any interaction with Hugh and Antonio. I neglected to eat or sleep. My rational mind recognized I was spiraling, but I couldn't seem to cease.

Two days remained until Suárez expected results. After poring over plant keys and materia medica devoted to poisonous plants, I was almost certain the pod had come from wisteria. Despite searching in the Generalife and the main gardens of the Alhambra, however, I had yet to locate any wisteria.

The internal voices from the past were my constant companions. I couldn't shake them, couldn't prove them wrong.

Returning to the house after midnight had become my routine. If the door swung wide, the hinge would screech, but two fingers wedged in the jamb would keep it silent. I searched the corners of the library. One gaslight was lit near the door, but that wasn't unusual. We left it burning in case of insomniac wanderings.

"Finally, you've returned."

My hand slipped on the wood, pinning my fingers in the space between the door and the hinge. "Argh! Fu—" Cradling one hand with the other, I probed the digits and joints. "Hugh? What were you thinking?"

He turned up the lamp, illuminating the room, and took a step toward where I crouched. "Are you okay?"

I could see he wasn't alone. He retreated across the room to Antonio's side. This had gone from bad to worse.

I stumbled to the settee, snagging a pillow to balance my arm on the ridged back. With the source of throbbing at shoulder height, my wits sharpened.

"We reasoned the only way to speak with you was by ambush," Hugh confessed.

My hackles rose. "I've been busy."

"Too busy to sleep?"

He wasn't wrong. I'd only returned to the house tonight because my lack of sleep was affecting my ability to function. In the middle of the afternoon, I'd fallen asleep face down in a flower bed. If it hadn't been for shouting among a group of workers, I might be there still.

"I've been doing both," I lied.

Antonio propped his elbows on his knees. "We need to discuss the case. What if there had been developments?"

"Have there?"

Antonio shook his head. "I went to Pelayo's townhouse, but the butler refused me entry."

My jerking movement dislodged the pillows from beneath my hand. "They refused? Don't they know who you are?"

"Perhaps that's why they refused," he replied. Did that mean Antonio was aware that Pelayo was friendly with the socialists? His sister had said as much, but I had no way to confirm it.

The bruises on my fingers were visible, even in the dim light. Distinctive creases remained across my fingers. Pulsating pain traveled from the limb to my chest in a rhythm: *Never enough, too weak.* Coronas ringing the library lamps danced to the throbs.

Hugh's clearing throat shattered my reverie. "I'm sorry. What was the question?"

Antonio responded, "Have you found anything?"

I wiggled my fingers, willing my concentration to hold. "Suárez gave me a week to identify what killed Pelayo, or I'll lose my position. I've been unsuccessful thus far. I have two days left. There are several potential sources, but the likeliest is wisteria. I have yet to find it growing in the Generalife. Not that it means anything."

Hugh and Antonio's nonverbal exchange swirled in the air. A miasma of reproach mixed with nausea percolated in my stomach. Hugh had defended my failure to accomplish my goals on Chiloé. His faith was unlikely to be secured by my recent actions.

Antonio's voice slipped through my self-castigation. "Suárez threatened you?"

I shrugged. "A warning."

"Having you dismissed from your job is a threat," Antonio insisted.

If I didn't move, this chaise would become my bed for the night. My knees wobbled when I stood. "Gentlemen, your questions will have to wait. I'm exhausted, and I must return to the garden at first light."

"We could assist with the search," Hugh prompted.

His offer was kind, but for a multitude of reasons, it obliterated my patience. "I am capable." My voice was harsh in the quiet library.

Both men froze.

Hugh raised his hands, palms out. "I wasn't questioning your abilities." My glower stopped his consolation. "Enough said. We'll wait for you to come to us."

Matias's pillow carried a faint whiff of his scent, the barest suggestion of juniper. Each day, the aroma faded a bit more, no matter how far I pressed my face into the linen. I plumped my cushion, careful not to disturb my hand. It gave off an angry drumbeat of pain that guaranteed sleep would be impossible.

Earlier, while I was rummaging through my medical kit to find arnica for the bruises, another bottle had fallen from the case, bouncing on the rug and under the dressing table. After crawling to retrieve it, I'd found a small container of rose hip oil. Maria had insisted that the rich oil would be beneficial for dry, chapped skin, common on ocean crossings.

I opened the lid and wafted it under my nose. The bright fragrance was redolent of Chiloé in the autumn: Wet soil, disintegrating leaves, crisp mornings. Glowing crimson globes hanging from leafless shrubs. Maria moving through the fog to collect them.

I missed her, Jaime, and the farm. We hadn't received a letter announcing their baby's arrival, but it should have been any day now. Maria's last missive claimed she was energetic and enormous. Given her previous difficulties carrying to term, my worries wouldn't abate until we heard they were well.

The bottle of rose hip oil glowed bloodred on the bedside table. Matias probably also had one for his medical kit. In the cold mountains, it would help with windburn. Was he warm enough? Surely the thick

Chiloé sweaters would be adequate protection. Had they found the wolves yet?

Of course, I missed my lover, but I missed my friend more, my closest friend. I wanted to discuss Suárez's threat with him. Tell him about Pelayo's sister begging me to solve his death. Gather his opinions on how my search for the plant could be different. This was not how I'd thought these weeks would pass. I'd assumed I would enjoy working in the Generalife, learning about the site and getting my hands dirty. Matias's absence would fly by. Hugh and I would reconnect.

Instead, my ill-advised habits had prevailed.

There was the thinnest line of light on the horizon, visible between a gap in the houses. A puff of a breeze entered through the crack in the door. The candle flickered.

Movement in the mirror on the other side of the room startled me. A woman stared back, her disheveled hair a halo of auburn flame. The candlelight turned her eyes into silver scrying pools. Deep purple shadows hollowed her face. Her skin was sallow, faded. She looked empty. Unmoored.

As so often seems to happen with a scientific discovery, a realization, or, in this case, the revelation of a clue, I stumbled upon the answer. Literally.

Bleary-eyed with exhaustion, I trudged along the paths of the Generalife, my bruised hand throbbing. A heavy basket of asters swinging from my arm. They were already wilting in the heat.

A large rock in the middle of the path threw off my balance. My ankle twisted and my injured hand landed on a stone wall, halting my fall.

A stone wall that had escaped my notice. It seemed to guard a small courtyard that had escaped my mapping.

After abandoning the heavy basket at the entrance, I ventured in.

Thick vines obscured the walls. Dark emerald arteries looped and twined everywhere. Thus far, it had been neglected during the restoration, probably due to its location away from the paths that led to the main garden. Its unkempt state didn't cloak its potential, not in my eyes.

In the center of the courtyard was a stone bench, weathered to a gleaming alabaster.

Helpless to resist the botanical puzzle of unruly plants, I ran my bruised palm along the Gordian knot of stems. A painful prick indicated a rose, which was confirmed when I found a few blooms. My fingers worked at the vines, trying to tease the other plants loose.

"Come out, little friend," I coaxed, tracing the runner until I encountered an unmistakable, leathery pod tucked behind the large roses.

It was wisteria.

The wisteria provided the structure under the rose vines, protecting it from the bricks. In the opposite corner, the wisteria was dense and twisted around itself. Hanging from those spirals were several large, leathery pods. My pods.

I dropped to my knees, fumbling in excitement to retrieve my dagger from its sheath.

Wisteria pods were safe to handle, but I used my knife to cut one loose, catching it with a handkerchief. Verifying this against the fragment at the house would confirm a match, but there was no doubt in my mind.

Here was proof Pelayo had been poisoned with wisteria seeds.

Work would have to wait. I wanted to return to the house to compare the specimens.

My exhaustion forgotten in the wake of my discovery; I scooped up my basket from the ground. Only the percussive sounds of running stopped me.

Leaving the basket for the moment, I clung to the wall to get a view of the path. Pilar was hurrying, her eyes on her feet, bottom lip caught in her teeth. The gardening crews hadn't arrived for the day. Why was she here?

My instinct was to avoid drawing her attention to this courtyard until I examined it. I stepped away, intercepting her on the path. She came to a stumbling halt before we collided.

"Is this where we are working?" Her eyes shifted over my shoulder.

I continued to block her view. "No, we'll start near the orchard. I wasn't aware of this courtyard. Have you seen it?"

"I have not. Anything interesting?" She balanced on her toes to peer in.

"Another area to add to the restoration. Shall we continue?" I led us away, hoping it was enough to dissuade her. My plan to compare the plants would have to wait.

We were under the shadows of the trees when I realized we had passed the beds and were on the outskirts of the orchards.

"We went too far. The beds are that way." I pointed the direction in which we needed to return. By chance, my eyes dropped to the dirt beneath the trees. It was ringed by footprints.

That was odd. I glanced around to see if anyone was at work, but the orchard was empty.

Pilar was standing over the beds with her hands on her hips when I approached.

"Here, on the right. We need to plant these, or they will wilt."

"Were you thinking about the restoration, señora?"

"Unfortunately, no. I should've been paying attention."

Pilar ducked her head as she accepted a bunch of flowers from my basket. "Were you thinking about the man who died?"

I flinched and almost dropped the aster. As I slowly placed the roots in the hole, I replied, "I didn't know the man. Did you?"

"No, no. I don't believe so. But it was a shocking thing to have happened. And you appeared to be involved . . ."

"Involved? The night of the reception was my first visit to the Alhambra. And when I met Pelayo, I was asked to assist—" Dammit. In my rambling, I had said too much.

Pilar was unfazed. She hadn't even reacted to his name. Not that I would've noticed, with my inane babbling.

She was efficient in her planting, patting the soil around the stems. "Are you an inquiry agent?"

I sat on my heels. "Ah, no. Though there is an aspect to this investigation that involves plants."

Pilar watched me with a guileless gaze. "Plants?"

"Yes."

"And you are certain this was a murder?"

"The doctor believes he was poisoned with a plant."

Pilar dropped her trowel, her fists clenching in the soil.

"Pilar? ¿Está todo bien?" Her reaction was interesting, for claiming not to have known him.

She retrieved the tool with a shaking hand. "Sí. Está bien."

My intuition said that pressing her at this point would be unwise. I didn't want her to become defensive. "Let's hurry and finish this planting. The flowers are drooping."

We worked steadily, excavating holes, placing the asters, and moving to the next flower bed. Soon, the bed was a swath of colorful blooms.

Meanwhile, Pilar didn't ask questions. I may not have received any direct answers, either, but her reaction was telling. One thing I had learned from interrogating Lucien was that the less you pushed, the more they revealed.

"That was the only work I have for you today. The other crew is weeding around the fountains. Perhaps you can join them?" I wanted to find Suárez to confirm the other plant was a match. If I didn't report to him today, he might dismiss me.

She used the side of her boot to knock the dirt from her trowel. "Are you leaving?"

"I am. I've work to do elsewhere."

"On the investigation? I can assist you."

"You work for the garden, not for me. I'll see you tomorrow." I needed a balance between gathering information from her and allowing her to get too close to what I might discover.

She hesitated, watching as I gathered tools.

I waved my hand. "Go on, Pilar. Join the crew."

I waited for her to join them. Pilar stopped to consult with the lead gardener. Her interest seemed to be more than simple curiosity. How involved was she?

When the gardener motioned to where he wanted her to go, I turned toward the offices. Once I reported to Suárez, I could decide what to do about Pilar.

Chapter Fifteen

Hours had passed since I'd returned to the palace to find Suárez. His evasive secretary refused to say when—or whether—he would return.

At the reception, a man working on the structural restoration of the Alhambra had alluded to a vast underground network of dungeons, cisterns, and hidden rooms that ran beneath the floors. If there were oubliettes, they must have patterned these offices after them. Not a wisp of air moved between the walls.

This was ridiculous. I ripped a piece of paper from my notebook.

Señor Suárez,

I have located the evidence. I will turn it over to Señor Navarro and return in the morning to see to my duties.

Sincerely,

Lady Wren

Writing my title made me cringe, but from what Antonio said, it held weight with Suárez. I extinguished the candle and wrenched open the warped door. My sore hand took the brunt of the movement, my lack of dexterity tumbling the note into the shadows.

I knelt, sweeping my hands across the foul surface, trying to locate it. Voices echoed from the empty hall beyond my door.

"You must know something. His family is anxious and pushing for answers. You said it was finished."

"Yes, yes, it will be. Pronto." The second speaker was Suárez. His response was conciliatory, deferential.

Was Suárez also getting pressure from the royal family? If what Pelayo's sister said was true, wouldn't they want the inquiry to be finished?

My fingers closed on the corner of the paper. I launched to my feet, dashing toward the courtyard to catch Suárez and whoever he was talking to. But it was empty, except for the tinkling sound of water.

"Linnea?"

A damp sensation beneath my cheek was the first sign I hadn't made it to my bedchamber. The unnatural angle of my neck was the second.

Words refused to form in my mind, only impressions. The contrast of the white handkerchief against the withered wisteria pod. Jagged crusts of bread. The sky-blue pattern on an empty bowl. Garnet dregs of wine in a glass. At some point, my exhaustion had won.

Hugh stepped into the library. "Ah, here you are."

I discretely wiped the drool from my face. Unfolding my limbs happened in increments: one joint, another muscle, until I was upright.

Hugh plucked a shriveled olive from the plate and popped it into his mouth. When he selected another, he noticed the wisteria pod and wrinkled his nose. "What is that?"

I folded the surrounding cloth. "Probably what killed Pelayo."

He discreetly slipped the olive pit onto the side of the plate. "You've found it?"

"I think so."

Antonio appeared, placing his hand on Hugh's shoulder. "Did I hear that you've identified the murderous substance?"

I hadn't noticed Antonio was in the room as well. Stretching the knot in my neck, I answered, "Poisoning from the seeds from a wisteria pod would have the same results as the doctor's description. Whether the dose was enough to kill him, we may never know."

Antonio used the end of a pencil to prod at the pod. "Are you certain?"

My wits were scattered. I stood to pour a glass of water from the carafe on the sideboard. "As sure as I can be. Assuming the poison came from the Alhambra, which is a leap."

Antonio nodded. "Did you speak to Suárez?"

I debated whether to share the conversation I'd overheard, thinking of Izabelle's reservations about who held Antonio's loyalty. Greedily swallowing the last of the water, I decided not to. "I left him a note. He was absent, with no definite return."

Hugh handed Antonio a glass of wine. The momentary relief from their attention allowed me to shake the sleep from my brain.

"Antonio, are you certain Suárez isn't involved? His manner is dodgy. He's rarely at the garden." I recalled Pilar's avoidance of him. "And when he is, the gardeners avoid him."

Antonio's regard was inscrutable. He twirled the stem of his glass. "He's on my list of suspects, but I didn't find any evidence that he's involved."

"Why threaten me, then? One moment, he's eager to have the investigation concluded, the next he discounts it." I tided the plant, folding it within the cloth. My notebook was also open on the desk; Antonio was gazing at it. I closed the spine with a snap and tucked it under my arm.

Antonio propped an arm on the chair casually. His eyes shifted toward Hugh. "Not to justify his behavior, but the royal family is impatient to have this investigation completed. Identifying the plant took longer than expected."

I hid my wince. *I* was the delay, he meant.

I buried the urge to press my palms to my abdomen. When had my doubts overridden my confidence?

Hugh must have sensed my turmoil. "That was harsh, Antonio."

Antonio scowled. "Suárez is not the only one harried by the royal family." He gestured to me. "She was avoiding us, so I have had little to report. At least now there is something."

A wave of shame engulfed me. There was no excuse for my delay. "I . . . I'm sorry it took so long. If there is anything I can do . . ." My voice was unrecognizable.

Wavering. Weak. Pathetic.

Antonio folded his arms. "We need more. I haven't been able to trace Pelayo's movements. He was at the reception that night to meet someone. I tried to get in contact with his family. However, his parents live in Jamaica. His sister, Izabelle, is traveling to be with them—distraught over his death, apparently. She is also a likely suspect, but the regent insists that Izabelle wouldn't have had the opportunity or motivation.

Our only hope is that someone at the Alhambra saw something. Can you continue to ask the gardeners?"

I wondered how I would stay involved without admitting that Izabelle had come to me. Given my previous reluctance, though, I didn't want to appear overeager. I dithered with my dirty dishes.

"Antonio, is that the best idea? It is asking a lot of her," Hugh interjected.

Thank you, Hugh, for helping with my deception. Even if he wasn't aware. "It's fine. I'm willing to help."

He wrapped an arm around Antonio's waist. "Good. That's settled. We haven't dined. Linnea, will you join us?"

A formal meal was beyond my capabilities. "Thank you. As you see, I've already eaten. After a bath, I'll retire for the night."

Antonio's nod was perfunctory as he strode from the library.

Hugh lingered. "I'm sorry he was abrupt. He isn't usually like that."

"He's being harassed." I locked the pod in the desk drawer and scooped up my other notebooks before turning to Hugh, my face schooled in a neutral expression. Waves of concern radiated from him, but I lacked the energy for reassurance. "Good night."

As I ascended the stairs, their contented murmurs came from the dining room. I was relieved they weren't arguing.

Languor from the warm bath made the short walk to my bedchamber more laborious than normal. Once inside, I padded to Matias's trunk, nudging it with my bare toes. The memory of his chaotic packing was bittersweet, tinged with regret. I should've slipped a letter into his books. Lingered in bed for another hour. Told him I loved him again.

I flipped open the lid. His tidy Navy habits had prevailed: clothing folded into thirds, the spines of books aligned, every inch of space utilized. The shirt on top was one Maria made, now worn thin. The linen was silk soft. I lifted the fabric, caressing it against my cheek.

Juniper, citrus, and a slight, salty tang of the sea. Matias.

The weight of the lid clunked shut. Walking like an automaton to the bed, I clutched his shirt to my chest, then tucked it beneath my pillow.

A sudden memory floated to the surface. My mother's nightgown. A ghost of her honeysuckle perfume wafting in the still air of the chamber. In my head echoed the words of my nursemaid telling a footman that my parents were dead. I'd run to their bedchamber to steal my mother's nightgown from beneath her pillow. I'd cried myself to sleep every night, holding it.

Uncle Liam had arrived a few days later to collect me. The nursemaid wasn't aware of the precious possession beneath my pillow when she'd packed the rest of my belongings. When the carriage rolled away from the house, my life had been severed in two: before and after. I never saw that house again. Solicitors sold the estate. Our lives moved on as if my parents had never existed.

In bed, my knees were snug against my chest, my arms aching from clutching them.

Relaxing my limbs brought instant physical relief, but the emotional residue lingered. Had my parents' marriage been good? Had my mother been stubborn, or my father argumentative? Had they preferred tea or coffee, rainy days or sunny ones? Uncle Liam never spoke about his sister—my mother. Even as a young child, I'd known it was a taboo subject. Liam and I existed in a vacuum, the two of us against the world.

Matias had told me about his mother, Viviana, and her songs and stories. His father had made mistakes, but in the end, he'd asserted his love for Matias. He'd been loved and wanted, even when he didn't think that was the case.

Had I ever been anything other than a burden? Uncle Liam had sacrificed his relationship with Hugh to raise me. He had given up the man he loved and had died without him. When I'd found out about Liam's choice, Hugh had assured me it was a mutual decision, words meant to comfort and placate my guilt.

Now Hugh had another chance with Antonio. I wouldn't come between them. And I would do everything I could to protect Hugh from experiencing that loss.

What about Matias? Was I fated to become a liability to everyone who came into my life?

I flung myself from the bed to pace the rug. What maudlin rot. I was missing Matias and overly fatigued. That was all this was.

Shaking my head, I grabbed a notebook from the pile—anything to distract from the onset of paralyzing melancholy. The book flopped open to the pages with speculations about the wisteria and Pelayo's potential killer. Tucked into the spine was a stem of dried rhododendron.

A flower I had not pressed between the pages.

I fumbled for a chair. My hand trembled, my mind racing to recall the meaning of rhododendrons.

Death. Murder. Danger.

Chapter Sixteen

A few hours of sleep were all that was possible after my discovery. Whoever had left the flower in my journal was either still in the house or had forced entry.

Which meant they knew I found something of significance.

Severiano was the only staff member who lived in the house; the other two went home at midday. If someone could get over the stone wall, the doors to the library were easy to access. Suárez was aware of my findings. Pilar might have been as well, if she was involved and aware of what was growing within that courtyard.

The cobalt night gave way to the grayish blue of a fresh bruise. I had abandoned my bed hours ago to watch the moon set from the cushioned bench of the balcony. When the swifts began to hunt for breakfast, I dressed in my work clothes. The streets between Antonio's house and the Alhambra were empty, which did nothing to lessen my anxiety. My body hummed like a tuning fork, vibrating with agitation.

When a figured emerged from the shadows as I passed through the Court of Myrtles, it sent my heart racing.

"Buenos días, señora."

A man stepped into the meager light, his familiar, intelligent eyes glinting in the predawn.

I pressed my palm to my chest to try to quiet the pounding. "Oh, Señor Prieto, you startled me. I'm usually alone at this hour."

We had been introduced one of my first days in the garden. He was an architect working on the restoration of the structures at the Alhambra.

Prieto gestured to our surroundings. "I wanted to see how the light enters the courtyard. It will give me a sense of how we should proceed with repairs. And you, señora—can you see the plants in the dark?"

I chuckled. "I prefer the garden early, when it is empty. Did you spend the night, señor?"

"No, I arrived about an hour ago." He gestured toward a small niche built into the wall. A tidy pile of blankets and a flask were on the seat. "Would you like some coffee, señora?"

He filled a tin cup from the flask. Enticing curls of steam rose from the surface. I gratefully accepted his offering. The first sip of coffee, spiced with cinnamon, made me gasp with pleasure. He grinned at my reaction.

We settled in the niche, side by side. His presence was relaxing. He wasn't nervous, or in a rush to speak.

From what I had gathered, Prieto had been involved with the restoration from the beginning. Maybe he'd known Pelayo.

Wrapping my hands around the warmth of the metal, I toyed with several lines of questioning, finally settling on a sideways approach. "I was warned when I began working here to beware of being alone. Apparently, some believe the Alhambra is haunted by ghosts—those taken prisoner or killed in battle. Are you not worried about those specters, señor?"

He laughed, the wrinkles around his eyes crinkling. "Ah, no, señora. No ghosts bother me."

I sipped my coffee, giving him a shy smile. "Too fierce, eh?"

He continued to chuckle, refilling my cup.

"Do you think it might be cursed? After all, that young man died here recently as well."

Prieto propped his ankle on his knee, settling against the stone wall. "Ah, yes. So tragic. Such a nice young man."

"You . . . knew him?" I asked tentatively.

"Not well. His family is involved with the restoration. He was curious and had many questions about the buildings."

A pair of swallows swooped low, chasing each other. We both followed their progress, their swirls and dives. "Did you see him at the reception?"

"I did, señora. Who would've thought that would be the last time? He appeared healthy to me."

Ah, so rumors had circulated that he was dead, but not that he was murdered.

"Was he interested in the gardens as well?" I asked.

Prieto had expressive hands that I associated with those of a musician. He ran them along the fringe of his blanket. "I saw him near the orchard on a few occasions."

The morning chorus of birds was growing in volume. Through the archway, I could see the city across the canyon, bathed in a tawny glow.

Our conversation was reminding me I wasn't an inquiry agent; I didn't know what the right approach was to gain information from people without making them suspicious. It felt awkward to circle around a topic. Still, at least I'd gained a few details about Pelayo.

"Thank you, señor, for the coffee. I won't keep you. When next we meet, I'd like to hear about your work."

He stood with me, taking the tin cup. "It's a challenge to please everyone. There are many opinions and few decisions."

"Indeed. I wish you luck."

"To you as well, señora."

One of the primary functions of the Generalife during its peak had been food production. Determining how to restore this area had been a point of contention among the gardeners. Some felt it should be planted with hedges to conform with the primary garden design; others believed we should maintain its original function.

I agreed with the latter. Although the soil was tired after many years of production and would have to be replaced, rows of vegetables could provide sustenance. The Generalife wasn't meant for status or design brilliance; it was about showing that the Alhambra fed the soul *and* the body.

I snorted at my philosophical rhapsodizing. Food was food. From what I had seen while walking through Granada, more food would be welcome.

As I strolled along the row of beans and peas, I brushed aside a wilted leaf to spy a late-season pea. *Compensation for a weary gardener,*

I thought as I crunched my plunder and ambled toward the orchards. From what I could recall of the footprint patterns, Pelayo hadn't walked further than where I'd found him. Had he planned to meet someone in the orchard the night of the reception?

Each stand in the orchard was named Grande, Colorada, Mercería, or Fuente de la Peña. These medieval trees continued to thrive, pruned each year to encourage fresh growth. Birds foraged in the warming air; the branches full of their mutterings.

I paused beneath the trees in the Mercería orchard, where I'd stumbled upon the footprints when Pilar and I had wandered. They were still there, a constellation of activity. More than the two or three workers I would've expected here.

The boot prints varied in size and were concentrated beneath two trees in an outside row, near the fortified wall. I followed their trail to an area where the stones had crumbled, allowing for a gap large enough to pass through. This was also where the soft soil ended. On the other side was a stone walkway.

Who was meeting in the garden?

Feeling ridiculous, I squatted low to the ground, peering across the surface of the dirt. It was just dirt with a few bits of leaf detritus.

I wiped my hands on my skirt. What made me think I was an inquiry agent? I didn't know a damn thing. My annoyed exhale ruffled loose strands of hair that tickled my nose. The force of my sneeze was enough to shift my precarious balance. I toppled onto my arse. As if I needed more evidence of my foolishness.

When I dug my hands into the soil to stand, something pricked my palm.

It was a scrap of paper with a rough edge. The print was smeared and illegible, but the paper and the type were unmistakably newsprint. The ink had a distinctly cobalt hue.

I followed the two sets of footprints again. From the main group, one set traveled from the orchard toward the palace. Not everyone had exited the garden through the wall after their meeting.

Once a week, we met as a team to share a rough schedule of our activities. It had been several weeks since the orchardists had worked on the trees, and they wouldn't return for a fortnight. I retrieved a branch from a pile of cuttings. Using the top to sweep, I created a smooth surface. My trap would reveal if another meeting occurred.

On my way out, I snatched an apple from the low branches.

While I was in the orchard, the garden had filled with workers. I waved to a few familiar faces as I dashed to my office to retrieve my tools.

With half the apple in my mouth, my hands were free to rummage in the basket I stored beneath the desk. I smacked my head on the underside of the desk as the door to my office slammed against the wall. My apple fell to the disgusting floor.

"You've arrived. Didn't you break your fast at your house, señora?" Suárez sneered as I scrambled to my feet, apple in hand.

"I've been here for several hours, señor. I was in the gardens."

The flesh of the apple was now speckled with unappetizing dust, I pitched it into the basket. His nose wrinkled in disgust as he wiped his palms on his waistcoat. "Do you have the evidence?"

Brackets of tension framed his tight lips. A bead of perspiration streaked from his eyebrow to his jawline. Interesting.

"El señor Navarro is giving it to the doctor who examined Pelayo." That was a complete fabrication. It was locked in Antonio's desk. "Can I return to my duties in the Generalife?"

He furrowed his brow. "I suppose. We must prepare the Patio de la Acequia for a private gathering this evening. The other gardeners are busy, so you will see to this task."

"It's a popular garden for visitors—isn't it in excellent condition?"

"It must be perfect. Members of the royal family will be in attendance, as well as the Ilustrísimo Señor Conde de Granada. He has pledged substantial personal funds to the restoration."

Years as an under-gardener had taught me to maintain a blank, placid countenance while receiving directives. Asking a senior gardener to clean a courtyard was unusual, but if this was what was necessary, I would do it.

"Señor Suárez, are there ever private gatherings in the orchards?"

He snorted in derision. "The orchard? Of course not. We wouldn't ask the royalty to stand in the dirt. They're interested in the formal gardens, not crops." Chewing on his lip, he examined the contents of my tool basket. "You've finished your part in the investigation?"

Would it be advantageous for him to believe my involvement was at an end? "El señor Navarro is responsible for the inquiry."

He responded with a curt nod. A nonanswer, but it appeared to suffice. "Please tidy the courtyard immediately, señora."

As I wiped the sweat and dirt from my face, it pained me to admit Suárez was correct: the courtyard was a disaster. It hadn't been tidied after a recent windstorm, and piles of dead leaves and branches clogged the pools. The same debris covered the stone walkways. In addition, the myrtles were overdue to be pruned.

After sweeping the walkways and cleaning the pools, I was a mess. My skirt was stained, and my hair was coming loose of its pins.

I was at the end of the rows of myrtles, cursing whoever had pruned them last. There was one more spot that was out of reach. I inched along on my knees, pressing my chest to my thighs to wiggle under the shrub. There was a branch I was determined to clip, and the sound of my secateurs snapping on the twig was gratifying.

My satisfaction was short-lived when I realized my hair was entangled in the branches. Scooting backward only ensnared more strands. The gnats were hovering, sensing a motionless victim. The ground beneath the hedge was covered in dead leaves and bug corpses, a level of intimate knowledge I could've forgone.

"Fuck."

My curse wasn't loud, but it was loud enough to be heard by a person now snickering nearby. I froze my shimmying.

"Do you need assistance, señora?"

His voice wasn't familiar, and few of the staff spoke English. A visitor? No matter who he was, my situation was mortifying. "Er, yes, please."

The stranger's fingers manipulated the branches, gently tugging on my hair to free it. An easing of the tension allowed me to turn my head enough to see that my savior was wearing expensive handmade shoes. Not a good sign.

"Señora, you are released."

I crawled out from beneath the shrubs, dawdling in the hope that he would allow me some dignity by leaving.

"Ah, Lady Wren, we meet again." It was the roué from the reception, the aristocrat. A patron of the Alhambra. Damn.

"Ilustrísimo Señor, thank you. Apologies for the rude language."

"It was amusing, señora. The myrtles were almost the victor."

As I was covered in dirt with a sizable hole in my skirt and my hair snarled into a rat's nest, I would argue that the courtyard had won. "It's fortunate I'm finished for the day."

"Why are you doing this? These duties are suited to an under-gardener, not someone of your . . . rank."

"I *am* a gardener, Ilustrísimo Señor, and content to fulfill whatever duties I am assigned." Something about his manner made me defensive. I couldn't abide by snobbery, and this man embodied it.

He frowned in revulsion while rubbing his fingers on the fabric of my skirt. I jerked it away. How dare he presume to touch me?

"You've arrived for the private viewing, Ilustrísimo Señor? I'll be out of your way in a moment."

The conde hovered as I collected my things. He was vigilant, following my every move. I was clumsy as I fumbled with my tools. Ready to bid him goodbye, I angled myself toward the exit.

As I attempted to escape, he interjected, "I'll accompany you to the offices. I must speak with Suárez."

My pace quickened, trying in vain to outpace him.

"Are you enjoying your position, señora?"

"I am, thank you."

"You haven't attended any parties since you've arrived. Have you not received the invitations? Most of our kind are in Madrid, but there is a select group."

"I beg your pardon, Ilustrísimo Señor, but I am not usually one for parties." I assumed these invitations had been addressed to Hugh, and he knew I would never attend.

"Nonsense. I'll make sure the invitations are sent." I was grateful to reach Suárez's office, but he was still speaking. "You will be in attendance this evening, señora, will you not?"

Suárez appeared at the door. I took satisfaction in his horrified expression. Was it my appearance, or the invitation?

"Unfortunately, not, Ilustrísimo Señor. I hope you are pleased with the progress of our restoration." I dipped in a curtsy, anxious to be away from them.

But his voice followed. "I expect to see you at a party soon, señora."

It sounded like a threat, not an invitation.

Chapter Seventeen

If I didn't know differently, I would have assumed a dance had occurred in the Mercería orchard. For the past two evenings, I'd swept the ground clear. Finally, this morning: boot prints. Many boot prints.

If I wanted answers, there was one logical solution: to spy on their meeting. How would I go about that? I had slept in Kew for years, disguised as a boy. Being in a garden at night was familiar territory. I didn't have those sorts of clothing, though.

I left the garden during my midday break to visit a secondhand shop. The shop was split into two sections, one for men and one for women. A pair of black trousers and a scratchy, charcoal jumper from the men's section would allow for freedom of movement and concealment. I told the shopkeeper that the clothes were for my husband.

Rather than waiting at the garden for nightfall, my plan was to return to Antonio's. Once it was late enough for the garden to be empty, I could sneak in.

I had intended to tell Antonio and Hugh about the rhododendron the day after I found it in my journal, but after a long afternoon of cleaning the courtyard, I had fallen asleep without removing my disgusting clothes. The next morning, I was in a rush, and then another day had passed. And another.

Izabelle's pleas rang through my ears. One more secret added to the burden. It was easy to find reasons to justify staying away from them.

The only person I might have confided in was Matias, which spiraled into my next set of worries. We had agreed that writing letters to each other wasn't feasible; he didn't know which towns they would stop in. The weight of all I was concealing was overwhelming. If I slowed down for even a moment, it would collapse on me.

When I slept, my rest was dreamless, an empty expanse. I didn't miss the nightmares, though they were replaced by a constant state of waking dread. My heart would skip a rhythm with no exertion. My vision swirled with vertigo.

I refused to turn to alcohol again. But my anxiety as getting worse. My only solution was to stay occupied. Distracted.

Maybe the risk I was taking tonight would help break the pattern? If it led to answers about Pelayo's death, it would be worth the gamble.

After eating a few slices of bread with cheese, I covered my hair with a flimsy, black scarf. Antonio's maid was meticulous in her cleaning, so it took a while to find enough soot to rub into my exposed skin. With a final examination of myself in the mirror, I looped a small, stained haversack across my chest, took a deep breath, and exited the doors to the balcony.

My stomach swooped at the view over the railing. Earlier, I'd studied the facade for the easiest route to descend the brick walls. That knowledge did not help my confidence now. My sweaty palms slipped against the railing, which made my pulse race.

I could do this.

With a final deep breath while on solid ground, I swung my leg over the railing and onto a narrow ledge. *Embrace the fear. Move.*

I pointed my toe, extending my leg like a dancer to reach the first hold. The slim, waxing moon cast adequate light to see my next destination, but not so much that I would be visible to someone on the street below.

As I moved from foot to foot, my descent was methodical: every muscle in my legs poised for the next rest, my breath synchronized with the movement. When my feet touched the ground, my knees dissolved. I collapsed against the wall, panting from the effort and ignoring the likelihood of having to ascend via the same route.

I had forgotten how trousers allowed for a greater range of movement. When I left Kew to work for Hugh, I'd had to accustom myself to walking in skirts. Tonight, the lack of fabric swirling around my legs meant I could move faster, keeping to the side lanes, dodging through shadows. People ambled along the streets, despite the late hour. It took half my usual time to reach the outer wall that ran the length of the Generalife.

The gate required a key, which I fumbled for in my pocket.

After locking the gate behind me, I stayed along the perimeter wall until I entered the cypress grove. The grove formed a gloomy barrier that allowed for an unobstructed view of the meeting place. I didn't know when anyone would arrive, so I would hide within the cypresses.

As I reached into my bag for a flask of tea, my unsteady fingers obeyed enough to tip a few sips into a tin cup.

Night closed in. Lamps winked off across the canyon. Bats hawked after insects in the trees above, their graceful aerobatics a welcome distraction. My hands ceased their trembling.

Gardens at night brought back memories of the years I'd lived at Kew while working as an under-gardener. Once the sun set, that vast expanse was my solitary refuge. Whether it was staying in the main garden beneath the trees or venturing near the Thames to be lulled to sleep by the softly lapping river, the solitary hours were a respite. Being around other people meant I was always playing a role, hiding that I was a woman—and away from Kew, I had to be even more vigilant.

I ran my palms on the rough fabric swaddling my thighs. Even these clothes felt familiar. Tugging the sleeves of the jumper over my fingers, I snuggled against the trunk. Warm tea in my belly and the whisper of nocturnal animals lulled me toward sleep.

A pebble ricocheting off a nearby tree woke me. It took a few moments to recall my surroundings. The moon had dipped behind the hills; the darkness was absolute. Multiple feet shuffled in one direction.

A low voice split the silence. "Raise the shade a touch. I can't see anything."

I pressed my spine against the tree trunk to remain concealed. A narrow beam of light came from a lantern placed on the ground. The pool of illumination ended a few feet from my hiding place.

"Let's make this quick. Every time we meet, we risk being discovered."

The lantern revealed the individuals from mid-calf to foot. There was nothing remarkable about their shoes. Every one of them wore boots and trousers.

"We're ready to implement the next phase of the plan. Our contact assured me everything is in order." Was it a man or woman speaking?

Another voice joined in, speaking in the low baritone of a man. "Do we need to do this? It doesn't gain us anything. What makes it worth the risk?"

I concentrated on the leader's reply, hoping to identify markers in their voice.

"We have no choice. We'll lose everything. They've attacked us once—what's stopping them from doing it again? We need to redirect their attention. We agreed, Rafa, and the debate is over. Nic, is the pamphlet ready?"

Pamphlet?

"We'll print it tomorrow after the shop closes. Ready for distribution in two days hence," a young man on the opposite side of the circle replied.

Someone spoke near me. "We have volunteers at the ready." He began to list several locations throughout the city. I committed the list to memory; there were a few locations I recognized, including several in the Albaicín.

The ambiguous voice I assumed belonged to the leader grew in volume as they drew closer to the lantern. "We shouldn't risk meeting for a while. Shall we agree to resume in a fortnight? By then, our other problem will be resolved."

There was a rumble of agreement, and the light was extinguished. Relying on my hearing to discern their movement, they seemed to travel toward the break in the walls, not through the Generalife.

I was about to stand and stretch when the shadows shifted in the clearing. A lantern glowed, the beam sweeping the area.

I froze, willing myself smaller, invisible.

In the wavering light, a figure fumbled in the branches of thick shrubs less than ten feet from where I sat. For a moment, a gloved hand holding a small notebook was visible before the lantern was snuffed.

I held my breath. My pulse thundered in my ears. When they passed close to my hiding place, I went motionless. Their breathing was audible—a sawing sound that made my skin twitch. Was it only a few seconds that passed, or minutes?

A desperate pinch in my lungs forced me to exhale in quiet increments. Repeated sprays of pebbles came from the trail that led to the garden, not the wall.

Was it someone who worked in the garden?

I waited, motionless, my breathing shallow as I thought through what I had heard. Had Pelayo meant to meet with these people? Had he been a member of their group? They hadn't discussed the contents of the pamphlet. Fortunately, they had shared the locations where it would be distributed. And what was the other issue that needed to be dealt with? Was it connected to the garden? It seemed an inconvenient location to gather, although it guaranteed privacy. Unless the pamphlet was particularly revealing, I would have to return in a fortnight to eavesdrop.

Cold seeped into my bones, making movement imperative. After one more scan of the area with my senses, I used the tree for support to stand while I stretched my cramped muscles. I walked to the shrubs, plunging my arms into the spiky branches. There was nothing obviously hidden— nothing I could find without light, at least.

A more thorough examination was warranted. I unwound a strand of wool from the bottom of my jumper and tied it to the base of a twig as a signal to myself of where to search.

On weak legs, I clung to the orchard's edge, toward the side path, which passed through a gate near the river. Concealed within the grove, I had felt safe, but in the open, the instincts of a panicked animal overrode reason. My breathing was rapid when I reached the welcoming glow of the streetlamps.

When Antonio's house came into view, it was a surprise. I hadn't marked the route on my return from the garden, lost as I was in a haze of nerves. I realized too late that I hadn't taken precautions to ensure I wasn't followed.

Severiano was smoking on the front steps. Damn. He would tell Antonio if I sauntered up to the front door dressed in these clothes, and Hugh would bombard me with questions. I was going to have to climb.

I darted around to the side lane, where I regarded the brick facade. On Chiloé, I had scaled a cliffside. Surely this wasn't any harder?

Refusing to overthink, I jumped for the first foothold. Climbing up was more taxing than going down; my arms shook with the effort. Each foothold required painfully jamming my toe into a brick.

Next time, I was going through the damned front door. To hell with being caught.

My exhaustion was so acute, I toppled over the railing onto the balcony, my knees cracking against the tile. The pain was excruciating. An involuntary whimper escaped me.

Through the open door of my bedchamber, a candle burst into light, searing pinwheels of color across my retinas.

"Dare I ask where you've been?"

Chapter Eighteen

Disbelief overrode the throbbing in my kneecaps. "Matias?"

I sprang into his arms. He smelled of rainwater and juniper soap, not of travel dust. His silk banyan soothed my cheeks.

My lips moved against the rough skin of his neck. "I didn't expect you for a few more weeks."

He stripped off my headscarf, working his fingers into my braid and positioning my head for a kiss. I whimpered when he stopped inches from my lips. "Can you wash off the substance on your face so I may kiss you?"

Flushing in embarrassment beneath the layer of soot, I withdrew behind the screen. The water in the pitcher was freezing. I gritted my teeth, scrubbing at my face until the water ran clean. My dark clothing was relegated to a heap in the corner to be dealt with in the morning. Or later in the morning, anyway.

Another several swipes of the frigid cloth across my chest made my teeth chatter. "H-H-How was your t-t-trip?"

"We'll get to that. Why are you returning to your chamber in the middle of the night by way of the balcony?"

"Mmph," I replied, delighted that the toothbrush in my mouth prevented a lengthy answer. Conflicted between wanting to spew every thought weighing on me and the need to hide my questionable decisions, I chose silence. No need to ruin our reunion. It could wait until tomorrow.

I secured the tie on my dressing gown and stepped out from behind the screen. Matias was propped against the footboard, arms folded. He needed a haircut. The whorls of obsidian locks framing his face didn't hide the lines of exhaustion or the lavender bruising beneath his eyes.

I rested my hip on the edge of the mattress, hovering over him. He appraised me from toe to head, using his thumbs to smooth my eyebrows. Removing soot or caressing me? Either way, his touch warmed my freezing body.

My arms slipped over his shoulders, cradling his scalp with my numb fingertips. Our welcome kiss was gentle—an introduction, an establishment of address, and a response. When it turned avid, he retreated, tugging me onto the mattress.

Once we settled beneath the coverlet, my worries relented. "I missed you, Matias."

He nuzzled my hair. "I missed you as well, but don't think I've forgotten my question. Or your clothing."

My drowsy serenity faded. I fumbled for an evasive yet succinct response. "A group has been gathering at night in the Generalife. I thought they might be involved in Pelayo's murder."

"And are they?"

"I don't know."

His grip tightened on my hip. "Why are you still investigating? And in the middle of the night?"

Anger flared, searing a path through my chest. I wanted to argue, to defend my choices, but I was so damn tired. And I *had* missed him.

"Can we discuss this tomorrow? It was cool in the garden, and I'm sleepy."

"I suppose," he replied.

My previously relaxed state was now elusive. Concern kept me on the edge of sleep. What would he think when I told him the truth? Would he agree with Hugh and Antonio that I wasn't capable? Should I tell him about Izabelle, even though it would mean breaking her trust?

After a few hours of rest, I woke when Matias's knee bumped my leg. He was face down on his pillow, one arm crooked above his head, the other cupping my thigh. His muscular back was bathed in the first rays of dawn. I could kiss those ridges. Lick the length of his spine. We could spend the morning in bed.

But if I did, someone might return for whatever was hidden in the shrubs at the Generalife.

With a single kiss to his shoulder in parting, I dressed and left a note promising to return for breakfast. Antonio and Hugh were abed, so I left through the front door, not the balcony.

On every corner was an enticement of pastries and coffee. The streets were busy. I moved with the crowd, evading the lure of the cafes. The sooner I finished the search, the sooner I could return to Matias.

I used my key as I had last night. With single-minded purpose, I bolted through the Generalife toward the orchard. Fog hovered in the garden. Once I reached the hedgerows, my skirt was damp with dew, the fabric clinging to my legs when I lowered to the ground to find my thread.

The thread was there, but nothing was in the shrubs. But I knew what I'd seen. I continued to search until my hands were a mess of scratches.

My fingertips finally encountered a slip of paper.

On the paper was a drawing of a coat of arms in cobalt ink, a crude representation of a knight's helmet beneath a smeared castle, and slashes below that looked like the upper marks of type. One edge of the paper was torn.

After one last exploration of the shrubs, I gave up searching. If I removed the scrap, whoever had left it might suspect their meetings had been discovered. I committed the details of the image to memory and returned it to the hedgerow. Wet through and through, I returned through the Generalife, my skirts slapping against my legs.

Despite the discomfort of my damp clothing, another thought persisted. What was wrong with me? I'd left Matias, who I'd been missing, in our warm bed to search for *that*? A piece of paper? What happened to the journal I'd seen?

A stranger had appealed to my sense of justice, and I had turned it into an obsession. Why? What was I avoiding?

Those provoking thoughts were enough to hasten my return to Antonio's house. Of course I wanted to talk to Matias, to hear about his trip. My leaving this morning hadn't been anything other than dedication.

Upon entering the house, I could hear masculine voices in the breakfast room. Perhaps a change of clothes was in order?

My stomach grumbled, arguing against that plan. Their conversation came to an abrupt stop when I entered. "Good morning, gentlemen."

Hugh sprang from his chair, as did the other two, unusually formal. They hovered while I filled a plate with a few pieces of toast and fluffy eggs. The silence stretched. I snatched the coffeepot and brought it to the table. Three pairs of eyes followed my motions.

I tried to ignore the irritating intensity of their scrutiny. "Matias, have you been telling them about your trip? You'll have to repeat yourself. I want to hear your stories as well. Has the entire party returned?"

"We haven't discussed it yet. We were talking about . . . other things."

My fork met the dish with a resounding clang. Was *I* the other things? "Indeed."

Hugh sighed, a dramatic exhale. "Linnea, why didn't you tell us where you were last night? We agree that you've taken unnecessary risks. What if something happened? You're a botanist, not an inquiry agent. You're overwhelmed and in need of our assistance."

A piece of toast lodged in my throat. Was Hugh inferring that I was incompetent?

I couldn't form words. The surface of the table blurred. Damn it to hell, I wouldn't cry in front of them.

I gulped. The toast descended. "You've *agreed*?" My voice shook with fury. "And reached an opinion on my abilities?"

Hugh's face drained of color. Antonio calmly tried to diffuse our escalating tempers. "We're concerned for your safety. You don't understand how complex this situation is."

I glowered at him. Matias squeezed my thigh under the table. In my distress, I had forgotten he was sitting next to me. "Linnea has a good reason. Don't you?"

His support was welcome, but it didn't ameliorate their condescension.

"I didn't tell you because I wasn't sure it was anything. There are clandestine meetings happening in the Generalife. I wanted to see what they were about before I shared. During our last conversation, you said it was fine to continue to ask questions."

Antonio leaned forward; anger forgotten. "Are these people connected with Pelayo?"

His eager body language and avid expression took me aback. Was it possible that Antonio was involved? Could his efforts to dismiss my conclusions be a way of dissuading me?

There were details I could share—the rhododendron, the pamphlet, and my conversation with Prieto—but I was reluctant to disclose them when I was this angry, or when I was unsure of Antonio's motivations.

I recalled our conversation about persecuting the socialists. Would Antonio accuse them at the exclusion of others? Would I be handing him and Suárez a reason to convict innocent people? Izabelle didn't trust Antonio.

The clock on the mantel chimed. I shouldn't be absent from the garden. Matias and I hadn't even spoken alone.

"I must go. Suárez's tolerance is strained. I don't dare miss a day."

If Matias was disappointed, he made a good show of understanding and squeezed my hand where it rested on the tabletop. "I'll collect you from the garden?"

I nodded. "Hugh and Antonio, there is nothing pressing about the situation."

I ignored Hugh's protests as I tossed my napkin onto the table. I hadn't finished my breakfast. Again.

Chapter Nineteen

A bed of mixed perennials behind a crumbling stone wall in the lower garden required weeding. Normally, it wasn't my task to clean the beds, but after that confrontation at breakfast, I needed the quiet.

Weeding was a satisfying activity, a tangible chore that brought order to something chaotic. Today, however, pleasure was elusive. Prior to this trip, Hugh's faith in my judgment and abilities had been steadfast. He had been my biggest supporter, despite my previous missteps. Until now.

I yanked at a weed, spraying my face with bits of soil. My pinafore was already covered in muck; more wouldn't hurt.

When I wiped my face, though, the linen came away damp. Bloody hell. My entire life, I'd been able to hide my emotions. Cut them off. For some reason, my fortifications were gone.

"Señora, are you well?"

Oh, bloody, bollocking—

"Hello, Pilar. Something in my eye." If she saw my face, it would be obvious that wasn't the case. I scooted the blanket beneath my knees to the next bed.

"May I assist?" She sounded eager as usual.

"I appreciate the offer, Pilar, but weeding helps with thinking. Conversation does not." Even I was surprised at my caustic words. What the bleeding hell was wrong with me? "*Lo siento*, Pilar. That was rude of me. I should work alone today."

"Oh."

She was hurt. My ill humor wasn't her fault.

I sighed in resignation. "Stay if you like. You're not the reason for my foul mood."

Her mouth tilted into a small smile while she attacked the weeds on the opposite side of the bed. We moved around the area, absorbed in our labor. She respected my need for quiet, humming under her breath and blithely pulling plants.

Her exuberant youthfulness soothed the rough edges of my demeanor. Insects buzzed around us, the sound mixing with the activity in the upper gardens to create a pleasing composition. When the bed was nothing but lush, churned-up soil, it kindled a soupçon of accomplishment within me.

"Where next?" Pilar asked, hitching up a basket of weeds against her hip.

The angle of the sun foretold the late hour. Somehow, the day had slipped away. "We're finished for today."

"Are you also leaving?"

As much as I would have preferred to delay my return to the house until my composure was fixed, my knees ached, my eyes were gritty, and I wanted this day concluded. But Matias hadn't arrived. Shrugging, I slung the blanket over my shoulder. "Not yet. There's correspondence to reply to. This position is not solely about playing in the dirt."

She chuckled, walking alongside me through the emptying garden.

"Linnea?"

Matias was waiting at the base of the stairs, propped against the curved banister. His folded arms rested on his chest; shirt sleeves rolled up in a way that displayed the ropey muscles of his forearms.

My entire body went hot.

Pilar inhaled through her teeth. "¿Quién es ese?"

I smiled at her thunderstruck expression. "Pilar, this is Matias Ward. He's my, er . . . friend?"

Matias snorted. "I'm at least that. Hello, Pilar. Es un placer."

She batted her eyelashes. "Señor, are you a gardener?"

"I prefer animals to plants. These gardens are magnificent, though. Linnea, are you ready?"

Their exchange was charming, between Pilar's innocent blushes and Matias's total obliviousness. "I am."

He took the blanket and folded it across his arm. "May I?"

I looped my hand through the elbow he offered. Pilar smirked, waving as she retreated.

When she was out of hearing, he interlaced our fingers. "I wasn't certain when to arrive. Is this too early?"

"My energy was fading. I must stop by my office first."

We continued past the fork in the path, toward the area where the offices were housed. As usual, the rooms were empty. I wondered if anyone else ever used this space.

"Are you enjoying your work?" he asked, picking up one of my sketches of a laurel-lined canal.

It was the perfect opportunity to confess. To tell him about Izabelle, about my desperation to prove myself after overhearing Hugh.

I glanced around the office, reminding myself how thin the walls were here.

"It's different from my previous positions. The head gardeners and administration have decided what will be planted, and my job is to make sure the work is completed. I suppose, in that way, it is a bit like when I was an under-gardener at Kew—except that besides those tasks, I have to respond to the general correspondence for the gardener on leave. I thought there would be opportunities to contribute to the design in the Generalife."

I stowed the basket beneath my desk. When I emerged, Matias had flipped the lock on the door and was sauntering toward me. "Not quite your usual role."

"It's good to return to basics. The Generalife was the grounds of the summer palace and home to the kitchen gardens, so there are possibilities for how they structure the design. A warmer climate means plants from Africa can thrive. The diversity is greater than we could cultivate at the Physic Garden or Kew. There's even a small medicinal garden I've contributed to."

During my monologue, he'd crossed the room and was herding me toward the desk. The flimsy structure gave a disconcerting shudder. He gripped my waist. "Do you remember the desk in Chiloé?"

How could I forget? "Y-yes, but—"

"Don't fret, I'll only steal a kiss."

I glimpsed his lopsided grin before succumbing to the coaxing pressure against my lips. Restraint slipped. The fervency of his mouth halted any thought.

His fingers tugged at my bound hair, which jolted me back to our surroundings. "Enough. The walls are parchment thin."

He rolled his forehead against mine. "You're right. I didn't expect that intensity."

I slipped my arms around his waist, pressing my ear to his chest and taking in his scent, the texture of his clothing against my skin, the movement of his lungs beneath my cheek. I'd passed the entire day disconnected from reality, floating in my mind until this moment. When we were physically close, words didn't matter. The world didn't matter. It was only us.

Following on the heels of that tender reflection was a spear of worry. *Don't get too comfortable. He'll leave again. Don't rely on anyone but yourself.*

With an exhale of annoyance at my internal dialogue, I ended our embrace. "Shall we return to the house?"

"The sooner, the better." He grazed the crease between my neck and shoulder with his teeth.

"Matias . . ." I shuddered at the sensation.

He continued to my earlobe, caressing it with his lips, sending another zing of arousal along my spine. "Did you miss me? Write me any more saucy notes?"

A giggle burbled from my throat. I gently pushed him away again. "Yes, I missed you. No saucy notes, but I would be happy to provide you with more details . . . in our bedchamber."

Winding our fingers together, I guided him toward the door.

On the walk back, Matias told me about the Sierra Morena. A rugged, challenging landscape that was difficult to navigate meant they'd had to rely on donkeys to carry their gear. His nights had been cold and the days short. An unseasonal dusting of snow had sent them fleeing to a lower elevation. But they'd had a few fortunate glimpses of wolves. Some of the other members of the expedition had wanted to set traps, but Fernández and Matias had agreed that doing so would be counter to their aims to observe without disrupting the pack. He sounded disappointed to have the trip cut short.

Even though a part of me dreaded his answer, I still asked, "Will you return?"

Matias tightened his grip on my arm. "I'm not certain. It depends if we stay in Spain. There will be another trip in the spring. Fernández suggested that if I accompanied them, he would share the writing credit for the paper with me—which is generous, and a first for me, to have authorship on a publication. In the meantime, I'll assist him in identifying and preparing museum specimens. He has crates of them."

I patted his knuckles. "He obviously respects you as a colleague."

Spring was too far away to worry about. Besides, of course I would support him going. This was what he had left the Navy to do. Who knew where things would be with us, anyway?

Upon entering the house, Matias marched us up the stairs to our bedchamber. Once the door was closed, he pushed me against the surface. While we kissed, he fumbled with my buttons. I couldn't contain a laugh that vibrated both our lips. His hands fell from the fastenings.

"Am I rushing? Did you want to talk first? It's only—"

I flung my hat across the room and unbuttoned his shirt. "No, I don't want to talk. Unless it is to tell me what you want."

His deep chuckle rumbled beneath my fingers. Never had we undressed so fast.

Chapter Twenty

The bathing chamber was outfitted with a woodstove and integrated pipes that led to a cauldron of water. Warm water filled the tub via a faucet. My toes curled around the rim of the wide copper tub, inching along the metal to brush against Matias's furred, well-defined calf. The muscle twitched underneath, and I ducked my smile beneath a wave of scented water.

"That tickles." He nibbled a tender spot on my neck. "Was your aim to make me amenable to anything? If so, I surrender." His languid slump returned his head to the edge of the tub.

I scratched my fingernails from his upper thigh to the crest of his ankle. "One worthwhile thing I accomplished in your absence was mentally measuring this tub, hoping we would both fit. My calculations were accurate." Upon arriving at my destination, I propped his foot on my knee to massage the instep, digging my fingers into the tight, calloused areas. His groan echoed off the tiles. "Shush. We don't need everyone to hear."

"If you think they don't know, you're deluded."

I applied my fingernail to the bottom of his foot, causing an undignified squeal. Water splashed from the tub onto the tiles when he lunged for my wrist. "Stop that." He gathered my hair in his palm, using the leverage to force me into his arms. With his lips on my temple, he whispered, "Are you relaxed enough to talk? You've been trying to hide it, but I know there's more happening than you've shared. It's time, mi amor."

I allowed my head to loll against his damp shoulder. He was right. But how did I begin? And how much should I reveal?

"The gardening is interesting, if not what I expected. Pilar is a surprise. I haven't been a good mentor, though. Despite that, she's eager and enthusiastic." I brushed the edge of my thumb along the veins of his forearm. Auburn glints among the dark hairs of his arm matched the copper of the tub. "Once I identified the wisteria, I thought my participation in the investigation was finished." I hesitated.

Izabelle had asked me not to tell. And the letter from Sir Thiselton-Dyer, though I hadn't seen the missive myself, was too humiliating.

Matias thought I was a confident, capable woman. For him to see me as anything less than that would be devastating and potentially catastrophic for our relationship. The woman he'd left his family behind for wasn't needy. She was strong, independent.

Matias shifted, trying to see my expression. My words tumbled forth. "When we were trying to find Tomas and Cristobal's killer, it was personal. We were responsible for their well-being. Tomas was a member of my crew, and Cristobal was a friend. These circumstances are not the same. I met Pelayo briefly. Yet . . . I can't let it go. Antonio is an excellent inquiry agent, but I want to solve this mystery."

Nervous about my disclosure and what I wasn't saying, I twisted my hair in a coil, wringing the drops from the strands. The water had cooled, along with my amorous mood.

I used the sides to rise from the slippery tub. My dressing gown hung nearby. I donned it, securing the knot. A water-stained lounge chair occupied one corner of the room. I sat cross-legged, the folds of my dressing gown covering my legs as I finger combed the snarls from my hair.

Matias hadn't moved from the bath, but his shrewd gaze tracked my agitated movements. "You're still holding back."

Damn. It was a double-edged sword, having the man I loved know me so well. I would have gladly fallen on that weapon rather than answer, but if I didn't confess to Matias, I never would.

I shuddered with the welling of emotions. "Hugh called in many favors to secure funding for the trip to Chile. He convinced Kew, the museums, and the academics to support us. And he did it for me. Because he knew I was stagnating at the Physic Garden. I wasn't unhappy, but I was going through the motions. Hugh knew I might regret not overcoming my fears, so he pushed. He saw the problem and wanted to help. And I failed him." Tears spilled over, scalding my cheeks with droplets of shame. "Instead of returning from Chile with crates of discoveries and accounts drafted, I arrived with a hold worth of plants and—"

"Me." Matias's voice was low, wounded. Water splashed on the tiles as he exited the tub. His wet feet squelched on the floor. He retreated to the opposite side of the room. I watched him brace himself against the wall, hands on his towel-clad hips. "Has Hugh said you failed him?"

I shook my head. "Not in so many words. But I eavesdropped on him and Antonio. There have been . . . rumors about my behavior on our trip. It is obvious they have doubts. Our conversation this morning was proof." I wanted to protect him from knowing that Felicity Ward was the source. He had suffered enough at her hands.

"What rumors? No one was with us on Chiloé. Anything being said is just hearsay." He strode over to his pile of clothes. Keeping his back to me, he shook out his trousers. "Is this why you're reluctant to discuss a future with me? Not because a lack of trust or confusion over your feelings, but because you feel guilty?"

He didn't turn around as he lobbed those dreaded questions. Fuck.

"I love you, Matias. But I'm scared that I don't know how to love and not be consumed. What happens when we have to confront those rumors in person? What will it do to my career? To yours? My existence is built around my drive to succeed, to prove that I'm equal to any man in my profession." My voice took on a hysterical edge. The questions and doubts disgorged into a veritable refuse heap of insecurities. "Who am I, if not a botanist?"

Matias paused, hanging his head. Droplets of water dripped from his curls to the floor. "Who said you can't be a botanist and my lover?"

A rush of anger sparked impatience. "Everyone, obviously. They already are." My voice echoed off the tile.

Matias tugged his breeches on and retrieved his shirt from the chair. "I didn't think you cared about other people's opinions."

"I don't, but what if I lose everything and can't secure employment? You know how judgmental society is. As a man, they won't chastise you, but I might be banned from the places I've struggled to persuade to accept me."

The fears I had held at bay for weeks came screaming forth, revealing my terror that everything I had worked for was falling apart.

He threaded his arms through the sleeves of his shirt, hiding his expression from me. "Do their opinions mean more than mine? More than us? More than my love?"

It was all there, in his emerald depths: pain, doubt. I *did* love him. I knew he loved me. But would it be enough? Would it sustain us if it destroyed our careers?

And what would happen when he realized I wasn't worth it?

Shaking his head, he sailed past me without stopping. At the door, he paused. "I love you, but I can't force you. This relationship has to be a partnership. You need to be in or out."

I stepped from the house into the garden, reveling in the fresh air. It was redolent with citrus and thyme. The whir of cicadas was deafening.

Movement among the greenery drew my attention. Hugh was alone on the bench, staring up at the sky. When he saw me, he patted the stone beside him.

I sat, also turning my face upward. "It's a beautiful evening." He nodded, toying with the crystal glass in his hands. "How are you, Hugh? We always talk about the murder. What are you doing with your time in Granada?"

He looked surprised. Had it been that long since I'd asked? I wasn't normally so selfish. My overwhelming inner turmoil had left little room for anything else, but it didn't excuse my neglect.

He handed me his whiskey. "Helping Antonio. He has record requests or places that need to be located. And we enjoy each other's company. Taking walks and such." His smile was serene, content. "I'm at peace, which I never thought I would say. Those last few months in England were unbearable. My brush with mortality made me want to live—really live, not go through the motions."

I bumped my shoulder against his. "I'm happy for you. Truly."

I finished the last drops of alcohol. My inner storms were making me blind to those around me. There was more to life than my profession.

"Do you resent me, Linnea? Do I smother you?"

I lowered the glass to the bench. "Far from it. I'm grateful for everything you've done. If anything, I feel guilty."

"Guilty?"

A loud trill from a nearby cicada drew our attention. Hugh jostled the rosemary shrub and it flew away. I didn't want to discuss this again, but apparently, he did. After my argument with Matias, I had to let go of at least one burden, or I was going to break.

"You've given me so much—more than I've given you. And for the past several years, I've floundered. Failed."

He tensed, straightening his spine. "Failed? In what possible way have you failed?"

"Drinking after the shipwreck. Languishing at the Physic Garden. Not producing anything substantial from my trip to Chile. Forming a personal attachment with a colleague." I hung my head, staring at the shiny tops of his boots. I couldn't look at him. "And . . . I heard you mention the letter from Sir Thiselton-Dyer."

Hugh's face blanched. He whirled on the bench, taking my shoulders as if to shake me.

"Why didn't you tell me? We could've discussed it. You haven't failed me, Linnea. Never. Perhaps you didn't accomplish what you had hoped, but by trying, by being in my life, you have succeeded in my eyes. That is what love is. It doesn't matter what happens. You want the best for the other person."

Behind my eyes, there was a warning pulse of pressure. For someone who avoided outbursts, it was the second time this evening that I was teetering on a precipice. I didn't know how to contain everything I was feeling, or how to find the words to express it. For years, I had been numb, secure behind walls of my creation. It was too much.

Hugh placed two fingers beneath my chin, forcing my face to rise. His profound study demanded my full attention. "I can try to reassure you, but my words will never be enough. You must believe."

The common theme of Hugh and Matias's statements did not escape me. They were imploring me to let go, to trust them. But I didn't know how to take the first step.

Frustrated, Hugh dropped his hand away. "I can't help you if you won't speak!"

I straightened, gently detaching his hands. "Hugh, it isn't up to you to solve everything."

He folded his arms, looking down his aristocratic nose. "We've traveled in circles again. You say I'm not smothering you, yet you push me away at every opportunity. It never used to be this way. Why now?"

The truth was it had always been that way. I had simply been an expert at pretending.

Antonio saved me from responding by appearing at the edge of the garden. "Hugh? Ah, there you both are. Tea?"

We were to assemble in the library after our meal. While we ate, Matias saved me from participating in conversation by talking about his trip. The group mused on the behavior of wolves and how it had changed now that the population was declining. The wolves were reclusive by nature, but now it was to the point of invisibility.

I understood how they felt. Hiding was protection.

My lack of participation went unnoticed, or at least unremarked upon. I sipped my wine and pushed food around my plate. My appetite had been absent for weeks. Matias stared pointedly at my plate until I took a bite.

When the meal ended, I sprinted for the library.

I pressed my hip bones against the surface of the large table, taking comfort from its solidity. On the surface, I arranged my notebook, the handkerchief containing the wisteria, and the dried rhododendron. The men arranged themselves around the room. Antonio remained near the table; Hugh at the sideboard, preparing drinks; and Matias a few steps away, arms crossed.

I cleared my throat, bringing our meeting to order. "I've not updated you on my progress."

They listened without interruption as I recounted my identification of the wisteria, my conversation with Prieto that had drawn me to the orchard, and my surveillance of the meeting.

"Tomorrow is the distribution day for the pamphlet. With luck, the contents will shed light on the reason for the gatherings." My throat was dry from speaking. I paused for a sip of water. "Antonio, we discussed this, but do you have any new thoughts on why Suárez was amenable to my participation and then changed his mind? There's no evidence that he is the murderer, but given his strange behavior, I don't think we can discount him."

"There's nothing in his background or governmental position that connects him with either the socialists or Pelayo. That said, I'm outside the circle of influence. I'm useful because I solve their problems, but I'm not one of them." Without waiting for a response, he continued, "This pamphlet—you didn't get any clue as to its subject?" He pressed his fists against the table, the muscles in his arms flexing from the exertion.

Had Antonio purposely steered the accusations away from Suárez?

"They did not discuss the contents. We'll know soon enough. Ah, as to that . . . if they were involved in Pelayo's murder, they may recognize me." With a fingertip, I pushed the dried rhododendron forward. "Someone broke into the house to leave this flower as a warning in my notebook."

A wave of reaction passed through the three of them—which would have been humorous, if they didn't all look ready to throttle me.

Hugh glared at both entrances to the library. "In the house? When?"

"How long ago did this happen? Did you question anyone?" Antonio chimed in.

"Severiano did not see anyone enter. I didn't have the opportunity to ask Sarita or Felipa. Honestly, I was distracted by Suárez's behavior and the meetings in the garden. I intended to discuss it with you—"

Hugh brought his palm down on the table. The papers jumped from the vibration. "And you are telling us *now*? Didn't it occur to that we were all in danger?"

I winced. It hadn't. What the hell was wrong with me? "I'm sorry, Hugh. I didn't think."

"No, you didn't! What is going on with you, Linnea? This isn't like you."

I had never seen Hugh so angry. His face was flushed with fury. Antonio placed a quelling hand on his arm.

Matias spoke, trying to be the voice of reason. "What's done is done. Let's review the facts and avoid unhelpful recriminations. Linnea will procure a copy of the pamphlet, and we will decide how to proceed—assuming she wants our assistance. Linnea?"

Hugh tried to interject, but Antonio clutched his hand.

Matias was giving me the space to regain my sangfroid. "Matias is correct. I can't change my decision now. We need to move forward. To that end, I would like Matias to accompany me to retrieve the pamphlet. If this group is responsible for the threats, they know who I am. Matias has been here the least. Once we have the pamphlet in hand, we can regroup."

Antonio replied, "That sounds reasonable to me. Hugh?"

Hugh's expression said he didn't agree, but he would accept it. "Yes, it sounds reasonable."

Chapter Twenty-One

Matias and I might have been occupying the same bedchamber, but we were worlds apart. Our intimacy had washed away with the bathwater yesterday.

After a stilted exchange of good mornings, I fled the bed.

He was sitting in a chair near the balcony when I emerged from the screen. Sunlight streamed through the lace curtains, turning his irises viridescent. His pillow had left a crease pattern on one side of his face. I could read the agitation in his body, though he was trying to keep it contained, trying to balance his conflicted emotions while navigating an interaction with someone unpredictable. Me.

The moments when I caught a prophetic glimpse of our downward trajectory were becoming more frequent.

Better to be the one who left than the one left. Protect yourself.

My coiled panic spun me toward the other side of the room. Gathering my boots, I plopped into a chair.

"Where do we collect the pamphlet?" he asked, splitting the tension. We were becoming experts at avoidance tactics.

I tied my laces. "The closest location is the steps near the Convento de las Tomasas."

"A hermitage?"

"Built to worship San Cecilio, the patron saint of Granada. It also houses a Roman cistern. We can go early to conduct reconnaissance in the neighborhood. The distribution won't begin until three o'clock."

"Linnea?" Matias lingered by his chair; his fist clenched around the curved back.

Was what he wanted beyond my capabilities? Was that his unvoiced question? How often could we go back and forth this way until we broke?

Detachment was the safest option. "Ready?"

The Convento de las Tomasas was simply a building, identical to the others in the neighborhood. Behind a wrought-iron fence, the cistern was a sinister hole in the brickwork. It was an odd location to choose to distribute pamphlets. The Mirador San Nicolás was nearby, which was a recognizable landmark, but the popular plaza would be too visible if they wished to be discreet.

We decided that I would wait for Matias at San Nicolás. A public place with a shifting crowd made blending in easier. Most of the visitors were occupying the stone wall that faced the Alhambra. The view was breathtaking—the Alhambra glowed rose gold in the afternoon light, the Sierra Nevada mountains rising in soft peaks beyond. A few trees dotted the plaza, though not enough for any significant shade. We aimed for empty spots to sit along the edge of the opposite wall, navigating around a roving group of musicians. Their proximity made conversation challenging.

"How did you meet Pilar?" Matias shouted to be heard over the musicians.

I waited until they wandered away to answer. "She approached me on my first day in the garden."

"You weren't told you'd have an assistant?"

"Communication between the staff is inconsistent. La señora Sánchez-Martín's instructions were meager. Occasional informal gatherings are the senior gardeners' idea of oversight. Suárez's duty seems to be pandering to wealthy donors."

A group who sat on his other side crowded us closer together. Matias turned toward me, furrowing his brow. "Doesn't that strike you as odd?"

In truth, I hadn't questioned it. "I assumed it was the way of things in Spain, or because I'm a woman. It wouldn't be my first experience of such exclusion while performing my job."

"Hmm." He wasn't convinced. "From what you've said, Suárez is a slippery character. First, the position at the Alhambra offered out of nowhere, and then Pelayo murdered practically at your feet—"

His point was valid, but "out of nowhere" rankled. "It isn't as if I don't have the qualifications," I retorted.

Matias pressed his knee against mine. "That isn't what I meant."

I was reserving judgment about Antonio's motivations in the investigation, but I'd taken his advice in our first discussion to heart. As for Pilar, it appeared there was much to consider.

"Antonio told me to be careful not to mistake curiosity as facts. Was it peculiar that la señora Sánchez-Martín approached me about filling the gardener's position the same evening Pelayo was killed? Yes. But does it seem so because we're examining the situation in retrospect? Few people knew we were traveling to Granada. The same could be said for my impression of Suárez. Is he that different from other high-level managers I've met, or is it the circumstances?"

A resonant chord on the guitar curtailed our discussion. We listened to them play until the clock chimed the hour—Matias's signal to depart.

Heat emanated in visible waves from the stones of the plaza. People clustered beneath the few trees for the tiniest scrap of relief. An afternoon haze cloaked the mountains, and the air rippled over the canyon, turning the Alhambra into a floating mirage. Damp strands of hair dried in curls against my temples.

Soon, it was nearing four o'clock, an hour since Matias left. I wasn't sure how much more I could bear. Swooning was a possibility.

On the periphery of my vision, a familiar forest green skirt caught my attention. The wearer navigated around the crowds beneath the tree.

Pilar.

She turned toward the other corner of the plaza at the same moment a woman with a voluminous skirt obscured me from sight. If I shifted a bit to the right, I could see Pilar, but she couldn't see me, as long as the skirt stayed put.

Whoever she was meeting had yet to arrive, or so I gathered when she stopped at the opposite end of the wall. Pilar stared at the view, fidgeting with the cuffs of her blouse and smoothing her ruffled hair self-consciously. Who was she waiting for? A beau?

I debated whether to stay hidden or assuage my curiosity. Once Matias arrived, she might see me anyway.

When Pilar turned away, I crept up to her. "Pilar! Enjoying the view?" She spun around, her features pinched in alarm. "Am I disturbing you? You're meeting someone?"

"No! As you said, the . . ." She gesticulated across the canyon.

Pilar might have been talented at gardening, but she wasn't at lying. Was this the wrong strategy? She might become more guarded, which wouldn't answer any of our questions. I drew away from her, shifting my weight. "I'm sorry to have interrupted. *Hasta mañana*."

"Please, señora, stay. I would enjoy your company," she implored, her hand reaching toward me.

Her eager assurance was at odds with her agitation, but my curiosity kept me from refusing. "This is an unusual place for you to visit. I thought only tourists frequented this plaza."

"Everyone enjoys a beautiful vista. I wished to be above the city. Have you recovered from yesterday?" She was beginning to relax, although she kept her attention fixed on the entrance.

"I was well, just a bit tired."

"And the man with you? He is your prometido?" she asked impishly, diverting the topic of our conversation. I would allow it for now.

"Fiancé? No, a friend, or—or a *novio*, I suppose."

"A novio?"

Her naïve blushes were charming, but I didn't wish to make this detour. "Shouldn't you be at the Alhambra, Pilar?"

"Today is my free day," she snapped.

Her reaction took me aback. Why was she so defensive?

I retreated a step and smiled at her in an attempt to break the sudden tension. "Ah, it is mine as well. Do you come here on your days off?"

She rocked her body from side to side, the bell of her skirt swishing against her boots. "Sometimes."

At her evasive answer, I steeled myself to increase the pressure of my queries, but whatever she saw behind me split her face into a sly grin.

"Here you are." Matias tipped his head, acknowledging Pilar. "Good afternoon, señorita."

Pilar flushed at his greeting, her lashes fluttering in demure perfection.

Matias nudged by her to loop his arm through mine. "Have you seen enough?"

Despite my concerns about overheating, I wanted to see who she was watching for. Even Matias's arrival hadn't broken her focus on the entrance. "Pilar, I'll see you tomorrow. Enjoy your visit."

She swiveled away. "Sí, señora. Hasta mañana."

I definitely wasn't leaving now. Tightening my fingers on Matias's arm, I steered us toward the crowd beneath a tree.

"We aren't leaving?"

"No, she's acting strange. Let's wait to see if whoever she is waiting for arrives."

Matias maneuvered through the people until he could slump against the trunk of the tree, below the height of those around us. I bounced on my toes until I could watch her through a gap. He tilted his head near my ear. "Why strange?"

"She's meeting someone but didn't want to tell me who, or have me around. Were you able to get the pamphlet?"

"Yes." He lifted the edge of paper from inside his waistcoat pocket. "A young man, eleven or twelve years old, was distributing them. Dirty face, soot beneath his fingernails. He was an enthusiastic peddler. They weren't trying to be subtle. I returned by a circuitous route in case I was followed."

"I assume you were not?"

"Not that I saw."

A drip of sweat trickled between my shoulder blades. Matias's curls drooped across his forehead into his eyes.

He tugged a handkerchief from his pocket to mop his face. "How long are we going to stay? This is unbearable. She probably has a beau."

"Aha," I exclaimed with gratification when a tall woman in a hat approached Pilar. She pinched Pilar's arm near the elbow. Pilar's wince was visible from across the plaza. Not an affectionate greeting.

Matias halted my impulse to go to her with a hand on my waist.

The woman towered over Pilar. Her lips moved faster, her hold on Pilar's arm tighter.

"She looks furious. I wonder if that's her cousin." I stretched taller, testing the limits of Matias's grip.

"If so, it isn't a warm relationship. Have you seen the cousin at the Alhambra?"

I scrutinized the woman. Her hat was large and obscured her face. "Pilar said she works elsewhere. I can't make out her features to recognize them. Can you?"

He squinted at the pair, shaking his head. Pilar was prying at the woman's fingers, trying to free her arm.

"She's hurting her." I lunged again in their direction, but Matias blocked me.

"Wait. If it gets worse, we'll intervene."

Pilar stared at the ground, cowed by the woman's display. When her lecture ceased, Pilar ripped her arm away, pointing toward the exit and then the Alhambra.

"If only we could hear what they are saying," I said, pressing against Matias.

She marched a few steps away from Pilar, and her voice carried. "Ven!" she demanded, calling Pilar as if she were a dog.

Pilar glared at the woman but followed her command anyway.

"They're coming this way." I faced Matias, stepping between his legs.

Our position was borderline scandalous. My senses were filled with him, perspiration mixing with a faint trace of his cologne. My body didn't care that we were in public, or at odds; it pulsed in response to his nearness. Already flushed from the heat, my skin steamed with embarrassment at my arousal.

I kept my head lowered and thought of cool things. *Ice. Nordic lakes. Snowstorms.*

His fingertips crept over the crest of my hip. My breath hissed through my teeth.

"They're gone." Matias's voice was gruff. Did he feel it too?

I stepped away, relieved that the distance lessened my lust. "Did you see her face?"

"They were moving too fast. What do you think that was about?"

I fanned at my perspiring face. "No idea. Do you think I should confront Pilar, or pretend we didn't witness it?"

"I wouldn't mention it. Get her talking about her family. If that's her cousin, they weren't happy with each other."

"It wasn't an acquaintance, not the way they argued."

A bead of sweat trickled down the side of my face, along my neck, to my collarbone. Matias followed it with burning eyes. Even he was rosy, and he had a higher tolerance than I did for these temperatures—or whatever it was that was putting us both in this state.

"Matias?" His hand reached for me again, but I didn't allow him to make contact. I couldn't. We were in public. "We should go," I croaked.

Without speaking, he moved enough to allow me to pass. We didn't talk on our return to the house. The spark of sexual tension crackled between us.

Several glasses of mint tea and discarded layers of clothing later, I settled in to read the pamphlet. Matias reclined on the chaise beside me while I read aloud: "*To the people of the Albaicín: We survived death and disease, only to be driven from our homes by wealthy aristocrats. No one will protect us. The prime minister disregards the rights of the people, choosing to fill his pockets and those of the rich. Our king is gone. The regent is a tool for those in government to manipulate. They don't care that we are starving, or that the asylums are full of orphaned children. The privileged elite grow and prosper at our expense. We must rise and protect what is ours.*" I offered the pamphlet to Antonio, who had entered the library as I read. "It goes on in that vein, giving examples of rich colonists who have returned to Spain to buy up entire neighborhoods."

"So, they are probably socialists. But are they involved in Pelayo's murder?" Matias added, mirroring my thoughts.

"Why risk meeting at the Alhambra if they killed someone? Antonio?" I turned toward him, curious to gauge his response to the socialist tract.

He shrugged. "Unless it is safe because someone is protecting them."

I ran my finger down the pamphlet. Cobalt ink. Rough paper. Similar to the fragments in the orchard.

I was wary of leaping to conclusions about their motivations and anxious to dissuade Antonio from acting, ever mindful of Izabelle's warning. "It could be a trap. Someone trying to set up the socialists to take the blame. Someone like Suárez? Does he know why you are in Granada?"

Antonio rubbed at the stubble on his chin, ignoring my questions. "Or are you the distraction?"

A sense of foreboding enveloped my body with sticky, warm indignity. The room blurred. What if I was the dupe, the sacrificial pawn in this game?

But to what end?

My mind enumerated the unusual events and my actions since arriving in Granada. At what point had it begun? Who was involved? La señora Sánchez-Martín? Izabelle Rodriguez Pelayo? Suárez? Pilar?

Matias slipped a cool glass of tea into my clenched fist. A thin strand of awareness anchored me to their continued conversation.

"Pilar may be part of the plot. The timing of her approach was calculated. We need to know more about her," I interjected, awkwardly cutting off Antonio mid-sentence. "We can agree that we can't be sure who is involved. A different strategy is needed to identify them. We can begin with Suárez. He has an office at the Alhambra. If he believes that I'm a bumbling aristocrat, he won't be expecting a search. It should be simple to access the room. He's rarely there."

My flood of conjectures was meant to distract from my internal spiraling. Antonio's keen scrutiny implied his consideration. He didn't argue with my plan, though. "If you can be discreet, we have nothing to lose. Matias, what can you tell me about the person handing out the leaflets?"

Matias recounted the same description he'd given me earlier.

On wobbly knees, I wandered over to my evidence table. The wisteria, the rhododendron . . . was it a game? A distraction?

"Linnea, do you have anything else to add?"

"No, I'm sure you've covered it." At least, I assumed he did, since I had no idea what he was asking.

I vaguely marked Antonio's departure. Matias also left for a meeting with Fernández. In the echoing stillness of the library, familiar voices rose to a clamor.

You are not an investigator. You are not a worthy botanist. They only chose you because you are easy to manipulate.

Two years ago—even one—I would've quieted them by consuming a bottle of whiskey. Today, I flung the doors wide, allowing the incessant buzz of the cicadas to obliterate the voices.

Hours later, it occurred to me that we had neglected to tell Antonio about the woman with Pilar.

Chapter Twenty-Two

"Almost there. Come on, my lovely," I coaxed, wiggling my bent hairpin into the tiny lock mechanism and shifting on my knees in front of Suárez's desk to get a better angle. As usual, the offices were empty. This early, the staff were on the grounds taking advantage of the cool morning, and Suárez wouldn't arrive until the fashionable hour, if he arrived at all. Antonio had said that Suárez was from a wealthy family, vassals of the monarchy placed in high-status positions. His interest in the Alhambra wasn't a vocation.

With a click, the lock surrendered, and I returned the pin to my cornet. Inside the drawer were pen nibs, scraps of paper, several dried leaves of laurel, and a slim folding knife with a brass handle. Not willing to concede that the drawer contained so little, my fingertips probed the panels of the desk for hidden compartments. No unusual seams or bumps.

I crawled under for a closer inspection.

The outer door to Suárez's suite flew open. Outside the door, two people were arguing.

Frantically, I searched for a hiding spot. The people had paused in the antechamber, giving me a few seconds. The furniture was sparse: two leather chairs and the desk.

Under the desk was the only option.

I hugged my knees to my chest, wedging myself into the furthest corner.

The drawer was still open. I eased it closed from underneath. If he found me here, I would lose my position, not to mention what it would do to the investigation. I struggled to quiet my rapid breathing.

"It's not my place to decide what's to be done with that fountain. Cease bothering me," Suárez snarled, stomping into his office.

"But señor, to achieve what is required, we must add a pedestal to the marble feature. It is expensive and will make the entire structure unstable. I don't want to waste funds—"

"Prieto, how else can I say it? No one cares about your opinion. The Ilustrísimo Señor Conde de Granada requested the alterations, and he provides the funding. Do you believe you know better than a conde? You're a gardener."

"Señor, I'm an architect," Prieto replied coolly.

"I care not."

Running footsteps intercepted them before they entered the office where I was hidden.

"Señor Suárez, the Ilustrísimo Señor Conde de Granada is at the gates. He demands you attend him immediately." The young man who served as Suárez's secretary had a shrill voice when he was hysterical.

"You see, Prieto? A conde. I solve problems for people in his class. Do the work as you've been directed."

Two people retreated. I remained huddled beneath the desk, waiting for the third to move.

"Cabrón arrogante," Prieto grumbled. More creative cursing followed him out of the office.

My legs prickled from sitting motionless. I couldn't venture from this cramped position until my feet regained feeling. I wiggled them, squirming at the sensation.

My rocking motion scraped my shoulder against a sharp edge of the drawer. I reached up to rub at the contusion, only to encounter an extra bit of metal protruding.

When I pushed with my fingertips, a small compartment popped loose near my ankle.

Maneuvering to my knees, I slid the compartment ajar. At first, it appeared empty, but I squeezed my hand inside the opening until I found a rolled piece of parchment. My narrow wrists had proven their worth. Triumphant that my risk had paid off, I inched forward, the parchment clasped in my palm.

What remained of an official-looking red wax seal marked the outside. Half the seal had crumbled from the parchment. I carefully unrolled the paper, squinting to read the narrow print.

Eliminate the problem. It is your responsibility now.

Well, that was unhelpful. The other side of the parchment was blank. No direction, no names.

Was the seal in the wax recognizable? A kind of vine? A knight's helmet? Little of the mark remained. Not enough to decipher. If I used my hand lens on it, the details might be legible.

After a moment of debate, I pocketed it.

Outside, el señor Prieto stood at the edge of a courtyard, scowling at a broken fountain. I hoisted the basket of tools I had retrieved from my office higher on my arm and stepped beside him. "*Buenos días, señor.*"

He turned, his grimace melting into a smile. "Ah, Señora Wren, buenos días. It's lovely this morning, isn't it? Not so hot yet."

"Indeed. Are you repairing this fountain?"

Prieto sighed, tilting his sketchbook so I could see the design. The crumbling fountain that occupied the center of the courtyard had been reimagined. Its classic pedestal was to be replaced by an ornate one shaped like the leaves of artichoke—a horrifying deviation from the original Islamic features.

"Er . . ." I searched in vain for a positive aspect to remark upon.

Prieto swiped his felt hat off his head. "You can say it. It's hideous. A wealthy benefactor insists we alter the fountain during reconstruction. He has funded the *improvements.*"

"But it will ruin the character of the feature, not to mention the historical accuracy." I didn't bother to soften my disgust. It was going to be a monstrosity.

"I've argued the same, to no avail." His earlier anger had lapsed into resignation. I could understand why. When one worked for wealthy patrons, it was providential to choose your battles.

"Is there no way to change his mind? I could try," I offered, though I doubted my efforts would matter.

Prieto replaced his hat, tapping the brim. "I appreciate the thought, señora, but I don't believe even you could make a difference."

"Best of luck, señor."

He continued to shake his head at his sketchbook as I departed for the Generalife.

My destination was the walled garden where I'd found the wisteria, a place I had avoided whenever Pilar was present. I surveyed the busy Generalife, searching for her. She either hadn't arrived yet or was working out of sight.

It wasn't solely Pilar's notice I was avoiding. If the rhododendron left in my journal was a warning as I suspected, then someone knew I had identified the substance used to murder Pelayo. Hugh's anger at the possible danger to the household—due to my secretive nature—haunted me. If I was being overly vigilant now, it was for good reason.

Trailing roses dominated the walls of the courtyard. My heaviest leather gloves were necessary for attacking the thorny vines. Spindly young specimens required pruning to allow the mature plants space to grow. This species of vine produced flowers with a scent reminiscent of steeped tea liberally laced with honey. Although the petals of these roses were not as beautiful as the early-season blossoms, their fragrance was intoxicating. As I knelt at the base of the wall, I amassed a pile of petals, intending to dry them and observe how the aroma developed.

"Oof, it smells like a perfumería." Pilar was closer than I'd expected. Her boots, crusted with dust, were right next to my knees.

"How are you today?" I asked.

"Estoy bien, gracias. I'm surprised they're blooming. Is it because they're sheltered from the heat?"

One of the vines was as thick as my wrist. I tapped it with my pruners. "In part, yes. These vines are old—they've had many years to adapt to the conditions. A plant that produces seeds throughout the growing season has a better likelihood of reproducing next year, continuing the species."

Pilar knelt next to me, examining the verdant wall. "Cómo?"

"If the rose produces seeds for a few weeks in late July and it coincides with hot temperatures, or no rain, or too much rain, there's a chance none of the seeds will survive. If a rose can produce seeds again in late August, it gets a second chance to establish for the next year."

"Ah, I think I understand."

We sat on our heels, taking in the network of climbers. In some places, it was so dense that the bricks supporting it had disappeared. "Plants are resilient. The harsher the conditions, the stronger they become. They produce more blooms and more seeds. It is as if they do it to spite the savagery of existence. I suppose you could say that is true of some people as well. Don't you think?" I hoped my analogy would strengthen her trust, but my ramblings had been too esoteric—or were lost in translation, judging by Pilar's puzzled expression. "From what you've said, it sounds as if you've faced struggles."

She trailed her pruning shears along a line of the bricks. "No more than any other person born into my world."

I smirked, chagrined at the hypocrisy of my aggravation. She had her fortifications that were difficult to breach, as I had mine. "Your world? As opposed to mine?"

"You went to school and traveled."

"I was fortunate to have resources others did not, but you've received an education and this job at the Alhambra—instead of working with your cousin?" I allowed my observation to settle, then directed her to the next corner. "Can you finish that wall? I'll do this one. Remove anything spindly, but leave the large vines." Interspersing my question with instruction would keep the tone of the conversation more casual, less interrogational.

"Yes. My cousin," she replied, snipping as directed.

"How much older is she?"

"Fifteen years. She was an adult when I was born. I wouldn't have a home without her. She made sure I went to school. We nursed each other through the cholera."

Pilar and I were similar in many ways, except she had her cousin, while I had always been alone. "You are close?" I ripped an entire vine, exposing the stained wall.

"Very."

"Let's move to the other end. These vines can remain." I led the way to the southern corner, where the wisteria and roses intertwined in great arcs of green with thick, brown pods. The woman I'd seen with Pilar at San Nicolás was older, but her hat had obscured her features. A fifteen-year difference would make her cousin near my age.

"What are those?" Pilar pointed to the pods.

I hesitated a moment, then turned fully toward her to observe her reaction. "Wisteria. You probably saw them bloom early in cascades of purple flowers. These are their seeds."

"I wasn't here earlier." Her expression remained curious, not agitated.

I froze, the blades of my pruners poised over a stem. When had she arrived? "Leave the pods. Trim them here and here." I pointed to two areas, and she went to work. "Were you employed elsewhere?"

"I still work at a café, and I help at the counter in the print shop where my cousin works."

Print shop? I had forgotten she had mentioned the print shop before. Was this how the meetings were connected with the garden?

Pilar finished her task and bent to the weeds erupting at the base of the wall. She knelt, tearing at the roots. I was plotting my next question as I gave the vine at my feet a distracted yank. It sent me toppling onto my arse.

Pilar's laugh was a bright ascension of notes. It was the first full laugh from her I'd heard. I smiled in delight. "That one was really attached." We wrangled the cuttings into a pile near the door. "Once we finish clearing this area, we can move on for the day. I'll return with a wheelbarrow for these," I said, nudging the pile with my toe.

After a few minutes of clipping and tearing, she asked, "Señora, that man you were with—your novio. Is he also an aristócrato?"

What was it about my relationship with Matias that was so fascinating to her? I was impatient to return to my questions about her cousin, but I reminded myself that this was how a friendship was established, in an exchange of personal information. If I wanted answers, I had to be transparent.

"No, his father was a translator. Matias joined the Royal Navy when he was a boy." I nudged her toward a snarled area. Matias had family, but from age twelve, he had been as alone as me. We were both guarded, with good reason. What would it take for me to trust him?

Her next question caught me off guard. "He is in the military?"

"Not anymore. He's a naturalist and studies animals." My mind wandered off again, thinking about Matias's joy at the work he was doing with Fernández. He had served for years in the Navy to have these opportunities.

"How did you meet?"

"We met because of our professions. He traveled with my godfather. Do you have a *novio*?" I tried once again to pull the focus from me.

Her cheeks flared scarlet. "No, my cousin wouldn't approve."

"Do you do everything your cousin says?" I challenged, hoping for a strong response.

Pilar's dark eyelashes settled on rosy cheeks, shrouding her emotions. With a vehement tug, she removed several feet of roses from the wall. "I do. I owe her my life. It is right that I do as she says."

I broke off a wilted blossom and carried it to a stone bench. "Earlier it sounded as if you want more. Love? Adventure?"

Pilar followed me reluctantly. "Working at the Alhambra is an adventure. Most people I know don't work somewhere like this."

I reached in the basket to retrieve a water flask. After partaking, I offered it to her. "Are you hoping to gain an apprenticeship?"

She examined the simple flask and eventually took a drink. "My position is temporary."

"Why temporary? Your knowledge of plants is growing. You're a hard worker. I'll give you an excellent recommendation," I reassured her.

"Maybe with your recommendation, I could stay." She shook her head. "No, it's foolish to hope."

I handed her the flower. "What do we have if we don't have hope?"

She gave me a youthful grin. "You have been a good—you have been kind to me, señora."

"We're friends, aren't we? You know about my life; I know about yours." I bumped our shoulders together.

"I would like that. I don't have many friends."

Before I could reply, a group of visitors led by Suárez entered the courtyard. We leapt to our feet. Pilar moved slightly behind me, blocking her from their view.

"And this is a pocket courtyard that we are renovating. Ah—this is Lady Wren, a visiting botanist from England, assisting with our restorations. Lady Wren, please greet our visitors and describe the botanical work you are doing."

With reluctance, I stepped forward and removed my gloves. As introductions were made, Pilar slipped from the courtyard.

When she passed Suárez, she ducked her head, avoiding his notice.

Chapter Twenty-Three

Usually, in the evening, we could rely on the breezes descending from the Sierra Nevada to provide relief from the heat, but not tonight. Restless energy vibrated throughout the city.

Hugh and Antonio were out for the evening, as usual. Neither Matias nor I could settle in the stuffy house. He suggested a ramble through the Albaicín as a distraction.

We weren't alone in our plan; the streets were thronged with people. I loved these evening hours in the Albaicín. Music floated from the cafés. Children darted through the crowds. Older couples leaned on each other as if it were the only way to stay upright. Courting couples exchanged flirtatious glances. Friends gathered over a glass of wine at the outdoor tables. Laughter burst from my chest as a tousle-headed boy squirmed between us, squealing in delight as he evaded his friends. Matias pressed his palm to the small of my back to steady my wobble. "Everyone is on the streets tonight."

"I love the joyful chaos." A puff of wind stroked my skin, redolent of cypress and citrus. "We're fortunate to be in this part of the Albaicín, near the gorge and the river. At least we get some relief from the heat. The center of the city must be stifling."

"My body is struggling to adapt to the temperatures. It was much cooler in the mountains." Matias swiped at his forehead with his wrist.

Once, I had asked him if he wanted to return. Some self-destructive inclination within prompted me to ask again, "Did you wish to remain?"

"I lost track of time when I was tracking and observing the wolves, and the landscape was beautiful. But no, I was ready to return." He arched his back, laughing. "My body was not happy sleeping on the ground. I'm getting too old. And there was no companion to steal the covers."

His teasing broke my descent into a melancholy mood. I covered my mouth with my hand in mock horror. "Me? You're the thief that steals my pillow!"

Matias tucked a loose curl behind my ear. "It's good to see you smile. It's been rare."

His observation stung. I dipped my head. "I'm sorry. My mind has been elsewhere," I said, contrite.

He gestured to a café. "Would you like to stop for a glass of wine?"

I was relieved that his focus had veered away from me. The tables were ringed with groups of merry people. Their exuberance was more than I could tolerate. "We aren't far from the river trail. I haven't explored it yet, and it's bound to be pleasant beneath the trees."

We drifted together as we walked, our fingers interlacing. Pausing at the apex of the bridge over the Darro, we watched the water ripple. On one side of the path, the walls of the Alhambra glowed in the evening light, but we meandered toward the grove of trees on the opposite bank.

Matias tightened his grip on my hand as we picked our way to a spot along the river, where the tree roots were exposed. "Let's sit for a few minutes."

I settled on a root, propping my feet off the ground to keep my skirt clean. Matias's hip bumped against mine as he settled alongside me. I snuggled into him, resting my head on his shoulder. He slipped his arm around my waist with a contented hum.

Voices in the distance faded while we were serenaded by the tinkling sounds of the river. Despite the sexual tension between us, we both had been avoiding extended physical contact. Or being alone. I wasn't sure how to regain intimacy with him after our argument. I didn't want to promise more than I could give. He didn't deserve that.

Matias traced the lines on the palm of my hand. "Your preoccupation—it isn't solely the investigation, is it? It's also what you said the other day."

Matias's perceptiveness was maddening when directed toward me. My impulsive words in the bathing chamber had lingered, wounding him days later.

"On the *Cormorant*, I was reminded of the consequences of my decisions on Chiloé. Although we were circumspect around our shipmates, I'm sure they knew we were a couple. But no one said anything to either of us. Nonetheless, I suspect they were judging me." I paused. I should tell him about Sir Thiselton-Dyer's letter. But if I did, Felicity Ward's actions would add to his distress. To what end? If it wasn't her gossiping, it would be someone else. "We might be comfortable being unconventional, but we know how other people will see it. And when we arrive in England—"

"Reality will be waiting for us."

I raised my head, surprised he finished my sentence. "Are you concerned too?"

He released my hand, wiping his palms on his thighs. "I've been thinking about what you said the other day. You're right. I have a family to consider. I can't be selfish. My actions could hurt my half sister, Josephine. We both know how damaging rumors can be. I wouldn't want something I did to affect her, or her future." Matias drew a line in the dirt with the toe of his boot. "I admit, I thought Fernández's offer was fortuitous because it would give us both space to consider what we wanted."

A band of pressure tightened around my chest. How would this work if we weren't both committed? If we kept running from each other? If we kept secrets?

"And did you reach any conclusions?" The words emerged as a squeak.

He stared at the river, the tension in his jaw carving divots around his mouth. "Not really. The consequences we are so concerned about are speculation. Well, they were. It sounds as if rumors are already circulating."

I didn't reiterate that the gossip was about me, not him. Or so I assumed. Maybe now that Hugh knew I was aware of the letter, he would allow me to read it. Until then, I wouldn't reassert the likelihood I would bear the brunt of any scandal.

The rippling sound of the river tempered my worrying. We sat motionless while the shadows deepened, obscuring the opposite bank. What more could we say? A resolution was out of reach, perhaps not even achievable.

With a resigned exhalation, I spoke, "We should go. It's getting dark."

He nodded, brushing off his trousers and offering a hand to help me from the ground. "I'm sorry, Linnea. I wish—I wish—"

"I know. I wish as well." I embraced him, leaning into his solidity.

I wasn't ready to surrender yet. We would keep trying to find a way.

We climbed up the bank. I pointed toward the gate in the Alhambra walls. "There's another entrance to the Generalife adjacent to the river. When you visited the other day, I didn't get to show you my favorite spots. There's a night-blooming jasmine in flower. I passed it several nights ago, and the scent is ambrosial."

"I'm in no hurry to return. Lead on."

I used my key to open the recessed door, guiding us on the path. To distract from the awkwardness that remained, I babbled about the origins of the Generalife, sweeping my hands in grandiose gestures. "Imagine the sultan sprawled beneath a fragrant bower with his many wives."

"It conjures quite the image, doesn't it? An ideal place to sleep during the summer months. The cool air from the river, the swish of the trees . . ."

"The attentions of a bevy of women . . ."

"I wouldn't say no to that. Ouch."

I smacked him on the arm, relieved that we could joke. "It's along this path."

A dark pool oozed from the bower entrance, saturating the packed earth. With dawning horror, I recognized the metallic smell.

"Matias—"

Someone was face down in a pool of what appeared to be blood.

"Fuck," I choked, lifting the hem of my skirt. Matias grabbed my elbow to keep me from entering.

"Let's wait. I'll find help. Given the amount of blood, it is unlikely we'll be able to do anything for them. Stay here."

He ran off toward the Alhambra gates, stones flying in his wake. I waited until he was out of sight. As I neared the body, I could see the skirt had distinctive embroidery at the hem.

"Oh no. No, no, no." I reached for her, falling to my knees.

The dark plaits, the delicate birds. I knew who it was.

Chapter Twenty-Four

My breath burned in my lungs. I fought against the pressure, arms flailing. Something pinned my legs, restraining me from hip to ankle. The scream that formed in my constricted throat emerged as a weak moan.

"Linnea—Linnea, stop."

My eyelids came unstuck, allowing in a sea of swirling, painful lights. "Matias?" When I furrowed my brow, needles of pain shot across my hairline. "Ow." I pressed my fingers to a large knot above my eyebrow, covered with a bandage. "What happened?"

Through my blurry vision, Matias shimmered into form, sitting on the edge of a bed. I recognized the heavy velvet window dressings. Our bedchamber. But how did we get here?

Matias's hand was on top of the covers, next to my thigh. He was dressed in wine-colored breeches covered by a banyan, hair mussed as if he'd been raking his fingers through it. His skin was gray with exhaustion.

He reached for my hand that rested on the bandage, guiding it away. His warm palm encased my icy fingers. "We were hoping you could tell us. When I returned with a guard, you were unconscious."

My head swam, the room blinking in and out of focus.

Matias brushed a fingertip across my cheek. "Mi amor?"

I clenched my eyes closed. "My head . . . hurts. Was it a dream? When?" Garnet droplets. Colorful birds worked in thread. The garden. My eyes flew open. "Pilar!"

Matias's fingers twitched on my leg. "Pilar isn't here, mi amor."

"No, no. Pilar was injured. Dead?" A pulse of pain accompanied my desperation to make him understand. "She was on the ground. I was touching her."

"It was her? You were alone when we returned."

I couldn't make sense of what he was saying. "Alone?"

He fussed with the blankets, rearranging them on the bed. Avoiding eye contact. "You were the only one in the bower."

"It was her. She was dead," I repeated. Why couldn't he understand? "You saw the blood! How could someone remove a body without leaving evidence?" Agitation made my heart pound, synchronized with the throb in my skull. I sagged into the pillows, paralyzed by the pain.

"We didn't search the area. Transporting you to safety and to a doctor was my priority. He believes you were struck by a cudgel." Matias's recitation was reserved. His calming manner should've been soothing, but it spiked my agitation. What wasn't he saying? He feathered a kiss on my eyebrow. "You were unconscious for hours. We were instructed not to leave you unattended. I removed your clothes but could only give you a cursory cleaning. Would you like to take a bath?"

My hands rested on top of the coverlet, blood caked in the creases and fingernail beds. A crashing swell of nausea swept in with the force of a tidal wave.

"Mmph—chamber pot—"

One appeared just in time. I heaved until stars flickered behind my eyelids. Matias gathered the hair off my neck. "Finished? Love?"

I shuddered. Lifting my head was excruciating. He handed me a glass of water. A cautious sip helped steady my ship. Swallowing past the raw fire in my throat, I sobbed, "Why can't I remember?"

He pressed a soothing, damp cloth to my nape. Cloth: cool. Stomach: angry. Head: hellfire.

I cataloged the sensations until I settled, recalling his question. "A bath would be welcome."

He removed the cloth. "There's a hip bath here in the chamber."

"Oh. Maybe not." Perching in a hip bath would be beyond me in this state. Could I make it down the stairs to the bathing chamber? I might as well have been faced with crossing a desert. On foot. With no water. Or clothing.

Without any warning, Matias hinged over the bed, hefting me into his arms.

"Matias, no," I groaned.

"Hush. It isn't far."

Our descent on the stairs was precarious, my vertiginous position heightening the nausea. I ground my molars, determined not to cast up my accounts. We were both panting when we reached the bathing chamber. He lowered me into a chair.

When he turned to fill the bath, I said, "Thank you, but I could've endured a hip bath." My appreciation was sincere, though my voice was weak.

"But you didn't have to."

I fumbled with the tie on my dressing gown, sliding it off my shoulders. "How will we get upstairs?"

"Let me worry about that."

It took our combined efforts to remove my chemise. Once I was naked, he carefully transferred me from the chair to the tub. Warm water lapped at my shoulders. I remained boneless while Matias took up the soap, lathering my hand.

"Your silence is distressing. Talk to me," he coaxed.

Words swirled in my head; a swarm that wouldn't settle into anything coherent.

"Doesn't it feel as if we have already lived this? My head injured? Carrying me to the bath?"

"If you could avoid head wounds in the future, we could prevent repeating this situation." His wry smile turned down at the corners. "I shouldn't have left you."

I could have argued that I was an independent woman that didn't need him to take care of me, but even in my semi-lucid state, I knew that would be absurd. After all, the man was currently washing my listless limbs.

Clouds of dirt and blood bloomed in the water. He pulled the plug to drain the tub. I wrapped my arms around my legs, huddling for warmth while I waited for the hot water. My few recollections from the night were fragmented.

Matias and I walking. Blood on the path, and a body in the bower.

Birds embroidered on the dress. Thick braids of dark hair. I couldn't recall her face, though. The firmness of her shoulder beneath my fingers, and then . . . nothing.

I rocked my closed eyes against the tops of my knees to clear the images. "How long were you gone?"

Matias dropped the soap he was using to wash my hair. I retrieved it, handing it to him.

"A quarter of an hour? It took a while to locate a guard. The Alhambra was empty."

"Enough opportunity for someone to remove a body?"

He paused his scrubbing to consider. "Possibly. I had hoped you would stay outside."

My throat thickened with unwelcome nausea. I waited for it to lessen. "I wasn't willing to leave her. We needed help. I doubt staying out would've kept me from being harmed."

Pitcher in hand, he guided my head back. "Have you remembered anything?"

I tipped to my left to make it easier to rinse my hair. The warm water and the gentle massage of his fingers on my scalp eased the pressure. "I remember us walking. Details of her dress, her hair. And then my memory is blank."

"You're certain it was her?" Matias's voice was as tender as his touch.

"Yes. No. I'm *not* certain." I jerked in distress, my stomach lurching at the sudden movement. "I may—I think I might—"

He thrust a chamber pot into my hands. It was sturdy porcelain decorated with delicate violets. The diabolically cheerful flowers danced in front of my eyes as the nausea receded.

Matias wrapped my hair in a towel while I was upright. He cupped my shoulders, whispering in my ear, "Are you ready to get out?"

I nodded, placing the chamber pot on the floor as he lifted me from the water. He approached with a spare towel and my dressing gown over his shoulder. Once I was dry and clothed, he boosted me into his arms to begin the laborious journey upstairs.

Matias, struggling to ascend the stairs while his dazed burden clutched a chamber pot to her bosom, must have been an amusing sight. Someday in the future, we might find it humorous. Not now, though. I cringed in mortification.

He set me on the bed with careful control before collapsing beside me. I turned my head on the pillow to caress his hair in affection.

Matias was rosy from exertion. The curls at his temples were damp with perspiration. He nuzzled his head into my hand. "I don't like this. You shouldn't be this ill. You're pale. I'm going to send for the doctor."

I threw my thigh over his legs, pinning him in place. "Rest for a few minutes. You carried a grown woman up two flights of stairs."

He stroked my bare thigh beneath the dressing gown. My body refused to summon even the tiniest flicker of desire. He loosened the linen around my hair, and a mass of damp locks pooled on the pillow.

I lifted a snarled hank, grimacing. "It's going to be a tangled mess."

"Stay where you are. Once I've sent the message, I'll braid it."

I burrowed under the covers, exhaustion getting the upper hand over consciousness.

"Don't fall asleep! The doctor said that once you're awake, you must remain alert." He removed the coverlet, ruining my cocoon.

"Can I close my eyes?" I growled.

"Yes, but don't drift off. I'll be right back."

My heavy lids dropped, and behind them danced tiny, embroidered wrens.

Chapter Twenty-Five

"She was seriously injured at the Generalife. As the supervisor of the restoration, it is my responsibility to assess her condition. You involved the police, and they have questions that must be answered. Why won't you allow them to interview her?"

"Señor Suárez, Lady Wren briefly gained consciousness. However, the doctor insists that she be kept calm and in quiet surroundings until she is recovered." Matias's use of precise English belied his anger. His usual accent was softened by his life at sea—rounded, Spanish-flavored vowels. With Suárez, he could've been speaking to Parliament.

I embraced my pillow, taking comfort from the lavender-honey fragrance of my soap. After the doctor visited, declaring that I could sleep, mere seconds had passed between his exit and oblivion.

"Señor Suárez, Mr. Ward has advised you of Lady Wren's condition. That will have to suffice. May I escort you to the door?" Hugh's forbidding tone brooked no argument.

Suárez's protestations were halfhearted and grew fainter as Hugh led him away. I braced for waves of pain as I opened my eyes, but there was only a slight tinge of discomfort that eased as they adjusted to the sunlight.

Relieved, I sat, swinging my feet to the floor. I tentatively pressed them into the rug. Once the haziness cleared, I shuffled to the privacy screen. A visit to the chamber pot, a splash of cold water to my face, and a quick brush of my teeth were life-altering. Matias had braided my hair last night but couldn't brush it first, so it was a knotted mess. As I unwound the strands, curls sprung free in every direction.

Matias entered the room to find me at the dressing table. "What are you doing out of bed?" he clucked in an excellent imitation of a hen.

"I'm well enough to brush my hair."

He unceremoniously snatched me from the chair and strode to the bed. "Fine, but you'll do it here."

"Stop picking me up! You'll do yourself an injury. How do you think I got over there? I can walk," I protested.

"You were unconscious for twenty-four hours. You will sit in that bed until I'm certain you're healed," he retorted, tucking the coverlet around my legs.

I was insensate for a full day and night?

He retrieved the brush from the table. "Where's your bandage?"

Teasing at the knots in my hair, I replied, "There was a tiny scratch. A bump doesn't need to be covered."

"That was not the doctor's recommendation," he scolded.

"Matias." No one had ever flapped and fussed over me like this. It was endearing, if a bit annoying.

"Would you like something to eat?"

My stomach responded with a loud grumble.

"That's a yes. I'll fetch breakfast. Hugh is impatient to see you. May I send him in?"

Tidying my hair had reignited the throbbing. My wound smarted. I would keep that observation to myself.

Hugh must have been hovering. As soon as Matias opened the door, he strode through. "You're awake. Shall I fetch the doctor?"

"I'm on the mend. And the doctor said I was healing as expected."

He pursed his lips. "He did, but you've been asleep since he left. That can't be normal. What happened? Matias said you were attacked where you found a body?"

The rush of questions aggravated the drumbeat in my skull. "I know you want details, but can it wait?"

Matias approached, bearing a tray loaded with piles of golden toast, a couple of eggs scrambled with fresh herbs, and—blessed cherubs—coffee. I ignored my slight nausea to take a bite of toast and chased it with a gulp of coffee. Our cook knew the way I preferred it: inky, no milk or sugar.

At my gusty sigh, Matias chuckled. "An excellent measure of Linnea's state is her reaction to the first sip of coffee."

I chewed another bite, considering them both. "I appreciate your concern, Hugh. And I'll be happy to provide you with the details. After I eat."

Hugh watched as I scooped a forkful of eggs. "Very well. Rest, please." The heavy door slammed in his wake.

Matias came around the opposite side of the bed and stole a slice of toast. "Sorry, not leaving."

I stretched to kiss his grizzled cheek. He hadn't shaved for a few days. The wiry stubble prickled my lips. He crinkled his nose and continued chewing. I returned to pillaging the tray. In the upper corner was a small dish of deep red jam.

The knife in my hand clattered on the plate.

My mind flashed to pools of blood. The green of Pilar's skirt. I clenched my eyes, trying to banish the vision.

"Amor?" Matias wrapped his fingers around my trembling wrist.

"I—I need—" My eyes bounced around the chamber, cataloging the signs of normality: the tray on my lap, the drapes swaying in the breeze, and the stack of books on my writing desk.

A vase containing a single fuchsia rhododendron bloom.

In a move worthy of a gothic heroine, I pointed my quivering finger involuntarily. "W-w-where did that come from?"

Matias frowned. "The flower? The household staff left it, I assume."

I pressed my palms to my face, the pressure a welcome relief. Matias's concerned gaze didn't budge when I lowered my hands. A lump lodged in my throat at the sight of the food.

Cradling the warm cup of coffee in one hand, I used two fingers to push away the tray.

"Finished? You've barely eaten anything."

"Can you tell me again about last night? Maybe it will aid my memory."

He slouched against the headboard. "You wanted to show me the night-blooming jasmine. We were almost at the bower when we encountered the puddle. There was a lump that looked like a body inside the courtyard, surrounded by what appeared to be blood. I told you to stay on the path while I went for help. I ran through the Alhambra looking for assistance, but it was empty. No one responded to my shouts. Finally, I located two guards at the gates. One went to find a policeman, and the other came with me." His fingers traced the lump on my forehead. "When we returned, you were unconscious in the pool of blood. Neither the guard nor I left the bower. I was concerned about you. Your breathing was slow. You were unresponsive, and you had that nasty contusion." Matias grimaced, lifting the glass of the water on the tray and draining it in one go. "The police carriage brought us to the house. We called for the doctor." He hesitated. "Do you realize how serious this was? You were unconscious for hours."

I recognized the fear in his voice. If our roles were reversed, I would've been frantic as well.

"Matias, I'm fine. You were with me. I wasn't doing anything reckless."

He took the hand not wrapped around the coffee cup and cradled it to his chest. "You believe it was Pilar? And that she was dead?"

Between surreptitious glances at the rhododendron, I clutched the cup with both hands to mask my trembling. "With that much blood? Who could survive?"

"We may never know. What made you sure it was Pilar?"

"The skirt had embroidered birds on the hem, like Pilar's." I was convinced that it had been her in the courtyard, but I didn't have any proof. We had nothing except the wound on my head. Matias wasn't saying outright that he didn't believe me, but his skepticism was obvious. "Someone was in that courtyard. I didn't imagine her. You saw it." My voice wavered with frustration.

He came off the bed and stalked across the room to the open window. "I didn't see it well enough to say. If you say it was Pilar, I believe you."

My stomach lurched, rejecting even the coffee. I didn't need his pity. After placing the cup on the side table, I lay down, pulling the coverlet over my head.

The bed shifted as he pulled at the fabric. "Why are you hiding? Are you feeling ill?"

Overwrought and in pain, I couldn't formulate the reassurance I knew he needed. "Matias, love, I'm well. I just want to close my eyes." It was the best I could do.

I dozed for several hours, drifting between moments of lucidity. Matias and I spoke little during those periods. He remained in a chair near the door. The ruffle of the journals he was reading whispered across the room like a breeze through leaves. Sitting upright went well; my dizziness seemed to have subsided. I tested my balance on the balls of my feet.

Matias watched the proceedings without interjecting. His attentiveness followed me when I went across the room to the privacy screen, and then onward to retrieve my notebook from the desk. I used the end of my pen to rotate the rhododendron in the vase. Was it a coincidence, or a threat?

With slow, careful steps, I returned to the bed. My journal split open to a clean page.

Tapping my pen on my lower lip, I considered my dilemma. If Pilar was the victim, why would someone kill her? Why remove the body? If her cousin was involved with the socialists, it made sense that they would protect her, not target her.

What did I know of Pilar? Was she involved? How could I obtain the answers? I needed to examine any evidence remaining at the Generalife, and find about Pilar's life outside the garden. Where did she live? What was her cousin's name? And what about the socialist group? Izabelle said Pelayo had been a member.

Antonio said he tried to be impartial, but could he, with the influence of the monarchy?

And if I didn't ask for his assistance, was there another way to gather insight?

Hugh knocked on the door and spoke without entering. "Matias, Linnea—dinner will be served soon if you would like to join us."

Matias set down his stack of paper and replied, "Thank you." He stretched his spine with a groan. "Would you like to go downstairs?"

A change of scenery would be welcome. "I do. I'm tired of being in this bed."

Matias came to my bedside. From the furrow between his brows, I could see he was considering picking me up. I stood first, giving him a conciliatory kiss. "I can walk. No more carrying."

"Fine, but we'll walk at the pace of octogenarians."

I obeyed. We descended the stairs like arthritic tortoises.

Chapter Twenty-Six

Our bedchamber ceiling had eighteen beams. I counted end to end, hoping to induce sleep. A spider web decorated the corner of the second beam from the balcony. Two of the beams were discolored, signs of a leak in the roof.

Dinner was forgettable. I was a useless conversationalist. I had worked up the gumption to ask Antonio for assistance in gathering information on Pilar, then promptly excused myself to wander while they enjoyed their after-dinner beverages.

Nighthawks had emerged to hunt for insects. Their quarry flittered through the beams, making for easy pickings. White moths remained within the shadows of the low shrubs. Visible, yet unreachable. I recalled the journal article Matias had shared with me that afternoon. It had been written by a zoologist, Edward Poulton. He described how some larvae appeared to blend into their surroundings in a defensive response to avoid predation. The naturalist attempted to link his observations to other insects and animals who also used their surroundings to hide.

What if I could disguise myself to get closer to the socialists? Could I infiltrate their group to determine if there was a connection to Pelayo's death?

Outrageous? Yes. But possible. Was attacking me a warning to stop interfering? If so, I didn't want to put anyone else at risk. Hugh's frustration at my obliviousness to the group's safety remained at the forefront of my mind. I refused to be so imprudent going forward, at least with their well-being.

My preoccupation over these questions and the possibility of going undercover whirled in my overactive brain. Matias shifted, murmuring in his sleep. Could I convince him, Hugh, and Antonio that it was worth the risk?

I started counting the beams again from the opposite direction.

"Please tell me you weren't planning to sneak away?"

I was hinged at the waist, boot in hand. Despite the damning evidence, my intention had been to tell Matias. "It isn't what it looks like."

He snatched the boot, crouching to my level. "Why can't you trust us? Trust *me*?"

"I do trust you, but this situation is my responsibility. What if my questions drew attention to Pilar? Nothing about this investigation makes sense. Are things truly as I perceive them? If you hadn't witnessed the blood, everything about that night would be in question. Whoever is toying with me has stooped to harming innocent people—"

Matias interrupted my impassioned babbling, "Are you certain Pilar is innocent? You saw her argue with that woman. And she has evaded your questions."

I plucked my boot from his hands. "She is—was—a private person. There's nothing unusual about that."

"Where are you going? It isn't wise to strain yourself."

After tying my bootlace in a double knot, I came to my feet slowly. Any signs of my injury worsening, and he'd never let me leave.

"I want to see if there is any evidence left at the Generalife. The possibility of finding anything is slim, but I have to try." Pressing my palm to his chest, I implored, "Will you accompany me, please?"

He held me in place with a firm hand on my nape, glaring at the strands of hair that covered my wound. "I suppose."

Rushing into the bower, I skidded to a stop when confronted by a pristine courtyard.

The soil had been scraped clean. Vigorous activity had damaged the jasmine's leaves. A delicate scattering of petals was all that remained. No material or prints.

The squeak of a wheelbarrow drew me from the bower at a run. I had to stop that worker.

When I skidded to a halt in front of him, he looked rightly alarmed. "*Buenos días. ¿Quién ordenó limpiar esta área?*"

"*El señor Suárez, señora.*"

He continued along the path, adding to a sea of footprints. I drifted in his wake, dazed with disappointment. This section of the garden wasn't open to the public, so there had been no reason to rush with tidying. I supposed it was foolish to think that it wouldn't have been disturbed, though.

One set of wheelbarrow tracks diverged from the others. I traced them to the outside walls, and to the door we'd entered through that night. Could someone have used a wheelbarrow to remove the body?

My key to the garden door had been on the dressing table this morning; I'd assumed Matias had found it when he removed my bloody clothing. I clutched it in my palm, the teeth biting into my flesh. Had I locked this door? I couldn't remember. We'd found the body immediately after entering. Whoever it was must've already been in the garden.

A stout breeze was moving through the canyon, swirling the branches of the cypresses on the riverbank. I walked toward the water. A glittering rock in the shallows caught my eye. I bent to retrieve it, shaking the drops from its surface. When I rotated it, raised veins of different materials refracted the light.

I clenched the stone in my fist, took a deep breath, and hurled it into the Darro with a frustrated bellow.

Matias burst through the door, hastening over exposed roots. "Are you well? What—why did you scream?" His color was high, his pupils wide with panic.

My skin crawled in mortification at my immature outburst. "I'm sorry. Any evidence is gone. The body is gone. My bloody mind is gone. What is the point of trying to piece together this snarled mess?" I squatted on my heels, too overwhelmed to stand. Ants swarmed around my feet, spilling out of cracks between the roots. If I lay down, would they carry me away?

Matias's boots entered my peripheral vision. "It's too soon. We shouldn't have come."

An ant crawled up my toe. "I'm failing, utterly and completely failing. I'm failing Pelayo, who I didn't even know. I failed Pilar. I am failing—"

"You don't know that it was Pilar."

For whatever reason, hearing him reiterate that bit of logic dropped me to my arse. Staying with the ants was a good plan. Wrapping my arms around my knees, I pulled deep breaths into my lungs. *Calm down, Linnea. Focus.*

When I regained some semblance of control, I propped my chin on my kneecap. Matias's composure was feigned, a thin facade over his crackling agitation. His hands flexed into fists, the muscles in his jaw clenched. Searching for evidence had been a pointless exercise.

I forced myself to stand. "We can return to the house. Suárez had everything removed. There's nothing to find."

On our way through the Generalife, I detoured to the courtyard where the wisteria grew. I wanted a glimpse of the last place Pilar and I were together.

"Is this it?" Matias asked from the opposite side, pointing to the dried wisteria pods hanging on the vine.

"I believe so. The texture of the pod matches the piece I found." My joy at discovering the wisteria seemed ages ago.

"Someone has been working in the courtyard."

"Yes. Pilar and me." I swept aside some rose petals and sat on the stone bench. Disappointment weighed heavily upon me. Matias remained standing along the brick wall.

"How often do people enter this courtyard?"

I sighed. What was the point of his questions? "Rarely. It was excluded from the restoration plan. When we started our work, it was untouched."

"Did you use a wheelbarrow?" His head was bent, muffling his words.

"No." I pointed to the heap of wilting vines. "I meant to return with a barrow to remove those."

"Look."

With an exaggerated exhale, I left the bench. He pointed near the freshly pruned roses. At the base of the wall, a section of churned soil held the imprint of a distinctive boot print—and next to it was the track of a wheelbarrow tread.

Rising hope lifted the fine hairs on my arm. "Someone found the courtyard convenient for a siesta?"

He knelt by the track. "Or someone moved the body with a wheelbarrow. That would explain the lack of bloody footprints and the speed at which it vanished."

Our theories corresponded. But I was cautious. "There's no way to confirm our suspicions. They would have to have been hiding here when we entered the jasmine bower. There was no reason to suspect we would show up. It was a spontaneous decision to come to the garden."

Paired with the tracks on the river trail, an escape via the orchard would be a likely scenario. Were we fitting the facts to our assumptions, though?

The late-blooming roses were finished, their final petals crushed in the dirt. I selected a few intact ones and slipped them into the pocket with the gate key. A memento of Pilar. When we pruned the roses, I'd thought we were at the beginning of our friendship, not the end.

Suddenly, debilitating exhaustion settled like a heavy cloak across my shoulders. My knees threatened to buckle. I slumped against the brick wall. "Can we leave? I'm . . ."

Matias moved with haste to support my weight. "Are you well?"

I didn't have the energy to reply. We stumbled to the entrance, fortunate that a hired hack was dropping someone off. The soporific swaying of the carriage lulled me to sleep immediately.

When we reached the house, I managed the stairs inside, but no further. I was content to splay on the chaise lounge in the library.

Matias unfurled a blanket and swaddled it around my shoulders. "I'm concerned about you, love."

"Need . . . to shut my eyes. All will be well."

His scowl was the last thing I saw before plunging into a vivid dream.

I ran through the Generalife, calling for Pilar, dodging in and out of courtyards. My lungs burned with exertion. I kept running. I had to find her. Angry voices came from the orchard. I spun around, my feet slipping on the loose rocks in the path. I fell hard on the surface, abrading my palms and knees. From my prone position, I saw the door beyond the orchard was ajar. Ignoring the pain in my limbs, I ran through it.

Three ropes hung from the cypresses: Matias, Hugh, and Antonio each stood beneath a noose. Pilar paced in front of them. Her dress was a vivid ruby red, a garish flag against the dense forest. She turned as I approached.

"Ah, here she is. It's your choice, señora: them or you."

A thick, muscular bicep pinned my arms to my sides, and the cold metal of a pistol pressed against the base of my neck. I tried to turn my head, but the person dug the barrel into my flesh.

"You claim to love these people, yet you're always running away. What will it be?"

"Them. Of course I choose them," I shouted.

"Why, Linnea? Is your life unworthy?"

"Compared to theirs? Yes." I stomped my heel into the arch of my captor's foot, but they didn't react. Why didn't Matias, Hugh, and Antonio flee? No bindings or guards restrained them.

I fought my captor's hold, distraught. "Run! Why won't you run?"

Matias stared at me; defeat etched on his beloved face. "It's too late."

"Why?"

An explosion rocked the forest. Trees toppled like a house of cards. The arms surrounding me vanished, as did everyone else. On my knees in the rubble, I was alone. A sob burst forth, emerging as a soundless croak. One remaining cypress wobbled on its roots, and then fell toward me.

I pitched upright on the chaise, the blanket slipping off me. My whole body shook. The library was empty. The door was closed. Sunlight streamed through the garden, shadows shifting through the movement of the trees. Anguish gripped my body. I muffled my sobs into handfuls of fabric.

The meaning of the dream was obvious. One of my greatest fears was bringing harm to those I loved through my actions, and being unable to prevent it.

My men were in danger. Whatever I was embroiled in at the Alhambra was poised to spread beyond the garden.

I picked at the blanket, returning to my suppositions. What if I could infiltrate the socialist group? I was convinced that was where the answers were. Could I do it if I pretended I was too ill to continue inquiries or work in the garden? Hugh, Matias and Antonio would have to agree to maintain the pretense—and they would be safe because it would appear that I had yielded. In truth, being confined to the house, or my room, would fracture my sanity.

With shaking fingers, I loosened the tangles in my hair. Each segment I completed of my braid sealed my commitment to this plan.

A triple knock on the door warned me of Antonio's arrival. He didn't look well. Dark circles ringed his eyes, and his shoulders drooped.

"Good afternoon. I have some information. May we meet in the courtyard? Hugh and Matias are waiting."

Chapter Twenty-Seven

A canopy of branches shaded the table that held our afternoon tea. Leaves danced in the gentle draft. It should've been a soothing scene, but the body language of the men set the air alight.

As Matias took the seat next to mine, he said under his breath, "You're awake. Are you well?"

If that dream was a hammer, my mind was glass shattered into a hundred pieces. How did one explain such an occurrence? I managed a one-shoulder shrug and focused on distributing the tea from an ornate silver teapot into individual cups. Even with an unsteady hand, not a drop spilled.

"Antonio, you have information?" I prompted amid the weighty silence.

He sipped from his cup, making us wait.

"I located the print shop that produced the pamphlet. The man behind the counter wasn't forthcoming. Understandable, since they print contentious materials. I wasn't able to confirm Pilar's cousin's employment." His evasive eye contact said this wasn't the bad news. "I went to the house where they live. The neighbors' confirmed Pilar hasn't been seen. She tends to her vegetable garden every day, but the neighbors said it has been neglected. Her cousin didn't return while I was waiting. Of course, none of this is confirmation that Pilar was murdered. Only that she's missing."

Heat from the cup seeped into my palms. Was it possible that she was alive? Whose body was it, if not Pilar's?

While I mulled over his disclosures, Antonio continued, "But there's something else. The Alhambra doesn't employ Pilar."

Tea sloshed onto my hand. With a muttered curse, I set it down.

"She told the garden staff she was your assistant. They assumed you brought her with you from Cádiz."

She lied to me.

Matias squeezed my shoulder. "Linnea?"

My voice shook. "I'm such a bloody idiot. Her attention flattered me into complacency. A willing participant in her merry chase."

"We don't know that for certain."

"No? What else could be the reason?"

"Maybe she was blackmailed, or otherwise forced to lie to you. Her admiration was probably genuine. We can only speculate about the circumstances." Matias was trying to slow my spiraling conjectures.

Hugh added, "You understand that as well as anyone, Linnea. No one forced you to dress as a man at Kew. It was how you chose to further your career."

"That was different. I wasn't hurting anyone," I retorted.

"And we don't know that she intended to harm anyone either."

Hugh might have been correct, but rationality was beyond me at the moment. She'd hurt me. And if she was dead . . . we would never know her motivation. "Anything else, Antonio?"

"Suárez is as he appears: a social climber supportive of the republic and the monarchy. Ultimately self-serving."

Matias picked up a teaspoon, spinning it between his fingers. One of his tells when he was deep in thought. "Pelayo might have been connected to the socialists, but we don't know how. Is it Suárez? Pilar? Pelayo's murder set everything in motion."

"Or did it?" I interjected. "What if I was part of the plot from the beginning? La señora Sánchez-Martín's invitation appeared spontaneous, but if it wasn't? Maybe they wanted a clueless aristocrat to fill a role. Someone gullible. And I met the qualifications."

They spoke over each other, piling on the reassurances, but I disagreed. I *was* a suitable scapegoat. And I hadn't yet told them about Izabelle.

"Gentlemen, cease, please. Your efforts to console me are kind, but our energies would be better used to trace the origin of my invitation. Who told Lourdes Sánchez-Martín about me? It's been years since I published anything, and I'm not known in Spain. She approached me at the Alhambra deliberately. And I haven't heard from her since I've taken up the role." I paced from the table to a nearby orange tree, bending a branch to sniff at a fading bloom. "Antonio, what do you know of her?"

"Her reputation is well established. I'm not aware of any details about her personal life. I'll see what I can gather, though. Also, one of the under-gardeners confirmed that Pilar was in the Generalife when they departed for the day."

Was she the victim or not? There was the tiniest glimmer of hope that maybe it hadn't been her, but if not her, then who had been in the bower? If I went undercover, I might track where she vanished to, if she was alive. If I remained at the Generalife, there was no chance of that happening.

I walked a circuit around the paving stones. Antonio jotted something in his notebook. Hugh and Matias drank their tea. Infiltrating the socialists was our best bet. I had to be patient and pick my moment to spring the plan on them.

Antonio gave a frustrated grunt. "Why didn't we think to investigate Lourdes Sánchez-Martín after Pelayo was murdered? She introduced you to him."

I returned to the table, sipping the last dregs of my cooled tea. "Because there was no reason to believe they were connected to me."

None of them could argue with that conclusion.

There is something about two in the morning. The soul is in communion with the night; veils are opaque between the conscious and the unconscious. It's also the hour one relives their deepest regrets. Or, in my case, it is the hour when you find yourself wandering a graveyard.

Matias was asleep when I abandoned our bed again. Concerned that my restlessness would wake him, I snagged my cloak, intent on a walk. I wandered until I came to a tiny neighborhood cemetery. A wrought-iron bench at the edge of the gravesites beckoned to me.

It was admittedly a stupid idea to be wandering about in the middle of the night so soon after the attack, but the state of my mind was fraying. The thought of staying in that house gave me a panicky feeling. Pilar was either dead—murdered—or lying to me.

I swaddled myself within my cloak, trying to contain the bottomless antipathy I felt for myself. Why was I so invested in finding the truth of this situation? Yes, Izabelle had appealed to me. Her situation had spoken to some of my greatest fears: A man controlling your life so you couldn't even find out the truth of your brother's murder. Being shipped away to a family that wanted nothing to do with you.

Deep in that blind-ego part of me, though, I knew my motivation wasn't entirely altruistic. I was still fighting, determined that I had something to prove to Hugh, Antonio, and Matias. More importantly, I wanted to smother those negative internal voices. This pattern of failures needed to cease.

I hugged my arms around my chest.

The metallic clang of the gate fractured the hush of the graveyard. Alert, I slid my hand under the cloak to my dagger in my boot. A figure passed into the light of the waning moon.

Matias.

He nestled beside me, draping his arm around my shoulder.

I intertwined our fingers. "You found me."

"I'll always find you." He tightened his hold on me, as if I were so insubstantial, I was at risk of floating away. "Are you brooding?"

"How can I sleep?"

"Linnea." He coasted his hand down my braid to where it vanished into my collar. "Why are you fixated on this?"

I sighed, unsurprised that he'd perceived the direction of my thoughts.

"I want to find the truth about Pelayo, and if Pilar was also a victim. I know I can do this, and I don't think anyone else will bother."

"But are those reasons to put yourself in danger?"

Why was I reluctant to tell him about Izabelle? A part of me worried that he would discount her appeal, even though I knew that was against Matias's nature. But what if he told Hugh and Antonio? I'd made a promise to Izabelle. Would he think going undercover was too dangerous?

To hell with self-preservation. I decided to broach the subject. "I have a proposition. Will you listen first?"

He squeezed my hand. "Of course."

"Prieto, the architect at the garden, said something that makes me think Pelayo may have met with the socialist group." A lie. It had been Izabelle who said it. My skin crawled, knowing I was willfully lying to Matias. "Whether it was assisting or spying, I don't know. Antonio can't find out that information. He's too well-known in Granada. And if Pilar has vanished and is alive, she might be in hiding." I took a deep breath, reining in my eagerness. "I want to go undercover in the neighborhood where Pilar and her cousin live to insinuate myself into the socialists." In my rush to share, I'd simplified things somewhat. Would he tell me I couldn't do it? Would he support this endeavor, even if it was a bit unhinged? "Well?" I prompted.

Matias released my hand and strolled to the nearest headstone. I contained my impatience, allowing him to consider. "You've thought this over?"

"For a couple of days."

Worry bracketed his jaw and brow as he returned to the bench. "If this is the best course of action, I'll support you however I can."

He didn't want to concede, but he would do this for me. I hooked my fingers in the waistband of his trousers to draw him closer, pressing my forehead to his abdomen. "I have to do this, Matias. I *have* to."

After a couple of passes over my hair, he flipped my hood over my head. "I know. Mi cielo, let's return to bed. It's cold."

I took his hand, letting him lead us out into the streets.

An overenthusiastic sparrow on the railing was making a racket that threatened to split my head in two. Daylight streamed through the curtains. When I walked my fingers across the surface of the bed, I didn't find a warm body. I never slept late.

I dressed with little thought given to my clothing choices, stopping just long enough to dab some ointment on the receding lump on my head and brush my teeth. Matias wouldn't tell Hugh and Antonio about my plan without me, would he? That inkling turned my final preparations into a frenzy. I was securing my braid as I exited our bedchamber.

When I peered over the railing into the interior courtyard, Matias, Hugh, and Antonio were visible through the greenery.

"Is she well, Matias?" Hugh's voice was barely audible.

I hid behind a rose-scented pelargonium, fondling the leaves between my fingertips while eavesdropping.

Matias's exhale carried. "She's obsessed with this investigation. She thinks it's her duty to find the murderer."

I *was* obsessed. But couldn't he understand why? He had been the same way when the murders were happening in Chiloé. It stung to think that he couldn't see the similarities between us.

Hugh rested his hand on Antonio's shoulder. "Antonio is the inquiry agent. Maybe we can convince her to let him take over."

That was not happening.

Antonio patted Hugh's hand. "If that is what she wants."

The fabric of my sleeve brushed the plant, breaking off a flower. It floated into the courtyard and Matias's hair. He brushed it away, tilting his face back to squint. Even from this distance, I could feel his perceptiveness.

Matias was pouring my coffee when I reached the table.

"Good morning, gentlemen. It's later than I thought."

Hugh slipped the plate of *tostada* across the marble. "You must've needed the rest, my dear."

Inside, I quaked with nervousness, but I tried to appear serene outwardly. I took a bite of *tostada*, dabbing at my mouth with the serviette. Everyone shifted in their seats, pigeons on a roost. "How is everyone this morning?"

Hugh refilled my cup with coffee, even though it was three-quarters full. "We're concerned about you."

An unfeminine snort slipped out. "Let's talk about something else. How are you?"

Hugh's mouth gaped, effectively diverted by my question. "We—we're fine. I'm helping Antonio with an investigation into a local businessman."

Antonio gave Hugh a fond glance. "I didn't expect Hugh would be such a talented investigator. It's refreshing to have an assistant."

A glow of happiness surrounded them. Despite the darkness that had plagued me since arriving in Spain, the diversion was worth it to see Hugh's contentment.

Hugh cleared his throat, blushing. "That's enough of that."

Matias folded his serviette into triangles, tapping it against the table-top. I stilled his wrist with a finger. Under my breath, I said, "And you? How are you?"

He gave me a crooked smile. "Tired but well, mi amor."

Our few words of normality seemed to assuage the unease. Hugh launched into an amusing anecdote about being followed by a pack of children in the Albaicín. His enthusiastic recounting meant I could consume my breakfast without their scrutiny. Antonio interjected with a tale of a similar experience with a child that helped him with an inquiry. The boy had realized he could blackmail him for money and refused to hand over information until Antonio purchased a new dress for his grandmother.

"I was happy to purchase the dress for his abuela. She was even more formidable than her grandson and remains a contact to this day."

Bonhomie lingered in the air. I'd intended to discuss my idea with Matias again before approaching Hugh and Antonio, but the moment was too perfect to ignore. In this state, they would be open-minded.

At the next natural lull in the conversation, I charged in. "I've had an idea that I'd like to share." Matias's head snapped around, knowing what was coming. "A way I can get closer to identifying the murderer."

Antonio's eyes narrowed. Hugh braced a hand on the tabletop.

I lobbed my artillery. "I think I should go undercover."

Chapter Twenty-Eight

Full marks to them: they didn't shout. Instead, their responses were infinitesimal. Hugh's jaw flexed. Antonio's eyes lit up with interest.

Antonio would be honest if he thought this was an abysmal idea. My concerns about him being involved hadn't vanished, but he knew Granada. If this scheme was to be successful, I had to have his input.

"Antonio, are any of the staff in the house?"

Without asking why, he stood from his chair and left the room. Hugh, Matias, and I sat in silence until he returned. "Sarita is out at the shops, and Severiano is outside, smoking. We'll hear him when he returns. Let's speak quickly. He was half finished with his cigarette."

With one more swallow of coffee for courage, I made eye contact with each of them. "I'll get straight to the point. Antonio, you're recognizable and known in Granada as an agent who works for the government. If this case is related to the socialist cause, your position is a hindrance. Fewer people know me. I haven't traveled outside our neighborhood in the Albaicín, only from the Alhambra to here, and rarely anywhere else. Even the other gardeners might not recognize me if I'm in disguise. My hair is my distinctive feature. If I change that . . . people will see what they want to see."

Antonio laced his fingers together, speaking with care. "Whoever struck you saw you, so I would refute that you are unknown, but with the right changes"—he glanced at Hugh and Matias—"it might work."

His tacit approval was enough endorsement. My chest tightened with excitement.

"I'll color my hair, find lodgings in that part of the Albaicín, and get a job in a café. You've said yourself that people are guarded. I must earn their trust. My story will be that I followed a lover to Cádiz and was abandoned."

The metal chair beneath me squeaked as I wriggled in animation, but it wasn't loud enough to cover Matias's scoff at "lover." He leaned forward. "I'd prefer to come with you."

Antonio intervened, "Coming up with a plausible story for two people is difficult. A woman alone is vulnerable, which makes others protective. How do we handle Suárez and your duties at the Alhambra?"

When sleep had eluded me, I had reasoned through this scenario. "Suárez believes that I'm gravely injured, correct? He'll have to be persuaded that I need at least a fortnight to heal. That should be adequate. It will have to be."

I waited for Hugh's argument. He was quick to do so.

"You think this is reasonable? Won't she be in danger?" Hugh implored.

I bit my lip. *Patience, Linnea, patience.*

Antonio came to my defense. "She won't be in any more danger than continuing to work in the Generalife. If the murderer believes she has conceded the field, it will embolden them. Linnea's correct—I'm at an impasse. Everyone knows I work for the government."

Matias reached for my hand beneath the table. "Will we be able to contact you?"

I turned to Antonio, rather than Matias. "No contact. Don't you agree, Antonio?"

"No contact between her and this house. We must convince the staff that she remains in her bedchamber. If they are turning away visitors at the door, rather than one of us trying to intercede, it will be more believable. Matias, you've put on a protective show for Suárez. That should aid our deception."

Gooseflesh pebbled my arms. Instead of existing in a fog of dread, I was clearheaded and focused. When I went undercover, no one would question my choices. Immersion in another persona wouldn't allow for complacency. In my absence, Hugh could help Antonio. Our adversity wouldn't burden Matias. Instead of continuing to fail everyone, I would be doing as Izabelle had asked. I would find justice for Pelayo and find the truth of Pilar.

A breakthrough to the murders felt tantalizingly close.

I dropped Matias's hand, launching from my chair. "Are we agreed? If so, I propose to leave the day after tomorrow. I would leave today, but

I must darken my hair. I have clothes that will suit a woman serving in a café. Antonio, are you familiar with any women's boardinghouses in the neighborhood near Pilar's house?"

Antonio stood. "I'll make a list."

Hugh wasn't contributing to the conversation. His face was an emotionless mask. "Everyone is in agreement, I see. What can I do? Are you certain we can't have communication with Linnea?"

Antonio paused by Hugh's chair. "People will be hesitant to confide in Linnea because she's English. She must gain their acceptance quickly. If they suspect she has a connection to this house or the aristocracy, she'll never achieve it."

Hoping to fend off any other objections, I added, "An apothecary will have the ingredients necessary for hair dye. Matias, can you collect them? We must avoid alerting the house staff to anything unusual. If I retire to my bedchamber now, you can say I've relapsed."

I turned away from them, darting for the stairs before Severiano entered. Matias found me pillaging a trunk and tossing clothing around the room.

I pointed at a scrap of paper on the desk. "There's the apothecary list. Thank you for going."

"Walnut husks? Indigo?"

"Walnut husks will create a dark brown shade, but if that isn't adequate to cover the red, I may have to use the indigo."

"How long will it last?"

"Long enough. I always wanted to be a brunette. Red hair is conspicuous." I lifted one of my auburn locks. It wasn't a true red, but it stood out as bright as a fox on a snowy field.

Matias sat on the bed, watching as I considered each item of clothing. "What if you're discovered?"

"What is there to discover? People disguise themselves for many reasons. As for the lack of communication, how is it any different from when you were in the mountains?"

He rubbed the back of his neck. "You're right. It isn't any different." He tugged at my hand, drawing me into the space between his thighs. "I've barely accepted your plan, and you're leaving."

My fingers tunneled through his hair, disarraying the ebony waves. "I know, but I can't wait. Whoever attacked Pilar believes I'm injured. It is an ideal time to leave. Would you fetch the valise on top of the wardrobe?" I came to my knees to brush my lips over his brow, releasing him quickly. A gesture of physical solace, an acknowledgment that we were retreating within our self-imposed emotional walls again.

Matias handed down the battered velvet valise. Into it went one somber dress and one skirt; I would wear the other skirt and take three shirtwaists, two pairs of thin wool stockings, no jumps, and two thread-bare chemises. Except for a few items, such as the dress I'd worn to the Alhambra reception, my clothes were threadbare. I'd purchased most of them for the expedition to Chile. They were functional rather than stylish, and suited to my temporary persona.

My journals were too risky. I selected a slim, new, empty notebook I bought in Cádiz, along with a pencil and a small volume of Keats's poetry. A hopeless romantic would have poetry among her scant belongings.

"I'll leave you to your packing. Willow bark, witch hazel, and other medicinals will help convince the staff and Suárez. Maybe even a little laudanum. Suárez might believe you are in the grip of the poppy."

Absorbed by my packing, I hadn't noticed Matias remained. "Speaking of Suárez, I'll pen a shaky note to him," I chuckled.

"Given the way you're moving, I assume you are feeling improved?"

I tucked the last shirtwaist into the valise. "Putting a plan in action speeds along one's recovery."

His expression told me he was dubious.

Using a mortar and pestle Matias had fetched from the kitchen, I crushed walnut shells, lavender buds, and the juice and peel of a lemon into a thick paste. Once applied to my hair, it would render it a glossy coffee hue.

The process turned my nail beds beige, which lent authenticity to my disguise. Although subtle, the lavender and lemon oils tempered the overwhelming vegetational odor of the dye. I remained in our bedchamber, except for a brief sojourn to rinse my hair. Matias scouted the way and stood guard outside the door while I took what would be my last warm bath until I returned. Most boardinghouses had basic bathing facilities; if I was fortunate, I would have warm water in a pitcher.

Antonio had passed through Matias the list of women's boardinghouses and names of two cafes that were hiring. Tomorrow would be my last full day in the house. Antonio and I planned to spend the morning reviewing the layout of the neighborhood. He would share any other insights he thought would be of benefit. A fortnight was not a lot of time to infiltrate the group and find a killer.

Cups rattling on a tray heralded Matias's entry. He froze when he saw me.

I rubbed a towel over my hair. A strand had escaped and clung to my cheek. The dye had worked. My bright locks had dimmed to a dark brown.

"I'll be happy when that rinses out."

I shook the mass around my face, striking a provocative pose. "Prefer ginger to brunette?"

He captured the loose hair, winding it around his finger. "Yes, on you."

The seductive aroma of strong coffee wafted from his tray. "Even for me, it is a bit late for that."

"I assumed you wouldn't be sleeping soon, anyway, and I wanted you to try this drink. A guide on our trip prepared it when we were in the mountains. It's called *carajillo*. Spanish soldiers drink it. I can attest to its ability to warm you on frigid nights." He placed the tray on the desk and handed me a cup.

I sniffed at the demitasse. My eyes went wide at the cloud of alcoholic fumes rising from the surface. "That's potent. Brandy?"

Matias swirled the liquid. "Traditionally, it has rum, but Antonio didn't have any. So yes, brandy."

My first sip was cautious. I let the liquid flow across my palate. The coffee was brewed strong, mixed with the alcohol and a gentle lacing of sugar. It was powerful. "Ohhh . . ."

"I knew you'd like it. It reeks in here. Let's savor these on the balcony."

I followed him over the threshold. Early evening crowds meandered the streets. Our balcony was tucked against the house in the shadows, hidden from sight. We settled on the padded bench, sipping our *carajillo*.

He nudged my shoulder. "Are you nervous?"

I hadn't allowed myself to consider the nature of my anticipation. "Impatient more than nervous. I'm excited about the challenge. When I dressed as a boy at Kew, the stakes were lower. At least I get to dress as a woman."

Matias paused as the strains of music from the café below fell silent. "I forgot about your days masquerading as a boy."

"Believe me, I haven't." Especially after my nighttime sojourn to the garden.

"Were you scared? Did anyone get close to discovering you?"

Despite the many years that had passed, I could recall the constant sensation of apprehension: a daily tightness of the stomach, though that might have also been hunger. Finding funds or opportunity for meals wasn't always a priority.

My satin robe pulled tight across my thigh, stretching the fine embroidery. Never would I have imagined back then that I would own something so beautiful.

"I was scared every day—not of the garden staff unmasking my gender, but of being hurt if someone saw through my disguise." Sharing the details of my early years at Kew wasn't something I did, even with Hugh. Matias had been on his own at a young age as well, though. He would understand. Hugh had met me when I was pretending to be a boy, but he wasn't aware of what it had taken to survive. Matias's life in the Navy had been challenging in similar ways. "I couldn't afford the expense—or the questions—that would've come with sleeping at a board-inghouse, so I slept in the garden."

His hand gripped my forearm in alarm. "In the garden? Outside? For years?"

I pressed my head to his shoulder in reassurance. "Yes. There was usually a potting shed for shelter during poor weather, but I preferred the grounds."

"What did you do if it was cold?" Matias was agitated now. I could see him imagining me, young and vulnerable. He wasn't wrong. My existence had straddled a thin line of destitution. The small amount of money I'd inherited from my parents and Uncle Liam didn't become mine until I was twenty-five years old. After that, I was employed by Hugh.

"I would linger at a pub until closing and return to the garden to sleep. There are a lot of sheds at Kew in which to hide. And they were relatively safe, compared to the streets."

His hand tightened. "Linnea, were you harmed?"

I reflected on the many definitions of harm. I assumed he meant sexually. To that, I had an unequivocal answer. "Physically, the occasional bruise. I was savvy enough to avoid dangerous situations, for the most part."

"What does that mean?" His eyes flashed in anger toward the threats in my past.

There was a reason I avoided speaking about those years. It brought on dark memories and lingering shame. "A few times, I fought my way out of uncomfortable circumstances."

Matias set his demitasse on the ground, rearranged the pillows, and scooped me into his lap.

My face rested in the perfect spot between his shoulder and neck. I fluttered my lips against his skin. "What did I say about picking me up?"

"Hush. I need to hold you," he murmured, shifting me closer.

Using the tip of my nose, I followed a line from his earlobe to the hinge of his jaw. He shivered. "No doubt you had similar experiences. You were a young boy in the Navy."

"I know what you are glossing over by using vague terms. And yes, the Navy was comparable. Physical discipline was frequent, whether meted out by the captain or fellow sailors. I kept my thoughts to myself and my fists at the ready."

I nodded my head against his shoulder. "But we survived."

"That we did."

My body hummed from the caffeine coursing through my veins. Images and memories flashed through my mind. We'd both endured many things to reach this moment, on this balcony. More than once, I'd contemplated ending my life after the shipwreck. If I had made that decision, I never would've met Matias, or experienced these moments with him. Never traveled to Chile.

I burrowed into his warmth, and the voices below us merged into an ensemble. An étude of early evening in the Albaicín. When we existed in these circles of intimacy, we could share from our hearts, and our barriers retreated. When the fortifications were reassembled, we struggled. How would we get past our stubbornness?

The aftertaste of the sweet carajillo turned sour in my mouth. I was fighting the inevitability of change. To move forward with Matias, with my career, something had to give. Thrashing around in this liminal space wasn't helping us.

Burying my face in his collar, I took comfort in his breathing and let the moment be.

Chapter Twenty-Nine

I covered my yawn with the back of my hand, but it drew Antonio's attention nonetheless. "Were you able to get any sleep?"

"An hour or two. My brain wouldn't settle."

We were meeting in my bedchamber to maintain the illusion of illness. Our chairs were arranged in front of the extinguished hearth, and Antonio tapped his fingers on the brocade pattern that covered the armrest. With Antonio, I couldn't tell if his fidgeting was impatience or concentration.

He lifted a finger toward the music playing outside the open windows. The musicians at the café across the street were playing a popular flamenco tune. "Have you seen flamenco performed?"

"Only a brief performance in the port at Cádiz."

"It has gained popularity in the last several years, which is a mixed blessing. There's a desire to adopt flamenco as a representation of modern Andalusian identity—ironic, given the treatment of the Gitanos. As you have witnessed all over the world, if those who possess wealth and power want something, they take it."

The voices came to a dramatic crescendo and transitioned to clapping.

"Everyone listens to flamenco. It isn't reserved for the elite." I gestured outside.

Antonio's fingers had ceased moving, and he leaned forward, arms resting on the chair. "Por supuesto. Our government wants flamenco to be equated with Spanish identity to set us apart from the rest of Europe. Flamenco is unique to Spain, or at least that is what they want the world to believe." A slight flush bloomed high on his cheeks. His agitation was a rare sight. Even on the night we found Pelayo, he had been steady, unemotional.

"Why do they want to be perceived as different?"

"They wish to be distinct from the rest of Europe, even if it ignores centuries of discrimination." Antonio held his hands out in front of him, flipping them palm up to palm down. "I am descended from the Arab-Berber people, some of my ancestors were enslaved people, but because my skin is light, I'm treated as if I am white. Spain wants to pretend it embraces everyone, but it's a facade, just like how their embrace of flamenco is superficial, a way of claiming something that is not their own. They want the performance, not the people."

I gripped the arms of my chair, processing his explanation. Matias had described a similar experience to Antonio's. He had been raised in his father's English family, but in Chile, he wanted to be accepted by his Chilean relatives. It was a struggle I could recognize but knew my privilege kept me from truly understanding.

"Oh, I see. They're claiming flamenco the same way they steal the neighborhoods."

Antonio's smile reassured me that I had passed muster. "The returning rich are buying up land to build palacios. By buying, I mean they are forcing the people from their homes so they can acquire them."

If Spain was similar to many places I had visited, it was more common for people to have a home or land than money. Being removed from their home would leave them with nothing. "How is that allowed?"

"They have a direct conduit to those with influence, and they are wealthy. They can exploit whoever they wish. Faced with such inequality, how are the voices of the people heard?"

The topic had peeled away Antonio's reserve. These were issues that mattered to him. My concern that he wasn't on the side of the socialists would mean that the conflict with him ran deep.

He walked to the open window, sweeping his hand toward the city. "We optimistically believed that the republic would represent our voices, but that hasn't happened. Because our government alternates between the conservatives and liberals, there's an illusion that the concerns of the people are represented, but that isn't true. Eventually, the corruption will be obvious to everyone. People are starving and being removed from their homes. Desperation will lead to violence."

I joined him at the window, remaining behind the curtain. The picture he painted was fraught. On the surface, Spain appeared to be at peace, but the undercurrents of what he described were bubbling. How long would the country remain balanced on this fulcrum?

I leaned against the casement. "Is this why you are investigating the socialists? Because the government thinks they will turn violent? Or is it because they are alarmed that people will fight the corruption instead of passively accepting it?"

Antonio bowed his head. "My position is precarious. As an inquiry agent, I can't reject their employment because of my beliefs. Your situation will also be tenuous. They must believe that you understand their way of life. They work, they eat, they sleep. It isn't the life of an aristo."

I bristled at his assumption. Maybe Hugh hadn't shared much about my past. "Did Hugh tell you how we met?"

"Only that after school, you worked at Kew, dressed as a boy. I gather this isn't your first foray undercover."

I tempered my tone. There was no need to be defensive. Antonio didn't know me. This was an opportunity to forge a bridge to understanding. "For two years, I labored, ate, and slept in the gardens. Under-gardeners are given the hardest menial jobs. I was dirty, hungry, and desperate. Because I am white, British, and have the privilege of education, I know my experience of the world is narrow, but I think I can be of service here." He had revealed much about himself during our conversation. It was fair to do likewise.

"I know you're not a stranger to hard work." Antonio fixed me with a stare. "However, you can dye your hair to blend in, but you can't change your skin. These people have experienced prejudice you cannot understand."

He was correct. It was a fair reminder. "I know, Antonio. I know."

Antonio placed a companionable hand on my shoulder. It was a welcome gesture, a recognition of our difficult but productive conversation. "On to your plan. My cousin owns a stationery shop near the boardinghouse. Here is the address. I'll visit every couple of days, so you can leave a message for me if you need to be in touch."

"I'll only send one if it is critical."

Antonio patted my shoulder again. "You're perceptive. I'm confident you will be successful."

"Thank you, Antonio." It meant a great deal to receive a compliment from him.

With a brisk nod, he exited the room, leaving me with much to ponder.

My belongings were assembled, and a hive of bees had taken up residency inside my stomach. Was this too impulsive? Was this the right course of action, or was I rushing headlong into a situation? Was I fleeing my abysmal behavior? Pushing Hugh away instead of confiding in him. Refusing to commit to Matias. Lying to them all.

Imprudent or not, I wouldn't reconsider. Some good had to come from this. I would find the murderer, meet my obligation to Izabelle, and prove to myself, and to them, that I wasn't defined by my relationship with Matias—or my failures.

Matias returned to find me seated ramrod on the bed, hair braided, a packed valise at my feet. His expression fell. "You're going?"

I picked up the valise. "I am."

I entered his outstretched arms.

He cupped my face. "Are you doing this because of us? Please don't put yourself in danger. We can come to a compromise."

A panicked, trapped sensation gripped me. If I didn't follow through, we wouldn't know who killed Pelayo, and possibly Pilar. I would've failed. I had to go.

I *had* to go.

I rested my forehead on his. "Do you remember when you said that part of the reason you went to the mountains with Fernández was for perspective? I need that, too, Matias. And I don't want you to compromise. You deserve so much more."

Our kiss was gentle and sad. It was the end of something. Pulling away from him was difficult, but there was consolation that this wasn't Chiloé. We weren't saying goodbye forever.

"I'll return before you know I'm even gone. Fernández has plenty of obscure, moth-eaten specimens to hold your attention." I kissed him again. "I love you, Matias. I *do* love you."

Matias raked his fingers through his hair with a rough exhale. "I love you too. Please be safe."

I handed him a sealed note. "Hugh was gone all day, but I should slip away now while the kitchen help are away. Will you make sure he gets this?"

I tied a kerchief around my hair, picked up the valise, and walked to the door. I tried to resist giving into the impulse, but I needed one more look back.

Matias stood next to our bed, one fist clenched at his lower back, the other wrapped around the bedpost. He was resigned, exhausted. And very dear.

Before I could change my mind, I closed the door behind me.

I sneaked down the back stairs through the empty kitchen. An argument on the street between two carriage drivers provided cover as I joined the stream of people walking deeper into the Albaicín.

Albaicín

Chapter Thirty

La señora Sandrina's *casa para mujeres* was shabby but clean. Her one available room faced the alley. La señora insisted it was the quietest of her bedchambers. Judging by the brisk physical transactions occurring below at high volume, her claim was dubious.

Two paces took one from the bed to a small window, two and a half from the end of the bed to the door. A chamber pot and washbasin were included, but linens were not. I had anticipated that; Antonio had contributed a worn set to add to my valise. Scratches around the dodgy door lock reinforced my decision to not bring anything valuable. The lone chair could be wedged under the doorknob while I slept, at least adding a slight measure of security.

For an additional three pesetas, la señora could provide an evening meal, but based on the evil smell emanating from the kitchen, I would fend for myself.

This part of the Albaicín was another world from the wealthy, lush gardens of Antonio's neighborhood. And it was blistering hot. I was reconsidering my decision to don a kerchief. In front of the speckled wedge of mirror, the style accentuated the two stones of weight I'd lost, making my cheekbones more prominent, which furthered my disguise. It also covered what remained of my injury. I probed the spot gently. Without the linen covering it, the small bump was still visible. I poured a bit of my precious water into the basin to splash my face. Water was fetched once a day from the communal pump, and each boarder was limited to one jug unless they wished to make the trip themselves.

With a last glance at my chamber and a deep breath for confidence, I ventured into my new neighborhood.

The streets were even narrower here. Neighboring balconies were in such close proximity, one could join hands over the gap. I felt eyes watching me as I wandered.

An advertisement for a waitress was in the window of a café a few blocks from the boardinghouse. I had never worked as a server, but I wasn't a stranger to hard labor. Still, it took an extra dose of confidence to cross to the café, where a robust man sat outside, smoking.

I sat at one of the outdoor tables, and he ambled over to take my order. While I waited for my meal, I observed the activities around the café. During the heat of the day, I was the only one dining. People moved in a constant stream. When they stopped to say hello to each other, the conversation was brief. My meal was served with an emphatic clatter of the plate, which made me flinch. The man's well-groomed mustache twitched in amusement.

I bit into a *tostada*. It was the perfect blend of warm bread and bursting tomatoes. And my coffee was bitter, rich heaven. If this was the fare on offer, I would be proud to serve it.

When it was obvious I'd finished, the man approached to collect his payment.

"Señor, are you seeking a waitress?" My voice wobbled with nerves.

He narrowed his eyes, assessing my suitability, beginning with my hands. Garden labor was demanding. My fingernails were cracked and stained from soil, but scrubbed as clean as I could get them. His eyes scanned the kerchief on my head and the make of my clothes. I sat motionless during his perusal.

He tucked his hands in the pockets of his white apron. "Hmm. Return at the dinner hour. We'll see if we get on. Inglesa, yes? You better not be lazy like most ingleses."

There was that quiver at the corner of his mustache again.

"No, no, I'm a very hard worker. Thank you, señor."

He grunted, "Raúl."

I hesitated for a moment. I hadn't decided on an alias.

"Leonore. Leonore Ward." While not a huge fan of the opera, I was a fan of Leonore. She was famous for disguising herself as a man. And Ward was close enough to Wren. That it was Matias's surname . . . would make me feel less lonely. My feelings about how marriage shackled women meant that this was probably the only situation in which I would claim Matias's name.

Raúl lifted his chin and glared. "Leonore. Don't be late."

I bobbed my head, hustling away. Instead of returning to the boardinghouse, I wandered the neighborhood. My string bag I purchased during my first day in Granada had been a late addition to my belongings. Now it held my purchases of a small loaf of bread and several oranges. To store much more than that in my room might attract rats.

Turning into a narrow lane, I stumbled upon a small bookstore—a welcome surprise this close to my lodgings. A bell chimed when I opened the door. A shower of dust rained down on me.

The space behind the counter was empty, but the books on the shelves were well cared-for, tidy, and dust-free. Next to the counter was a display of pamphlets. I browsed the books while sauntering toward the display. The books were an intriguing mix of titles: classical texts in Greek and Latin mixed with novels. Radcliffe and Austen. There was even a section of political treatises—Locke's volumes, as well as Hume's.

I was leafing through a dog-eared copy of *Two Treatises of Government* when a voice broke the silence. "Buenas tardes, señora. Are you searching for something in particular?"

Squinting in my direction, a man cleaned a pair of wire-rimmed spectacles with a stained handkerchief. His voice was a rough tenor. Brushing a strand of ebony hair off his brow, he replaced the spectacles. The lenses enlarged his coffee-rich, thickly lashed irises. He cocked his head like a raven—the huge, canny ones that ruled the Tower of London. I placed his age near mine.

He turned his attention to the book in my hands. "That's a unique choice."

"Oh, it was accidental. I prefer Gothic novels." I slipped it back into the gap.

Despite my airy tone, he continued to look skeptical. "The next row contains some of those."

His avidity made me uneasy. I tried to shake off his attention. "I'm browsing today. I'll return after I've earned a bit at my new position."

"These shelves are a lending library." He indicated the bookcases to the right of the counter, next to the pamphlets. "I'll note your name and address, and you can borrow a book for a sennight. It only costs one peseta."

"Really?" I said, moving toward the shelves, ignoring my disquiet for the moment. The books were either a representation of the diverse reading habits of the neighborhood, or aspirational on the part of the owner. Around the height of a child were primers and picture books. On the middle shelves were the novels; scattered among the Spanish editions were a few English ones. I spotted a slim edition of *Marianela,* a novel by Galdós. I hadn't read it yet but wanted to.

"Señora, English novels are on the second shelf."

I glanced up from the book. We were conversing in Spanish. My accent was more South American, but my Spanish was fluent. "I read in Spanish."

"Lo siento, señora. I assumed, as you are inglesa."

I was correct about the fervency of his observation. "How did you guess?"

He shrugged. "Your Spanish is excellent, but there is something . . ."

"I arrived in Spain several months ago—Cádiz, but I wished to be in Granada. So, here I am."

His stygian regard didn't reveal his opinion on that indiscreet disclosure of information. I would rather he ascribed my nervousness to being in a new place, rather than the real reason. I dug in my pocket for a peseta and slid it along the countertop. "I would like to borrow this one."

The man nodded, producing a register from beneath the counter. "Please write your name and the address of your lodgings. I'll enter the title of your book."

I hesitated; pen poised over the book. "I don't know the address."

"Where are you staying?"

Was it wise to share the location of my lodgings?

He seemed to sense the direction of my thoughts. "Or where you are employed."

"The café, a few streets . . ." I pointed in the direction. "Raúl is my employer."

"I know it. It's called La Sirena."

I adjusted my grip on the pen to alter my penmanship from its normal copperplate, necessary for labeling scientific samples, into sloppy, slanting letters. The bookstore owner read the entry upside down.

"Leonore Ward. I am Sebastián de los Rios, the shop owner."

"It was nice to meet you, Señor de los Rios. Thank you for the book."

He gave a slight bow. "Señora Ward, please don't forget to return it."

I tucked the slim volume into the string bag with my market goods. The bell clanged as I exited the shop. I sensed his unfathomable gaze following my retreat.

Chapter Thirty-One

When the clock struck six, the first wave of people invaded Raúl's café. Part of their daily routine seemed to be stopping on the way home or on the way to their second job to enjoy a glass of wine, a bite to eat, and conversation. Raúl and I circulated through the tables, taking orders. Once one group finished, another waved for service—an endless loop.

At first, discussion would cease when I approached, but after a glass or two of wine, they stopped caring. I couldn't think about the murderer, the socialists, or that I was undercover. My brain was working to juggle orders in rapid, sometimes slurred Spanish.

Carmen, Raúl's cousin, prepared the food in a minuscule kitchen. Her fare was simple: various toppings on bread, or the soup of the day. After I dropped off an order and returned to the dining area, the food would be waiting when I returned. Carmen scowled every time I entered the kitchen. During a brief lull, she forced a bowl of soup into my hands.

Tonight, it was *sopa de picadillo*, a clear broth with chunks of ham, boiled eggs, and noodles. I didn't register if it was good. It was simple fuel to sustain me through the night.

I should've requested a second bowl. When the true rush hit, there were no breaks. The crowd shifted from those on their way to those settling in for the evening. These gatherings were lively, and they lingered. If they lived in lodgings as small as the boardinghouse, there was no space to lounge. During the summer, tiny dwellings were unbearable until the evening cooled. As the temperature inside the café climbed, I was thankful for the intermittent breeze when I served the outdoors.

Coffee preparation was Raúl's sacred territory. A heady fragrance wafted from each cup I delivered—pure torture. When the clock rang out eleven bells, Raúl nudged the final customer out the door.

Gardening was demanding physical work, but I couldn't remember being this exhausted. My botanical efforts were solitary. The frenetic interactions of the café left me drained, my ears ringing. I wiped my hands on a rag Carmen tossed across the counter.

With a nod, she slipped out the back as Raúl bustled in. "An adequate job, Leonore. Return tomorrow at eight, eh? I'll pay your wages once a fortnight, assuming you last. Agreed?"

A glow of satisfaction at a job well-done crept past my fatigue. It was a welcome change from my niggling doubts over my competency as a botanist. "Sí, señor, thank you."

My progress was sluggish on the few blocks between the café and the boardinghouse. The soles of my feet protested each step on the cobbles. Despite my state, I noted that the streets weren't empty. Men lurked in the doorways and shadows. Their assessment prickled my skin.

I stared forward, reassured by the weight of my dagger in its sheath against my ankle. When the stairs of la señora Sandrina's came into view, I pushed through my lethargy to scurry across the threshold.

La señora Sandrina's was a glorious, silent contrast to the clamor of the café. A broken stair squealed in indignation under my weight. I recoiled, frozen in place, but no one opened their doors or shouted at me.

After I shoved the chair under my doorknob, I swayed in place. If I lay down, I would fall asleep.

I removed my boots, exposing my swollen, red feet to the air. Hobbling to the washstand was arduous. A light hum of sensation came from the knot on my head. It was fortunate I hadn't tried this a few days ago—I wouldn't have made it through the evening. Was it only this morning that I'd woken in a luxurious bed with Matias at my side?

I tried to stay awake to parse the day, but my eyelids refused. Through the window drifted the sounds of women chatting with prospective marks. It was insipid, bawdy talk, a patter that lulled rather than innervated me, which made for strange dreams.

My first few days at La Sirena passed in a blur. Midday often quieted enough to find a few moments of rest. I perched on a stool rescued from the back room, book in hand. Raúl said I was free to leave during the break, but I was content to read.

I was on the last pages of *Marianela.* It wouldn't rank among my favorite novels. Nela attempted suicide because she lost Pablo's love when he regained his sight and decided he preferred a beautiful woman. Nela died of a broken heart. Why did the woman always suffer in the end? Another predictable ending without consequences for the man.

In the days since I started waitressing, I had proven myself capable. As an investigator, not so much. Those who frequented the café were now familiar with my presence—their conversation didn't halt when I approached, but no one mentioned the socialists or meetings.

As I read the last page, Raúl slid a cup of coffee onto the ledge of the counter. After my less-than-subtle mooning over his coffee, I was finally being honored.

"Gracias." I sipped the rich brew. It was bliss. My sigh of contentment was more audible than intended. Heat rushed to my cheeks when Raúl guffawed, a deep, rippling laugh.

"Ah, I've seen you making eyes at my coffee."

I covered my blush by taking another sip. "It's heavenly."

"I'm pleased you prefer coffee to that foul brew the other ingleses drink."

I sputtered into my cup. "I've always preferred coffee to tea." But a preference for coffee was unusual for a working-class Englishwoman, and women in coffeehouses were relatively uncommon. I should've thought of that before speaking. For the most part, such errors were rare, but I had learned not to react when they happened. In this case, that meant returning to the pages of my book.

Raúl seemed unaware of the inconsistency. "You've worked hard. Here are your wages."

"I thought you paid once a fortnight?"

"I said that so you would return. I trust you."

"Gracias, señor." My appreciation was genuine. To maintain the guise of a struggling worker, I had brought the bare necessity of funds. It had been a number of years since I'd had to think about when I would be paid. Another complication was that the safest place to store money was on my body, and even that was risky.

"Señor, may I go to the bookstore? I'll be quick."

"The bookstore? Is that what you spend your money on? You'll be skin and bones. You can't eat books."

"I borrow books from el señor de los Rios's lending library," I reassured him.

"Away with you. People will demand their meals soon."

I leaped from my stool, swallowing the last of my coffee. Raúl laughed at my impatience, waving me away.

As I walked the streets to the bookstore, I realized that in only a few days, I had adapted to living in this neighborhood. Working at the café was exhausting, yet I enjoyed it. I labored in the gardens and in the wilds when I was traveling, but it was different from waitressing. When I worked for myself, I had the luxury of taking a break whenever I wished. If I had a day I wasn't feeling poorly, I could choose what I did instead. I missed Matias, Hugh, and even Antonio, but I also felt more myself than I had for months.

Living aboard a ship, or traveling around the world, or even dwelling in London meant I was usually surrounded by people. But my whole life, I had remained solitary within that chaos. A self-contained existence was comfortable for me. Hugh and I were used to spending years apart; travels that took you far away, had always been part of his life as well. Matias and I being together was relatively new. It wasn't that I didn't miss him, it was that I'd reverted to what came naturally.

The dust in el señor de los Rios's store was part of its charm. The bell sent another puff down when I entered. He was behind the counter, watching patrons browse the shelves.

Instead of lingering over the other volumes, I went to the lending stock. He nodded in recognition when I passed the counter. "Señora Ward."

I held up the copy of *Marianela*. "I'm returning this one."

He nodded and went to assist another customer with their purchase. I pretended to peruse the titles on the middle shelf while skimming the pamphlets: there were ones for remedies, the control of house pests, and news around Europe. Tucked behind one with a vicious rat on the cover was the socialist tract. Near it was a torn copy of *Jane Eyre*.

As I nudged aside the rat treatise, the cover of the pamphlet triggered a memory. The meeting in the garden! I'd forgotten that they had planned to gather again.

El señor de los Rios interrupted my frantic calculation of days. "Do you not care for *Jane Eyre*?"

My ability to mask my reactions had obviously failed. I found Jane irritating and Mr. Rochester a sulky bore, but it was convenient. Tapping the cover, I murmured, "I do not."

"Have you read *El panteón de los herejes* by Rodríguez? I believe there is a copy." He stretched across the counter to point to the book. "It is also Gothic, but the author is Spanish."

I read a few paragraphs. It would do. Another customer left the shop, and while el señor de los Rios's attention was occupied, I casually riffled through the pamphlets. I picked up one on the benefits of coconut for growing lustrous hair and placed it over the socialist text, scanning both texts together before replacing them on the shelves.

El señor de los Ríos was studying his ledger when I approached. "I would like to borrow this one."

He opened the register and wrote the new title next to my name. "You didn't wish to purchase a pamphlet?"

"Ah, no. La señora Sandrina has the pests under control, and I have plenty of hair." My tone was teasing, but his expression unaffected.

"There was also the other pamphlet."

I had to guard myself around this man. He was far too perceptive. "Ah, yes. I don't know about the politics of Spain, but I'm sympathetic to the situation described in the pamphlet."

"Are you?" He sounded dubious.

Motioning to the shelves, I rolled my eyes. "Governments don't understand the lives of most people, or maybe it is that they do not care. They wish for us to dedicate our lives to serving them without questioning inequities."

There was a pause. "You work at Raúl's café, yes? You seem too educated to be serving food."

I rubbed at the shiny counter with my thumb. Maybe I should rethink visiting this bookstore. His attentiveness could be dangerous. "I was taught to read in a ragged school set up by reformers St Giles."

"Yet you also traveled."

Lowering my gaze to the floor, I scuffed at the surface with my toe. "I fell in love with a sailor and stowed away. He promised we would stay in Cádiz, that he would . . . anyway, he caught a merchant ship sailing to the Bahamas." I swiped at my cheek, feigning the presence of a tear.

El señor de los Rios murmured, "I'm sorry, señora."

"I'm making the best of it. Speaking of, I need to return to the café. Bueno?"

He finished noting my choice. I mumbled a goodbye, distracted by my deduction. Tomorrow night was the meeting at the Alhambra. Would I risk attending?

The Alhambra was at least twenty minutes from the café. I wouldn't be able to leave until closing, which left a narrow window of opportunity. I considered whether I should notify Matias of my plan.

There wasn't time to deliver a message to Antonio's cousin's shop to alert them. I was on my own—as I claimed to prefer.

Chapter Thirty-Two

Fetid air clogged my breathing and slowed my steps. Not only had the temperatures soared, but it was the busiest evening yet at Raúl's. Sweaty, desperate diners filed into the café, clamoring for Carmen's gazpacho. Once word circulated around the neighborhood that we were serving it, everyone wanted a bowl.

Most of the café tables spent the season on the sidewalk at the edge of the square. Raúl said when it rained, we would move them in, but the drought showed no signs of breaking. Tonight, every seat was occupied. Pairs of men entered, slapping their dusty hats on their thighs and proceeding toward the rear of the café. Tables kept being added to accommodate the growing gathering. Orders were fired in my direction during pauses in their impassioned discussion.

I stopped Raúl on my way to the kitchen. "Is it a club?"

"Ah, this is your first jueves. They hold their meetings on Thursday nights. I don't mind—they buy lots of food and drink." He lovingly wiped clean his small stove, which was dedicated to brewing coffee.

I fluttered my eyelashes. "*¿Puedo tomar una taza, por favor?*"

"Sí, sí, off with you," he chuckled, waving his linen at my departing back.

I emerged from the kitchen, balancing a tray of bowls, and almost upended my armful into Sebastián de los Rios. "*¡Cuidado, señor!*" I snapped, struggling to balance the towering tray.

"Lo siento, lo siento, señora. I didn't see you."

I detoured around him, intent on delivering the soup. As I handed bowls to the men, de los Rios joined them. "What can I bring you, señor?"

"I'll have a gazpacho and a glass of wine, por favor."

As I darted toward the kitchen, Raúl passed me a cup of coffee. Carmen fulfilled my request for another bowl, watching in amusement as I drank my *taza* in one go. She had yet to speak, but when I asked Raúl why, he shrugged and said she would when she had something to say.

Fortified for another round of orders, I returned to the table with de los Rios's soup. The men were engaged in a fraught conversation, one man in particular holding their attention.

El señor de los Rios gestured to me. "If you have a moment, listen to what he says," he whispered.

I placed his bowl on the table.

"They're blind to the suffering, seeing only power, connections, and money. Now that they can't make their fortune in other countries, they turn their hungry eyes toward us. This morning, my sister and her four children were forced from their home. Every home in the area is under threat. Someone has corrupted the prime minister. He uses the flimsiest excuses to issue evictions. They claim that my sister and her children are a hazard to the health of the community because of rumors of cholera. A returning aristo family who owned a sugar plantation wants the entire block. And the government is complicit—nay, *encouraging* these actions! What should I do? There are already seven of us in our flat!"

The man next to him gripped his shoulder. "We'll help you."

Another man slammed his fist on the table. My heart skipped at the sudden display of violence. Perhaps I wasn't over my attack yet.

My breathing must have altered, for de los Rios turned his observant gaze my direction.

The man continued, "*We* must stop them!"

His words filtered in, but my eyes remained locked with de los Rios.

"Leonore. Leonore!"

It took a third repetition of Raúl saying my "name" until I responded. I rushed across the café. Was this the socialist group from the garden, or some other gathering?

Raúl insisted that I remain outside, since I was "too distracted indoors." It was late when the last group of diners departed from my tables. My plan to escape was foiled.

I glanced at the clock. Maybe if I left now, there was a possibility I could arrive ahead of them.

Inside, the men were still meeting, including de los Rios. While clearing the dishes and linen from the adjacent tables, I eavesdropped on their conversation. My head was bent as I cleaned when a man snapped his pocket watch and muttered, "Alhambra."

I went motionless, waiting for a response.

"We need to leave soon," another man said.

"What's the point? Every time we get close, they slip away."

"Not always."

"True. Why do we keep meeting at the Alhambra, anyway? It isn't convenient."

"You know why. They keep it safe for us."

"For now."

A serviette fell from the table. Crouching beneath the surface to retrieve it gave me a chance to think. It *was* them—the group meeting at the Alhambra.

Bloody hell, I had to follow. But as long as patrons remained, Raúl wouldn't allow me to leave.

A chorus of scraping chairs signaled their departure. El señor de los Rios came around the table to where I was hunched. I brandished the serviette, rising nonchalantly. "Señora Ward, can I make one last order?"

Over his shoulder, the men filed from the café, tipping their hats and patting Raúl on the back.

"You aren't joining your friends?"

"Not yet."

I stifled my frustration behind a neutral manner, wary of his perceptiveness. "Of course, señor."

"Can you ask Raúl to make a carajillo?"

"*Por supuesto.*" I wiped my clammy hands on the linen tucked in my apron, as he seated himself at the clean table. My job was more important than one meeting. If they met every Thursday, there would be other opportunities. Did de los Rios notice my close observation of their conversation? "Raúl, el señor de los Ríos would like a *carajillo.*"

"Would he indeed? I wondered why he didn't leave with the other men." Raúl narrowed his eyes in appraisal. "Hmm. Tell Carmen she can close the kitchen for the night."

I ducked into the kitchen to pass the message on to Carmen and stayed to help. We swept the floors and packaged up the extra food. Perhaps if I delayed, Raúl would serve de los Rios himself.

Luck was not on my side. He was still there when I emerged from the kitchen. Raúl waved. "El señor de los Ríos ordered another carajillo for you. He was waiting." Raúl smirked, handing over a tray with two cups. "I'll be out front," he added, pulling his pipe from his pocket.

Damn.

Fatigue and wariness slowed my steps. I placed the cups in front of him. "Señor."

"Please, señora, sit down. And call me Sebastián."

I sat sideways in the chair, as if I planned to leave at any moment. "Thank you. *Señora* will do, since we are not acquainted."

"Aren't we? Your accent is charming. You pronounce my name the Spanish way, but more melodically."

Rather than reply, I sipped the drink. Christ, it was strong. Every sentence exchanged was fraught with potential pitfalls. I must keep my wits about me.

"Have you had carajillo?"

"Yes, my *novio* enjoyed it, although he prepared it with rum," I lied with aplomb.

"He must have traveled to have access to rum."

I took another large swallow, angling further away in my chair. "It's been an exhausting day, señor. I don't mean to be rude—"

"Sebastián."

I relented. "Sebastián."

"Would it be acceptable to call you Leonore?"

I sighed. Was it worth fighting him? At this point, I wanted to be finished with this conversation and in my bed. "Sí."

He adjusted his glasses, sliding them up his nose. The lenses magnified his cryptic scrutiny. "I won't keep you, but I wished to hear your thoughts on the topic earlier."

Why did he care about my opinion? "It's terrible. How can they force people from their homes?"

"It is happening all over the Albaicín."

"Is anyone trying to stop it?"

"We are. I thought that was clear."

There was a slight tremor in my hand as I returned the cup to the table. "I didn't hear much. As I said, a busy day."

El señor de los Rios blinked slowly. He was always watching, like a clever, nefarious raven.

"Have you traveled to England, señor?" He tilted his head at the abrupt change of subject—another corvid-like gesture. An uncontrollable giggle burbled from my chest. "In London, we have a place called the Tower. Have you heard of it?" Without waiting for his response, I rambled on, "It has a gruesome history. A flock of ravens inhabit the Tower. Are there ravens in Granada? I don't remember seeing them. Did you know a group of ravens is called a conspiracy? Anyway, you remind me of them, señor. The ravens."

The corners of his mouth stretched into a smile. His expression took me aback. He was profoundly handsome when he was less grave. I continued with my observation.

"I imagine that those ravens, the descendants of birds that witnessed atrocious, bloody events, are born with a recognition of the fallibility of people. They know that we are busy, silly sacks of bones that will be replaced by more useless humans."

His laughter cracked through the café. Raúl stuck his head inside. Heat raced up my body. I should have eaten this evening.

"I'm sorry. I've no idea where that came from."

"Dios, Leonore. You aren't like anyone I've ever met."

I waved at the table. "Tired. Brandy."

"Yes, well." He opened the small watch pinned to his pocket. "I've kept you late enough."

We both rose from the table. "Thank you for the carajillo, señor."

"You're welcome." He gave me a shy, lopsided smile. "I have another shipment of books arriving tomorrow if you want to stop in. The older volumes are rotated into the lending library on delivery days."

I twisted a towel between my hands. Returning to the bookstore might be imprudent. Sebastián de los Rios noticed everything.

I was pondering the benefits versus potential traps when he ambushed me with a kiss on my cheek. "Buenas noches, señora."

I muttered, "*Buenas noches.*" He strolled from the café, stopping to say goodbye to Raúl. The spot on my cheek tingled.

I rubbed at it with the back of my hand. Where did that come from? Was my manner flirtatious? There was a pier glass behind the station where Raúl made his coffee. El señor de los Rios was reflected in the mirror. He'd paused for one last glance.

His words echoed in my mind. *I've kept you late enough.* Did he keep me at the café so I couldn't follow his compatriots?

Chapter Thirty-Three

Movement on the street was at a standstill. Up ahead, a carriage was wedged sideways across the road. Though picturesque, the narrow streets weren't built for wide carts. When a shop received a delivery, traffic in every direction was halted. There was nothing to do but wait.

I rested against the wall outside a tobacconist and dug out the note I had written for Matias. A week had passed since I arrived, but I hadn't made significant progress. At least another week would be necessary. The socialist group meeting at Raúl's was the same one from the Alhambra, and Sebastián de los Rios was a member, so infiltrating them was critical.

Raúl didn't wait for me to drink my first cup of coffee before the teasing began.

"I believe you have an admirer, Lenore." Raúl waggled a finger in my direction as he pushed the steaming demitasse across the counter.

I squirmed, uncomfortable with his insinuation. "It's nothing. We discuss books. Can I leave during my break today?"

He wiped droplets from the countertop. "Ah, off to visit your novio?" I scowled at him, which made him laugh so loud, it echoed off the walls of the café. "Sí, adelante."

The blockage had cleared. I walked on toward the stationer. Maybe I was too cynical, but I wasn't convinced de los Rios's actions were innocent. Was our shared drink a diversion? His flirtation felt suspect, given how standoffish he'd been at the bookstore. Again, the motivations behind his interest, whether it was friendship or something else, would take time to uncover.

My note to Matias was brief. Antonio was confident of his cousin's discretion, and coded phrases assured our privacy.

Mr. Ward,

I will be detained longer than previously arranged, at least another sennight. Please respond at this address if necessary. All is well and proceeding as expected.

Yours,

L

I sped up, conscious of the passage of my limited break. Being at the mercy of someone else's schedule was not a situation I had dealt with in many years. My older body also wasn't used to the work demands. Yet most people would never experience the luxury I had been gifted. Raúl was Hugh's age, but he would labor in his café until he physically couldn't any longer.

At the stationery shop, I used my sparse wages to purchase a small notebook. I handed over my note for Matias, along with my payment and a coded phrase: "Here is a receipt for hot cross buns for your ailing cousin."

The clerk's face was impassive, but he stowed the note beneath the counter while giving me my change. Hopefully, it would find its way to Matias.

A glance at the clock tower showed I had less than an hour to return to La Sirena. Upon entering the bookshop, I stumbled over several crates that blocked the entry. Was returning to de los Rios's store reckless? Mayhap. But after much internal debate, I decided it was worth the risk.

Balancing on one foot, I rubbed at my stubbed toe. El señor de los Rios peered around a stack near the counter.

"I'm sorry. They were just delivered," he said, contrite. His hair fell into his flushed face and obscured the lens of his spectacles.

"I can help for a little while," I offered, mindful of taking any opportunity to gain information.

He brushed the strands of his hair away. "I wouldn't want you to risk your position."

"At least we can move these crates from the entryway. It won't take more than a quarter of an hour." I came to the opposite end of the crates.

"Thank you." He lifted one end while I took the other. We moved them to a stack near the shelves. When I easily hefted a half-full crate, he scowled. "You're remarkably strong for a woman." At my distasteful expression, he rushed to defend himself. "I don't mean to be rude. I wouldn't have thought carrying dishes built such strength."

"Señor, trays of dishes are heavy. I'm back and forth in the kitchen all day." *Or hauling loaded wheelbarrows, shovels, and rakes*, I didn't add.

"Sebastián, por favor. Especially when you are scolding me, which I deserved." He wiped his forehead with the back of his hand, smiling.

That smile of his was dangerous. It lulled me into forgetting my subterfuge. I returned to the crates, hiding my swift blush. We worked in silence until the clock on the counter chimed. "I must go. Raúl will be impatient."

"May I show my appreciation with another carajillo this evening?"

I dusted my hands on my skirt. Sebastián might be the key to accessing the socialists, but I had to be cautious. I reassessed the advantages. Wasn't it worth taking the chance for the knowledge?

"A glass of wine instead?' I offered. "Between the coffee and the brandy, my sleep wasn't restful."

The corner of his mouth twisted in a sly smile. My comment wasn't intentionally provocative. Dammit.

I hurried toward the door. "Good day, señor . . . Sebastián."

"Until this evening, Leonore."

My last stop was one I'd been avoiding. From my pocket, I unfolded a scrap of paper that held Pilar's address. It wasn't far from La Sirena, but I had delayed visiting. The grief, guilt, and betrayal were still raw, though working as Leonore was a reprieve from the clouds of melancholy. Leonore didn't carry the weight of Linnea's life, but Pilar's house was a reminder of what waited for me.

Rather than lingering in front, I walked past the house into the shadows of an alley. The curtains were drawn, and the pots of flowers on the balcony were wilted. Someone had swept the stairs clean. Her cousin?

An older woman was on her steps a few houses down. I left the shelter of the alley to approach her.

"*Buenas tardes*, señora. Do you know Pilar Molina?"

She propped her broom against her hip and glared. "Who's asking?"

"Pilar is my friend. She invited me to visit."

"I haven't seen her in weeks. Maybe she moved. That cousin of hers is there, though, leaving at all hours."

"*Gracias*, señora." I departed so I wouldn't raise her suspicions. I took a one last look at the house. No obvious clues as to the fate of its inhabitants. Were Pilar and her cousin so private that the neighborhood would be unaware of her demise? She said her family had always lived in the area, so presumably, they were acquainted with their neighbors. If one feared for their safety, it would make sense to stay out of sight.

My body ached with misery. Dark clouds of despair built with each step away from Pilar's. The gravity of my situation was as resounding as thunder.

A murder I wasn't solving.

Missteps with Matias.

My floundering career.

I greeted Raúl and tied on my apron. Leonore's life was simpler to navigate. This must have been what people recovering from amnesia felt: the blanks of memory suddenly filling in with the pleasant and rotten parts of your life.

A steady flow of patrons kept me from submitting to the doldrums. Even though I was at half my usual momentum, I attended my tables. Raúl intercepted me on my way out of the kitchen with an outstretched *taza*. "Leonore, drink that. Problems with your novio?"

Not this again. "Raúl, I don't have a *novio*."

"If you say so, querida. If it isn't your novio, what's the matter?"

I gulped the liquid. It was scalding. "Those need cleaning." I pointed to two cluttered tables, taking a step in their direction.

Raúl put his hands on his hips, blocking my exit. "They can wait a moment."

"I was thinking about a friend who died recently. Thank you for the coffee." I dodged him, skittering away. Neither Leonore nor Linnea were inclined to confide in strangers. Our friendship was developing, but not enough to reveal my inner torment.

The constant demands of the café were exhausting, yet also a welcome reprieve from thinking. Raúl claimed that tomorrow would be quiet, as many people would attend the market in the plaza. "They fill their bags with food but still come for Carmen's soup."

The evening crowd thinned, and we started cleaning and organizing for closing. I was relieved that Sebastián hadn't appeared. Maintaining my mask was a chore. I wanted to return to my tiny room in the boardinghouse and retreat into solitude.

Someday soon, I was going to betray Raúl—a realization that turned my empty stomach queasy. I wouldn't be the first waitress to scupper on him, no doubt. And what about Sebastián and Carmen? Two other people I was playing false. Why hadn't I considered the ramifications of this endeavor? Sebastián might lead me on a merry chase, but it didn't reassure my conscience.

I dove through the door that led to the alley and took gulps of the fetid air. It didn't ease my nausea.

When I emerged from the kitchen, Sebastián was chatting with Raúl at the counter. Raúl waggled his eyebrows; I scowled at him when Sebastián turned. His shoulders slumped at my expression, which spiked my guilt again. Raúl also noticed his dejection.

"Ah, don't worry, my friend. Our girl's been grumpy all afternoon. No doubt she thought you wouldn't arrive."

I glared at Raúl. He ignored me to scrape at the surface, even though he'd already cleaned that spot.

"*Buenas noches*, Señor de los Rios."

"Leonore. Are you finished for the evening?"

Raúl answered for me. "Sí, she's finished."

Before I could make an excuse, Sebastián interrupted, "You promised a glass of wine."

These two were going to be the death of me. I couldn't get a word in edgewise.

Raúl placed the glasses on the counter. "Leonore, I will assist Carmen."

"But—"

"Enjoy your wine with your . . . friend."

The swinging kitchen door cut off his annoying chuckle. Sebastián was already moving toward a table outside.

I removed my apron, folded it into quarters, and sat with it cradled in my lap.

Sebastián lifted his glass. "Salud."

"*Salud,*" I replied.

Our glasses held a crisp *vino blanco*. It was refreshing, tart as a fresh apple. We could have a brief conversation, then I would return to my original plan of brooding the rest of the evening. My patience would have to hold for a bit longer. "Did you unpack all your crates?"

"I did. I brought a book I thought you would enjoy." He slid a tattered volume across the table. It was by Rosario de Acuña.

"*Ecos del alma,*" I read from the cover.

"It's poetry. She's a progressive woman, a socialist."

I was touched by his thoughtfulness. My fingers stretched over the cover, which was warm from his hands. His act of kindness caused the tears I had kept at bay all day to well up. *Bloody hell, Linnea,* I thought, *pull yourself together.* "I'll read it quickly so others may borrow it."

"It's a gift. I want you to have it."

"Oh no, it's too generous. I couldn't accept it."

The streetlamps were sparse in this corner. The light spilling from the windows was the only source of illumination. As Sebastián bent forward, pinpricks of the diffused candles became flames in his pupils.

"I would like us to become better acquainted." His hand reached across the surface, his rough palm cradling my fingers. At the minute wince that traveled up my arm, Sebastián pulled away. "Unless you aren't interested."

I demurred, "Sebastián, we've just met." *And I am with someone,* I thought.

"True, but I know how you came to be in Spain. You like to read. You're sympathetic to our cause."

"But I don't know anything about you, other than you work in a bookstore." My fumbling for reasons was painfully obvious.

"I *own* the bookstore."

"Ah."

"Can we try?" he cajoled.

I gave a half shrug. My presence here was temporary. Getting closer was unlikely to affect either of us beyond some slight disappointment.

"Would Raúl allow you a half day tomorrow? He closes in the morning for the market. I would like to take you to hear someone speak. And we can be together, away from the café or bookstore."

I swirled the last swallow of wine in my glass, uncertain about the wisdom of encouraging him. "I can ask. There's no guarantee he'll agree."

Sebastián smiled at someone behind me. Raúl and Carmen were watching us from inside the café.

Troubled, I shot up from my seat, the sound of the metal chair legs screeching off the buildings. "I should finish cleaning."

"May I walk you home?"

I couldn't escape, not without making this situation awkward. Raúl would notice and ask questions.

"Give me a moment. I'll meet you here."

"And you'll ask about tomorrow?" he pressed.

"I will."

I kept my face averted while stowing my apron behind the counter. The entire situation made me nervous. Logically, I knew these chances must be taken if I wanted answers. Eavesdropping in the café wasn't enough.

"Raúl, may I have tomorrow morning off? I would like to go to the market."

"To the market, eh? Alone?" Raúl tipped his head toward the table outside.

I didn't reply.

"That would be fine, but arrive by eleven. Market mornings are our opportunity for a thorough cleaning of the café."

"I will, thank you. *Buenas noches*, Carmen, Raúl."

Sebastián smiled when I joined him. I tried to shake off the exhaustion. Our walk was a chance for a subtle interrogation. We traveled a handful of steps before I asked, "Did you attend school?"

"I did. My grandfather taught at the Universidad de Granada. My family believed in education for everyone. Because of his political activities, my grandfather was dismissed from his position when my father was young. He found employment in a bookshop. The owner eventually sold it to him. My father worked there until he passed away, and I took over." Sebastián removed his spectacles to rub his face.

"I'm sorry for your loss. Is your mother alive?"

"No, my parents and grandparents are dead. Is your family in England?"

I hesitated. To be a convincing liar, it was best to stick close to the truth. While I deliberated my reply, a group of men ahead of us halted their conversation, watching us draw near.

"My parents died in a railway accident when I was young."

A man split from the group. Sebastián also noticed. He looped our arms together and whispered, "Just keep talking."

"I lived with my uncle for a while, but when he died, I went to a girls' home."

"That must have been difficult." He tightened his grip on my arm, but the man appeared to have lost interest in us. We had reached the bottom of my stairs anyway. I pulled from his grasp. "Did Raúl give you the morning free?"

"He did, but Sebastián, I don't—"

Sebastián laid his finger over my lips. "It's only to hear someone speak. I think you'll enjoy it. Nothing will happen that you don't wish, Leonore."

"I must return to the café by eleven," I insisted.

"May I collect you around nine?"

"Yes, nine."

His lips brushed my cheek. "Dulces sueños." He flashed me a cheeky grin.

Tomorrow might be the opening I needed to press him about the socialists. At least, that was what I assured myself, but an ill feeling radiated from my abdomen to my toes.

Chapter Thirty-Four

Another morning of gritty eyes and precarious balance. My lack of sleep had become chronic. I descended the stairs gingerly. According to la señora Sandrina, there were other occupants, but I had yet to meet one.

The mistress of the boardinghouse was glaring out the window that overlooked the street.

"Señora, ¿está todo bien?"

"There is a man. Men are not allowed."

I stood next to her to peer through the glass. Sebastián was early. "Ah, that's my friend."

"Friend," she mumbled, spinning away in a swirl of skirts.

I paused, the door handle gripped in my palm as I built my fortitude for another day of acting. "Sebastián."

"Buenos días, Leonore. You look lovely."

I was wearing an old skirt paired with an unstained shirt. Baths were not provided, but I had hauled up enough water to wash my hair in the basin. A small bar of lavender-honey soap, a rare indulgence while undercover, made my ablution luxurious. I'd spent a few extra minutes braiding my hair and winding it into a cornet. The lump from my attack was gone, and it was a relief to go without the kerchief on my head.

Each step of my preparation had been jarring. I was primping to walk out with a man I was manipulating for information. It gave me a queasy, off-balance feeling.

Which was magnified when I saw that Sebastián had also made an effort. He wore a crisp ivory shirt tucked into navy breeches. His evergreen waistcoat was embroidered with blossoms. All his garments were of excellent quality, fitted to his body to highlight his slender, muscular form.

"The embroidery on your waistcoat is very fine. Are you sure you wish to wear that to the market?"

He smoothed his hand over the threadwork. "I've smiled more with you in the last few days than at any time in recent memory. That is worth the waistcoat."

His compliment cut deep, provoking an internal wave of guilt. My brain scrambled for a response. "Have you been unhappy?"

He joined his arm with mine to escort us off the steps. "Not unhappy. Distracted. Organizing our group has been a challenging undertaking. No one agrees on a plan of action, so our goals keep shifting. Our leaders are not decisive."

How convenient that he'd gone straight to the topic of their gatherings. "You aren't one of the leaders?"

"I prefer to be in the background. I enjoy reading the underlying philosophy to understand how to apply it to our situation. Others want action."

My arm remained pliant in his grip. "Action?"

"We must make our discontent known, our voices heard."

The street merged with a larger one, where we were absorbed into the main flow of traffic. More carriages and people made conversing tricky.

"Do you mean violence?" I asked, my nose brushing the skin beneath his ear.

I regretted the casual touch. His reply was choked. "I . . . I do not. At least, I hope not. We're determining our strategy. With the government eager to stifle dissent, we must be cautious. Some questionable decisions have already thwarted us."

We passed the café. Raúl was visible through the window, mopping the floors. I wondered how far I could extend this line of conversation. Too many questions would raise his suspicions. "What kinds of decisions?"

His brow furrowed. "The usual. Saturday mornings, I close my shop to attend the market. It's a convenient place to gather and recruit."

His change in subject was clumsy but effective. *Gather?* Alarm spiked through me.

"Recruit? Is that what we are doing today?" My disguise was superficial. If a member of their group worked at the Alhambra, they could recognize me.

Sebastián must've sensed my unease. He slipped his hand down my arm to press our palms together. "There is no obligation for you to do anything except listen. The woman I want you to meet has revolutionary ideas. I think you'll like her."

I was not reassured. What if it was the woman from Plaza Larga? Would she remember? My palms were clammy. I drew my hand free, evading his notice by twining it through his elbow.

We turned into the narrow plaza, which was even more compact than Plaza Larga. The stalls were crowded, forcing people to shoulder through the space like a shoal of fish. Sebastián wound our arms tighter, pinning me to his hip.

I flinched away from the sudden physical contact, almost taking us both to the ground. He scooped my shoulders, helping me regain my balance. "Should we leave?"

Sebastián's arm was still wrapped around my shoulder, bringing our faces uncomfortably close. There was no denying the spark of attraction between us, but that was all it was—attraction. I was with Matias . . . and hadn't answered his question yet.

"I'm well. The crowd is barbaric."

"We're just going over there."

I recognized the voice without seeing her. The woman from Plaza Larga.

Sebastián nudged us toward the front. I stayed behind him. He wasn't as tall as Matias, but it would do. She was on a small box, which placed her above the mesmerized crowd.

"Friends, we have reached a crisis. If we don't act soon, we will lose our homes. We'll lose everything. The government must stop the wealthy from taking this land. Why are the liberals in charge of the government if it isn't benefiting the people? They are persuaded by money and power. Only action will get their attention!"

When the crowd cheered their encouragement at the end of her speech, I shifted sideways toward an opening.

Not only was she the woman from Plaza Larga, but she was also Pilar's cousin. Her face had been hidden at the Mirador San Nicolás, but there was no mistaking her height and manner.

In my dumbfounded state, I didn't notice that Sebastián had a brazen hand on my hip and was guiding me toward the stage. "Come, I want you to meet Novia."

A layer of fabric rested between my skin and his palm. My body shuddered in reaction.

Sebastián turned at my response, his head bowed with intention.

Was he going to kiss me? In the middle of the plaza? My hands raised to fend him off.

"Sebastián." A sharp voice from behind us stopped him.

I took the opportunity to press the back of my hands to my cheeks, gathering my composure.

"Novia, I've brought someone I'd like you to meet."

I bowed my head, watching her surreptitiously. She was as I remembered: tall, with keen, amber-colored eyes. Her hair was in a tight braid. No hat today. She wasn't pleased. Her patrician nose wrinkled as she regarded me.

"This is Leonore Ward. Leonore, this is Novia Torres."

She offered her hand, which I accepted with a limp grip. "You are not Spanish." Her nose wrinkled again.

"No, señora, I'm from England. I've lived in Spain for about half a year. Cádiz, and then Granada."

"And what brought you to Spain?"

I adopted a placid countenance, glancing at a nearby couple to indicate a lack of interest in this subject. "*Amor. Amor estúpido.*" I shrugged.

She gave a derisive snort. "For Sebastián?"

I put another step of distance between us. "Another man, a sailor. He left." I hung my head in feigned embarrassment.

"Novia, Leonore is sympathetic to our cause. I thought she would enjoy hearing you speak."

"Is that so, señora? Or are you like other ingleses who claim to support us, but withhold any true assistance?"

It was one thing to pretend to be someone I was not; it was another to question my convictions. I met her fiery leer, allowing my fury to shine through and convey a warning. She wasn't dealing with a weak, simpering woman.

"If there is something I could do, I would not hesitate."

She took my measure, withholding her final judgment.

A man in a blue hat interrupted our standoff. "Novia, it is time to speak again. I have the posters for you to review."

"Very well. Sebastián. Señora . . . Ward, was it?"

With that, we were dismissed.

"Sorry she wasn't affable. The pressures of speaking . . ."

"And I'm English," I retorted, my temper simmering.

"That's of no matter. Novia is egalitarian." Sebastián obviously hadn't heard the speech she gave at Plaza Larga. "Shall we stay so you can hear her address the crowd again?"

I wasn't anxious to meet la señora Torres again, but hearing her speech once more might provide insight into their cause—and actions. "If you would like."

We retreated to the edge of the plaza, another surge of people replacing us. Sebastián purchased two oranges. He peeled mine for me, graciously handing it over inside a handkerchief. I savored the tart, refreshing juice and the scent, which helped disguise the fug of overheating people. He beamed when I popped a piece into my mouth.

Shame burned through my chest. The act of suppressing a cough made my eyes water. I was brimming with hidden motivations, and he was enjoying himself.

Novia's speech was in the same vein as earlier. Much was said about acting, but nothing specific. I listened with half an ear while mulling over the case threads, beginning to weave them together. The design was developing, I could feel it.

Sebastián watched Novia speaking, rapt. How did he fit into this?

When her speech reached its climax, Sebastián tilted his head toward the exit. Once we were free of the plaza, we ambled in silence. I was preoccupied with the revelation of Novia Torres and whether she was involved in the murders.

Sebastián interrupted my woolgathering. "That was more crowded than I expected."

"My ears are still ringing."

His chuckle was forced, artificial. I slanted a glance, trying to determine what had altered his mood. "There is a small park one street over. Care to rest for a bit?"

We weren't far from the café. I acquiesced, following him to the small strip of green tucked along a wider street. Children were playing a game at one end, absorbed in their activity. We sat on a bench beneath the spreading branches of an oak.

Sebastián removed his spectacles and cleaned them with a handkerchief. Instead of replacing them, he slipped them in his pocket. Without the barrier of the lenses, his magnetism was more potent. "That disturbed you."

I didn't expect a direct confrontation, but so be it. *Let the dance of obfuscation begin.*

"Not disturbed. It was a lot to reckon with—the crowd, la señora Torres . . ."

"I assumed you would agree with her."

"I do agree," I reassured him. "With her motivations, anyway. La señora is a vibrant speaker who rallies people, but her incitement lacks substance. She rouses the crowd to act, but she doesn't have solutions."

Excitement brightened his face. "Precisely! We produce pamphlets and posters, but we aren't organized enough to take real action. Something that produces results."

I prodded, "Such as?"

"Attempts to persuade the people in power. You can imagine the success of that endeavor."

"Did those people work for the government? The prime minister? Contacts at that level would be the likeliest to make a difference," I encouraged, anxious to identify a link.

"We operate as a collective, but I'm not part of every decision. Novia has associates in the government that are supportive of our goals." He bumped his thigh against mine. "What are your plans? Your dreams? Do you intend to stay in Granada?"

"That was a lot of questions, Sebastián." I put some space between us on the bench.

"Forgive me. I am curious."

Weaving my fingers in my lap, I tried to conjure answers that weren't lies. "It's not in my nature to remain in one place. And dreams? What are those? When one works to survive, there is little room for dreams."

It was Leonore's story, but it was mine as well. Matias had asked me to promise to consider our future. It was a promise I had every intention of keeping, but when I tried to imagine what it could be, a pessimistic curtain obscured my imagination.

Sebastián's voice came from a distance. He was sprawled on the bench, stretching his arm along the seat behind my back. "Dreams ease the everyday struggles. After my father died, imagining possibilities helped. When an entire day passes in the bookstore without one customer, contemplating the future is a balm."

Part of my mind remained on Matias. I tried to bring my attention back to Sebastián.

"And what are your dreams?" My curiosity was genuine. I was eager for a glimpse into the brain of this enigmatic man.

"Some are vast, such as equality for the people of my country and assisting those struggling to survive. I'm aware those dreams must be accomplished, along with others. But I have personal aspirations too. To travel, maybe to France? To have a companion of the heart and mind, a family. For my bookstore to remain in business."

"A companion, not a wife?" My impetuous query tripped forth.

He observed the children running across the grass. "The person is more important than calling them my wife. Are you content alone?"

But I wasn't alone. I almost said as much, which took me by surprise. Not only because it wasn't Leonore's story, but because the loneliness was different now. It was self-imposed. Matias was there for me. Nothing was equivalent to what we shared: Laughter that made my sides hurt for days. Exchanges of ideas, emotions, affection. I had Matias *and* Hugh, despite my attempts to retreat from them. The isolation I felt here was because of their absence.

"My past has made it challenging for me to trust. Being alone means I'm less likely to be hurt." I played with the fabric of my skirt. Ah, how the truth had snuck into the deception.

Sebastián rested his hand on my knee. "Do you believe that? That it's better to be alone? Did your novio hurt you so much?"

A few inches would bring our lips together. The possibility made me withdraw.

"Life has." I stared into the distance. "Did your parents have a happy marriage?"

He angled away, thoughtfully removing his spectacles from his pocket and securing them with a sigh. My distant manner had provoked his necessary detachment.

"Yes, their marriage was happy. Despite his disenchantment at being dismissed from the university, my grandfather was a kind man. My father inherited his qualities. They cared for each other and were affectionate. I was their only child. After she died, papá was devastated. He never remarried—never even looked at another woman. Although he lived another ten years, I don't think he stopped wishing he could join her. Both my grandfather and my father died of cholera."

"I'm sorry, Sebastián. That's a great deal of loss in a short period." He was trying to find hope amongst loss. I admired that quality, and felt awful that I would disappoint him.

"Yes, well." He stood from the bench. "It's time to get you to La Sirena. Raúl will be displeased if I'm responsible for your tardiness." He caressed my fingers as we walked. "Leonore, please consider staying. Raúl likes you, and even Carmen approves. You would be an asset to our cause."

I refused to lie, to promise him anything. It would be wrong on many levels to reassure him. We stopped at the corner opposite the café.

"Don't answer now. Just consider it, please. If not for those reasons, then because I want to know you. I feel . . ." He withdrew his arm and dug his hands into his pockets.

I waited, even though I knew it would be kinder to stop him.

"We have a connection I haven't experienced. Don't you want to explore it?" His face was open, vulnerable.

I was disgusted with myself, not him, but as a result, my reply was acerbic. "I'm a riddle to be solved?"

Regardless of my intentions, my emotions weren't an experiment.

"No, it's—it's hard to explain. But you feel it, too, don't you?"

I fiddled with the cuff of my shirt, crafting a diplomatic answer. "I'm not leaving soon. Thank you for this morning." I thought to soothe any hurt feelings with a friendly kiss on the cheek, but his keen manner shuttered the impulse. Mutely, I spun on my heels toward the café.

Raúl and Carmen greeted me while I retrieved my apron. I watched Sebastián stare motionless at the café as I tied it on. When I looked again, he was gone.

Chapter Thirty-Five

After our outing yesterday, the pieces spun in my head, refusing to join together. Tonight would be different. I would stay alert and keep my thoughts in order.

Propping my elbows on his spotless bar, I begged Raúl for an extra-strong cup of coffee.

"You're going to be awake all night, querida. Or is that the idea? Una cita with your novio, eh?"

Carmen's snicker wafted from the kitchen. I ignored them both in favor of sweeping the floors. Raúl could heckle me all he wanted, as long as he also made the drink. "He's a friend. I don't have many friends."

"What are we, eh?"

"You're the *jefe*, Raúl."

With a twinkle in his eye, he placed a thick, dark cup of coffee on the counter with reverence. "That is how shepherds drink their coffee. Mastica, querida."

After depositing the broom in the closet, I returned to the bar. My first sip was a jolt to the brain.

"It's perfect," I gasped.

Raúl tucked his towel in his apron pocket. "We'll see if you think that tomorrow, after a night without sleep."

Raúl's words were prophetic—and the floor of my bedchamber was more disgusting than the one at the Alhambra. Fishing beneath the bed for the pencil I had dropped from trembling fingers brought me too close to the boards. I washed my hands, patted my perspiring face with cold water, and filled a cracked teacup. I was twitchy and dying of thirst. A walk would take the edge off the stimulation, but at this hour, it was too dangerous.

The tip of my pencil had broken off when it rolled under the bed, and I didn't trust my shaky hands to sharpen it. I threw it onto the desk with a clatter. My list would have to be mental.

Tomorrow I would return to the stationer. Matias should've replied to my message. I closed my eyes, imagining my favorite bench in the garden behind Antonio's house, surrounded by herbaceous breezes and a canopy of stars overhead. Matias and I sharing a glass of wine and some kisses.

I frowned. While we had been affectionate, there was a distance to our interactions. Why was I just noticing now? I backtracked to the moment things had changed: the day of our argument in the bathing chamber, when he had given me his ultimatum. And I had . . . ignored it? A sensation of warmth bloomed at the base of my spine and crept to my nape. I rubbed at the physical manifestation of my frustration. He had asked me if I was in or out, and I left. I *left*? Like a child running from danger?

Someone slammed the front door, and the walls of my room shuddered. The cogs of my brain reengaged. *Fix this. Solve it. And then you can go to him.* I slid my dagger from its sheath and picked up the pencil. Scraping the layers to produce a fine edge had a steadying effect on me. I jotted down words to clarify the situation:

Socialists
Who protects them at the Alhambra?
Novia Torres=Pilar's cousin
Government officials? Aristocrat?
Motivations?

Sebastián must have attended the meetings at the Alhambra. Novia Torres was probably the leader whose voice had been hard to distinguish. She would have had access to the garden through Pilar. But what about the murders? Did Novia know Pelayo? Was his murder connected, or a coincidence? And how did Pilar fit? Despite their argument at the plaza, Pilar had said they were close. Wouldn't Novia protect her? Sebastián must have known Pilar. He was an enigma. I couldn't judge if his interactions with me were friendly or flirtatious, authentic or counterfeit—or did it seem that way because I was deceiving him? He was intelligent, independent, and a bit of a mystery. Unfortunately, the sort of person I found intriguing.

The bedsprings screeched in protest when I flopped backward. There was no obvious pattern; the links were flimsy. I needed solid evidence.

Sometime after my second hour of staring at the ceiling, monstrous self-loathing arrived. I should have been focusing on Matias, on my work at the Alhambra, on how to fix the mess brewing in England. Instead, here I was, going in circles. I sighed and punched the wad of clothing that was my pillow. To top it off, Raúl was right: I was wide-awake.

As soon as I set foot in La Sirena, Raúl buckled with laughter. "Was it worth it?"

I grumbled inaudibly, accepting his peace offering of more coffee. How could I love this drink so much and hate what it did to me? Evil brew.

The effects of the beverage propelled me through the morning. During the midday lull, I went to the stationer to collect my messages. A new coded phrase came with the handover: *A receipt for removing wine stains.*

There were two notes, one from Antonio and one from Matias.

L,

If you are making progress and feel it is best to remain, then I trust you. However, if you do not appear on 2 October, I will come find you.

Yours,

M

L,

This is to let you know that the person in question has still not been seen, and the person in charge continues to question your absence. You must return soon.

A

Chapter Thirty-Six

A night of sleep helped focus my intentions. My best option to get answers fast was Sebastián. To break through his facade, I needed a new tactic. I decided to question him at his bookstore. He would be less defensive in his own space.

Raúl was waiting at the door when I arrived. He was expecting the delivery of a cart of kitchen goods and insisted that it was simpler for them to handle it alone. I had a few hours off while they unpacked the cargo. It was fortuitous timing for a visit to Sebastián.

His bookstore was wedged between a rag-and-bottle shop and an empty storefront. Both windows were thick with grime, obscuring their interiors. Sebastián's walkway was swept clean. Upstairs, delicate curtains swirled in the open windows. Did he live there?

The clang of the bell drew the attention of a group of boys gathered around the lending-library shelves. Sebastián took the momentary advantage to defend the books from their eager pawing.

"Boys, you may each have a turn. Be patient. How can I . . ." he trailed off when he noticed me.

"Sebastián, that bell rains dust every time someone walks in the bookstore. May I clean it?"

He glanced at the boys. "If you wish, I'll fetch the stool."

I slipped the bell from the hook, cradling it in my other hand. Using Sebastian's clean handkerchief that I'd kept since sharing oranges in the plaza, I scoured each ridge and line. Distracted by my devotion to the task, the boys almost toppled me from the stool when they barreled out the door.

Sebastián rushed to steady me, resting his hand on my lower back. I offered the bell for inspection. It was stained, but no longer dusty. "If you have a lemon, I can remove the tarnish."

He examined it and handed it back so I could rehang it. "That isn't necessary. It is much improved. Thank you. I should've paid attention to the state of it."

"It was no bother."

Sebastián's hand was gone from my back, but we remained in closer proximity than normal. Daylight reflected off his spectacles, hiding his eyes. His tousled hair gave off a strong rosemary fragrance. A seam at the shoulder of his shirt was pulling apart. The air in the store was motionless, anticipatory.

I stepped off the stool, breaking the tension. Sebastián cleared his throat to mask the hitch in his exhale.

"Now that those miscreants have left, you can see what I received in the last shipment."

He motioned to the shelves and took his place behind the counter. I perused the new books, gasping in delight to find a plant guide to the mountains of southern Spain. I snatched it from the shelf, rifling through the pages. Marvelous illustrations were interspersed throughout the dense text. Matias would love this book as well.

Except there was no way a serving girl could afford it. With a regretful caress to the tattered spine, I returned it to the shelf.

"You can borrow it. I'm surprised that's what caught your eye."

"It isn't on the lending shelves. I have a fondness for plants, and it . . . made me think of someone."

"Plants? That's unusual."

Sebastián swished a duster over the nearby stacks. My nose prickled from the bits it scattered. "In England, I apprenticed with a gardener, and he taught me to love plants." It assuaged my guilt to allow the truth to slip in once in a while.

He leaned against the shelves. "Have you been to the Alhambra yet?"

I ran a finger along the wood so I didn't have to look at him when I lied, "I haven't. It isn't a place for people like me."

"Of course it is. I've visited."

I channeled my delight at his confirmation of being at the Alhambra into eagerness. "You have? Was it amazing?"

He laughed at my enthusiasm. "From the little I've seen, yes, it is beautiful."

"Are people not allowed to walk through the entire garden?"

"Ah, well . . . I've only been at night."

Even better.

My face contorted into an expression of confusion. "At night?"

He fidgeted, straightening the spines. "You overheard us discussing it that night at the café. We meet at the Alhambra."

His gaze was piercing. I tried for innocence. "Oh, is that what you meant? I lose things in translation." His flat perusal didn't alter when I asked, "You've been there for meetings?"

"Yes." His voice was even, emotionless.

Sebastián was turning wary. If I was prudent, I would retreat. I pitched my voice to a flighty octave. "Well, you're fortunate! On my first day in the city, I ended up in a neighborhood near the Alhambra where they have beautiful private gardens. What are those tall purple trees?" I pretended to search my mind for the name. "Jacarandas! So different from England."

Sebastián gestured for me to follow him. "Come look at this section."

That was a near thing, but my act seemed to have convinced him. He handed me a lovely, illustrated book of plants from the Alhambra. It had been written shortly after Irving visited, prior to the restoration. I stroked the pages with reverence. "Oh, Sebastián, this is remarkable."

"Do you think so?"

"Yes, look at the maps." I tilted the page that described the layout of the orchards.

A flicker of alarm danced through his countenance.

My subtle manipulation was successful. He snapped it shut, pushing it toward me. "Keep it. Consider it a trade for cleaning my bell."

My hands cradled it, then pushed it back. "No, you already gave me a book."

He flattened his palms, fending it away. "Please, Leonore, allow me this."

"It's too generous."

"It isn't." He bent toward me. "You have something . . ." His thumb brushed over the arch of my cheekbone and continued on, caressing my jaw until he cradled my face.

Mesmerized by his gentle touch, I was rooted in place. He removed his spectacles, setting them on a nearby shelf. My brain would not engage. My body wouldn't respond. *Move*, I thought. *You need to move now.*

Matias was the only person I had kissed in two years.

Sebastián's kiss was compelling. Gentle, yet impatient. His lips were warm, plush. My hand on his shoulder was intended to force him away, but his affection called to the loneliness inside me, swirling into the corners where I felt hollow.

I fisted the fabric of his shirt. He gave a hum of approval, tracing my lips with his tongue. He tasted of citrus. His mouth was silk, stroking with confidence, not dominance.

What was I doing? I broke his hold, stumbling against the bookshelves. My fists clenched around the book, my whole-body trembling.

Shaky breaths escaped through my open mouth. Each one was sharp with regret and shame.

Sebastián fumbled for his spectacles, then settled them on his nose. His face was calm, but his hands were unsteady. "Must I apologize?"

I raised my chin, struggling to remain calm. Words deserted me. I shook my head.

"Good, because I can't ask for forgiveness. That was—"

My voice emerged scratchy, strangled. "Don't say it."

He propped himself against the bookshelf, the thin fabric of his jacket pulling tight across his biceps. "You regret it."

"I knew this would happen if I came here," I chided myself.

"Yet you came." Sebastián pushed off the shelf, drawing closer.

"I did." My cramped fingers eased around the spine of the book. I shoved it at him. "I should go."

"Take the book, especially now."

"Is it payment?" I was appalled at his implication.

He was horrified. "No, no. I just . . . I want you to have it."

"I'll borrow it. But I don't intend to keep it."

I had to pass him to leave. He captured my arm, squeezing. "Please don't regret this, Leonore."

I felt sick at the sound of that name. To him, I wasn't Linnea. He didn't know me. My throat was thick with nausea, with tears. I had betrayed Matias, and I had betrayed myself.

"I'll see you tomorrow night," he said, not waiting for my response.

"Tomorrow?"

"It's Thursday, our meeting night. Maybe you can join."

Coward that I was, I didn't glance back as I fled. In the crowded street, I searched for a place to gather my wits. Finally, I spied a dark corner of an alley up ahead. I propped the book on the wall and pressed my forehead against the cool bricks.

Fuck.

Sobs ripped from my chest in great heaves of shame. I could've stopped him. I could've stopped myself. And I didn't. *I* didn't.

Dammit. Every curse I'd ever heard at sea welled in my mind. I pressed a palm to the bricks, uncertain whether vomiting would help or not. Sebastián had confirmed that he had been at the Alhambra. But what was the cost? My self-respect? Would I destroy everything good in my life for the truth of this investigation? I should collect my things and never return.

Instead, I did what I always did. I straightened my spine, picked up the book, and got on with it.

Chapter Thirty-Seven

Twice during the night, I packed my valise, only to unpack it after a few minutes. Sitting alone in my chamber wasn't helping. When dawn broke and the danger of darkness had passed, I left the boarding-house.

In a daze, I walked to the small green area a few streets away. I kept thinking about what Matias had said on the *Cormorant*. He had been taught by his mother, who was a *machi*, that there were other ways of knowing. Answers that visited us through the unobservable, through our intuition. The few times I had managed to slip into this alternate path of perception were when I was within nature.

A house must have once stood in this run-down lot. Charred bits surrounded the remaining foundation stones. Anything salvageable had been scavenged long ago. Volunteer plants covered the compacted earth—whatever could blow in and take root. This lot had one plant in particular that I wished to visit.

In the middle of a pile of rubble grew a hawthorn tree. Somehow, amidst the destruction, this tree had survived.

I sat on a broken stone near the trunk. The tree was small, but the branches spread in a wide canopy. Clumps of green, unripe berries hung from the top branches.

Hawthorn was one of my plant familiars, companions I returned to when I was struggling. When I was studying the medicinal uses of hawthorn at the Chelsea Physic Garden, I came across a reference to it being a gateway to other worlds. At its roots, you could present your true self and ask the plant for guidance. Whether that was accurate or not, I was willing to try. I had reached a crossroads.

I had been naïve to believe that being undercover would be similar to dressing as a boy to work at Kew. In that situation, I'd risked only myself. In less than a fortnight, I had drawn people into my snarl: Sebastián, Raúl, Carmen, and, by extension, Matias, Hugh, and Antonio.

A withered berry plopped to the ground near my boot. I picked it up, rolling it between my fingers. How did plants protect themselves? By growing a thick outer layer, sprouting thorns, producing toxins. Some of those defenses were more effective than others. But what about a group of people? How would one go about guarding them?

What if the socialist group was defending itself? Or someone?

My thumbnail bit into the skin of the berry. The tough layer cradled a few seeds, safeguarding the next generation of plants.

The hawthorn may have shown me an alternative scenario for the murders, but it wasn't straightforward. Realizing that the group was protecting someone wasn't a surprise. After all, even the night they had met at the café, they'd spoken of how to keep their communities and families safe. I pondered that aspect, pushing Sebastián's kiss to the furthest corners of my mind.

At La Sirena, Raúl and Carmen were bustling around the kitchen.

"*Buenos días*, Raúl, Carmen," I said, lingering at the entrance. After the turmoil of the previous night, it was a relief to see their faces.

"Ah, here she is. You're late, querida. We were concerned you weren't coming."

"Am I late?" I glanced at the clock.

"As you can see, no one has arrived yet. You usually arrive earlier. I was worried."

My breath caught on a stab of guilt. I *would* vanish someday soon. "I'm ready to work."

"First, you need coffee. I know you. Nothing happens without coffee."

"Especially your coffee, Raúl."

He went behind the counter to prepare my cup. I hopped on a chair to keep him company until the first customer arrived.

"Tonight is the meeting, so it will be hectic. Are you rested?" Raúl bent over his small stove. "El señor de los Rios will be here, but that isn't an excuse for laziness," he scolded me, holding a steaming cup out of my reach.

I rolled my eyes, snatching it away. "I told you, he's a friend. Nothing more."

"There are sparks between you. Friends, indeed."

The coffee in my mouth tasted of bitter betrayal. Over my internal self-recrimination, I retorted, "Does he have many novias?"

Raúl's laughter was bombastic. I winced at the volume. "*Now* she asks. The only women he's ever with are the women in that group."

"There were only the men last week."

"A few mujeres attend. A tall woman, the strident one, is la señora Torres." He rolled his *r*'s dramatically. "And a few older women. A young, pretty one as well, but I haven't seen her in a while."

My eyes watered as my swallow of coffee scalded my esophagus. Pilar? "What happened to her?"

"No idea. She came to the café for the meetings. I saw her at the market, so she must have lived nearby. She was always with la señora Torres. Maybe she decided the meetings didn't interest her. They are a zealous lot."

Our first customer came through the door, shouting hello to Raúl and promptly concluding our discussion. I tied on my apron, prepared to work another day that, with luck, would have some answers at its end.

Raúl was correct; it was pure madness. My meals were taken propped against a wall in the kitchen, shoveling whatever Carmen prepared into my mouth.

More people were in attendance at this evening's meeting. Sebastián caught my eye when he arrived. I ignored him, a flush of chagrin scalding me from toe to face. I should've resisted that kiss.

But the crowded café didn't allow me to linger on those thoughts. They were jovial tonight. Even the man who had been concerned for his sister was in high spirits, slapping his compatriots on the back in greeting.

When la señora Torres arrived, the men settled into pattern cards of deference. I rushed to the table to take her order. She stared at me while I waited patiently. "Aren't you la inglesa I met at the plaza?"

"Sí, señora. What can I bring you?"

Her scrutiny was unflinching. If she intended to intimidate me, she wouldn't be successful. Pilar's cousin or not, I didn't owe her my esteem.

"Un vino blanco y una sopa, por favor."

I was given a temporary reprieve in Carmen's calming presence. Then another customer was waving from across the room. After taking that order, I returned to the kitchen with an armful of bowls, backing through the door while giving Carmen the next request. I nearly stumbled when I spied Sebastián seated on a stool beside the washtub.

Carmen glanced at him, then gestured toward the alley. I followed him through the door, staring at my feet while I tried to get a word in first. "I can't be away long, it's so—"

Sebastián's kiss was an ambush, a determined sneak attack. This time, I didn't freeze. I shoved him away firmly.

"Sebastián," I warned, my palms against his chest.

"I've wanted to do that since you walked out of my shop."

The partially open door loomed in the periphery. "It, um, isn't private."

He glanced at the door. "Does it matter?"

"It matters to me. Sebastián, this isn't—"

Raúl's voice boomed from inside. "Leonore? Where's that girl?"

I snatched my hands away. "I have to go."

"Will you join us later?"

"La señora Torres—"

"She requested that you meet with us. I think she wants more women involved."

I paused. "Even though I'm not Spanish?"

"LEONORE!" Raúl shouted.

Outdoor patrons remained at the tables until after closing, so I wasn't able to eavesdrop on the meeting. When the last diner left, I hastened inside. The group was deep in discussion.

Sebastián waved to me when he spotted me cleaning the empty tables. I sidled up to Raúl. "May I listen to the meeting for a bit?"

Raúl had scolded me for abandoning my tables earlier, and his mood had been off since. He stacked the coffee cups, replying, "You want to get involved with that lot?"

I shrugged. "I would like to understand their cause and—if I can—help."

"They drink and talk about what they will do, but nothing changes. The people who have the power will do as they like." He tossed the rag into the heap. "Go on, then."

Sebastián fetched another chair and placed it next to him. Everyone was silent, watching me taking my seat. Their scrutiny was unnerving.

Sebastián cleared his throat. "This is Leonore Ward. She works at the café and is interested in joining us."

I faced a sea of silent, skeptical faces. La señora Torres rested her chin on her palm. "*You* think to join us? What makes you think you can understand?"

I took a deep breath, moderating my tone so as not to sound defensive. "Do you think our situation is different in England? We have a monarchy. We have a parliament, similar to the republic. People are starving there, just as people are starving here."

She smirked while I spoke. Was it respect or ridicule?

Sebastián interjected, cutting off her reply, "I believe Leonore has something to contribute."

La señora snorted in response. "Oh, you do?"

The men laughed with her. I braced myself for their derision, but she surprised me by changing the topic.

They discussed another area in the neighborhood that was being threatened. More wealthy merchants were returning from abroad and wanted to build their houses on the currently occupied lots. Through a combination of harassment and bribes, the houses had been slated for demolition.

"Thirty people dwell in those homes. Where will they go?" one man asked.

Everyone solemnly contemplated the fate of those families.

La señora Torres raised her voice. "We must stop it. If the architectural plans were to vanish, it might buy us time to apply pressure."

"Do we know someone with the power to stop the development?" a thin man at the neighboring table asked.

"Maybe. Or maybe we could use the plans as blackmail," she retorted.

"Plans are replaceable."

"Not without considerable expense. A delay may allow us the opportunity to find someone to intervene on our behalf." Her face glowed with fervor.

"So, how do we get the plans?" The man who asked swiped the hat from his head, slapping it against his palm. "It won't be easy to slip into their offices to steal them."

She nodded. "No, we need someone invisible."

A prickling at the base of my nape was my forewarning. Novia Torres narrowed her feline gaze in my direction.

"Sebastián, this sounds like the perfect job for you and your new friend."

Chapter Thirty-Eight

Sebastián's opaque mask was back in place. "Why us?"

"She claims she wants to help. Plus, the two of you can sneak into the office. You can both pass for wealthy."

Sebastián pointed at our clothing. "How? I work in a bookstore. Leonore works in a café."

"You're both educated. Or at least, she speaks as if she is, and if your clothing is tidy, you will pass."

The other men around the tables shifted, muttering sounds of agreement.

"It would give us leverage," said the man next to me.

Another one mumbled, "Especially since our other plans have failed."

What other plans? If this was what it would take for me to gain their trust, I would do it, but it didn't lessen my unease. Was she setting a trap?

She wouldn't do that to Sebastián, would she?

La señora raised her hand, halting their conversation. "We are a collective, and we only act if we can agree. Does anyone disagree?"

For a moment, I considered speaking up. Her plans were barreling ahead without careful consideration. Under the table, Sebastián pulled on the corner of my apron. He must've sensed what I was thinking.

La señora Torres nodded. "Very well. I'll make the arrangements with Sebastián. We'll have the plans in hand at our next meeting."

The meeting concluded, the men rose from their chairs to file out. I slid away from the table to leave with them, but Sebastián grabbed my hand. "Stay. She'll want to discuss with us."

I whispered, "I didn't agree to commit a crime."

"Hear her out? Please?"

He didn't release my hand, which la señora noted. She regarded us as a cat eyes a mouse. Was her anger a facade? If I had lost my cousin, someone I had known my whole life, I might expect to be impulsive as well.

Unless she had killed Pilar. That couldn't be, could it? I was staring at her, but she didn't shy away. Raúl's voice ended our standoff. "Leonore, we're ready to close."

I nodded, pulling my hand from Sebastián's. "If we are going to discuss this, it will have to be later," I said, rising.

They came to their feet. "Novia? When should we meet?"

She fluttered her hand at me. "She agrees?"

"You know I'm committed to our cause. Whether Leonore participates or not is up to her," Sebastián said through clenched teeth.

I chimed in, "I'm willing to listen to your plan. But I'm not making any promises."

The three of us walked toward the entrance of the café. Novia paused at the door. "We must meet somewhere private. At the Alhambra?"

Oh no, it couldn't be there. I scrambled for a reason to avoid the garden. "It's too far. I can't be away from work for very long. I'm Raúl's only waitress."

Sebastián touched me again, placing a hand on my back. His physical familiarity needed to cease. "We can meet at the bookstore. I'll close so we won't be overheard."

Novia nodded. "Very well. Tomorrow? Eleven?"

"That will do for me. Leonore?"

"Assuming Raúl approves, yes."

Sebastián stayed as la señora walked away. "Leonore, I . . ." He came a step closer, his hand exerting pressure on my back.

Novia's voice sliced through the moment. "Sebastián, we have other business to discuss."

He stepped away. His immediate acquiescence was telling.

"She calls and you run?" I observed unkindly.

His face darkened. "It isn't like that."

"Hmm. *Buenas noches*, Sebastián." I didn't allow him to reply as I shut the café door behind them and threw the lock. It was petulant, but I was annoyed that I was being drawn into Novia's machinations.

Raúl was irritable, and it wasn't just because I was leaving to meet Sebastián and Novia. My concentration was suffering. Even though it wasn't a busy morning, I had gotten several orders wrong. Another night with little sleep while I puzzled through the endless twists of this investigation. I tried to connect Pelayo, Pilar, Novia, Sebastián, Izabelle, the socialists, and the café. All it gained me was a bed covered in scraps of paper and a sore head.

Today marked a fortnight undercover. A breakthrough had to happen soon. My days were running short. Novia's plan could be a trap, but it could also be my only chance.

I opened Sebastián's door. The clean bell rang out with a crisp tone. He gave me a wry smile when he saw the direction of my glance. "Leonore, can you flip the sign to cerrado and turn the lock, please?"

I hadn't noticed Novia lurking among the back shelves. I flipped the sign.

I had been correct; Sebastián lived above the store. The stairway to the next floor was narrow. Bright sunlight spilled from above, illuminating the dust mites. The high ceilings of the flat made the small space seem larger. The walls were whitewashed, the floors burnished wood that gave off the fragrance of lemon oil. A threadbare velvet chaise and well-worn chair had been placed around a low table. The living area adjoined a tiny kitchen, and the other room must be his bedchamber. In the corner, a woodstove emanated banked heat. Sebastián removed the cover from the top to balance a coffee percolator.

"There should be enough heat to boil the water. It will take a few minutes."

Novia walked to the windows, flicking the curtain aside to peer down at the street. I sat on the green chaise. The velvet was worn in patches, giving it the texture of a dog with mange. It was so large, I wondered how he had gotten it up the stairs.

"How long have you been in the Albaicín?" Thus began Novia's inquisition.

"Not yet a month, señora."

"There's no need to be formal. You may call me Novia. You came to Granada for a man?" she fired back.

"Cádiz. I traveled to Cádiz with him. I came here alone." I kept my face averted, picking at a loose thread on the chaise.

"Are you waiting for him?"

Enough. I snapped my head up, defensive. "I am not. What does this have to do with why we are meeting?"

"I'm curious. Few women are brave enough to travel alone—or have the funds to do so." She crossed her arms, defiant.

"I didn't like Cádiz. I worked in a café until I earned enough money to come to Granada. One of the other waitresses was born in the Albaicín, and her descriptions were intriguing."

"And you are lodging at la señora Sandrina's?"

I assumed Sebastián had shared that information with her. So, they had discussed me. Not unexpected, but it was a fortuitous reminder to be cautious. "Sí."

Sebastián sat beside me on the chaise. "Novia, can we move on to your thoughts about the architectural plans? Leonore needs to return. Your questions will have to wait."

I shot him a grateful smile, then returned my attention to Novia. She eschewed a chair to skulk near the windows.

"The plans are kept at an office near Plaza Nueva. An architect working on this project has the chambers adjacent to a minister, his patron. There's also a registry in the building. You can pretend you are newlyweds."

I suppressed a snort of amusement. Newlyweds? "Aren't couples required to marry in the church in Spain?"

"Yes, but it's customary to have it recognized by the government registrar. It is becoming common for those who aren't religious. Your task is simple—enter the office and remove the plans."

Sebastián attended to the now-hissing pot, speaking over the burbling coffee. "And you think the plans will provide enough leverage to delay the evictions?"

She accepted the cup he offered. "I do. These people will do anything for money. Without the plans, their progress will be delayed. It will give us space to find other ways to influence them."

"Any architect worth their salt produces duplicates. If these people have the funds to build, they can recreate them," I observed, balancing my cup on my knee.

Novia scowled. "Stealing the plans will give us an advantage and stall the transaction. It's worth the risk."

She wasn't the one risking anything. It went without saying that I was expendable. But Sebastián?

"If we're caught, we'll pay the price, not you. Sebastián, what's your opinion?"

He stood behind the chaise, over my shoulder, silent. The corners of Novia's mouth turned up in a slight smile. She was confident in his answer.

"I am willing."

I was wary of his submission to her. "That's it? You don't have concerns?"

Novia slammed her cup down on the end table. "I must go. I knew I could rely on you, Sebastián. Others have pointed out that you're quiet at our meetings and avoid getting involved in actions, but I have faith in your loyalty. We all valued the contributions of your father and grandfather. It's your turn."

She didn't wait for his response. Her heavy boots thudded on each step with her descent.

When the chime on the door rang, Sebastián sighed heavily. "She prefers to have the last word. We must go. She unlocked the door—anyone could enter." He gathered our cups and dumped them into a tin washtub.

I felt offended on his behalf. "She has no right to speak to you that way."

He whirled on me. "What do you know of it? She's right, my father and grandfather were leaders. I've been preoccupied with my business for the last several years, and I'm not inclined to lead. But I am as dedicated as they were."

"No one doubts—"

Angry, he interrupted, "You don't know. You aren't from here. If you would rather not be involved, I understand. I can do it alone."

I studied the whorls on the floorboards. Should I refuse? Was this a sign to pack my belongings and return to Antonio's house?

"For the deception to be believable, you need a couple," I said, my voice uncertain even to my ears. "Raúl was vexed at my absence today. If we are doing this tomorrow, I can't make him annoyed."

Sebastián tried to draw me into his arms, but I resisted. He scowled in confusion. "What is it, Leonore? I thought . . ."

I shifted my weight to my back foot. "You're a friend, and I'll do this, but that is all there is between us. Friendship."

"Hmm," he said, taking my hand. "But tomorrow we'll be married."

"We will *pretend* to be married." I tried for a stern admonition. His lips pressed against my fingers made it hitch at the end.

"The walk to Plaza Nueva will take a while. What will you tell Raúl?"

I turned toward the stairs, stepping into the dark hallway. "I don't know, but I'll come up with something."

We entered the empty bookshop. Despite his concerns, it seemed as if customers were not queuing up to enter. He took his place at the counter. "So—tomorrow. At noon? We can walk from here. If you bring your clothes, you can change in the flat so Raúl doesn't pry."

"Is that appropriate?" Alone together while I undressed was too far, even for me.

"I will stay here in the shop," he soothed.

"Noon," I agreed. "Until tomorrow."

The crowd absorbed me as I walked, content to be anonymous among the swarm of people. Tomorrow, I might stroll into a trap, or I might do something worthwhile. Either way, it would be an end.

Chapter Thirty-Nine

"I'm sorry, Raúl. I promise to return before it gets busy this afternoon."

His glower didn't relent. He shoved through the kitchen door, grumbling, "What's the point of having a waitress if you aren't here?"

I retrieved my bag of clothes from where it was hidden beneath a broken table in the corner. Raúl's tolerance for my absences was thinning; it was just as well that this was almost over. I paused at the door, looking around the café with fondness. I had found a purpose. The work was demanding but rewarding. Some of my plant discoveries could be used for medicine, but the people I worked for didn't care about that. Instead, those specimens were grown in glasshouses to be planted in rich people's gardens.

I twisted my hands in the handles of my bag. Those same people would mock the profession of a waitress, yet in the café, we cared for people. They were hungry and we fed them. I was a witness to their laughter, their low days, their celebrations.

Later, I could reflect on how this experience might have changed my thoughts about my floundering career. Right now, there were plans to steal.

Sebastián was pacing when I arrived, the store practically vibrating with his restless energy.

"You can go upstairs and change. I'll finish closing the shop."

He tidied the lending shelves. A pamphlet slid from the stack, sailing across the floor to land near my foot. I picked it up and handed it to him. "Are you well?"

"A bit nervous."

He continued to bustle around the shop, so I left him to it and climbed the stairs to his flat. Wind swirled the flowered curtains around the open windows. Raúl had claimed that the wind meant the heat was finally breaking. He'd been cheerful until I had requested another absence.

Sebastián's bedchamber was orderly. A small stack of books was next to his bed: poetry, atlases, and a Spanish copy of Jeremy Bentham's book on utilitarianism. His dressing table held a brush and a set of miniatures that must have been his parents. There was also a delicate flower arrangement: a late-blooming rose and several sprigs of lavender.

Where had Sebastián gotten those flowers? Growing space in this neighborhood was rare. Their presence reminded me of the rhododendrons left in my chamber. Yet another mystery I hadn't solved.

I withdrew my clothing from my bag, a skirt and shirt that were the finest I had brought undercover. Maria had stitched intricately embroidered dolphins around the cuffs. While I loosened the button on my work clothing, I inched open the door to his wardrobe. He owned a few sets of serviceable, colored waistcoats and shirts. The boots on the shelf were worn; the left one had a hole in the toe.

A squeak from the stairs announced his imminent arrival. I pulled the clean blouse over my head and was fastening my skirt when he tapped on the door. "Are you ready?"

"Almost," I replied, bundling my clothes into my bag.

Sebastián lingered in the doorway, examining my outfit. I ran my palms over my hips, smoothing the wrinkles. He came closer, tracing the threads on the cuffs. "Pretty."

I nudged the vase on the dressing table. "Where did you get such lovely flowers?"

"A friend grows them." He reached around me to lift a rose and tucked it into my braided cornet. "Now you look like a bride."

The word *bride* made my stomach roil. I wasn't anyone's bride, least of all his.

"It will wilt," I protested.

"No matter. It belongs there. But we need something else." He opened the drawer to the dressing table. The speckled looking glass across the room reflected a stranger. It was the first time I had seen more than my face in a mirror for weeks. The woman in the glass was pale and thin. Her tightly braided hair had obvious glints of auburn. She looked like an apprehensive bride with that wildness in her eyes, especially when the dark-haired man approached her.

Sebastián met my eyes in the mirror. I broke away, staring at the toes of my boots rather than the reflected scene. He kissed each of the fingers of my right hand. I closed my eyes with a hiss, which turned to a gasp at the sensation of metal. A thin gold ring with a glowing opal encircled my third finger. It was luminous.

And so wrong.

My breath lodged in my lungs as if I had taken a blow. My voice emerged thready. "Sebastián."

He tipped my hand toward the window. The stone caught the light, refracting into shards of color on its surface. "It was my mother's. The stone matches your eyes. So changeable."

"What if I lose it? We can't risk your heirloom. It's priceless." I tried to remove the ring, but he stilled my fumbling.

"I want you to wear it. There is no significance, no declaration. It's part of our act. A bride would wear a ring." He wriggled his fingers. "I'm wearing my father's, see?"

A crack bisected my chest, a black gorge spewing emotion. Pain arrowed through my veins. This was wrong. This was *all* wrong. Pinpricks danced at the base of my skull. Here it was: the crucible. I had traveled beyond safety.

Either I moved forward and faced what was on the other side, or I left.

Sebastián's arm came around my shoulders. My lungs recalled their function, although my first breath was constricted. "Are you well? Did I upset you? I thought this would help us play the part."

The solidity of his form pressed against my side was a temporary comfort. His body was different from Matias's. Matias was muscular from a life spent at sea; Sebastián was slight, lean.

I reminded myself that we were doing this for a purpose. Our theft would help the families that might starve and lose their homes. Sebastián's face was, as ever, inscrutable. I couldn't judge his sincerity, his motives. Even the slight spark of attraction didn't feel entirely genuine.

I moved, putting space between us. "We should go. Our window of opportunity is short."

He blinked. "You go ahead. I'll be there in a moment."

I gathered my bag. Why did he want to be alone up here?

On my way to the door, he spun me around. Once again, he disarmed me with a frenzied kiss—and ended it before I could stop him.

I lurched toward the exit. "I'll meet you in the shop."

We matched our strides as we walked through the city to Plaza Nueva. In our neighborhood of the Albaicín, the shops were thronged with people, but as we passed through the affluent areas, it emptied. The people who lived here had servants who saw to their needs. I preferred the bustle of the other neighborhood. What would it feel like to live like this again? When I was younger, it was easy to ignore inequities and focus on my little square of existence. As I grew older, I couldn't look away.

A beam of sunlight glinted off the ring where my finger rested on Sebastián's arm. At least I knew *that* was not my path.

Sebastián caught me looking at it and tightened his grip. "We're almost there."

We turned the corner, coming to the edge of the plaza. It was enormous. I hesitated, pulling Sebastián to a stop so I could catch my breath. Contrasting square tiles stretched to the horizon, and the center was split by a grove of trees. The scale of the space was breathtaking.

"You haven't visited?"

"No, it's . . . impressive."

"Did you know that the Darro runs beneath the plaza?"

"It does? Extraordinary. And the opulence of the buildings . . ."

He nodded, lifting a finger to point at the center structure. "That's where we are going."

It wasn't just an office. It was the Royal Chancery of Granada. Once a palace, it now housed the courts. My knees wobbled. "You neglected to specify that this was the building we would be robbing."

"It's where the records are held. Many professionals prefer offices near the courts."

I whistled through my teeth. "*Joder.*"

Sebastián choked at the expletive. "Have you changed your mind?"

I patted his arm. "I haven't. Just reassessing the risk."

"Let's go. The sooner we're done, the sooner we can . . ." He didn't finish his sentence. What would happen after we accomplished our task?

I couldn't think about that now. We strode toward the riveted main door. To enter, we passed under a cartouche and two regal stone ladies. The echoing marbled main room was open to the public. Small groups of people wandered the edges, viewing the monarchy memorabilia. Several corridors branched off the room, including one labeled Registros.

We strutted along the hall, summoning the possessiveness of proud newlyweds. When we passed two men in expensive suits, Sebastián slipped his arm around my waist.

Novia had told us the architect's office was six doors from the entrance to the corridor. Sebastián tapped my waist when we reached it, then stood cover while I knocked lightly and then tried the door. "Is it locked?"

"Of course." Fortunately for us, my skills extended to lockpicking. I withdrew two pins from my hair and knelt in front of the lock.

"How do you—never mind, I don't want to know."

"Shh," I hushed him. The lock was simple. With a few twists of the pins, it gave way. We slipped inside, locking ourselves in. "You search the shelves. I'll take the desk," I said, heading for the ornate ormolu desk in the center of the room. How could an architect work at this monstrosity? It was a garish behemoth of scrollwork, more for appearances than function.

Sebastián rummaged through the shelves. The single drawer on the desk was locked, so I used my hairpin again to open it. This one was trickier, the smaller mechanism difficult to manipulate.

"Nothing on the shelves." Sebastián loomed. "Can you get it open? We must hurry."

"Just a moment," I muttered. With a ping, the lock sprang free.

The drawer was filled with parchment. On top of the pile was a set of plans for an enormous home. I sifted through the pages. There were designs for at least six residences. Beneath them was a letter from an official on behalf of the prime minister, granting permission for the area to be cleared.

I gathered the papers and was rolling them into a tube when another drawing caught my eye. It was a plan that I recognized: the layout of the Generalife.

I lifted the small square from the others. In the bottom left corner was written one word: *Pelayo*.

"We need to go!" Sebastián hissed. Voices were approaching in the corridor.

I finished rolling the plans and tucked them beneath the back of my skirt, secured by my waistband. The Generalife drawing went into my pocket. "I'm ready."

The drawer clicked when I closed it, the lock reengaging. We hurried to the door. I peeked around the frame. The corridor was empty.

"It's clear. *¡Vamos!*"

I didn't bother to lock the door. I grabbed Sebastián's arm as we took our first steps down the hall. He tried to rush, but I slowed him. We didn't want to draw attention by dashing from the building.

We turned into the vast public room. Freedom was near.

A laugh resonated off the abundance of marble, drawing the attention of everyone, including us. Why did that laugh sound familiar?

I slowed in front of a display of royal robes, turning my face into Sebastián's shoulder to take a subtle look. The man had his back to us, but I recognized his stature.

It was Suárez.

His party was headed in our direction. I yanked on Sebastián's arm, encouraging him to move quicker across the slick surface. His foot skidded, almost sending us both to the floor. He gave me a furious glower. "What is wrong with you?"

"We need to leave now," I whispered, parading us around the outskirts of the giant room.

"Why—"

"Lady Wren?"

Fuck.

Suárez's voice carried across the hall. We were near the entrance. Just a little further. "Lady Wren, is that you?"

I shoved the door open. Releasing my grip on Sebastián, I ran from the building, frantic for somewhere to hide.

There!

Without glancing behind us, I headed for a narrow space between two buildings. Taking shelter behind a half-destroyed crate in the small alley, I crouched low, the papers in my waistband cutting into my flesh. Footfalls paused at the entrance.

"Leonore?"

I poked my head around the crate and whispered, "Here."

He came to where I languished on the grimy surface of the alley. From his expression, it was where I belonged. "Did that man recognize you?"

I adjusted the bundle in my skirt, peering around him to the street. "Can we discuss this elsewhere?"

Sebastián folded his arms, blocking my exit. He had reverted to being a cold stranger, embodying that celestial remoteness that made me associate him with ravens.

A chill passed through me. It was the beginning of the end.

Without speaking, he rotated on his heels. I followed, pausing at the mouth of the alley to check both directions. Sebastián slowed when I came alongside him but continued to ignore me. We were nearing our neighborhood when he gestured to a small grassy area. He sat on the bench, hunched forward. I stayed on my feet to face his inevitable accusations.

"How does that man know you, Leonore? I assume he does, given your reaction."

I ran my thumb over the outline of an embroidered dolphin. What would I tell him? "It's complicated."

I didn't think it was possible for his expression to become more aloof. Tension rippled through his muscles. "Was any of it true?"

His voice held an undercurrent of vulnerability. I reached for him, but he reared back. My hand dropped to my side. "Yes, Sebastián. Some of it was true."

Closing his hands into fists on his thighs, he growled, "Who are you working for?"

My eyebrows shot upward in surprise. That was not the question I was expecting.

"I don't work for anyone. Someone I care about was harmed, and I'm trying to find out why."

"Do I know the person?"

"I'm not sure. Her name was Pilar."

He came to his feet so fast, I staggered away, hands out to fend him off. I didn't think he would hurt me, but his agitation was like a fast-moving storm. "Pilar? You mean Novia's cousin?"

I stood my ground. "Y-yes. How do *you* know Pilar?"

He circled the bench. "No, no more. Don't say anything else. I must speak to Novia."

"You need to speak to Novia? Can't you be honest?" I scoffed. After everything, he couldn't tell me without involving *her*?

"*Honest*, Leonore? Is your name even Leonore?"

I flipped up my shirt and thrusted the rolled-up documents into his hands. "Here. I played my part. This is what you want from me."

They knew where to find me, and they could be the ones to decide how this would end.

Chapter Forty

I tried to act as if nothing had changed. With my apron over my smart clothes, I attended to the full tables. My bizarre mood and automaton-like manner kept Raúl from prying. When the rag I was using to mop up a spill snagged on Sebastián's ring, I rotated the stone inward and tried to ignore it. Despite the situation, I didn't want to be responsible for destroying his heirloom. No doubt Sebastián and Novia would arrive, eventually.

Cleaning the kitchen with Carmen in companionable silence helped calm my nervous anticipation. I expected each person who opened the door to the café to be Sebastián.

As the hours ticked by, my impatience surged. I couldn't even say goodbye to Raúl and Carmen. They stood near Raúl's coffee counter, confused by my behavior yet giving me space. I fought the sense of despair that threatened to knock me to my knees when I closed the café door behind me for the last time.

Back at the boardinghouse, my valise was packed and open at my feet. Should I leave or wait? Perhaps the papers *were* all Sebastián and Novia wanted from me. A crinkling from my skirt pocket reminded me I had the map of the Generalife. I unfolded the paper, holding it near the candle until every mark was visible. Smudged beneath Pelayo's name was a set of numbers that appeared to be a date and time.

It was the date of the reception. What did it mean? Why was this with those plans?

I glared at my valise. I was strongly tempted to flee, but I was so close to finding the murderer. If I left, I might never find the truth. But now that Sebastián knew I wasn't who I claimed to be, it was unlikely he would cooperate. If the socialist group had murdered Pelayo, they could turn violent. Was remaining here reckless?

And I had been seen by Suárez. He would put pressure on Antonio for answers.

Shoving the map deep into my pocket, I lay on the bed. I would wait. Tomorrow would arrive soon enough, and then I could make a decision.

My exhaustion must have been more acute than I realized. I didn't recall falling asleep. I also didn't remember my bed in the boardinghouse being this hard. Or this cold.

Without opening my eyes, I stretched my toe to snag the thin sheet at the bottom of my mattress. Instead of encountering a wad of blankets, searing pain sliced my thigh.

My eyes snapped open . . . to absolute darkness.

I blinked frantically, but nothing changed. No light was visible. Just deep, unrelenting blackness.

Other disconcerting sensations emerged as my lethargy diminished. My hands were immobilized in front of my body. My heart was hammering in triple speed, mirroring the throbbing coming from my temples. There was a rawness in my throat that no amount of swallowing soothed.

Calm, Linnea, calm. I tried to ignore the thundering of my pulse, counting off breaths. The air shifted as my eyes grew accustomed to the dark. The shadows undulated in strange ways.

Had I been drugged?

Despite my deep breaths, prickles of sweat dotted my nape. I clenched my fists as a wave of nausea flickered across my consciousness. I resisted the urge to cry. When I tried to raise my hands to wipe my face, another rush of pain halted the motion.

Give up. Give up. Curl up in a ball and go back to sleep.

With everything in me, I resisted the urge to follow those commands.

Find something to focus on.

Where was I? I wiggled my fingers along the surface. The floor was coarse, very fine dirt. What did I smell? Perspiration from my panic. A slight smell of mildew. I could hear the distant drip of water.

My awareness swam, overlapping this moment with being trapped in the caves of Chiloé.

I turned my face to touch my tongue to the ground. Somewhere in my mind, I thought, *What the hell are you doing, licking the floor?*

Not surprisingly, it tasted of dust and ancient rock. I rolled on my hip to bring my knees up. Another point of pain, but I came to a balance, swaying. The surrounding space shimmered and billowed. This was not normal. Whatever they had given me, it hadn't worn off. I couldn't seem to make my mind function.

For a moment, reality slipped. Interlacing my fingers, desperate for some form of contact, I encountered something unfamiliar. I caressed the metal with the opposite thumb. A ring? Sebastián's ring.

But thieves would've taken a ring.

Clarity broke through the fog. My knife—I had my knife. Contorting sideways, I inched my fingers down my leg until I reached my boot. Since my assault in Chile, I always had my knife.

The sheath was empty. Whoever captured me had left the ring but taken my weapon. They'd known I had it.

I was defenseless and drugged. The stale air scoured the inside of my nostrils. Was this my fate? To be buried alive? Where was I?

I focused on the distant sound of water, trying to restrain my erratic mind. Could I be in the Alhambra? I recalled dungeons on the maps, oubliettes that prisoners could not escape. They had been lowered on ropes from the ceiling and left at the mercy of their captors.

My terrified gasps reverberated off the stone walls. My lungs burning, my consciousness wavered again. If I didn't slow my breathing, I was going to faint.

Straightening my legs, I lost my balance and fell backward. My sore shoulder knocked into a wall. I rested against it, enervated and dejected. A sheen of sweat coated my face. What was the point? I slumped, emptied of the will to fight. If I was in the dungeon, no one would find me.

Hot rivulets of tears dripped from my face to my hands. This was what my foolhardy actions had wrought. If I was here, what might my attackers do to Matias, Hugh, and Antonio? Wasn't this what both Hugh and Matias had warned me of? I wasn't an investigator. Too many risks. For what purpose?

I didn't have a drop of religiosity in me, yet I prayed for unconscious-ness. And some benevolent deity—or drug—responded to my call.

Low sunlight turned the filaments of grass into a sea of golden irides-cence. My senses flooded with the scents of sea lavender, ocean breezes, and him.

Matias's chest rested beneath my cheek. The linen was rough, but through it was the comforting heat of his skin. His fingers worked through the knots of my hair, massaging at my scalp, lifting and spreading the strands. I came to my elbows. His face was radiant with the last beams of daylight. I traced the shape of his lips, the line of his jaw. When I kissed him, it was a vow. My body hummed with it. I was his; he was mine. That was all that mattered.

Night fell suddenly, the sun shuttered in an instant. I was alone in the grass. Above me hung the Pleiades, not another star in the sky. No moon. No Matias. The wind gathered speed, and the grass flattened to a carpet. Another gust. A crash of waves.

Awareness returned with the bite of a rope into my wrist. A lick of air dried the tracks of tears on my face. Someone was coming.

Halting footsteps approached. Two voices raised in argument. Two men. I feigned unconsciousness as they drew near. I could smell them. They bore the scents of cigarillos, bergamot, and bay rum.

"She should be awake. How much laudanum did you give her?"

I froze, suffocating on the overwhelming smell of cologne. My brain was slow to translate their Spanish. Laudanum? Rough linen was tied over my eyes. Smooth fingers probed the side of my neck.

With every bit of will I possessed, I waited until they moved away be-fore swallowing.

"Her pulse is strong. She's fine. Are you going to do it, or do I have to?"

Acrid cigarillo smoke wafted in my face. A cruel grip on my chin forced my mouth open. Metal pressed against my lips, and the cool fragrance of mint stung my sinuses. My thirst was so acute that my throat immediately contracted when the first trickle of liquid flooded my mouth. Sweet mint tea laced with bitter laudanum.

Alarmed, I gasped. The man took advantage, dumping the tea down my throat. It overflowed, trickling over my cheeks and into my collar.

"Why?" I implored, collapsing from the wall to the dirt floor.

No one answered. Their steps echoed as I plummeted into the abyss.

Chapter Forty-One

"How did you find her?"

"Pilar told me where she was."

"We thought Pilar was dead."

"Ah, she isn't dead." The speaker sighed. "It's a long story."

"And Pilar knew to bring her to this house?"

"Sí."

"If she doesn't wake soon, I'll send for the doctor again. The laudanum should've worn off."

"Are you her hermano, señor?"

The other man snorted. "Ah, no. Not her brother."

His laugh sparked a surge of adoration through my body. Mental images flashed on top of each other: an island, a ship, his face. It was Matias.

An involuntary whimper of confusion and pain escaped.

Matias's hand brushed my forehead. "Linnea? Are you awake?"

"Linnea? Her name is Leonore."

Oh no. I recognized that voice as well. Was this another bad dream? Maybe if I went back to sleep, this wouldn't be happening.

"I know you're awake. Please open your eyes." His voice was tight and brittle. Matias was troubled.

My lids were reluctant, heavy and sticky. One opened, then the other. Blinding sunlight seared my retinas. My vision struggled to adjust. When it did, I wished for unconsciousness.

Matias sat on the bed to my right. He was canted toward me with a stormy expression. Sebastián was on my left—near the bed, but not on it. He was ready to bolt for the exit. Great. All this scene needed was—

"Is she awake?" Hugh sprung like a jack-in-the-box from behind Matias's shoulder.

I groaned, burying my face in my hands.

"Are you going to cast up your accounts? Should I fetch the chamber pot?" A hand rested on the back of my head; I was certain it was Matias.

"She needs some space. Hugh, can you ask the kitchen to prepare a bowl of broth?" he ordered.

"I can. Señor?" Hugh addressed Sebastián.

Matias and Sebastián replied together, "He stays."

"I'll stay."

When the door closed, I inched my fingers away. Coming to my elbows took a Herculean effort. I propped myself up, willing the room to cease spinning. Matias handed me a glass of water. The taste was ambrosial. I gulped it.

"Don't drink too fast, or I'll have to fetch that chamber pot."

My stomach concurred with an unhappy gurgle. I propped the glass on my covered abdomen, taking in the scene. Matias and Sebastián in one room felt like the remnants of my intoxicated nightmare.

Physically, they were different, yet they shared a similar essence. Probably why I found them both attractive. That brought back the horror of the situation. I tentatively rubbed my temples. My brain was disordered.

My voice croaked when I spoke. "How did I get here? I was . . ." My vision flickered with black spots. A dungeon, or a cave? Or was that a dream?

Once again, Matias's hand on my body grounded me. Gesturing to Sebastián, Matias replied, "He brought you here, said you were in a dungeon below the Alhambra. But he hasn't introduced himself. Presumably, you know who he is."

I sipped from my water before responding, "Sebastián de los Rios, this is Matias Ward."

"Ward? You said you weren't her brother." Sebastián blanched. "You aren't her marido?"

Matias frowned in confusion. "No, I'm not her brother or husband. Linnea, what happened? Who did this?"

For a moment, my concentration scattered. A dungeon, he had said. Not an oubliette? So, it hadn't been a nightmare—or it had been, but not one created by my subconscious.

"I don't know," I mumbled. "There were two men. I didn't recognize their voices. I was bound. Blindfolded. Laudanum in the tea." Mint tea, bay rum, and the acrid taste of the laudanum coated my tongue. In my rush to wash it away, I spilled water down the collar of my nightgown, which brought back the memory of the tea. And my captors. My whole body shook in terror.

"Dammit," Matias said as he pried the glass from my death grip. His voice gentled. "No more questions. You aren't well. And he doesn't even know who you are."

I blinked up at Matias. Who was I? Was this real?

"Linnea Wren, Sebastián. That's my real name," I choked on the words.

Sebastián grew paler, clenching his hands into fists. "That man at the Chancery—he called you Lady. Are you a Lady?"

The Chancery? Ah, yes, Suárez. "I am, but I don't use it. I didn't grow up in the aristocracy. Sebastián, how did you find me?" My voice was gathering strength, but my body still trembled.

"Pilar came to me and asked for my assistance."

"Pilar!" I shot upright. A bad idea. My sharp inhale of breath triggered a deep cough. The dust from the dungeon remained in my lungs. Matias refilled the glass of water.

When I took it from him, he noticed the ring. He set down the pitcher with a clatter. "What is *that*?"

"Oh, right. Er—" I yanked it off, offering the ring, palm out, to Sebastián. He fixed me with his corvid-like perception, baffling as ever as he shook his head from side to side. Refusing to take it.

Matias's face was thunderous. Beneath that was devastation.

I rushed in, eager for him to understand. "We pretended to be a married couple to steal the plans. I can explain. But first, who attacked me? Where has Pilar been?"

I swayed, and Matias steadied me by gripping my elbow. "I don't think we should discuss this right now. You need time to heal."

Everything was gray and fuzzy at the edges. "My mind is . . . cloudy, but I need to know . . ."

Sebastián's voice pierced the fog. "I should return to my store."

I couldn't let him leave until I understood how the pieces fit. I tried to move from the bed, but my body refused. "Stay? Please? There are things to discuss. I need your help." Even in my altered state, I knew that if Sebastián left, he wouldn't return.

He glanced between us. "But my store—"

"Stay until she's coherent. We have plenty of bedchambers." Matias's suggestion was magnanimous, but his tone was not.

"Very well. I'll stay, but not for long."

"Thank you," I sighed. His acquiescence was a relief.

I went slack against the pillows. Matias moved away from the bed to escort him but stopped to kiss my forehead as he passed.

Sebastián marked the gesture, again shaking his head as he closed the door behind him. I set the ring on the side table for safekeeping. Matias glared at it, then came around the bed to toss back the covers.

He gathered me against him. My face went to the space beneath his jaw. A place on his body formed just for me.

"I was so frightened," I whispered against the skin of his neck. Saying it was hard, yet necessary. I hadn't ever admitted weakness to anyone. Tears clogged my throat. "I don't understand . . ."

"Rest now." His voice rumbled beneath my ear. "You're safe." His arms were tight bands around my shoulders. Unconsciousness beckoned, tendrils unfurling, caressing.

My voice came from outside my body. "I was so close to the answers, and then everything fell apart."

"That's an understatement. You returned home unconscious from enough opium to fell an elephant. I've never been so scared."

Cool fingers rested against my feverish skin, reminiscent of the man in the cave. Adrenaline spiked through my body.

"Your pulse is erratic. Dammit, Linnea. The doctor said there was a chance you may not wake up. They nearly killed you."

I whispered, "Who? Who nearly killed me? Pilar—"

Dreams didn't arrive to confront me on the other side. Stretched in my unconscious was a barren plain of shadows.

Chapter Forty-Two

When I woke, I knew where I was. I lay with my eyes on the ceiling, ordering the facts—or what we knew of the facts. Someone had imprisoned and drugged me. Pilar was alive and had assisted with my rescue. Sebastián was inside Antonio's house.

"How are you?"

It wasn't the voice I was expecting or wanted. Sebastián was splayed in a nearby chair. Unsure of where to start, I didn't try.

Lavender smudges ringed his eyes. His inky hair was disheveled, his cuffs stained, and several days' worth of stubble shadowed his jaw. He'd stayed as I requested. If he was guilty of conspiring with my captors, he wouldn't have, would he?

"Where's Pilar?"

He jerked in the chair. That wasn't where he thought I would begin. He rested his elbows on his thighs. "She—she's safe."

I struggled to sitting. Proceeding directly into a confrontation with him probably wasn't the best tactic, but it might be the only way to get some answers.

"Did you know all along?" I accused.

He frowned. "Did I know what?"

"Who I was? That I was looking for Pilar?"

"No, no, of course I didn't know."

I couldn't decide if I believed him.

"What were you doing? Why so many lies?" His tone was defensive.

"Trying to find Pelayo's murderer. Then Pilar was killed, and she was my friend. I wanted to find the culprit before anyone else died."

He rocked in the chair. "Who *are* you? This house, those men—*Lord* Martin and Mr. Ward. *Ward*?"

"She has no obligation to tell you anything." Matias approached my bedside with a tray.

Sebastián sprang out of the chair and retreated across the room. I rested my heavy head against the bed, turning toward Matias. He offered me a steaming cup. As I reached for it, I searched his face and body language, but he gave nothing away.

"Thank you, Matias, but Sebastián should receive an explanation, as long as he's willing to do likewise."

The cup contained hot, sweet tea. I wrinkled my nose. Not what I was expecting.

"Hugh thought it might be better than something too enlivening," Matias said, placing the tray on the bedside table. "Just try it."

To placate him, I sipped it. I didn't mind black tea, but sweetened was not my preference. It was as awful as expected. The cloying taste was an unpleasant reminder of the drugged tea.

"Right. Answers," I said, abandoning the cup.

Matias sighed, taking the chair beside the bed. Sebastián moved one from my writing desk closer. I waved at him. "He needs to know who I am first, so I'll begin there."

Their twin expressions of annoyance would've been humorous if not directed at me.

"My name is Linnea Wren, and I'm English, as I told you. I'm also a botanist who has traveled the world. I have been employed by several botanical gardens in England. Matias was a naturalist on my last expedition to South America. We came from Cádiz to Granada, and shortly after I arrived, I was offered a temporary job to assist with the restoration of the Alhambra."

Sebastián's eyes widened. "Pilar told me about you. I didn't know it was *you*. You've published articles, books—"

"You knew Pilar was my assistant?"

"She told me about the woman she worked with at the Alhambra. Novia suspected you were allied with the aristócratos, but Pilar thought not."

So, Pilar was a spy. Was everyone I met since arriving in Granada lying to me? What about Izabelle? Had she lied as well?

I felt a rush of anger, chagrin following quickly on its heels. I had lied to them too.

Matias spoke up, halting my descent into self-pity. "Linnea?" He was poised to stop this at the slightest hint of discomfort. I wanted to get it over with.

Taking a bracing inhale, I pushed on. "When Pelayo was murdered, I was asked to assist with the investigation. I was attempting to find the murderer while working in the garden. And then Pilar was attacked around the same time I discovered your meetings in the orchard. I came to your neighborhood to ascertain if your group was responsible for the murders."

"You found a job at the café, and—"

"—met you and the others. By chance, Sebastián, not by design." His cryptic countenance was as immovable as a marble statue. I slanted my eyes to Matias. He wasn't any less opaque. "What was your role in all of this, Sebastián?"

He avoided making eye contact as he moved toward the balcony. "Novia and Pilar know more than I do. All I did was give Pilar a place to stay." He was lying. "I can't be gone from my store any longer."

I tried to intercept him but pitched from the mattress toward the ground. He reached me before Matias could. I took advantage, gripping his forearms.

"Who attacked me?" I demanded, digging my fingers into his muscles.

"Pilar burst into the bookstore and asked for my assistance. I went with her to the Alhambra. You were in a dungeon beneath a gallery. We carried you out and brought you to the house. That's all I know."

I released him, slumping onto the bed. "Did Pilar recognize who took me?"

"Maybe. I'm not sure. Look, I need to go. I'll ask them to come and speak with you."

"Tomorrow?" I said, not having any idea what day it was. I scooped up his ring from the bedside table. "Don't forget this."

He held it in two fingers. For one second, he showed his wistful regret before turning away. "Until tomorrow."

"Thank you for rescuing me." My gratitude was the least of what I owed him. And it was sincere. I didn't believe I would ever escape that dungeon.

"It was Pilar. She's the one who deserves your thanks."

As the door closed behind him, Matias scoffed, "He knows more than he's saying."

I needed to move. Matias was there in an instant to lend me his arm when I wobbled to my feet.

We lurched toward the balcony. He lowered me to the cushioned bench but remained standing. The air was crisp and scented with citrus. The acidic fragrance cleansed the sticky shame that clung to me.

Matias rested against the railing. His physical distance felt meaningful. "Will you tell me what happened?" he prodded gently.

I clasped my knees to my chest and wrapped my arms around them. My memory was jagged, so I closed my eyes, which wasn't a good idea. Immediately, a rush of panic descended. Gooseflesh broke out on my arms, followed by a cold sweat.

You're safe. I exhaled.

"Last I recall, I was in my bed at the boardinghouse. Earlier in the day, Sebastián and I went to the Royal Chancery of Granada to steal some documents. Suárez saw us as we were leaving. I think he recognized me. After my shift at the café, I returned to my lodgings. I was debating whether to stay or return."

The cushion dipped beside me. His body remained tense, though. I cupped my palms over my eyes, taking a few slow, deep breaths.

"We don't have to do this now."

"Just a moment." I exhaled. "It was dark. At first, I thought I was dreaming of the cave in Chiloé. But my hands were bound, and I was . . . befuddled. They took my knife. I couldn't think. Between the panic and the drugs . . . I thought I was going to die."

The last word emerged on a whimper. Matias hugged me to his side. It was the reassurance I needed to finish.

"Two men arrived. One of them gave me tea with laudanum. That was the last I remember."

"You couldn't see them?"

"No, there was no light at first. And then I was blindfolded. One of them smelled like cigarillos, the other one smelled like cologne—bay rum and bergamot."

He tightened his grip around my waist. "Who do you think it was?"

I waited for my pulse to return to normal before replying, "I'm not certain. Sebastián knew I was not who I had claimed to be, but Suárez also saw me. Bay rum is a common cologne. I don't remember Suárez wearing it, nor have I seen him smoking cigarillos. But that means nothing. He could have hired someone."

"Who is Novia?"

I fiddled with the end of my braid. "Novia Torres is Pilar's cousin. She's the woman we saw confront Pilar at the plaza, and who I saw speaking at Plaza Larga. And the leader of their group."

My eyes drifted closed, lulled by the soft wind wafting over the balcony.

Matias shifted away from my side. I opened my eyes to watch him retreat to the railing, withdrawing into himself. "And why were you wearing his ring?"

I shivered at the suddenness of his detachment.

"We were sent to steal some documents. Posing as a newly married couple gave us a reason to be in the building."

Matias bit his lip, not looking at me. "It sounds as if your experience was . . . complex."

My focus was slipping again. The aftereffects of the laudanum were lingering.

"I missed you. How are you? How were your last several weeks?" Desperate to connect with him despite the exhaustion threatening to pull me under, I reached for his hand. He did not step forward to take it.

"You need more rest. The doctor said it might be several days until you feel normal. Whoever drugged you came very close to administering a lethal dose. Shall I help you to the bed?"

He wasn't going to tolerate my efforts to distract him. So be it.

"I'll stay, thank you."

Pausing with one hand on the stone wall, he leveled a final observation. "El señor de los Rios is acting like a jilted lover, not an acquaintance."

Heat scalded my cheeks. "He's not my lover. It wasn't my idea for us to masquerade as a married couple. The ring was a part of our disguise."

Matias's hands fisted at his side. "That was all that happened? Pretending?"

Lying to Matias wasn't feasible. I was too transparent, and I simply wouldn't do that to him—even though what I said next might cause a fatal blow to our relationship.

"He kissed me."

He tapped his fist on the doorframe. "Did he force you?" His voice was finely honed steel.

I flinched. "No, no, he didn't force me. I justified my participation as vital to the investigation."

I was loathsome. If our roles were reversed, I would be devastated.

"There's one person who holds my heart. You are the only one I want."

Whatever I expected in response to my confession, it wasn't silence.

"Matias?"

"I need space, Linnea."

A sudden gust of wind swept across the balcony. Dried leaves skittered across the tiles, dancing in the air. Strands of hair blew across Matias's face, splitting his countenance into fragments and obscuring his emotions. My heart clenched, missing a beat, and it wasn't from the laudanum.

Chapter Forty-Three

Our bedchamber echoed with Matias's absence, so I eschewed it for the balcony.

In a state of half consciousness, I watched the action on the streets below, parsing my emotions. Matias was furious, hurt. And I had to balance determining who was trying to kill me with mending what I'd ruined between Matias and me. At the moment, I didn't have the energy to do any of it.

Hugh brought a dining tray out to the balcony and took a seat on the bench. "How are you?"

Tears leaked from my eyes. I brushed them away with the back of my hand. "I wanted to be of service. But even that desire was selfish, and now I'm paying the price."

Hugh drew me into his arms, pressing his lips to my temple. "You've worked yourself into a state, my love."

"What if I can't fix it? What if he doesn't want me anymore?"

"Matias kept vigil over you the last few days. A Cerberus at the door who prevented anyone from entering, including me. He's scared. We were scared. We almost lost you."

Hugh held me through the tempest of sobs unlocked by his words. I'd thought I was going to die without seeing Matias or Hugh again, and it was made worse by regrets over my behavior with Sebastián. I kept acting in ways that I was ashamed of, charging headlong into situations without thinking through the ramifications. It was antithetical to the logic that had ruled my life up to this point.

He rocked me gently to the city sounds and the gusts of mountain air. Hiccups of breath signaled the cessation of my outburst. Hugh released me to produce a handkerchief from his pocket. I used the linen to tidy the damage.

"Better?" he asked.

"I'm sorry. I don't know what came over me."

"You've had a scare. You've always been stubborn about shouldering your burdens alone. This time, it was almost a fatal mistake."

I thought about my close brush in Chiloé. "Well, maybe not just this time."

He tried for a mock stern expression, but failed when he noted the tremor in my lip. "It's time, my girl. Time to let us in."

I blotted at my cheeks and nodded slowly.

"Now come. You need rest. Your dinner is cold. Let's get you settled, and I'll fetch a fresh tray."

I obeyed, following him into the bedchamber and allowing him to fuss over my comfort. After returning from the kitchen, he stayed, entertaining me with a story about a rich baroness and her lost terrier. I managed a piece of toast and an egg before my eyelids grew heavy.

Hugh kissed my forehead and tucked the coverlet under my chin. I was asleep before he reached the door.

A dip in the mattress woke me. The room was lit by a single taper on my side of the bed. It was a fresh candle, as if someone knew that if I woke in the night, I would need it.

"Matias?"

His hand landed on my hip. "I didn't mean to wake you."

"I'm glad you did," I replied. I traced his eyebrows with my thumbs and brushed the tips of his lashes. Pinpricks of candlelight were reflected in the depths of his irises.

His mouth found mine, his kiss demanding. I bit his lower lip lightly. He coasted his hands along the sides of my breasts, over my hips. "We shouldn't—are you feeling well?"

"I need you, Matias. I need this."

My kiss was a desperate question, and he answered with passion. I explored his mouth. Familiar, yet also novel. After weeks apart, it felt like a rediscovery of what burned between us.

His hands pushed my nightgown from my shoulders. He brushed his mouth along the underside of my breast. My cry of pleasure as he engulfed my nipple in the scalding warmth of his mouth turned him frantic. His drawers were quickly dispatched to the far reaches of the bed.

Matias mapped my body with his hands, stroking down my ribs, circling my waist, and cupping my breasts. I wrapped my arms around his broad shoulders, wanting him closer, every bit of our skin touching, but he pinned my wrists.

I went slack when he rolled me onto my stomach. The hot bar of his arousal pressed into the small of my back.

I wanted to connect, to see his eyes so I could glimpse what was in his soul. But Matias wasn't going to allow for a slow savoring.

Exerting a slight pressure on my hips, he lifted them higher, slipping a pillow beneath me. The callouses on his fingertips swirling on my clitoris emptied my mind.

I submitted, giving over to him. To the sensations. To whatever he wanted.

Matias's exploration was tender yet urgent. I moaned into the mattress, imprisoned by pleasure.

Pinned in a submissive position, I couldn't reach him or draw his response. He kept me there for what felt like eternity, ascending the cliffs of arousal and drawing away from the edge when I was about to plummet. My worries about us drifted away. Pain—gone. Sensation scrubbed the slate of my mind clean.

His gruff voice vibrated against my ear. "Touch yourself," he ordered, guiding one my trapped hands between my legs.

I balanced on an elbow, reaching between the mattress and my body. My first two fingers were exploring the wetness he'd created when he filled me.

"God, that feels—" He didn't let me finish thrusting further inside. I craved his force. His loss of control.

"Keep touching us," he commanded.

Grazing the base of his cock where I was stretched around him, I circled my fingers, squeezing. He snarled, restraint shattering. His thrusts were frenzied, his grip on my hips bruising as he hit a place within me so deep, I shied away. Ripples of my orgasm were building. It wasn't going to take long.

"Matias," I croaked, meaning to warn him.

"Now. Come now," he compelled.

And I obeyed, detonating, contracting around him. He followed me with an animalistic growl.

We both dropped to our backs, panting. Viscous sexual satiation flooded my limbs. I couldn't have moved even if the room was on fire.

My gaze wandered along the length of his arm to his curled hand on the sheet. I pushed it open, caressing his palm in concentric circles. His chest expanded and contracted. I could tell by the rhythm that he wasn't asleep either. Would I shatter the peace of this moment to press him for conversation?

I was rousing my fortitude to do so when he spoke. "Can we please not have any discussion tonight? Can we be in this moment?"

While our joining had been pleasurable, it hadn't returned us to a place of intimacy. And it seemed I wasn't alone in feeling that distance. "If you wish."

A bubble of emotion lodged beneath my breastbone. We weren't all right. He was slipping away.

I was awake when the first drops hit the windows. Thunder rumbled in the distance. I shifted from beneath the covers, moving soundlessly over the floor and down the stairs.

The wide leaves of the rhododendrons were slick with rain. Another roll of thunder shook the paving stones under my bare feet. The storm was picking up momentum.

I ran to a small patch of grass at the center of the garden. My toes curled into the wet blades as the clouds unleashed. Scents trapped for weeks in desiccated vegetation burst forth. The air was redolent with thyme, cypress, myrtle, stone, minerals, steel. I sank to my knees.

My dressing gown plastered to my skin, my face wet with a combination of rain and tears. A fork of lightning split the sky. For a brief second, I could see the Alhambra between the buildings, backlit and wrathful atop its throne. Thunder followed on its heels.

I instinctively clenched my fingers into the sod when the intensity of sound seemed to cleave the earth. The drought had broken. The deluge had arrived.

Chapter Forty-Four

Matias waited for me at the top of the staircase. I hadn't returned to our bed the previous night. Soaked through, I had dried the best I could and slept in the library.

He was obviously assessing my stability as I walked toward him. I sailed past, intent on proving I was well. Halfway down, a loud knock vibrated the door.

I glanced around the foyer for Severiano, but the hall was empty. When I pulled open the door, the trio on the step froze in place: Novia mid-sentence, Pilar with a fist poised to knock again, and Sebastián staring straight ahead, expression carefully blank.

At the sight of Pilar, I was flooded with relief, followed by bitter betrayal. She flushed, grimacing at the ground.

"*Buenos días.* Please enter." My voice betrayed my internal apprehension.

Novia marched past me, nose in the air. Pilar and Sebastián scuttled behind her. Matias led the way into the library. A tray of refreshments dominated the large center table with coffee, tea, and biscuits. The sweet smell of rain lingered in the room despite the closed doors. Novia and Pilar sat together on the brocade settee, Sebastián in a chair. Matias and I occupied the seats opposite.

Summoning my minimal fortitude, I projected calm congeniality instead of demanding answers.

"May I serve anyone a cup?" I gestured to the tray. All three declined, so Matias and I didn't partake either. "I'm hoping we can have a discussion that is mutually beneficial—"

Novia snorted. "Help? What help can you possibly give *us*?"

"Despite what you believe, I wasn't working against you. I was trying to find Pelayo's murderer, and who I thought was Pilar's killer as well."

"You were spying on us!" Novia shouted.

I gestured at Pilar and snapped, "So were you!"

Pilar placed her hand on Novia's arm. "Prima, please let her speak."

Everyone settled, readjusting in their seats. I gripped the curved armrest of my chair. "One of you should begin. This story predates my arrival in Granada."

Matias paced away, unfastening the door to the garden. The rain-scented air dispelled the fraught mood of the room.

Novia sat forward on the settee. "How did you come to be in Granada, señora? Or is it Lady?" she sneered.

"I'll answer your questions, but I think I deserve an explanation first, since I'm the one who was attacked. Twice. And you can call me Linnea."

Pilar nudged Novia. She gave a curt nod. "Interest and momentum in our cause have been building for the past six months. More people were attending our meetings. Printings of our pamphlets were selling out. But to make substantial change, we needed powerful people involved. Alonso and I met by chance at a literary gathering. He attended, expecting a party. I was there as a representative of the printing press. His interest in our cause was genuine, though. As an entitled son of an aristocratic family, he was the last person I expected to join us. People thought he was frivolous, but he wasn't. Alonso pressured acquaintances in the prime minister's office to intervene and halt the evictions. At a reception at his cousin's house, he learned about the proposed development in our neighborhood. We assume that, through his actions, he drew the attention of the wrong people."

Novia seemed unusually subdued. She'd also referred to Pelayo by his first name. Had they shared more than camaraderie?

She averted her face from us. "Alonso said he was being followed. He received threatening letters ordering him to cease putting pressure on officials. They made him more determined. He attended the reception at the Alhambra because whoever he suspected of intimidating him was also invited. You're aware of how that ended."

"To have killed a member of the royal family, they must've believed they would get away with it," Matias contributed from across the room.

"Of course they did! To guarantee their part wouldn't be revealed, they plotted to accuse *us* of his murder. She was already in Granada before he was killed," Novia said, pointing at me. "Someone intended to frame us. We were told you were investigating and had to act before they set up any other traps. Pilar has always been interested in plants. It was simple to arrange for her to pose as your assistant. The Alhambra management assumed you'd hired her."

If my meeting with la señora Sánchez-Martín was deliberate, who was responsible? If Novia suspected me, why remove Pilar from the Alhambra?

"Why did you fake Pilar's murder?" I asked.

During our conversation, Pilar had relaxed. She allowed Novia to explain without contributing.

"I also received hostile letters. They knew Pilar was my cousin, and that she was working at the Alhambra. She would be their next victim if we didn't stop. We decided to kill her ourselves. That way, the author of our letters might believe that we had turned on her, and you would believe it was your fault. Either way, it bought us an advantage—enough time to steal the plans so that we would have leverage. We didn't plan on you finding her 'body,' though."

I recoiled from the visceral memory. The blood. The clothing. My utter despair.

"Where did the body come from?" Matias asked while I attempted to rip myself from my recollections.

Pilar finally spoke. "We created un . . . espantapájaros, I don't know how to say it in English. We dressed it in my clothing."

I struggled to translate the word. Oh. She meant a scarecrow—a dummy.

I swallowed again, pushing past the rising nausea. "And the blood?"

"Pig's blood. From the butcher," Novia replied.

Staring at the bookshelves, I catalogued their organization, attempting to clear my mind of the raw images. "And who attacked me? Was it so I wouldn't foil your deception?"

"We didn't attack you," Pilar said with vehemence. "We don't know who did."

No one could've predicted that Matias and I would visit the garden that night. I supposed it could've been a coincidence.

"Who did you expect to find the body?" I addressed this question to Novia.

"It didn't matter, as long as they alerted Suárez. He must be involved, but we haven't determined how. We've been following him for months. Whoever it is, they have ties to the highest people. We thought maybe it was you, but you vanished after Pilar was—"

"It wasn't me."

"What about el señor Navarro?" Novia suggested.

Matias and I conducted a wordless exchange. What if it *was* Antonio?

I felt ill at the possibility. Antonio had been aware of almost every aspect of the investigation, including where I stayed in the Albaicín. I pinched the skin on the bridge of my nose. If I was unknowingly in league with our villain, I wouldn't admit it in front of Novia.

Matias saved me from answering. "Let's leave the question of Antonio aside. What happened after Pilar disappeared?"

"The letters continued to arrive. But they now claimed that we would be convicted of Pelayo's murder, and to prepare ourselves. But we won't surrender without a fight. I thought once we had the plans, we would have something to bargain with, but the letters have stopped. And when we discovered who you were . . ."

Pilar picked up the thread. "We panicked. We couldn't take the chance of you recognizing me or getting any closer to Sebastián. When he returned from the Chancery and told me the name Suárez called out, I feared for our safety."

"You didn't know who I was until that day?" I asked Sebastián.

He shook his head.

Novia replied, "No, we didn't know who you were. Only Pilar would've recognized you."

I turned from Novia. "Sebastián, you've been quiet. What was your role?"

"Pilar stayed at my family's house. I live above the bookstore, as you know, but I haven't sold the house. I took supplies to her. Novia and Pilar told me about the threats, but we were keeping it from the other people in the group."

Pilar lurched forward, grabbing my hand. "When Sebastián told me what happened, I knew we needed to speak. I went to your lodgings, but in the alley, I saw two men put you into a closed carriage. They were delayed turning into the street, and I hired a hackney to follow. When they arrived at the Alhambra, they were met by another man with a wheelbarrow. You were unconscious." Her grip tightened as she spoke, her voice distraught.

"She returned to the shop to fetch me," Sebastián said. "We hid and waited for the men to leave. In the dark, we weren't able to see their faces. The place they put you in was down a very steep staircase. Fortunately, Pilar knew the dungeon could be accessed via a shorter set of stairs with an exit to the outside walls. We were able to carry you that far."

I reached for the urn to pour myself a cup of coffee. The container sloshed in my unsteady hand. I spoke rapidly, hoping no one noticed my state. "So, you suspect that whoever murdered Pelayo has ties to the government. Someone who thinks they can convince those with power that you killed Pelayo. And now Suárez thinks he saw me at the Chancery, where they've no doubt discovered the missing plans. Bloody hell."

We sat in silence, absorbing the magnitude of the situation.

Inside, I was a swirling mass of confusion. Was anything that had happened since I'd arrived in Spain as it appeared? It felt like being pitched overboard off a ship. Up was down, down was up, and all was chaos. Nothing was solid. I hadn't been chosen to work at the Alhambra because of my reputation. And Izabelle? Was our meeting genuine, or was she in on it as well?

My relationship with Pilar was a facade. Antonio might have been lying to me, and to Hugh. And then there was my desolation over the fracture between Matias and me.

My cup rattled in the saucer as I abandoned it to pick up my notebook. I could wallow later, when I didn't have an audience.

"First, it's clear I must return to the Alhambra immediately. The murderer must realize by now that I've escaped, but they don't know how much we know. We have to lure them out. Second, Novia and Pilar require protection. Is there somewhere outside of Granada you can go?"

Novia came to her feet. "We won't run away. This is our fight. Our city."

I stared up at her, pleading. "They attacked me. Either of you could be next. I can assist with your travel. And it won't be forever. Long enough to determine who is behind this and the source of the danger. What about France?"

Novia shook her head.

Pilar stood next to her, touching her back. "We should think about it. She's right. Leaving would keep us safe."

A sudden starburst of pain exploded behind my right eye. My notebook fell from my hands.

Matias knelt at my feet. "Are you well? What is it?"

"Just a headache, I think. Give me a moment."

He shot up to standing. "We don't even know who did this! You made her a target." Matias rounded on Novia. "She was dosed with a life-threatening amount of laudanum. The doctor wasn't certain she would regain consciousness. I'm sympathetic to what you are trying to do, but at what cost?"

"At any cost! I'm willing to sacrifice my life," Novia shouted.

Sebastián stepped between Novia and Matias. "That is your choice, Novia, but to ask or demand it from others is not the way. And arguing is not either. We must go. And I don't believe Leonore—Linnea is well enough for much more."

I wanted to protest, but he was right. I wasn't.

"Novia and Pilar, please decide soon if you want my help to leave the country. If this house is being watched, you've both been seen." I fumbled for the arm of the chair. The room was wavering. I choked my way through the last things I needed to say. "I'll send a message to

Sebastián with a suggested time to meet." Novia began to argue. "Yes, Novia, we're going to talk again. With luck, we'll know how to resolve the situation. I'll return to the Alhambra tomorrow as bait for our murderer."

Chapter Forty-Five

I left Matias to escort them from the house. Instead, I took refuge in the garden. A methodically shaped oak dominated one corner of the space. Its branches were dense enough to provide shelter from the drizzle. The fragrance of the plants, a companionable embrace, surrounded me. A nearby rosemary bush dominated the mélange, evoking my conversation with Hugh at Holloway House prior to our departure on the *Cormorant*. After much prodding, I had confided my insecurities about guiding an expedition, traveling to Chile, and completing my research.

Instead of emerging from that experience reinforced, I was shattered. Since coming ashore in Spain, my shortcomings had been confirmed, exploited. I'd been spinning, running, desperate to escape the unrecognizable person in my skin. I hated her. I didn't want to be her.

Pressure built in my head, reminiscent of a deep dive underwater. On instinct, I buckled, resting my head on my knees. Matias's voice filtered through my huddle.

"Do I need to carry you to the bedchamber?"

From my prone position, I mumbled, "I'm well." I wasn't, but how to explain the dissolution? *Woman drowning in self-pity?*

His boot prodded my toe. "Is it wise to return to the Alhambra tomorrow?"

Probably not, but I had this feverish need to see this to the end.

"Suárez has no doubt raised the alarm after he saw me. That he hasn't come to the house is suspicious. Maybe he's hoping for a confrontation, or maybe he'll feign ignorance. Either way, the next move is mine."

"Why was stealing the plans necessary? I don't understand what that was supposed to accomplish."

I raised my head, the garden whirling into focus. Matias was tossing an acorn in one hand, looming above me.

"They're planning to clear the neighborhood. People will be forced from their homes. Novia thought stealing the plans from the architect's office would give them a chance to stop it." He threw the acorn aside. I continued, "I also found a drawing of the Generalife with Pelayo's name on it. Given what we heard today, we can surmise why they were together."

"So, there's a connection between Pelayo and the house clearings." Matias rubbed a spot of moss on the stone walkway with his boot, absorbing this information. "What are you going to tell Hugh and Antonio?"

I rested my chin on my fist. "I need Antonio to get Pilar and Novia out of the country. If Pilar can persuade Novia. But I can't risk saying too much. Not yet."

His fingers caressed a branch, then snapped off a dead end. I flinched.

Matias grimaced at my reaction. My fragile composure was too obvious to him. "What do you need from me?"

How did I interpret his request? My first inclination was to ask for nothing, even though that was at the root of our estrangement. I couldn't solve the problem of what was happening to us, but I could concede this patch of ground.

"I need someone to guard my flank. Can you do that? Pose as an assistant? There are so many people in the garden, no one pays attention. Look at Pilar. If they were successful, we can improve upon it. You'll see things I'll not be able to. And I think, for now, we should avoid involving Antonio and Hugh."

"You're becoming quite the master—or is it mistress—of disguise, aren't you?" He didn't give me his answer immediately. He leaned against the trunk of the tree, his face betraying the swirl of his thoughts. "Yes, I'm willing."

I slumped at his resigned tone. He would help me, but we were delaying the inevitable—a more difficult discussion.

"I'm going to lie down. My headache has returned."

He remained beneath the tree after I departed. I held in my tears until I was behind the closed door of our chamber. And then I cried myself to sleep.

"—and that is how the play ended."

I interrupted their conversation when I entered. A ghoul manifesting at their pleasant party. The lingering effects of two massive doses of laudanum should've worn off by now, but that hadn't been communicated to my brain. My skin prickled, my mind hungered for oblivion, and reality was distorted. A phantom in body and mind.

Hugh offered me the decanter of whiskey. I declined. His glower darkened. "Are you well enough to leave your bed?"

"I'm well, Hugh."

Antonio and Matias sat near the fireplace. It was my first encounter with Antonio since I'd returned. I couldn't help but scrutinize his every expression.

"We're anxious to hear about the past fortnight." His concern seemed genuine.

Another side effect of the withdrawal was that I was as fractious as a dog with fleas.

"May we eat dinner first? They're ready for us." I set off toward the dining room, ignoring the murmurs in my wake.

I avoided Matias's concerned glances when he took the seat next to me. I tore into a roll with rabid enthusiasm. Perhaps evidence of my appetite would set them at ease.

Hugh was the first to break the atmosphere. "When you requested our absence today, I assume someone from the Albaicín visited?"

My hunk of bread lodged in my throat partway. Everyone stared while I willed it past my gullet.

"We met with several people I became acquainted with while waitressing. I owed them explanations for my ruse. Now that my identity is known, I won't be returning to the café or the neighborhood. Tomorrow, I'll return to the Alhambra."

Antonio responded, "Already? Is Suárez involved?"

I reached for my glass of water before answering, "I'm unsure of Suárez's role."

Spoons clanked, glasses chimed, and no one spoke. Another sip of the vegetable potage soothed my abraded throat, though Carmen's soups were better. Severiano, Antonio's footman, closed the door behind him after serving the next course.

While we sampled the roasted chicken, Hugh huffed. "Are you purposely withholding information?"

I returned the fork and knife to the edge of my plate. "We've reached a critical point. I want to focus on our next steps."

Hugh's eyebrows pinched, his thoughts plain. I could see him wondering why I'd been open with him yesterday but was being guarded today. Everyone returned to their meals.

I sawed off another bite of chicken. It was very good.

Antonio abandoned his food for another sip of wine. I regarded him discreetly while continuing to eat. We dressed informally to dine, so the flush that spread from his chest up his neck was visible in the open collar of his shirt.

"It's me, Hugh. She suspects I'm involved." His tone was harsh.

Activity at the table halted. My fork was halfway to my mouth. I couldn't decide whether to finish the bite or lower it.

Antonio had made that leap quickly. Was it because he was working with them, or because he wasn't?

"Why would she think such a thing? Antonio wouldn't harm you!" Hugh's voice rose along with his indignation.

I lowered my utensils, formulating the best way to diffuse his temper. "I'm not accusing Antonio. We've reached a precarious stage. I'm trying to be circumspect in how we proceed."

Hugh turned to Matias. "You approve? Won't she listen to you?"

Every muscle in my body tensed. I clutched the handle of my knife, the whorls of the design imprinting on my palm. Matias kicked my foot beneath the table. "This is her investigation. She knows what must be done."

My grip eased on the knife. His support meant everything. I whispered, "Thank you."

Mollified, Hugh poked at his chicken. Our conversation the night I broke down had repaired some of the distance between us, but my suspicion of the man he loved was straining those bonds. "Isn't this when you draw your allies close? To make sure you are protected?" he mused.

A full wineglass sat at the edge of my place setting. My hand itched to take it. I chose the water instead. It tasted of the terra-cotta pitcher, but at least it was cool.

Antonio's gaze was averted, fixated on cutting his meat into tiny pieces. Did I believe he was involved?

Matias cleared his throat. Too many seconds had passed since Hugh's query. "I'll ask for assistance if I believe it is necessary."

Antonio and I glowered at each other. His warm brown eyes had always seemed trustworthy. Now they were flat, guarded. We had armored ourselves.

A niggle of premonition crept up my spine. I hoped it was the right decision. If he wasn't involved, I was damaging another important relationship in my life. If he was, well, that might also destroy it.

Chapter Forty-Six

Under the door of the library, flickers of light danced. I slowly twisted the knob and opened the door. One of the large leather chairs faced the hearth. I came around the side.

Shadows from the candlelight hid Matias's face. He didn't acknowledge my arrival.

Drifting in front of him, I slid my feet over the bare tops of his feet. My cold soles kissed his warm skin. His head was resting on the back of the chair, tipped toward the ceiling. The collar of his shirt was unbuttoned, his neck and collarbone bare. When my hand slipped into the opening of the fabric, his throat undulated.

My voice emerged thready. "You never came to bed."

His eyelids fluttered. Why was he reluctant to open them? But he did. Flames danced in the mossy depths. His reserve reminded me of my moment with Antonio. One by one, they were shutting me out. Because of my actions.

"You weren't in bed this morning," Matias retorted.

"I couldn't sleep. I thought we would be together again tonight."

"Why? Nothing has changed. Was it because I defended you at dinner? I've always defended you, Linnea. You just haven't noticed."

His barb hit home.

"To have you understand me is a gift, one I haven't appreciated enough. I'm sorry." I tightened the knot in my dressing gown. "Have I ruined things between us, Matias?"

We had been honest with each other in the past. I was relying on his candor now. There was a glimmer of potential forgiveness. But how often would he extend that mercy?

A deep exhale deflated his entire being. "I don't know."

"Oh."

I stepped away, but he prevented me from fleeing by taking my hand.

"I've never felt so conflicted. I told you I won't accept a relationship, a love, that is one-sided. I still feel that way. But when I thought you might die—" Matias raised his other hand to swipe down his face. "Fuck, Linnea. I don't know how I could go on without you. And that frightens me because you keep these walls between us. Then you show up with another man's ring on your finger. It makes me wonder if it is me that you are reluctant to commit to, not the situation."

Each word struck with the precision of a dart. The room wobbled, my vision blurring. My reply was disconnected from my body.

"No, no—I would never—not with anyone other than—" I wanted to say it, I did, but I couldn't form the words. No matter how much I loved him, I was too afraid of binding myself to anyone. Even him.

My wavering sight worsened. I heard the scrape of his chair and felt the pressure of his hand on my elbow. "You need to be in bed. Why do you keep pushing yourself?"

It was a valid question. "Because I missed you. Because I need to fix this."

His chest rose on his deep inhale and exhale. "I don't know that we can."

Matias's arrival was not subtle. The door bounced off the wall. After last night, I was uncertain of him. We'd parted with much between us, and nothing resolved. He never came to bed.

"Linnea, are you in here?"

I was frozen, toothbrush in my mouth. I spat into the bowl. "I am."

When I peeked around a corner of the screen, he was closer than expected. My erratic movement caused the panel to rock. He steadied it, a slight smile lifting the corner of his mouth. "Are you planning to emerge?"

I nodded, stepping out while working the knot loose in my dressing gown. "Yes, I was about to dress."

He moved toward the chair at the writing desk. I gave him a gimlet eye.

"You don't honestly want me to leave? I've seen you naked. Recently."

"Fine," I grumbled, selecting a dress I'd designed for garden labor. The rough, taupe fabric hid stains. It also sported several pockets, both obvious and secret. Two compartments were concealed on the underside of the hem, and one was stitched to the interior of the bodice. Ideal for carrying weapons.

I buttoned the front of the dress, scrutinizing Matias's outfit. He wore a tattered set of breeches and cracked, old boots, and resting on his knee was a floppy felt hat. Perfect for masquerading as a gardener. I turned to the dressing table and opened the drawer where I kept my weapons. A small knife rested between two stiletto-type blades on a bed of velvet. Furthest to the left was the spot where my missing dagger usually lived. Presumably, the men who had removed it from my boot sheath had disposed of it.

"I have a knife in each boot," Matias said from behind me. I gathered my remaining weapons and sat on our bed. When I flipped my skirt to my hips so I could secure a stiletto in my garter, Matias coughed. "So, what's our plan?"

"Today, let's focus on reactions. I'll return to my duties as if nothing has changed. I don't expect anyone will interfere. We have the advantage of surprise by arriving without warning. Unless, of course, Antonio alerted them."

Matias kicked out his dusty boots. "I'm not convinced he's involved. What would he gain?"

"Whoever killed Pelayo has connections to the Alhambra and the government. They've threatened the socialists. Antonio had the opportunity and access. His involvement must be eliminated first."

He watched me tie my boot and the remaining weapons into place. "You realize that if it is a government official, it may be impossible to bring the murderer to justice."

I paused with my elbows resting on my knees. "I know, but if I can keep Novia, Pilar, and Sebastián safe, it will have to be enough. The carriage will deposit you at the lower gate to the garden. Here's my key." I handed him the key. "I'll meet you at the entrance to the Generalife at the bottom of the stairs. No one seems to pay attention to the movements of the gardeners."

"And if you don't appear?"

I considered where would be an inconspicuous meeting place. "Do you remember where my office is located?"

"I can find it."

"I'll go there to collect my tools. Look for me at the office first. If I've been delayed, that's where I will be."

Matias scowled, rising from the chair. "Unless you're kidnapped again."

"In daylight? Unplanned? That seems unlikely. And I'm prepared to fight." I patted my skirts and bodice. This was as ready as I was going to get. "Shall we?"

From what I could recall, my office was undisturbed. I hadn't returned to the Alhambra since after Pilar's staged murder. I'd been in a haze of grief and a concussion, so I couldn't state for certain that nothing was different.

No one seemed surprised at my return. As usual, Suárez was absent. My basket of tools was underneath the rickety desk. Everything seemed accounted for, nothing unusual. Glancing around the space once more, I sighed, mentally preparing myself to enter the garden. I was nervous, my palms slippery on the handle of the basket. Returning to the scene of the crime without knowing the identity of the murderer . . . Was I purposely being reckless?

The swollen door screeched in the frame when I bumped it open with my hip. My heart lurched in my chest, spurred into a triple beat. "Bloody hell," I murmured. My reactions were too erratic. I needed to be calm.

Trickling water ran through the troughs on either side of the stairs. I trailed my hand in the spillway as I descended to the Generalife, cleansing myself for battle.

Matias waited at the base, his hat pulled low over his face. He turned at my approaching footsteps. As I came to his side, he whispered, "I was worried."

"Apologies. It took a few moments to gather my things."

My hectic internal state must've been obvious. His eyebrows drew down in concern. "I promise this is the last time I will ask. Are you certain about this?"

"Yes, I want it resolved."

Matias glanced at the gardeners milling about with a haunted, pensive expression on his face. "That doesn't mean there will be a satisfying conclusion, though, does it? I know that from experience."

At that moment, Suárez appeared on the path from the lower garden. He hadn't noticed us yet.

"Dammit. Here comes Suárez. Keep to the path on the far side of the garden. Try to keep us in sight."

Matias set off on a side path. I bowed my head, pretending I didn't see Suárez. From the high-pitched shout of my name, he hadn't been warned of my arrival. "Lady Wren! You're here! I thought you wouldn't return to us."

"Apologies, señor. My recovery was slow." I squeezed the handle on my basket, willing my heartbeat to slow.

He tucked his fingers in his jacket pocket with a lighthearted glare. "I thought I saw you." I maintained a serene countenance. "At the Chancery."

"The Chancery?"

"At Plaza Nueva?"

"I'm sorry, señor, I've yet to visit Plaza Nueva. I was confined to the house," I said placidly.

"Whoever she was, she bore a striking resemblance to you."

"I'm an only child, señor. Maybe it was my evil twin?" I laughed, downplaying his accusation.

"Hmm. You're here to work? In the garden? Or the investigation?"

"The garden. The investigation is almost concluded. I believe I've identified the murderer."

He bloomed a florid crimson, the shade of a bougainvillea, and a vein in his forehead pulsed. I hoped he didn't suffer an apoplexy before we proved his involvement.

"Off to work. I have much to accomplish." I strolled away, listening for his response. Hearing none, I sped onward, not daring to look again. I headed for the wisteria courtyard, assuming Matias was following.

I set the basket on the stone bench. My hands were shaking. Suárez was bombastic, but I wasn't convinced he was the killer. The man was flustered under pressure.

I recalled Suárez's reactions on the night of Pelayo's murder. He'd been surprised but not distraught, and he'd swiftly moved into action. Nothing that indicated obvious guilt.

When I heard someone outside the courtyard, I wielded my pruning shears. Matias ducked through the entrance.

"Notice anything?"

"He was surprised. He didn't return to the Alhambra until you entered the courtyard. Is he the murderer?"

I flicked a shriveled pod on the wisteria vine. "Suárez is too obvious. From the beginning, he's been obstructive. But I believe he is being manipulated by someone else. Suárez is the type of man who bows to power. He relies on those he considers his betters to dictate his actions."

Matias moved to the wall, cradling a pod in his palm. "It's such a strange plant."

"They originally came from Asia, but they've grown popular in Europe."

He traced the looping vines with his leather-gloved finger. "Persistent thing, isn't it?"

I nodded. "I'm missing something, Matias. Someone who was at the reception who visits the garden." I shifted my basket to the side to sit on the stone bench. I closed my eyes to engage my recall.

Lourdes Sánchez-Martín.

Pelayo.

Suárez.

The aristocrats.

My memory conjured a sea of vague faces. Who had returned to the garden for one of Suárez's events?

"Oh!" I exclaimed, my palm slapping the bench.

"Who?"

"El Ilustrísimo Señor Conde de Granada. He was at the reception. He's a patron of the garden, and he's always here for meetings. Suárez worships him. Maybe he is just an involved individual, but he has the status to murder a fellow aristócrato and get away with it. And the access."

Matias placed the basket on the ground to sit beside me. "Did I meet him?"

"He was the dashing roué who snatched me away at the reception."

How could I be sure it was him? What was his connection with the Albaicín? And how could I lure him to the garden?

Matias twirled a wilted cutting. "I don't recall him. He's been at the garden again?"

"Yes, on several occasions. He meets with Suárez and attends the parties. We need to know more about him."

"You know who will have that information?"

I sighed. "Antonio. I also need to ask Novia, Pilar, and Sebastián about him."

"Shall we go now, or work?"

"Work, of course." I smiled, pointing to a spade. "How do you feel about shoveling?"

Chapter Forty-Seven

Matias and I spent the afternoon redistributing soil in the courtyard while I perfected my plan. It could easily be adapted, no matter who we determined was the culprit. However, a favor from Fernández was critical. If he was willing to lend us the final item, we had the makings of a trap for a murderer.

"Do you think we can borrow it?" I accepted a spade from Matias, propping it on my shoulder to carry it to my office. We had passed the hours running through various scenarios. Our exchange of ideas reminded me of how we could be together. It had been ages since we had touched that compatibility.

"I do, but he'll want to chat. I won't return until late."

"It'll be worth it."

We were finishing earlier than I usually did and parting at the gate so he could continue to Fernández's house. He hesitated, jamming his hands into the pockets of his breeches.

"Would you prefer not to ask him?"

"It isn't that. You haven't been alone outside the house since—"

The garden was crowded. "We're surrounded by people. I'll leave the tools in my office and return to Antonio's house. You can't always be with me."

Matias removed his leather work gloves, then slapped them against his thigh.

"Matias, I promise I'll go straight home." I gave him a weak smile with my assurance.

Our discord was taking its toll. The lines that fanned out from the corners of his eyes were deeper, the brackets around his mouth more defined. His eyes appeared bruised. He hadn't been sleeping well. I had conflicting urges to hold him in my arms and shake him.

"I'm not trying to be controlling. I'm just concerned," he insisted. I reached for him. He stepped back. "You're meant to be my employer."

"Yes. Of course." I flushed with embarrassment at his rejection. "I—I appreciate that you wish to protect me. But others will question your constant presence." I passed near him, brushing the tips of our fingers together in a subtle gesture of tenderness. "Good luck with Fernández."

He passed through the gate. I lingered at the exit so I could watch him stride toward the carriage stand.

Although the garden was busy, it was tranquil inside the buildings where our offices were housed. Strange that no one else ever used the offices. I paused beside the door to one of the other spaces. It was ajar, so I nudged it open.

There was nothing in the room except cobwebs. I continued down the hallway. The next door was shut, but I tried the knob.

Again, empty. Dots of perspiration misted my forehead. Every room was unoccupied except for mine. Was I jumping to conclusions, or was this suspicious?

I leaned the spade against the wall inside the door, attempting to quiet my riotous thoughts. Suárez had an office, and his secretary occupied the antechamber. But why was I alone in the corridor? Once more, I checked the rooms. They were all empty.

On the way to the house, I decided I would have to ask Antonio about the conde. Trying to gather the information on our own would take too long. Now that I had revealed myself at the Alhambra, we had a limited window to gain the upper hand.

Severiano wasn't minding the door, but Hugh and Antonio were home. Their lively discussion filled the house, and Hugh's unreserved laughter drew me forth. They were arguing about an actor in a performance they'd attended last evening, so engrossed in their playful exchange that they didn't hear me enter the room.

Antonio's arm was over Hugh's shoulder. Hugh was hugging Antonio's waist. It was the first time in the years I had known Hugh that I had seen him physically close to someone who wasn't me. Rather than being embarrassed, I found it comforting to witness their affection.

"I'm sorry to interrupt. Good afternoon, gentleman."

Hugh tried to leap away from Antonio, but Antonio kept his arm in place. "You've returned sooner than I expected." Hugh's fidgeting betrayed his discomfort, despite his efforts to appear nonchalant.

"My tasks were less arduous than I expected. Antonio, I wondered if I might have a word?"

Antonio's arm fell from Hugh's shoulders. His expression was opaque; it was not for nothing that he was an accomplished inquiry agent. "Of course." He exchanged an eloquent look with Hugh.

"Hugh, you're welcome to stay. It isn't confidential," I reassured them. Once we were settled, I dove into my request, trying not to sound overwrought. "I need information about someone I've encountered at the Alhambra. However, my request comes with conditions. This discussion must not leave the room. My reasons for asking about this person will also be withheld."

Hugh scoffed. "Is that necessary?"

Antonio didn't hesitate. "I agree."

"El Ilustrísimo Señor Conde de Granada is a frequent visitor to the garden. What do you know about him?"

"The conde? Hmm. He's a favorite adviser to the regent, and he wields considerable influence. While he doesn't have an official governmental role, he's often with the regent. His family is one of the wealthiest in Andalucía."

"And what are his interests?"

"Property, mainly."

"Property?" I echoed, concealing my excitement.

"Yes, his family had extensive holdings in the colonies. When those collapsed, the conde turned to property to keep the coffers full. He finds land and houses for wealthy families, and they compensate him. The currency varies. However, it wouldn't do to exchange actual money."

"Does that mean they pay him in favors?"

Antonio gestured. "Or whatever they want."

A drumbeat of veracity resounded through me. Here was the thread I had been searching for.

"And the conde donated funds for the Alhambra restoration?"

"I believe so. That was why he was at the reception. His interest in plants stems from traveling to his family's plantation holdings. The garden at his home is extensive—I'm surprised no one mentioned it to you. It's near the cathedral."

My eyes were drawn to the chrysanthemum pattern of the rug at our feet. If each piece of this mystery was a petal, they were unfurling, one by one.

Antonio's voice startled me from my thoughts. "Are those all your questions?"

"Yes, that will suffice for now."

"Linnea, the conde is a powerful man with many connections. If you are thinking he is involved . . ."

I rubbed my palms along the ridges of my chair. "I understand."

Hugh came to my side. "If we can assist—"

I covered his hand with mine. "All is well." I met Antonio's eyes over Hugh's shoulder. "However, it might be best to distance yourself from me."

Antonio stood in one smooth movement. "I would recommend—"

"Señor, there's a visitor at the door." Severiano awaited Antonio's reply from the study's threshold.

"Thank you for the information, Antonio," I said, slipping past the two men.

My former Albaicín neighborhood was familiar yet strange. I wasn't the same person walking these streets. When I'd first arrived, it was to find answers, to solve the murder of a stranger and a friend. Now it was clear that I was a pawn in someone else's game. Izabelle's request had never been simple; I knew that when she made it. The twists and turns of a murder investigation often plunged you into vulnerable territory you would never expect. We learned that in Chiloé.

After recording my thoughts about the conde, I had spent the nighttime hours pondering the repercussions. Why did I continue to keep my interaction with Izabelle from Matias? She had asked that I not tell anyone, but there was also a less altruistic reason I kept it from him. My desire to prove that I could best my opponent. And it kept me from having to face what was happening to my reputation in England.

At least Matias and I had slept in the same bed. Fernández had kept Matias at his house until late; I woke after he had already joined me. Antonio and Hugh hadn't brought up my questions over our meal. I could feel the impatience emanating from Hugh. His conversational topics reminded me of the countless dinners we'd hosted at Holloway House for funders: inane, meant to fill the silence with no real depth.

I didn't argue when Matias insisted on accompanying me to Sebastián's store. Even I could admit that returning alone to the area where I'd been attacked and drugged was foolhardy.

"How was your evening with Fernández?"

His steps faltered. "He was happy to accommodate our request."

"Did he ask why we needed it?"

"He did not. He was too excited about a paper published about Siberian wolves."

I wrapped my hand around his arm. He didn't move away, but the muscle flexed under my palm.

"He values your opinion. Rightly so. I'm glad you have someone who respects your insights and abilities." I was looking ahead to the turn into the close where Sebastián's store was, but I felt Matias's regard. "Here's Sebastián's shop."

That damn bell clanged as we entered. I glanced up, smiling at the memory of cleaning it. And then my stomach dropped when I recalled what else had happened that day.

Sebastián's back was to us. He was arranging books on the lending-library bookshelves. "I'll be with you in a moment."

"New books for the lending library?"

Sebastián whipped around, and a heavy volume in his hand crashed to the floor. Impulsively, I knelt to retrieve it.

"Was it damaged?" Matias asked.

Sebastián broke our eye contact as he took the book from my hands. "It's fine. I'm fortunate to have you grace my humble shop." His tone was barbed.

Not surprising, I supposed.

"I apologize for interrupting your day, señor." Sebastián wrinkled his nose at the *señor*. I charged on. "There's someone I suspect might be involved with the threats. I wish to speak to Novia. I thought if we came here, you could contact her. We shouldn't chance being seen together."

Sebastián casually propped his hip against the counter. "It might take a while. She'll need to leave the print shop."

I conferred with Matias. He nodded his head without me needing to ask. "We can wait."

Sebastián reached behind the counter for his hat. "I'll turn the sign and lock the door. You can wait in my flat. You remember the way, Leo—Linnea?" The smirk he aimed at Matias was not subtle.

He'd paused to flip the sign when an idea came to me. "Sebastián, do you have the papers we stole?"

"I do. We decided it was safest for them to remain here. They're in my chamber, on top of the wardrobe." He pulled the key from around his neck. "We won't be long."

I waited for him to walk out of sight, and then pointed to the door that led to the stairway. "We can wait up there."

Matias followed me into Sebastián's flat. It hadn't changed. That day we had stolen the plans felt distant, but the memory of our conversation and our kiss lingered. "You've visited his lodgings?"

"Yes, we met with Novia and prepared for our theft of the building plans."

Matias scowled, lifting a book from the side table. "Did you live near here?"

"Both the café I worked in and my boardinghouse were close. It's a small neighborhood." I pressed my hand to his taunt back. "I'll fetch the plans."

Sebastián's bedchamber smelled of him: rosemary and books. A dried rose was stuck in the mirror frame. I touched the petals, remembering the twin I'd worn in my hair. I rubbed my thumb against my finger, recalling the weight of Sebastián's mother's ring.

Disconcerted, I spun to the wardrobe, standing on my toes to re-trieve the roll.

Matias was by the window when I returned, peering through the sheer drapes.

"Will you help me look through these? I'm hoping the conde's name will be in here." I handed him a stack, then took up a seat on the settee. The first two documents were drawings. Matias sat across from me with a loud sigh. I glanced up. "Did you find something?"

"No. I'm only . . . wondering." He hesitated.

"About?"

"Who you were with them. With him. If you were different."

At one point, I would have assumed that Matias knew no one was a threat to our relationship. I had destroyed that confidence. I set the pa-pers aside. "I don't think I was. I'm not that accomplished an actor."

His head was bent over his stack of parchment. In the strong sun-light of Sebastián's flat, his dark waves had streaks of brown and auburn. This was not the place to have a serious discussion, but I had to say something.

"Matias." He waited a moment before looking up. "I didn't stop thinking about you while I was here."

Could he see that it was true? A shadow moved across his face. He remained closed off, purposely obscured.

"But you kissed him." Those four words held a heap of pain.

"I did." I exhaled. "And I regret it."

Somewhere in Sebastián's flat, a clock ticked off the minutes. We worked in silence. I tried to focus on what I was doing, on what I would say when they returned, but the print blurred. Hope was waning when I reached the second to last scrap in my pile.

On the reverse of a rough sketch was a receipt to the Ilustrísimo Señor Conde de Granada for the design of five dwellings.

I had found our proof.

Chapter Forty-Eight

If remnants of our emotional exchange hovered in the flat, they vanished at the sound of stomping feet on the stairs, signaling the group's arrival. We shared one final, wordless look when Pilar burst through the door. She appeared happy to see me, while Novia bristled with impatience.

"I can't be gone for long. What do you want?"

I held out the plans to Novia. "This was among the papers we stole from the Chancery. Do you know the Ilustrísimo Señor Conde de Granada?"

Novia took the paper, carrying it to the window to scrutinize the print. "These are the palacios they are attempting to build at the edge of our neighborhood. And yes, I know who he is. He's been involved in many of the property schemes."

I breathed steadily, concealing my impatience. If I shouted, Novia would shut down, and this conversation would be at an end.

Pilar took the parchment from Novia, examining it herself. I softened my voice. "It didn't occur to you that he was involved?"

Novia slapped her hands on her hips. "Of course it did, but he doesn't dirty his hands with people like us. Two men from our group followed him for weeks, and it resulted in nothing. Just his normal schedule of socializing."

Could I be wrong? I resumed my seat on the settee, tracing the worn pattern on the cushion. "Was this before or after Pelayo's murder?"

She frowned. "Before. After Alonso received his first letter, we began gathering information on anyone with ties to the property developments. If nothing else came from it, we would have material for blackmail if we needed it. The conde has a predictable routine, nothing obvious we could use. Plus, he's a favorite of the regent. We didn't want his attention."

Around the room, everyone settled like a flock of birds. Pilar perched on the worn chair near the kitchen. Sebastián replaced the small coffeepot he had retrieved from the woodstove. Novia came to lean against Pilar's chair. Matias didn't move from his seat.

A slight, encouraging tilt of his head prompted me to speak.

"I fear his attention was somehow drawn, or Pelayo confronted him. I assume that when he was followed, his connection with the Alhambra was noted? He was also at the reception the night of Pelayo's murder. Suárez dotes on him. He jumps to his every request."

A storm of reactions traversed Novia's face: confusion and pain, which she quickly masked behind defiance. "How can you prove any of that? If he was the one, we would have known."

I assumed, given our previous conversations, that there had been affection between Novia and Pelayo. But I could see now that it went deeper than that. She guarded it, but she was reeling from the possibility that his death may have been preventable.

Novia had loved Pelayo.

I slanted a glance at Matias. If someone harmed him, would I rage as a vengeful goddess, or would I crumple? Fury, no doubt. Much as he was responding to my attack.

Novia's anger wasn't solely driven by the situation her community faced, but by the loss of someone she loved.

However, she wouldn't countenance my pity. I had to use my insight with care.

"You're correct. We need proof. He's done an exceptional job of obscuring his involvement. Does anyone have any ideas of where we can obtain solid evidence?"

No one spoke. A gust of wind blew the curtain inward; it billowed and undulated. An argument between a cart driver and a pedestrian filled the silence.

"Are you blind?" the man shouted. "I was right in front of you! Do you have more of a right to the street than me?"

Whoever held possession held the rights, especially if it was political and monetary clout. If there was one thing I'd learned from hovering on the outskirts of the aristocracy, it was that they saw themselves as above everyone and everything. Nothing was out of their reach. If they wanted it, they took it. To hell with those who stood in their way.

However, when confronted by one of their own . . .

It had to be me.

"We need to provoke a confession. He'll never negotiate with anyone he considers below him. A fellow aristocrat, though . . ."

Matias understood immediately. "No, Linnea, you can't face him alone. If he murdered Pelayo, then social standing is meaningless to him. Pelayo was an aristocrat too."

Indeed; the conde believed he was impervious. If he wasn't stopped, there was no telling the extent of the damage he could cause.

With a rustle of fabric, Novia was on the move. "Why would you do this? This isn't your battle."

I clenched my fists in my lap. Why *was* I doing this? What did I have to lose? They had made a fool of me, stroking my ego to use me as a pawn. But it was also because I was driven to find justice for Pelayo on Izabelle's behalf. And if this could help preserve those homes and protect those people, the risk was worth it.

"Because I can. No one should be without a safe roof over their heads. Because it is the right thing to do. Besides, if I publicly accuse him without solid proof or a confession, no one will be safe. He has the protection of the regent, probably the prime minister too. We need irrefutable evidence of his machinations. It is unlikely he'll hang for Pelayo's murder, so I need leverage for safety for you and your group. It may be the best outcome we can expect."

Pilar and Novia glanced at each other. Pilar spoke this time. "What leverage?"

"I'll have to take the chance that there will be something. You both must stay hidden until after I've met with him."

Sebastián propped his hip on the edge of the woodstove. "But what if he isn't the murderer, and you accuse him?"

I shrugged. "What other choice do we have? Except for Suárez, there's no one else who could've accomplished it."

Matias's glower promised a discussion of this later, when we were alone. The rest of them seemed to process my plan. Novia huffed. "If this is what you want to do, who are we to argue? Pilar, we must go."

"Wait." I stood from the settee to obstruct her departure. "You must hide for the next day or two. I have an idea of how to draw him out, but I don't want either of you to be a target. He probably knows Pilar is alive. He's aware that I am. I went to the Alhambra today to reveal myself."

Sebastián responded. "If Pilar hadn't found you, those men would not have let you go."

No one knew what I'd faced in that dungeon alone. Through many tears, I had made peace with my death. I was afraid, yes. But if I was losing Matias and my career anyway, what did it matter? Of course, I couldn't say that to them. "I couldn't hide forever."

Pilar joined Novia. She came and placed her hand on my shoulder. "Can I help? I am known in the garden, after all."

"I appreciate the offer, Pilar, but I think it is best that I confront the conde alone." I stepped away so they could pass. "So, are we in agreement?"

"If you want to risk yourself, it's nothing to us." Novia was dismissive, but now that I could read her, I knew she was masking concern. It was easier to be empathetic now that I had gained a deeper comprehension of her pain.

"I'll send word when it is finished."

Novia pulled on Pilar's arm, marching her to the door.

Matias came to his feet, turning toward the exit. "Are we finished here, then?"

"I believe so. Sebastián, thank you for your assistance." I moved to follow Matias.

Sebastián emanated indecision, shifting in place. "May I speak to you for a moment?" Matias paused at the threshold, his back to us. "Ah, alone?"

Matias's shoulders slumped in resignation.

But I felt I owed it to Sebastián to hear what he had to say. "Matias, you'll wait?"

"I'll be downstairs," he muttered.

We listened to him descend.

"Novia's question was a fair one. Why *are* you doing this? We don't need your pity."

I thought about the conversations we'd shared. He didn't just resemble the ravens in appearance; he had their perspicacity, an honesty that left no room for misinterpretation. "Do you remember what you said in the park?"

He tilted his head.

"You said that the thing that makes the struggle worthwhile is your ability to dream. To imagine a different future for yourself. If confronting this man means that one more child living in those houses can dream, then whatever minor discomfort I have to endure will be worth it. Pilar's freedom will be worth it. She has dreams, but she believes they'll never happen. Men like him don't care about destroying others because all he has ever known is freedom. He can't imagine a world in which he doesn't hold the power. I want to shake that foundation. Does that make me foolish? Perhaps."

Sebastian's pointed glare pieced my temporary righteousness. "So, you would sacrifice yourself for us?" He asked.

"Please don't make me out to be a martyr. The conde—if it is him—has disrupted my life as well. He's made a fool of me. He may have also cost me something irreplaceable. Through my actions, but because of his machinations."

Sebastián glanced at the door, correctly guessing that I referred to Matias.

He took a step, placing his finger under my chin. "You were part of that future. For a while, it was a grand dream."

On that day, for a fraction of a second, I'd allowed myself to consider the possibility as well. But it had been ephemeral. I wouldn't do that to him, or me, or Matias.

I said nothing. I kissed his cheek and descended the stairs to the only man I loved.

Chapter Forty-Nine

Matias waited near the shelves that contained the atlases. His hand lingered on one of South America.

The wizened floorboards of Sebastián's bookstore squeaked beneath my heels as I came to his side. "I miss it. Don't you?"

He fanned the pages, pausing at a sketch of the west coast of the continent. "I do. The place and the people."

I traced the outline of Chiloé Island. "Maria must have had the baby."

Matias replaced the volume on the shelf. "Er, she did."

"What?" My voice cracked. "Why didn't you tell me?"

"There's been so much happening. And you were gone when I received word. In all the chaos, I forgot to tell you. She had a girl—they named her Emelina."

"Emelina," I breathed. I couldn't believe he hadn't told me. His oversight stung. "Shall we go?"

We walked several blocks before he spoke. "I'm sorry I forgot. It wasn't intentional."

I was silent, then nodded. After all, given the amount of betrayal and hurt I had saddled him with recently, this was a minor omission. "It's fine. I'm happy to hear they are both well."

"I'll let you read Maria's letter. Even Jaime wrote a bit." We were side by side, but the distance between us felt insurmountable. "You didn't speak to Señor de los Rios for very long."

I slanted my eyes toward him. Did he eavesdrop? "There wasn't much to say. He wanted to understand my motivations for continuing with this investigation."

"I'm curious about that myself."

I was grappling with them, too, yet I sensed he might understand better than others after his experiences in Chile. We had reached the edges of Antonio's neighborhood. Up ahead was the cemetery where I had taken shelter after I thought Pilar had been murdered. Once we entered the house, the tasks that needed to be accomplished would take precedence.

I stopped, indicating the entrance to the cemetery. "Can we go in? I'll try to explain."

We wound through the headstones until we reached the bench beneath the stone angels. It took me a few minutes to order my thoughts. I hadn't noticed the gravestone beneath the statues on my last visit.

Asuncion Vazquez Torres

b. 1848

d. 1885

Ella llenó cada segundo de su vida con sonrisas, amor y felicidad.

Given the dates, Asuncion must have died in the cholera epidemic—Asuncion, who had filled people's lives with smiles, love, and happiness.

When I died, I didn't want to be buried underground. I wanted a sea burial. Let me sleep at the bottom of the ocean, to be nibbled on by creatures. What would my epitaph read?

Linnea Ailith Wren

b. 1850

d. ?

She filled our lives with aggravation, coffee, and bits of plants.

That seemed about right. I did almost end up at the bottom of the sea after the shipwreck. Maybe I needed to rethink my final resting place.

"Linnea?"

I was so lost in my musings on death that I had forgotten our purpose.

"Sorry, I was . . . distracted. What is your middle name, Matias? I know it begins with an *E*."

He furrowed his brow. "Edmund, after my father. Not very original. What's yours?"

"Ailith, named after a Scottish grandmother. By all accounts, she was ferocious."

"Did your ginger locks come from her?" He tugged at a strand that had come loose from my braid. The brown dye was wearing away but still masked its usual vibrancy.

"No idea. There's so much we never know when our parents die young, isn't there?"

Matias grimaced. "Or when we push them away."

"Or that." His regrets over the estrangement between him and his father were a deep wound. A hurt that couldn't be resolved, and was tied to the situation we'd faced on Chiloé.

"Do you remember how you were determined to travel to Castro alone? To protect Maria, Jaime, and me from danger when you were trying to unmask the murderer?"

"I still believe that was the right decision. We didn't know who was involved." His tone was defensive, as was the set of his shoulders.

"I'm not criticizing you. I'm trying to say that I understand now how complex our reactions are when the people we love are involved."

He folded his arms. "Hugh, Antonio, and I haven't been threatened."

"Not directly." I fluttered my lips, exhaling. "I'm making a hash of this," I muttered. "Sebastián doubts my motivations."

"I haven't questioned—"

"Please, Matias, let me try."

He nodded in acquiescence.

"I told him that it was, in part, because the people in those neighborhoods deserve to have a chance. Someone is robbing them of their property. If I can do one small thing to right that wrong, it will have been worth it." I smoothed the wrinkles of my skirt. "But it isn't the only reason. When we organized the expedition to Chile, I was riddled with doubts about my ability to lead. There were flashes of confidence when I was botanizing on Chiloé, but it was against a backdrop of the murders and our romance. As we crossed the ocean to Spain, every one of those insidious thoughts came to roost." I wrapped my arms around my body. *You can do this. You have to do this.* A vise clamped on my throat. My vision wavered, but I forced out the words. "What am I, if not a botanist? By now, word will have spread that not only did I not achieve what I promised, but that I took up with a man. I was worried about the consequences from the beginning. And then someone made sure I was set up to fail again."

Matias inched his hand across the stone to squeeze mine. I kept speaking in a flood of words I couldn't stop.

"Why me? I want to prove them wrong. At least I can do that, even if everything else is crumbling. And . . . Pelayo's sister, Izabelle, came to me after he was killed. She asked me to find his murderer."

"What? You hid this from me? From Antonio? Why didn't you tell us? Where is she?" He paced away in his anger, fists clenched on his thighs.

The hot track of a tear spilled down my cheek. I felt hollow after my confessions. If I lost him, what would be the point of fighting?

"I can understand wanting to regain some pride, but this is absurd. You trust *no one* with the truth. Not even me. You were willing to put yourself in danger for a *stranger*." His face was flushed with indignation.

My fury raced to the surface. I glared at him. "I'm putting *me* in danger—no one else. Men! You always want to control everything. Izabelle was snatched away by her husband. That's how it works. Men dominated my life, controlled my career, tempered the possibilities because of the reality of living in *their* world. Do you know how much fortitude it takes to be this person standing in front of you? *I* was alone when my uncle died. *I* survived that bloody school and pretended to be a boy for years, just to do the bare minimum at Kew. Years! Do you know how much resistance I've had at every turn? Men question my intelligence, my ability to do my work, my authority over them. Men undermine me and attack me, verbally, *physically*!"

He stood frozen in front of me as I hurled my pent-up emotions at him. I was panting from the force of my conviction.

"That is *not* me. You know it isn't. Yet you seem determined to place me in that role." His words were gravelly and sharp with hurt.

I banged my fist on the stone bench. The pain of connecting with the surface jarred some sense into me. "You're right. That is unfair. My distance was meant to protect us both."

Thunder rumbled in the distance, echoing the harsh, impetuous words I'd unleashed. We watched the horizon, watching for the lightning. The surrounding air was heavy with acrimony and resignation. I couldn't stop myself from adding more to the mix.

"I don't want anyone else there when I confront the conde. Especially you."

Matias scoffed. "That's not going to happen. I'll be there."

"Matias."

"No, you have your pride, and I have mine."

There was no point arguing with him. My eyes landed on the gravestone. "I don't regret falling in love with you, Matias. But I think it has become clear that I don't know how to be *in* love. My actions are hurting us both. Love shouldn't be like that."

His head was bowed. Strands of his hair hid his face. He sat motionless, remote. I allowed the silence to linger, hoping against hope that he would refute my statement. But he didn't.

With an elongated exhale, he lifted his head. "We should put your plan in action. There will be time for the rest."

I wanted to rail at him, to provoke his anger again. Instead, I stood from the bench and led the way out of the cemetery.

An owl hooted from the top of an oak in Antonio's garden. How long had I been standing here? Long enough for the sun to slip below the horizon. Matias and I had parted at the door when we entered the house. I'd come to the library to think about my explosion in the graveyard. After coming to the conclusion that there wasn't a solution, I turned my thoughts to the impending confrontation. To have the best chance of stopping the development, I needed someone with clout to overhear any confessions.

Antonio was the obvious choice; however, it meant telling him what I intended to do. If he was in league with the murderer, it would jeopardize the entire scheme. I tried to silence my racing mind by focusing on the garden beyond the doors.

Instead, I slipped into an abstraction. Confessing to Matias hadn't lightened the emotional weight. Rather than clearing the air in preparation for the danger I was facing, I had generated a hurricane.

"Mr. Ward, you're not joining us for dinner?" Hugh's voice came from the other end of the corridor. I retreated into the shadows of the darkened library.

"Ah, no. I received a message from Señor Fernández. He has an item I requested. Have you seen Linnea?"

The edge of the shelves dug into my spine where I pressed against them.

"I haven't." Hugh's tone was somber. "Er, Matias, I shouldn't . . ." My body flushed with humiliation. Hugh wouldn't tell Matias about my outburst, would he? Would Matias tell Hugh about Izabelle? "Is everything well between you and Linnea?"

As the quiet stretched between them, I found myself taking a step toward the door.

Before I interrupted, Matias said, "It's complicated."

A rustling of fabric indicated one of them had moved. I pressed my eye to the crack at the doorjamb. It took a moment for me to adjust to the lamplight. Hugh was resting his hand on Matias's shoulder.

"Matias, we've known each other for years. I've known Linnea since she was a young woman. She's wrestling with something that's making her more mercurial than normal. However, she loves you. She wouldn't be so conflicted if she didn't."

Matias leaned into Hugh's hand. He allowed Hugh to see the anguish he had been hiding from me. "She . . . ah, I should go. Thank you, Hugh."

I rested my forehead on the wall, tapping it in silent distress.

"I know you're there. You might as well come out."

Damn. Hugh was standing in the pool of light inside the library.

I sidled out from behind the door. "I'm sorry I eavesdropped."

"You're sorry you were caught," he teased.

I shrugged. He was right.

Hugh turned the switch on the lamp nearest to him. "How long have you been here?"

"Awhile. I was thinking, and then I lost track of time. Antonio's library is comfortable, but I miss our chairs at Holloway House."

Hugh clanked the glasses on the sideboard, pouring himself a drink from one of the decanters. When he lifted one toward me, I shook my head. He savored his sip, closing his eyes for a moment. "I thought I would miss my house more than I do." His stormy blue eyes glinted when he faced me. "I'm considering staying."

"In Spain?" I wasn't shocked, but he would be giving up a lot if he chose to remain. "What about your studies? The house? Parliament?"

Hugh tossed back the last of his drink and came to stand in front of me.

"I've not been on an expedition in years. And with all my traveling, I've hardly ever occupied my seat in Parliament." He surprised me when he drew me into a hug. The urge to sob into his shirtfront was tempting. I took great, gasping breaths of his cologne. "My girl, I'm going to give some advice. When you find someone who loves you, you move heaven and earth to make it work. Attraction and desire are commonplace, but love . . . that is rare. There is nothing in England that equals what I feel for Antonio."

A ball of nausea formed in my stomach. I broke Hugh's hold, skittering from him. "It isn't the same, Hugh. You—I can't make someone love me. And Matias . . . you don't know what I've done to him. I don't deserve—" My voice broke. I coughed, trying to cover my distress. "I'm happy for you, Hugh. If staying in Spain with Antonio is what you want, I will do whatever I can to help."

"Linnea, you deserve it too."

I took a shuddering breath. "That remains to be seen. Is Antonio in the house? I need to speak to him about tomorrow."

Chapter Fifty

*D*ear Matias and Linnea,
    Two days ago, on September 1, we welcomed our daughter, Emelina Viviana, into the world. The less said about the experience, the better. All that matters is that we are both well. Jaime is quite taken with his daughter. She's been introduced to the horses and the sheep. I told Emelina about her cousin and his adventures.

I hope you are both well. I've only received one letter from each of you, and neither of you told me much of anything. I want to know what Spain is like. Emelina and I will be staying close to home for a while, so please write and give us some new stories.

All my love,
Maria

Matias,
Maria makes light of it, but the birth was not easy. The doctor said Emelina is likely to be our only child. They are well now, but it will be a lengthy recovery for Maria. I wish you could've been here, primo. There are no words to describe this kind of love.
Jaime

I refolded Maria's letter and returned it to the bedside table. Matias had left it for me as promised. Emelina Viviana.

Not only did he not tell me about Emelina, but he also didn't mention that they named her Viviana, for his mother.

Everything in my body ached. I kept thinking about what Hugh said, that if you loved someone, you moved heaven and earth. Matias had done that for me. He left Chile on the *Cormorant* instead of staying with his family. He chose me. And what had I done? Pushed him away. Lied to him. Kissed another man.

My self-loathing was crushing me, a bone-deep misery that kept threatening to pull me under. But no, I had a murderer to confront tomorrow.

I flung myself backward, sprawling on our bed with arms and legs thrown wide. I'd spent so much time over the last several months worrying about the trajectory of my life. Instead of living it, I'd lit it on fire. Poof.

Laughter from the street came in through the open balcony doors. Why couldn't I be happy like other people? What was wrong with me?

Matias entered our chamber, narrowing his eyes at my position on the bed. "Are you well?"

"Mmph," I grunted.

"Is that an answer?"

"It's the closest I can come to an answer at present."

He loomed over the bed, tilting his head in consideration. With a shrug, he began unbuttoning his waistcoat. "Fernández fulfilled our request. I went ahead and took it to the garden."

"You did?" That explained the state of his clothing.

"I assumed I would attract less attention. I used your key to enter."

"Did you see anyone?"

He hung his waistcoat in his wardrobe and untucked his shirt from his breeches. "No, it was empty."

Matias pulled his shirt over his head. He examined the stains, then tossed it into the basket we used for soiled linen. He ran a hand down his chest. I bit my lip to keep a groan from escaping. It would be so much easier if I wasn't attracted to him.

"I think I need a bath after two stints of digging in the dirt today." He snatched up his banyan, tying it about his waist.

I sat up, scooting off the bed. "Would you like assistance?"

His pupils flared with hunger that he quickly hid. I couldn't take another rejection.

"You've assisted with my bath. Let me do the same for you." While he debated, I leaped up. "I'll go run the water for you."

He must've spent a while debating the wisdom of this because the tub was full when he entered. While he disrobed, I carried a stool over to the side. I propped a bar of soap on one knee and a linen cloth on the other. With his back to me, he lowered himself into the steaming water. His groan of relief had me gritting my jaw.

I wet the linen and created a lather with the soap. I tapped his right arm above the waterline. He obliged, draping it over the edge.

I scrubbed his fingers first, and then across his shoulders. His eyes followed my movements. I leaned around him to wash across his chest.

His head bowed, and he groaned again. It took great restraint to focus on the task and set aside my desire. How had he done this for me?

I moved to the end of the tub. He propped his foot up on the rim. I refamiliarized myself with every inch of his body: the bony turn of his ankle, the sinewed strength of his calf, his delicate patella. I spread my palm over the span of his thigh muscle, my small finger brushing against the evidence that he wasn't indifferent to my ministrations. My eyes snapped to his face. His color was high, with flags of red on his cheekbones. A sheen of humidity glinted on his upper lip.

But his eyes—oh, how they burned. The breath I exhaled was sultry, releasing desire that had set my insides ablaze. A quarter of an inch to the right, and my hand would be on him.

"Matias." My voice was husky.

He pinched my wrist, moving it the vital distance. His head dropped against the rim of the tub when I gripped him.

I teased him, varying my speed and pressure. The water lapped at my wrist. This would be just for him. I pressed my lips to the compass rose over his heart, darting out my tongue to taste his skin. His hand gripped my nape.

I thought he was keeping me in place, but he used his leverage to draw me up. His kiss was so ardent, I had to release him to balance myself. "I want you," he rumbled.

"You have me. This is for you, just you."

He ripped at the tie of my dressing gown. "No. Together."

He stood. Water cascaded over his body, but he didn't bother to grab the linen towel. He stepped from the tub, plucking me from the stool. As we kissed, he walked me backward, stripping me of my dressing gown and night rail. My arse met the fabric of the chair, but I had no idea how I got there. Matias pushed my legs upward. I was pinned in place, exposed, at his mercy.

He thrust home. My internal muscles gripped him, fluttering around the invasive. But he didn't slow. His forceful movements rocked the chair, thumping it against the tile floor. This was going to be fast.

Our faces were inches apart, panting in the humid air. I gripped his shoulders, searching for stability within the intensity of sensation.

"Why?" he growled in my ear. "Why do I want you this much?"

I couldn't reply. My breath sawed in and out of my lungs. On the edge of a peak, a devastating fall loomed. My fingernails dug into the skin of his arms when I exploded. A whimper escaped as I spasmed.

Matias strained under my hands. "Fuck."

He slumped, boneless, to the floor. Only the fragment of furniture under my arse kept me from joining him.

I looked down at his dewy skin. Our breathing was harsh in the small chamber. His exhalations made the strands of hair that had fallen around his face dance.

"We didn't finish your bath." I tried for light banter, even though I felt fractured in a million pieces.

Matias flipped his hair away. His hand shook when he put his palm over his face. "I knew this was unwise. We can't be within proximity to each other without this happening. And I am so angry with you."

"It's fine, Matias. It's only—"

"Don't say it!" His livid voice rattled the walls of the chamber, or maybe just me. "You know it isn't only that. And every time we do this, it makes it harder."

He pushed himself from the floor, striding toward the tub and grabbing the dropped linen on the way. After dipping it into the cooled water, he gave himself a perfunctory scrub, then snatched up his banyan, all the while refusing to look at me.

At his retreat, I drew my knees up. My clothes were too far away for my shaking legs to carry me to them. What did he mean by that last statement? Harder for what?

Was he leaving me?

"Matias, it makes what harder?"

He bent to retrieve my dressing gown. The silk slipped in his hands, sliding onto my knees when he stood over me. I pushed my arms into the sleeves, waiting, dreading his answer. I felt vulnerable below him in this chair, but I didn't trust the wobbliness of my limbs to keep me standing. Especially if he was about to end our relationship.

Judging by his face, he had retreated from me, at least as far as he needed to say his piece.

"Even as a young boy, I knew my parents loved each other in different ways. My mother loved us with her whole heart. My father and I were her world. She gave up everything to come to England with him, but it was a sacrifice she willingly made, one I have no doubt she would've made again if he asked it. On the other hand, my father's love for her was possessive, and sometimes dismissive. He would become obsessed with a text or a theory and forget us. Did I ever tell you how she died?"

I shook my head, gripping the tie of my dressing gown. Terror was gathering in me, an oncoming storm that was unstoppable.

"She was with child. I didn't know, not at first. She was a few months along. My father was away in Oxford, meeting with some academics about a text he was translating, when she started bleeding. We were alone in the house, and I didn't know what to do. As you know, she was *machi*, so she was calm. She sent me to the apothecary for herbs that would ease things. But when I returned, it was to a scene that haunts my nightmares. She was in the parlor we used as a music room, spread out on the floor in a pool of blood." Matias stared at a point on the tile, and I knew he could see it. Could recall every detail. "She looked so peaceful. I thought she was asleep. My father found us when he returned on the afternoon train. I have never witnessed such devastation. He wasn't the same man after that day. Neither of us were. His grief turned him into an automaton, abstracted from life."

I reached for him, and he allowed me to take his hand. "I'm so sorry, Matias." I couldn't contain my tears, heartsick for him, his father, and the unnecessary loss of his mother.

Matias crouched in front of my chair. "Don't you see, mi amor? I can't be them—my mother or my father. I love you—god, but I love you. But since we've been together, I've come close to losing you more than once. And when we thought you might not survive that laudanum, I felt the edge of that abyss. The one I would disappear into if I lost you. Just like he did."

I cradled his hands, turning them palms up and bringing them to my lips. "But I love you, too, Matias. Do you think it is any different for me?"

He drew his hands away. "I do. I fear I'm more like my mother, loving you blindly despite your preoccupations. Despite your recklessness. But unlike my mother, I want more. I want a career, a companion of my heart. I deserve that."

I was confused. "Of course you do."

"I'm afraid that we are both too strong, too driven, that there isn't room for us to nurture a relationship. We're solitary creatures. I can't force you to open up, to love me how I love you. Perhaps it would be better to go our separate ways before it destroys us."

His words blasted a hole in my chest, incinerating my heart. I fisted the silken fabric of my gown.

How do you fight for someone who doesn't want you to?

"Linnea?"

"If that is what you want." I heard my voice yet couldn't make sense of the words. Something inside screamed, *Fight! Fight for him, you idiot.* The part that was driven by doubt, though, said this was inevitable. And might as well be now.

He came to his feet. "We shouldn't have discussed this tonight, I know. Tomorrow will be a demanding day. I'm not going anywhere. I'll be by your side, and we'll discuss this again." A warm hand gripped my shoulder. "Linnea, are you hearing me?"

"Yes, I hear you."

Somehow, I found the wherewithal to stand, clean our mess, drain the tub, and follow him to our bedchamber. I lay next to him, but I didn't sleep. One thought kept circling my mind: *If I lose him, then I have nothing left to lose.*

Chapter Fifty-One

I broke my fast alone. Matias was sleeping when I left our bed. His arm sprawled out across my empty spot, face down on his pillow.

I sipped my coffee and waited. Every instinct was warning me to flee, a wild animal avoiding the pain, but today I couldn't. We had a murderer to catch, and I couldn't think beyond accomplishing that task.

Matias entered the breakfast room, yawning. "You woke early. Give me a few minutes to eat something and we can go."

I pushed my chair from the table. "I'll gather my things and meet you in the foyer."

He stepped in front of me, blocking my retreat. "Linnea, I know—"

I placed two fingers over his warm lips. "Not now. Please, Matias. I have to see this through."

I didn't wait to secure his agreement, running from the room like the coward I was.

"I assume you will enter through the back gate?" It was the first time I had spoken to him since we left the house. We were waiting a few streets from the Alhambra. Matias would take the path that ran along the river to enter the gate we used the night we found Pilar's scarecrow. I would go to my office to cast our bait.

"Yes, as we planned."

"I'll come to the courtyard after I speak to Suárez."

Matias jammed his hands in his pockets. "Do you think this will work? Will he come racing to the garden because Suárez calls him?"

"I think so. It's worth the attempt."

He furrowed his brow. "You will be cautious?"

"Yes, yes." I waved him away. "I'll see you in there."

I had ceased to care about my safety. I would see this to the end, and that was all there was to it.

The success of our trap depended on how tantalizing I could make the enticement. Suárez had to believe that I was about to reveal everything so he would summon the conde. But for the first domino to fall, Suárez had to be present—and of course, he hadn't arrived at the Alhambra yet. My spirits were plummeting. I wanted to resolve this situation today.

I snatched up my clippers in frustration, abandoning my office for the myrtle courtyard. Shaping the myrtles brought me a measure of contentment. The blades made a satisfying snap on the rogue twigs.

"Lady Wren, buenos días. What are you doing, working here?"

My quarry had found me first.

"It appeared unkempt, so I thought I would see to it. I was waiting for you, señor. I have some news." I stared at him, shifting my clippers between my hands.

He ran his thumb over his shiny cuff links. "Oh?"

I stowed my clippers in my pocket and shook out my skirts to delay the inevitable, trying to force him into a state of nervous anticipation.

"I'm pleased to share that I've identified Pelayo's murderer."

His expression brightened, which wasn't quite what I expected. "Was it the socialists? I knew they were the ones responsible. I assume the mess in the jasmine bower was because you were getting too close?"

I waited a beat, stroking the leaves of the myrtle, drawing out my revelation. "No, señor, they are innocent. I have evidence that points to corruption at the highest levels."

Suárez blanched. "Th-that's not possible. What evidence?"

"Nothing you need to concern yourself with. This goes beyond someone in your position." I dug the knife in deeper, reminding him he wasn't the one with power.

His face was turning an alarming shade of red. A vein under his jaw pulsed at a rapid tempo. "No one will believe you. It is farcical. Everyone knows it was the socialists. They attack anyone associated with the aristocracy."

"I have an appointment with a government minister this evening to share my conclusions." I hadn't disclosed any details to anyone, and I had zero evidence to back my claims. But it didn't matter. He was doing fine on his own, working himself into a fervor. "Since you assigned me this task, I thought it courteous to inform you that as of this evening, it will be concluded. If you'll excuse me, I have work to do."

Suárez was immobile, his fists clenched at his sides, mouth gaping. It delighted me to knock the man off his pins. I swiveled on my heel, aiming toward the Generalife. Now I had to count on his panic to bring the wolf to the door.

I located Matias in the orchard. The canopy provided relief from the sun, and we had a full view of the Generalife. Our communication was perfunctory, which maintained the illusion that we were coworkers. I set us the task of hand digging a new bed, and it was slow-going. The dirt was packed hard.

"This is what you do all day? No wonder you're so strong," he gasped, draping himself over the handle of the shovel.

I mopped my forehead with a handkerchief and dug into my basket for a flask of water. "Not every day. We rarely dig a new bed. Most of what we do in the Generalife is replace the neglected beds with new plants."

Matias reached for the flask. "It's been hours since you spoke to Suárez. Maybe it won't happen today."

I handed the water to him. "Given his distress, I suspect he ran to the conde. If he hasn't shown in a couple of hours, we'll retreat until tomorrow. I would rather avoid any confrontations after dark."

Once our digging was complete, I collected the scarlet, sun-hardy sage plants. I placed them equidistant from one another in the bed, and we dug corresponding holes. We were nearing the end of the row when Matias nudged me. "Mira."

Suárez appeared at the entrance to the Generalife, his hand shading his eyes as he surveyed the garden. It took him several scans until he located us. When he did, he hurried toward the buildings.

"You'll stay close?"

He nodded. I casually stowed away my tools. While I was kneeling, I patted the blades strapped to my garter and in the boot sheath. Insurance, in case the situation turned violent.

Chapter Fifty-Two

My stroll through the garden was a laughable display of indolence. I caressed leaves, sighed over the remaining blooms, and lingered at the fountains. It was, however, effective. As I walked, I gathered a gang of unsubtle stalkers, men who stayed in the shadows along the external walls, mirroring my advance toward the wisteria courtyard.

By my count, there were three of them. Matias stayed on the opposite side of the area. They paid no attention to him, which was what I was banking on. They were circling in when I entered the courtyard.

Matias had left the wheelbarrow where I asked, a few feet to the left of the stone bench. I set down my basket and moved the wheelbarrow out of the way.

My hands were shaking as I stripped off my gloves, but I felt formidable. The men entered the courtyard and took up positions that forced me to remain in the corner. Not that I had any intention of moving.

"*Señores.*" I inclined my head. "*¿Estáis perdidos?*"

None of them responded. I pressed my back against the wall. Would the conde show? Matias and I couldn't take three men.

A sharp weeding tool was at the top of my basket. I was considering reaching for it when the click of a cane approached.

The Ilustrísimo Señor Conde de Granada's appearance was the height of fashion. His suit jacket hugged his shoulders. His waistcoat was sapphire, decorated with intricate silver embroidery. On his hand, a bulky signet ring gleamed as he caressed the gold head of his cane.

He had gained so much opulence on the backs of others. Even the cane possessed a filigree design.

I studied the familiar shape of the design. It was a wisteria vine. His audacity made me ill.

"Buenas noches, Señora Wren. I see you admire my bastón. Lovely, isn't it?" He twirled the cane with a flourish.

"Forgive me, Ilustrísimo Señor, but I couldn't care less about your fripperies. Are these men necessary? I'm only a woman."

He smirked. "Only a woman, indeed. Señores . . ." The conde waved the men outside. They didn't go far. I hoped Matias had hidden himself well.

I came toward the conde, wondering where to begin. Unease spiraled through my limbs. Last night, I probably should've worried about my relationship less and planned for this confrontation more.

The conde kicked out a leg, balancing casually on his cane. "You're not what I expected. I assumed you would sleep late, order people around, and make a halfhearted attempt at solving the murder. I didn't anticipate such . . . striving." Disgust dripped from his pronunciation of the word.

I shrugged. "Then you failed to do adequate research before issuing the invitation. I assume that was where this began, with la señora Sánchez-Martín?"

He twirled his hand in the air like a flamenco dancer. "Oh yes, that is where this dance began. Poor Señora Sánchez-Martín must rely on recommendations to secure her commissions. She was so easy to manipulate."

The man would not stop moving. He unbuttoned the top fastening on his jacket, reaching in to produce a cigarillo. I resisted the urge to knock it from his hand.

"Why me? What purpose was there in my involvement?" I prodded.

He produced a small silver contraption from his jacket. With a few flicks, it produced a flame that he used to light the cigarillo. "You have so many questions, señora. Suárez said you had figured this out. I don't intend to waste my time weaving a story for you."

I waved my hand dismissively. "I know enough, conde."

Curls of smoke cloaked the space between us. He squinted at me through the wisps.

"We became aware of you because of . . . what is he, your novio? Protector? The two of you set the cat among the pigeons, didn't you? A few days in Spain were enough to bring you to our attention."

What was he talking about?

The realization hit me with the force of a punch. Felicity Ward.

"Ah, I see you understand. La señora Ward made some powerful friends during her stay in Spain. One in particular is quite devoted. He understands our situation in Granada, and when word reached us that you would be coming here . . . well, let's just say favors were called in."

My mind reeled. Felicity Ward was behind this? How? She must've had some communication with her friends in Spain before she boarded the ship to England. But who?

The conde straightened, taking another draw on his cigarillo. "Perhaps you don't know much at all."

Later, I would have to figure out the specifics of how this connected to Felicity Ward.

"I know you killed Pelayo, and why," I accused, trying to provoke a return to his involvement.

He chuckled. "Oh, please proceed. I'm curious what it is you think you know."

I pushed away the creeping sense that this situation was more complicated than I thought. Winning back some control was critical.

"Pelayo was helping the socialists. He was approaching people you would rather not know of your association, asking for their assistance. You tried threats, but he was persistent, to the point where you had no option but to silence him, despite being a distant member of the royal family." It had been a few seconds since he had taken a draw on his cigarillo. "How am I doing thus far?"

The conde had perfected his insouciant stare. He shrugged. "Más o menos, I'm curious to see how this will end."

I noticed the evidence that I had rattled him a bit, drawing confidence from his wobble.

"Pelayo was poisoned at the reception, and his body was deposited where I would find it. El señor Navarro is a favorite of the regent. He might've revealed your scheme. But someone who didn't understand the politics here would be ideal. And if the socialists were blamed, it would give you further leverage to threaten them." I sidled toward the wall, unwilling to turn my back on him, and looped two fingers through the wisteria vines. "But it didn't proceed as you expected, did it?"

"Not after they faked the murder of that young woman."

"And I vanished."

He tossed the spent cigarillo to the ground, grinding it with the heel of his bespoke shoe. "Vanished. Yes."

"It was you who had me kidnapped, wasn't it?" I wondered if the men who stood guard had been my captors.

The conde fixed me with his hooded glare. It was disconcerting how fast his blithe manner turned feral. I eyed the distance separating us. I didn't want him too close. Not yet. But I ignored any thoughts of self-preservation and forced my legs to move, pacing forward to meet him.

He reached around me with the tip of his cane, lifting a wisteria vine.

"Have you traveled to the islands of Asia, señora?" I shook my head, refusing to break eye contact. "My family worked the trade routes through those islands, and I traveled there frequently. That is where these vines originate. Some of the islanders believe wisteria represents passages, new beginnings, immortality." He snapped the tip of the cane upward; the vine flew off with a loud ripping noise. "When trade collapsed and we were forced to leave our land, my family returned to Spain. There are many aristocrats in the same situation. This is what you don't understand. Everyone in this country is desperate, but for some of us, our needs take priority."

I scoffed at him. His cane slammed against the underside of my chin, forcing it up. It was an unpleasant way to discover the tip was sharpened to a point.

"Pelayo didn't respect it, either, señora, not even at the end. He knew he was dying, and he wouldn't surrender. One has to respect that, I suppose." He adjusted his grip on the cane, drawing close so I had no choice but to stare into his flat, unfeeling eyes. "I have the support of the crown. Whatever evidence you have, it means nothing. Nothing. I snap my fingers, and those people in the Albaicín vanish. As will you."

I gritted my teeth against the radiating pain in my chin. "You tried that once, Ilustrísimo Señor. I don't vanish easily. People will ask questions. Especially el señor Navarro."

The metal punctured my tender skin. A warm trickle of blood coursed down my throat. *Courage, Linnea, courage. Draw him closer.*

"El señor Navarro won't be an impediment." The conde heaved an overdramatic sigh. "I tire of this game. It was diverting, but now it is tedious." He brought his cane to the ground, and I suppressed the urge to check my wound. "I suppose if you want a job done, one must do it themselves." He twisted the head of the cane, drawing forth a sword that rested within.

It was now or never. I had to provoke him again. "Do you get your hands dirty? Don't you have people for that?"

"For you, I'm willing to lower myself, one aristo to another. At this stage, I don't even care about the plans you stole. There are other places to build, a city full of neighborhoods waiting for us to claim. We are so far above you, señora. You are nothing but a nosy coñazo to be crushed."

If this was how it was to end, so be it. But I owed it to Novia and Pilar to try and negotiate.

I reached under the back of my blouse and withdrew the roll of documents. "You can have these. With terms."

He eyed the roll, advancing a step. "As I said, I don't need them . . . but it would be nice to tidy up a loose end."

I glanced over his shoulder. There was no sign of his men. He flicked the sword, bringing the tip to rest on my blouse, over my heart.

Panic made my hands slick. I almost dropped the paper. "There's more than the *palacio* drawings. Written evidence that you were involved with Pelayo's murder."

He huffed. The threads in the fabric of my shirt parted, and I felt the bite of steel. "No such evidence exists."

"You're wrong, Ilustrísimo Señor. It's inadvisable to have lazy lackeys who don't adequately dispose of your orders." I'd never attempted a more blatant bluff. One drawing of the Generalife with Pelayo's name on it and the anonymous letter from Suárez's office wasn't enough to accuse a peer.

The internal calculations he was engaged in were writ on his face. The lengthening shadows accentuated his furrowed brow.

"Release me, and you have the papers."

The conde roared with laughter. "You can't be serious? I have a sword on you. You know too much."

When he was distracted, I knocked the blade away with the roll of papers. An arc of fire seared across my chest as the blade sliced into me.

I shifted a few feet to the side. "Come and get them."

The corners of his mouth pulled into a smirk. He moved forward, brandishing his sword. And stepped directly into the buried wolf trap.

The metal jaws snapped on his leg, and he let out an inhuman screech of pain.

Matias rushed into the courtyard, followed by Antonio, a group of men, and a sheepish Suárez. The conde writhed on the ground, beating at the steel trap.

"Get it off! Someone get it off me!"

Suárez dropped to his knees and attempted to pry it open, slicking his hands with the conde's blood in the process.

"You can't get away with this! What have you done? The regent will—argh, Suárez, get it off!" the conde screeched.

I tossed the plans in the dust next to the two men. "You can have these. Antonio, I assume you heard enough to inform the regent?"

He nodded. "Yes, I have an appointment with her in the morning."

Matias reached for me. "Linnea, you're bleeding."

I plucked the linen away from my chest. "It's minor. I believe we are finished."

I was woozy, but I refused to swoon in front of the conde. Matias wrapped his arm around my waist, taking some of my weight as we exited the courtyard. Three men sat in a row on the gravel, hands bound, with policemen standing over them.

The conde's screams carried over the walls of the courtyard. The sweet sound of vengeance rang in my ears as we left the Generalife.

Chapter Fifty-Three

I dabbed at the wound on my chest with a wadded-up bit of cloth. The oozing cut was too shallow for stitches, and binding it would be impossible. At least the one on my neck had stopped bleeding.

Matias frowned from across the room. "We should've entered sooner."

"He wouldn't have stepped into the trap if you had."

"We could hear, but we couldn't see. I wouldn't have waited if I knew he had a sword on you."

"And then we wouldn't have his confession. He needed to admit to killing Pelayo loud enough for Antonio to hear." I reached for a fresh cloth. Matias hadn't let me out of his sight since we'd returned from the Alhambra. He'd even stayed with me in the bathing chamber while Severiano fetched the medical supplies. "Antonio should've returned by now. Can you keep him and Hugh in the library? I'll be along soon."

Matias shook his head but adhered to my request. When the door closed, I pressed my hand to my forehead. *Bloody, bloody hell, that was close.* Beneath the cloth was a diamond-shaped wound that was deeper than the rest of the injuries. Another few moments, and the conde might have driven the sword through my heart.

Then again, Matias had already skewered it last night, so maybe it didn't matter.

Hugh, Antonio, and Matias would require an account of my conversation with the conde. Matias had assured me that Antonio had heard enough to take the man into custody, but I knew there were revelations they weren't aware of. Matias hadn't mentioned anything about Felicity Ward, so he must not yet know about her connection. I couldn't remember the name of the man Antonio said she was involved with, but he had played a role as well.

There were too many loose ends. It would fall to me to reveal Felicity's part in yet another deadly scheme. At least Pelayo's death couldn't be attributed to her, for what that was worth.

My blouse was bloodstained and torn. The buttons were difficult to manage with trembling fingers. Bone-deep exhaustion was settling in, now that the adrenaline was fading. Between Matias's devastating words last night, my lack of sleep, imminent danger, and near death, it was a wonder I could stand at all.

I could, couldn't I? I gripped the armrests as I got my feet under me, using the chair to balance when my vision blurred.

Hugh handed me a glass with several fingers of whiskey. It had been weeks since my last drink. I savored the liquid burn scorching my insides, numbing my overexposed nerves.

Hugh raised his brows at the state of my clothing, then turned to Antonio. "You said she had a few minor scratches. She's covered in blood."

I laid a hand on his forearm. "My injuries *are* minor. It looks worse than it is."

The injuries *were* minor, but the weakness in my limbs was not. I tried not to stumble as I made my way to the settee.

"Antonio, thank you for coming to my rescue. Matias and I wouldn't have been able to subdue the conde's men without you and the police."

Antonio leaned forward in his chair, dangling a glass from his fingers. "Just doing my job." He swallowed the last drops. "You're aware that despite the evidence, he may escape prosecution. I'll attempt to convince the regent that his punishment should be severe, but his status will protect him."

I splayed onto the cushions. "I know. I had to try—for Pelayo, for Novia and Pilar, and for the people in that neighborhood." I couldn't succumb to my exhaustion yet. The last drink of whiskey fortified my composure. "There was more than just his part in the property scheme and Pelayo's murder." I steeled myself for this painful revelation. "Felicity Ward brought us to their attention."

"What?" Matias rushed forward. When I'd entered the room, I'd noted that he was holding himself apart, positioned near the outside doors.

Three faces of disbelief met my pronouncement. I knew her involvement would wreck Matias.

"The conde claimed that Felicity sent word to her inamorato. When we left for Granada, he sent my name to the conde as someone to be conscripted into the plans already in motion. We should've known she would attempt some measure of retribution. It isn't in her nature to surrender. And she *did* threaten us."

Matias dropped into a chair. It shuddered under his weight. "She did this? Again?"

"No, Matias. Her role was secondary. The conde was forcing people from their homes. Pelayo's murder was planned. They needed someone to create a diversion, someone who would turn suspicion on the socialists. They chose me."

Matias squeezed his neck. His distress was palpable.

I turned to Antonio. "Whose house was Felicity Ward living in?"

He thought for a moment. "El Ilustrísimo Señor Conde de Granada, I didn't consider investigating him. Once Felicity Ward departed Spain, I assumed her connections here were at an end."

I shrugged. "None of us guessed. We can't assume we're out of danger. The conde may still be seeking revenge on behalf of Felicity Ward."

Everyone retreated to consider the possibilities. The clock on the mantel ticked, and a sparrow called in the garden. There was no satisfaction in this outcome. The conde would go free and continue his destruction and intimidation. Had I accomplished anything? I had permanently disabled a man, ruined my relationship and perhaps my career . . . what now? Where did we go from here?

A knock at the front door surprised us all.

Antonio rose to see who had arrived. Hugh came to his feet as well. He took my glass from my hand and refilled it. "So, are you finished at the Alhambra?"

When he handed me back the glass, I swirled the liquid inside. Maybe it wasn't the worst idea to drown myself in alcohol.

"I suppose. My role there was a facade. I wasn't asked there because of my expertise."

It was demeaning to admit how easily I'd played into their manipulations. They'd assumed my hubris would bind me to the investigation and the Generalife, and they'd been correct.

When I let the floodgates lower, my stomach cramped with shame. My pulse throbbed in my ears. Failure after failure after failure.

I blinked frantically, searching for something else to focus on. Hugh stared into the bottom of his beverage. Matias was half turned toward the window, chewing on his lip. It felt as if we were still on a battlefield after the war was over, bits of shrapnel scattered everywhere.

Antonio led Pilar, Novia, and Sebastián into the room. He gave me an apologetic look. *Oh, bloody hell, not now.*

"I sent word to Sebastián when I left the Alhambra. I thought they should know that the conde was arrested."

I appreciated Antonio's forethought, but my reserves were almost empty, my emotions too close to the surface. I swilled the whiskey, hoping it would prove medicinal.

Matias and Hugh offered their seats to the ladies, then Matias excused himself before I could ask him to stay. I sensed that, like me, he was spiraling into self-recrimination and had no desire to hearing any parting words between Sebastián and I.

I was so focused on watching his exit that I didn't notice Pilar had sat beside me on the settee. "Señora, is it true? The conde has been arrested?"

Before I could respond, Antonio said, "Hugh, perhaps we should give them some space?" He motioned toward the door and escorted Hugh from the room. I was on my own.

"Yes, the conde was arrested. He admitted responsibility for Pelayo's murder and the threats against you."

Pilar's expression brightened. "Well, that is good news, isn't it?"

Novia's harsh voice cut through her positivity. "Did he agree to spare the neighborhood?"

I plucked at the stiff fabric of my shirt. "He did not."

Sebastián pointed at my stained clothing. "Were you injured?"

"A few scrapes."

Novia flung her hands in the air. "What was the point? Alonso died. The stolen plans gained us nothing. You could've at least secured protection for the people in those neighborhoods."

I hung my head. "I didn't have any room to negotiate. He was threatening me with a sword. I tried."

Pilar covered my hand, squeezing it, but Novia wasn't pacified. "What did you accomplish?" she snarled.

"Some vengeance for Pelayo," I muttered.

All three of them jolted. Sebastián was the one to ask, "How?"

"He walked into a leg trap meant for wolves."

Novia snorted. "I wish I could've seen that."

"It was . . . memorable."

Pilar nudged my knee. "Will we see you again?"

They surrounded me, this group of people I had met under the most unusual circumstances. Novia was so fierce, so dedicated to what must be done. I envied her fire, her motivation to fight for others. Sebastián deserved someone who would appreciate him. His keen insight and caring were gifts that shouldn't be squandered. Pilar, on the surface, appeared innocent, but she was as fierce as her cousin. She was also a friend.

I cleared my throat. "Probably not. My position at the Alhambra was a ruse. There isn't much point to my returning. Er . . . I don't know where I'll go next. Antonio will meet with the regent in the morning. We'll send word regarding the outcome, but I wouldn't be too hopeful."

Novia sighed. "The regent has enough to deal with. We do not rank among her issues."

"Maybe," I said, resigned. "But it was the best I could do. I'm sorry, Novia."

Her face softened in the way I had witnessed before, when we'd spoken of Pelayo. She had lost more than leverage in this struggle; she had lost the man she loved. And she loved him enough to continue to fight for him, for her cause, even after he was gone.

Meanwhile, I was a coward.

"Do you understand why we have been fighting so hard? What most of us must endure? I joined this movement because we are trying to change things to make things better for everyone. It felt as if we were close to a victory. Instead—" Her voice was kind. Not apologetic, but bleak.

"—they killed Pelayo and came after you," I finished for her.

We stared at each other. I wanted her to know that I knew. I recognized what she lost.

"We should go. If there isn't anything else to say . . ." Sebastián said.

I felt the effects of the whiskey as I came to my feet, swaying in place. There was one more thing. "I thought I could do more. I'm sorry for my deception and any distress it caused you."

Novia nodded. Pilar looked ready to object. Sebastián's eyes flashed in anger . . . or was it regret?

I cupped Pilar's elbow, halting her progress. "Pilar, would you stay for a moment? I have something for you."

I followed Novia and Sebastián into the entryway, then darted up the stairs to our bedchamber as quickly as my whiskey-addled state allowed. I snatched a bundle from my desk with Pilar's name on it. Matias hadn't retreated here; the room was empty.

Pilar waited for me near the bookshelves downstairs. I handed her a packet. It was a bit more than what she would have earned as an apprentice gardener. It had occurred to me during my hours of rumination that Pilar had been unable to seek wages while in hiding. I felt it was what she was owed.

"I cannot accept it." She tried to force the packet back into my hands.

"They're your wages for while you were unable to work. It only seems fair. Share it with Novia if you feel you must, but I wanted you to have your own money. You have an aptitude with plants, Pilar. I hope you will seek a position in another garden. I've included my address in London as well. I would be honored if you wrote."

Even in the low light of the lamps, her cheeks were flushed. "Thank you, señora."

"Despite the situation, I enjoyed working with you. I came to value our friendship."

She fiddled with the package. "I've never had a friend like you. I'm glad we met."

I followed her to the door. Novia was waiting for her on the cobbles at the bottom of the stairs. It appeared that Sebastián had already left.

I was a swirling mess of emotions: sad to be saying goodbye to them, remorseful that I hadn't done more. "Goodbye. Be well."

Novia gave a tight nod. Pilar lifted her hand in farewell. I leaned on the closed door, trying to breathe through the pain in my chest—not from the sword wound, but from emotions I couldn't contain. If my legs hadn't been so shaky, I would have run to the garden. Instead, I moved at an unsteady amble.

I didn't retreat to my usual bench. I was drawn to the small fountain at the center. Plants were my place of safety, my familiars. But today, nothing would help.

A rustling came from the path that I assumed was Matias, but Sebastián emerged from the greenery.

"I thought you left."

He came to my side beneath the branches of an orange tree. "I intended to leave with Pilar and Novia, but it didn't feel right. We won't see you again?"

"I doubt it. I'm unsure what I'll do next." Sebastián was skilled at hiding his emotions, but I could recognize his tells: a tightening of his jaw, the clench of a hand. "Sebastián, I *am* sorry. I didn't intend to hurt you."

He reached up, plucking a leaf from above. He spun the stem between his fingers. "Did I imagine that we had a connection? Was that false as well?"

Without thinking, I wrapped my hand around his moving one. "You didn't imagine it. Our friendship became more than I'd anticipated."

He turned his hand to grasp mine, running his thumb over the back. A sparrow chittered at us from the branches, almost obscuring his voice. "If you stayed in Spain, could we?"

I pulled my hand free. "Oh, Sebastián, no. I enjoyed our time together and value your friendship. But my heart belongs to another."

He folded his arms across his chest. "At least now you're honest."

I bowed my head. So many mistakes, so much harm.

"Safe journeys, Linnea. I hope you don't forget about us in the Albaicín. Your life is different from ours, but I think you understand and believe in what we are doing."

"I do. I very much do. Goodbye, Sebastián."

The shrubs blocked my view of his retreat. I returned to the fountain. Crystalline drops caught the sunlight as they tumbled from the bowl. My sparrow friend returned to flit in and out of the cascade of water. She blurred through my tears.

I covered my mouth to contain my sobs. Now that I'd started, I wasn't sure I could stop.

Chapter Fifty-Four

My soiled clothing lay in a heap on the floor behind me. I stood in front of the glass in nothing but my drawers. Who was the woman in the reflection? I ignored my unfamiliar, ravaged face to scout the terrain of my body. A line of red arched above my breasts, angry and inflamed. My ribs. The scar on my abdomen from my surgery. Weeks of recovery. Searing pain when I moved. A lifetime ago.

I cupped my hips, feeling the satiny texture of the drawers beneath my palms. Each freckle, wrinkle, and scar were familiar, yet it felt as if I were inhabiting a foreign dwelling. I slid my fingers up my body to my face, leaning closer. My eyes were swollen, which made them appear intensely blue-green-gray. Wrinkles fanned out toward my temples.

"What now?" Even my voice sounded odd in the quiet room.

I unpinned my hair, releasing the braid and separating the strands. The woman in the reflection looked even more unhinged with hanks of hair framing her face.

I registered the closing of a door but didn't move. Matias appeared in the reflection. "What are you doing?"

"Trying to figure out who this woman is." I pulled the skin over my cheekbones taut. Was that how I'd looked fifteen years ago?

Matias gripped my shoulders. His palms were dry and cool. They were soothing on my overheated skin. "Are you well?"

I grabbed my dressing gown from where it hung on the screen. "I honestly don't know." He reared back, as if surprised that I'd confessed my doubt. "Are you?"

"I'm still in shock over Felicity. Every time, I think she is gone. And then there is this." He handed me a letter folded in thirds. I scanned the lines while he summarized the contents. "It's from Josephine. Preparation for Felicity's trial is underway, and it isn't going well. She will be acquitted unless more evidence is presented. Josephine says Lucien wasn't transported. He's on a prison hulk on the Thames. She asked me to return as soon as possible."

Her fervent request for Matias was understandable. I gave him back the letter, then tightened the belt of my gown against my stomach, which had turned into a whirling pit of nausea. He didn't know about the letter from Sir Thiselton-Dyer, or Felicity's efforts to destroy what was left of my reputation. "Do you want me to come with you?"

He ran his fingers through his hair. "You are the most aggravating, blind, reckless woman I have ever known—and dammit, it would be easier if I loved you less. But I would rather lose you on my terms than through your intemperate actions. Yes, I want you with me."

I wasn't as dead inside as I thought because his words set off a hot flare of anger. "How is it my fault that I've been attacked? That I was kidnapped and drugged? I didn't do those things to myself."

He moved so we stood toe to toe. "How often have you put yourself in danger without asking for assistance? How many, Linnea? You've been impetuous since we arrived in Spain. It doesn't seem as if being with me makes you happy. Your work at the Alhambra didn't make you happy. So, what will?"

I wanted to shout, I wanted to rail at him, I wanted to tell him he was wrong. But he wasn't.

I pressed my fingers into my face. "I'm scared. I'm so scared. What if I can't move forward? What if I can't love you? I've failed at everything." I slid to the floor, my legs shooting out from under me.

He followed me down, kneeling. I curled into a ball on the floor, my dressing gown hitching up to the top of my legs, so far in the throes that the utter shock on Matias's face barely registered. I was helpless to stop this outrageous behavior.

Finally, Matias tapped my shoulder. "I brought you a glass of water. Can you sit up and have a drink?"

I peered at him through the barrier of my arms. He was exhausted. I was only making him want to run faster and further away. I sat up and took the glass. After a long drink, I cradled it in my hand. My mind's reaction to the overabundance of feelings was numbness. Inside, nothing stirred.

"Tell me what to do, Matias. Please."

He brushed a strand of hair from my forehead. "Let's return to England."

I took another drink, watching him over the rim. Why did he want me to accompany him now?

"But Linnea . . . I think we should make the journey as friends. Not lovers. It's too confusing."

Was he only capitulating because of how I was acting? "Don't do this because you think to placate me. I'm not trying to manipulate you. I would rather you leave me than be an object of your pity."

He flexed his fists at his side. His tone softened. "That isn't the reason. I'm not ready to part either."

I stood and retreated behind the privacy screen, not only to use a cloth to wipe my tearstained face, but also to hide my distress from him. He didn't know what it would cost me to return to those shores. I would have to tell him before we arrived.

His voice came from the other side of the panel. "Will you rest? Can I leave you while I go check on train schedules to get us to a port? I'm going to try to find where we should go for the earliest departure."

I clutched the linen in my fist. "I'm fine. I'll rest."

After he left the chamber, I crawled into our bed. Our bed. I didn't know that last night would be the last night we shared it.

I pressed my face into his pillow, inhaling his scent.

Chapter Fifty-Five

The dried rhododendron fell out of my notebook as I carried it across the room. I never did discover who had been in the house. I slipped the flower back between the pages. It was worth keeping, if for no other reason than as a reminder of Granada. Not that I needed one.

Matias's trunks were stacked in the corner, already packed.

In the days since our conversation, I hadn't seen much of him. He was sleeping in a guest room down the hall when he wasn't packing or finding us passage on a ship. Hugh tried to get me to talk about what was happening between us, but it was too raw. Too new for me to conjure up adequate words.

Antonio had met with the regent about the conde. She said that she would enforce protection for that neighborhood in the Albaicín, but she didn't promise that other neighborhoods would be spared, nor did she promise that he would be punished. They would prefer to pretend it didn't happen. It wasn't a surprise.

I closed the lid of the trunk on the last of my books.

"Lady Wren?" Severiano still insisted on calling me by that name, despite the months we had dwelled together.

"Yes?"

"A message has come for you, my lady."

Maybe something from Novia, Pilar, or even Sebastián?

Linnea,

You are needed immediately at the train station. There's been an emergency with the conde. Please meet me at Track 8, third carriage.

Antonio

An emergency? With the conde? Had he attempted to harm someone else? Why would Antonio need my assistance?

I snatched up my hat and left the chamber, stopping in the library and study to see if Hugh or Matias was there to accompany me, but neither were home. Recalling their frustration, I jotted a note, letting them know I was meeting Antonio.

I walked several blocks until I found a hired hack to take me to the train station. On the ride there, I had plenty of time to spin several scenarios.

The train station was bustling. Now that one could catch a train to almost anywhere, people seemed to have embraced this form of travel. Our trip from Cádiz would have taken more than a week if we hadn't been able to go by train. I followed the numbers posted until I located Track 8. It was at the end of the row, away from those boarding.

"Antonio?" I called, stepping from the platform to walk along the carriages. "Antonio?" The third carriage was a freight hauler. I peered inside the dark space. "Antonio?"

There was a rustling noise in the back corner. Had someone hurt him?

I hoisted myself into the carriage. "Hello?"

A hand slammed into my back, shoving me to my knees. The door clanked closed behind me with an ominous finality.

I pounded on the metal. "Help! Help me!"

But my screams were drowned out by the whistle of the train.

* * *

Author Notes

Garden of Shadows was written (in part) during the height of the pandemic, while *Voyage of the Pleiades* was being edited and queried. As a result, I was unable to travel to Spain to refresh my sense memories. Any errors in descriptions or locations are inadvertent. This is a work of fiction and while I try to be accurate, I am only human.

The reason it takes longer to write historical fiction (or at least, my books) is because I believe in taking a deep dive into research. *Garden of Shadows* was heavily influenced by *Sonidos Negros* by Meira Goldberg, which led me down multiple rabbit holes into this period in Spain's history. On the surface, it seems to be a time of peace, but as you dig into what was truly happening, you begin to see the shifts that led to a long period of unrest. Because I don't write "serious" fiction, these issues were simplified for the book. It is much more complex than I could portray here.

The Alhambra was also undergoing restoration during the period *Garden of Shadows* takes place. Robert Irwin's book, *The Alhambra*, is an excellent (English language) starting place for those that wish to know more. Controversy over the design choices by the restorationists continues to be a point of contention.

In a twist of fate, I was hired as lead writer for a documentary on our housing crisis in Chaffee County, while I was working on *Garden of Shadows*. *A Home in Paradise* has shown in multiple venues in southern Colorado and will soon air on Rocky Mountain PBS. The housing crisis I describe in Granada, happened in many cities in Spain during the 19th century. And it is something we still grapple with throughout the world. I traveled to England and South Africa while I was finishing the final edits of this book, and had conversations with residents of both countries about their housing crisis. This isn't an issue that is going away.

I'm fortunate to have the support of wonderful people in my life that help me get these books to publication. Tulani Bridgewater-Kowalski, is my sister in arms. My fellow coyote that scrapes me off the floor and prods me to keep going. Jenny Tananbaum is my voice of reason. Vanessa Trost tolerated many conversations about housing in Spain. My companions in the Writer's Room are the best group of co-workers an introverted writer could have.

Larissa Melo Pienkowski, thank you for editing yet another book. I can't imagine going through this journey without you on my team.

Copious besos to my beta readers.

And of course, much love to my readers. I appreciate every one of you.

Dave, you tolerate my rambling, my storyline induced fugue states, and my grumblings about poisonous plants and the patriarchy. Thank you for your support, taking me on emergency bike rides, and recognizing my need for an afternoon Aperol spritz. Love, your feral woman.

Amy Marie Turner is a Heartland Emmy-nominated documentary and commercial film writer. She also writes the historical mystery novels, the Linnea Wren series. Amy lives in the mountains of Colorado where, when she isn't dreaming up her next project, she talks to plants, rides her bike, and reads. www.amymarieturner.com

Sign up for Amy's Substack and Linktr.ee to be the first to hear about book releases and all of Amy's projects.

Printed in the USA
CPSIA information can be obtained
at www.ICGtesting.com
CBHW050017161024
15912CB00006B/98